THE CURE
for
MODERN LIFE

ALSO BY LISA TUCKER

The Song Reader

Shout Down the Moon

Once Upon a Day

THE CURE
for
MODERN LIFE

a novel

Lisa Tucker

ATRIA BOOKS

New York   London   Toronto   Sydney

ATRIA BOOKS

A Division of Simon & Schuster, Inc.
1230 Avenue of the Americas
New York, NY 10020

First Atria Books hardcover edition March 2008

ATRIA BOOKS and colophon are trademarks of Simon & Schuster, Inc.

For information about special discounts for bulk purchases,
please contact Simon & Schuster Special Sales at
1-800-456-6798 or business@simonandschuster.com.

Designed by Kyoko Watanabe

Manufactured in the United States of America

10   9   8   7   6   5   4   3   2

Library of Congress Cataloging-in-Publication Data

Tucker, Lisa.
  The cure for modern life / Lisa Tucker.
    p. cm.
  ISBN-13: 978-0-7434-9279-9
  ISBN-10:   0-7434-9279-X
  1. Friendship—Fiction. 2. Homeless children—Fiction. I. Title.
  PS3620.U3 C87 2008
  813'.6—dc22
                              2007029890

This book is for Miles because he wanted it to be.
And because he showed me it was possible to have all the
ordinary things: a family, laughter, happiness.

UNLESS someone like you
cares a whole awful lot,
nothing is going to get better.
It's not.

—Dr. Seuss, *The Lorax*

THE CURE
for
MODERN LIFE

CHAPTER ONE

The Kindness of Strangers

Was Matthew Connelly a bad man? He'd never once asked himself that question. Make of it what you will. Of course it would have surprised him to know that, as he walked toward the bridge that night, a little boy was asking the question for him. Because Matthew didn't notice people like this boy, he never wondered what they were thinking about, or if they thought at all. They were as invisible as the ants he'd crushed under his feet as he walked through the streets of Grand Cayman the weekend before, with Amelia and Ben, the happy couple, deliriously grateful to have found each other, all demons of the past behind them—and all thanks to him. His matchmaking was a good deed from their point of view, pure and simple. To Matthew it was something else entirely, something he didn't dwell on but accepted as another delicate operation in an extremely complex job.

The boy watching Matthew, who gave his name as Timmy or Jacob or Danny, depending on the situation, was only ten years old, but his mother said he was closer to forty in his harsh judgments of other people, by which she usually meant his harsh judgments of herself. And it was true; the boy took an almost instant dislike to Matthew Connelly. It wasn't just that the guy looked too young to be so filthy rich, with a fancy topcoat that had to cost more than it had cost to feed Isabelle for her entire life, or even that he was obviously in a hurry, striding up Walnut Street like he had somewhere important to be, though it was way past midnight. It wasn't even the loud, idiotic singing the man was indulging in as he walked, as though no one could possibly be outside on that frigid November night in Philadelphia except Connelly himself, who no doubt considered the journey a reason to pat himself on the back that he was always up for a little exercise. No, the real thing that condemned him, from the boy's perspective, was the position of his hands, which were jammed so far into his pockets that all you could see were the tops of what surely were the most luxurious leather gloves sold on the planet. So he wasn't cold, which meant there was only one reason his hands were like that. He was a selfish person, the kind who wouldn't lift a finger to help anyone else. The kind of person his mother called a "natural-born Republican bastard," even though she didn't believe in her son's hands theory, preferring instead the simpler principle that all rich people were bastards.

Still, the boy, who ended up naming himself Danny that night, had no choice; he had to try. He grabbed three-year-old Isabelle in his arms, groaning under her weight, and ran up the concrete stairs as fast as his scrawny ten-year-old legs would carry him. He had to be standing on the bridge when the man got there, blocking his path. As the guy came closer, Danny proceeded to yell and scream and cry: "Help! Please, mister! My baby sister! Help!"

The tears weren't real because he never cried, but the fear made his frozen hands shake harder. Isabelle had been throwing up all day and his mother had told him a million times that if you throw up for too long, you can die. Protecting Isabelle was his sacred duty and he would do it no matter what, even if he had to die himself. It was part of the code of honor he'd adopted a few months after his sister was born, when he'd sworn himself in as a knight. This was after he'd read a book about King Arthur and the Knights of the Round Table, which his mother had stolen for him from the library, but he wasn't playing some stupid pretend game. Even the book said that knights weren't only in the past, and anyone could be one. True, the boy had never met another knight, but that wasn't surprising since knights had to sacrifice everything to uphold the code, and that was hard, even for him. But whenever he wanted to renounce his knighthood and go back to being a regular kid, he remembered his honor and how no one could take it away from him—not his mother, not the cops, and certainly not this selfish asshole who wasn't going to stop, Danny knew, no matter how much he begged.

That Danny turned out to be wrong had nothing to do with his ability to judge men like Matthew Connelly. On that particular night, there was something about Matthew that even a very wise, very hardened ten-year-old boy/knight couldn't guess from the man's appearance. The rest, Danny had gotten right, uncannily so. It was true that Matthew was what most anybody would call rich, given his upper-six-figure salary; his stock options at Astor-Denning, the pharmaceutical company where he was a VP; the top-of-the-line Porsche 911 he'd bought with last year's bonus; his property investments across the city—though he was leasing the loft where he'd lived for the last two years, an upscale but not intimidating place, perfect for his friendships with scientists. It was also true that he was walking quickly, not because he had a flight to Tokyo in the morning, which he'd put out of his mind, but because it felt good to move; not as wonderful as it had on the dance floor, but still good. The idiotic humming was a carry-away from the club he'd just left, a way of remembering the woman he might have taken home with him if this were a normal night, yet it had been anything but.

At seven-thirty he'd gone out to dinner with a nationally known med school professor who'd agreed to testify before the FDA on behalf of Astor-Denning's new diabetes drug. Matthew's goal was to make this guy happy, to give him the right food, the right wine, the right conversation, even, if necessary, the right women. But the only thing the good doctor really wanted was to try MDMA: ecstasy. He was recently divorced; he thought he needed a drug that would "release" his emotions about his ex-wife. Matthew agreed to make a few phone calls, though he hoped he wouldn't have to listen to the guy's emotions as they were released. When the doc insisted that they try the drug together, Matthew's first reaction was to smile and nod and decide he wouldn't swallow it. The illegal part didn't bother him, but he didn't want to lose control of the meeting. But then the doc said they'd know they were "tripping" when their pupils dilated, and Matthew realized it might not be easy to fool this doc, even if the guy was high. Whatever happened, he could not let this important contact decide he was a liar. What the hell. The E was pure, according to his source, and he had a brilliant medical professor at his side. What could go wrong?

The fiftysomething, fat, balding doc had had the time of his life, running around the club, groping one woman after another, telling each of them, "I know I'm on X, but the way I feel about you is so intense, it has to be real." Matthew was much more subdued, but he enjoyed the experience, too. And he felt proud that he'd forced himself to leave the club alone—after the doc left with some blonde—even though the pill was still working, knowing it would give him a cheerful walk home, which, damn, he needed for a change. The trip to the Caymans last weekend, meetings and conference calls and putting out fires all day, wining and dining research partners five nights out of seven: all of this was making him feel unusually tired, though he was determined to prove that nothing had changed, despite the fact that he'd just turned forty. He was in great shape. He could always *party like it's 1999*, even if that particular phrase was one he kept to himself, fearing it would date him with the hot twentysomethings he invariably found himself attracted to rather than women his own age.

With the pill's help, he floated painlessly down thirty-one blocks from Old City to the bridge, no side effects except a little teeth-chattering. He lived on the West Philly side of the river to enhance his intellectual cred with academics, but the loft scored him points for being hip, too, because uptight people were afraid to live there even though the building was more like a suburban gated community than an edgy inner-city neighborhood, and his Porsche was probably safer there than anywhere in the city. Walking on the Walnut Street Bridge at night did make him a little nervous, which was why he usually took a cab home, but now nothing bothered him, not even some screaming kid standing near the stairs to the river.

When he reached the kid, he noticed the boy was holding what looked like a bundle of clothes, except that it was making sounds like a kitten (or were they words? Whatever it was, that sound was so sweet), and Matthew found himself bursting into a smile. "Can I hold it?" he said, pointing at the bundle.

He just wanted to see what could make that brook sound, but the dirty boy wasn't cool. He frowned and said, "What? Are you a perv or something?"

Matthew wasn't sure why, but the question made him feel so happy he started laughing. "No, I'm not," Matthew said, still grinning. "Am I supposed to be?"

The boy cursed under his breath. "You're drunk."

"Wrong again," Matthew said, and then he blurted out something he would never have told another adult, especially in his condition, given his strict policy of avoiding emotional entanglements. "I'll have you know that my father died of cirrhosis of the liver. I am not now and have never been drunk. So there." He stuck his arm out, pointing one finger playfully at the kid. "Take that!"

The boy looked away then, lost in thought, but Matthew was too busy trying to see over the top of the bundle to care what the dirty kid was thinking about. Even if he'd known the kid was thinking about drugs, he wouldn't have cared. What was the boy going to do, have him arrested for swallowing his first-ever tab of E? After a minute, Matthew said, pointing at the bundle, thrilled that he'd figured it out, "It's a little girl!"

"Duh," the kid said. "It's Isabelle, my sister." He pulled the blanket down just enough to expose the largest blackest eyes Matthew had ever seen. Doll eyes.

"She doesn't look like you," Matthew said. The little girl was a light brown color, while the boy was chalky pale, even under the dirt. "She's so adorable. Can I touch her?"

Before the boy could answer, the bundle shook and heaved like a volcano about to erupt, and Matthew took a confused step back as the little girl let loose with a stream of vomit that covered the boy's hands before spewing all over the ground, with one big splat landing on one of Matthew's handmade Italian shoes.

"She's sick," the boy said, sounding depressed. "That's why I stopped you. I'm sorry."

Matthew smiled at the humanness of it all. Puke. It happened to everyone, didn't it? It had happened to him a few hours ago, right at the beginning of his trip. "I know what she needs," he said, before he could stop himself. "Emetrol and Gatorade."

"Where do I get that?" The kid's tone was much lighter now, sweet even. "All the stores around here are closed."

Matthew thought for a moment. He was happy, but not stupid; yet he didn't see how this scrawny kid could pose any threat. Not to mention the downstairs guard at the loft: a 275-pound former boxer who would rush to his aid at the push of a button. He could give the beautiful baby the Emetrol and Gatorade and send them on their way, with cab fare for wherever they usually go at night, which he didn't want to think about. He wanted to stay happy.

"All right, come on." He looked up at the dark sky and laughed. "I haven't got all day."

"Great," the kid said. "Just give me a minute." He pointed below the bridge, presumably to the riverbank at the bottom of the stairs. "I left something. I have to get it or Isabelle will cry."

"We don't want that," Matthew said, though he was thinking that maybe he should go ahead and walk home without waiting for them. He'd just remembered the plane to Tokyo at 8:37 in the morning. His plan had been to be in bed by one-thirty, then up by five-thirty, showered, packed, and on the road to the airport by six-thirty. He'd sleep on the plane, too, but the four hours would buy him the energy to do the packing and stand in the annoying line at airport security.

He was still working out the details in a fuzzy-minded way—he could easily make it to the Philly airport by seven, but he'd have to take a cab, so he didn't have to park—when the kid handed him the bundle. "Just hold her. Stand right here."

The kid's voice was reluctant, and so was his expression each time he looked back while he rushed away, but Matthew didn't care. All night he'd felt like touching everyone, but holding this baby was like having a little bird in his hands, a beautiful bird that cooed delightedly every time his finger stroked her cheeks. This sound was better than dance music, better even than the Bach playlist on his iPod. It was like the voice of heaven, he thought. Why didn't the radio play this child cooing all day long? Why wasn't it being broadcast from the loudspeakers at Franklin Field right now?

When the kid returned, dragging a garbage bag—and a skinny woman—with him, Matthew was still talking to the baby, listening to her sweet, lilting babbles that seemed to be answers in another language, though he was pretty sure he heard the word *yes* and positive he heard multiple *nos*. But still, he felt better when the boy told him the woman was their mother. This made him feel peaceful and warm, knowing these two kids weren't out at night by themselves. They had a mom, though she was sick, too, obviously. During the short walk to the loft she puked twice, dry heaves, quick and quiet and over before the boy had time to stop. Unless he had no intention of stopping. He shot his mom several dirty looks, which struck Matthew as pointless. She couldn't help it if she was sick. Puking was human and oddly touching. The simple act of retching made anyone seem vulnerable.

They finally made it to Matthew's building and went up the elevator into his apartment. Matthew found the Emetrol in the guest bathroom medicine cabinet and told them the Gatorade was in the fridge; then he headed to his bedroom, just planning to change his shoes because the smell of vomit was bothering him. Somehow he ended up on his bed. What happened after that wasn't strange, since he'd swallowed two Ativans on his walk home, knowing E was an amphetamine and afraid he wouldn't get to sleep for hours, but it was extremely unfortunate, since he passed out before he had a chance to get rid of the boy and his mother and even the beautiful-voice baby, who he knew he wouldn't want to see in the morning. Without the pill's effect, music was just music and puking babies were an annoyance. And strangers looking for handouts were worse than annoying; they were weak and irresponsible and, nearly always, absolute believers that they were morally entitled simply because they were victims.

What Matthew thought of as the victim mentality taking over America was a perpetually sore subject for him, and never more so than in the last month when, as his boss so colorfully put it, Matthew had been driving a hundred miles an hour, in a convertible, trying to outrun a shit storm. The potential disaster had surfaced on an ordinary Thursday night when he was in bed with a woman, dozing after sex while she watched inane TV. Later he would wonder why no one on his media surveillance team knew that this pseudo news show was going to mention Galvenar, but at the time, his reaction was more primal. He went into the bathroom and punched the wall hard enough to make his knuckles bleed, though the wall, embarrassingly enough, was absolutely fine.

By every standard, Galvenar had been Astor-Denning's most spectacular success, and one of the most successful launches in the history of pharmaceuticals. The medicine was approved by the FDA for chronic pain, but it also had a stunning array of off-label uses, which had led to AD's stock climbing steadily ever since the drug had come on the market two years earlier. In the last quarter alone, its sales had reached 1.32 billion. Matthew had no intention of letting some idiot who fancied himself an investigative journalist ruin all this, especially with the non-news story that two men had died of heart attacks while taking a long list of meds that just happened to include Galvenar, which this jackass journalist had the nerve to suggest could be "the next Vioxx" and have to be withdrawn from the market, like Vioxx, for the "safety of the public."

That same night, Matthew started making damage control phone calls. First, the AD legal team threatened the network with a lawsuit if they didn't issue a statement that Galvenar had been specifically tested for cardiac side effects and judged absolutely safe, even in doses sixteen times larger than either of the men had been taking, which was all true: Galvenar wasn't even in the same drug class as Vioxx. After the retraction aired, Matthew had his staff reach out to journalists, suggesting they might want to ring in on the "scare tactics" used by this network to boost ratings. More than a dozen had taken the bait, including a handful who wrote for prestigious newspapers. In the meantime, the PR firm drones were planting more testimonials for Galvenar on sites like patientsays.com and manufacturing outrage in pain community chat rooms about television shows that didn't understand suffering, with frequent references to Galvenar, the gave-us-our-lives-back miracle drug. Then, over the last few weeks, Matthew had personally contacted all the scientists who'd signed on to the research results, just to gauge their reactions, but few of them had heard of this TV report and those who had thought it was another example of the public's ignorance about cause and effect. Finally, he'd gone with Ben and Amelia to Grand Cayman last weekend, without telling anyone about the trip, even his boss. His boss didn't know anything about that situation, but even if Matthew had forced him to hear every detail of the last twenty years, all the way back to when he and Ben and Amelia were in college, the boss might still have concluded that Matthew was being so careful it bordered on paranoid. But to Matthew, there was no such thing as too careful. Not when billions in profit were at stake.

Thankfully, it had all blown over now. Well, almost. On Saturday, a Japanese television station had picked up the discredited story, and now Matthew was going to Tokyo with a PR exec, just to make sure the newest big market for Galvenar wasn't having any second thoughts. His job was simply to present the clinical trial data again and emphasize the impressive safety record in the post-market, while the PR rep, a heavy hitter, played off what the Japanese (and the rest of the world) already believed: that the American media and government seemed to be obsessed with scaring the hell out of everyone, turning our country into a nation of frightened brats.

Matthew was all too aware that Japan and Europe didn't like U.S. pharmaceutical companies, whose products they considered vastly overpriced, but they didn't think the companies were Big Meanies. Only in America. He had dreams of telling all these whiners that the solution was simple: just stop taking any of the products from evil Big Pharma. Put your money where your mouth is. See how you feel about dying at forty, the way your great-great-grandparents did.

This point of view, harsh though it undoubtedly sounds, was not something Matthew had chosen to believe; he was sure about that. Of course he would have preferred to see the world the way he had last night on E, but he knew that rosy outlook was deeply and utterly false, a mere alteration in his brain chemistry, not in the way things really operated. Case in point: last night, he'd stupidly tried to help a poor family, and what was the outcome? He'd not only been inconvenienced, he'd been robbed.

He discovered this after his shower, when he was dressed and packed, but he couldn't find his wallet. He was already planning to wake up the kid and tell him they had to leave, but now he was furious. He grabbed the boy by the hands, lifting him from the hardwood floor (vaguely wondering why the kid hadn't slept on any of the furniture or even on the thick oriental rug), and said, "All right, you little thief. Where the fuck is my wallet?"

The boy rubbed his eyes. "I tried to warn you. Don't you remember? I kept shaking you, but you wouldn't wake up."

"If I wouldn't wake up, then how could I remember?"

"I tried to stop her. I even tackled her, but she shook me off."

He smirked. "You're saying the baby robbed me?" Then all of a sudden it hit him. The baby was still asleep, tucked into the corner of his leather couch, with throw pillows all around her. Of course he wasn't talking about his sister; he was talking about his mom, who Matthew suddenly knew wasn't sick like the little girl. She was sick like an addict. This was why the kid hadn't sympathized with her last night. Of course.

"You're telling me your mom rolled me?" He was shouting. "I let you in to help your sister, and you bring along your mom, who you know will steal whatever isn't nailed down?"

"I wanted to tell you to lock everything up, but you passed out." The kid's voice had an edge to it, but then he said, more quietly, "I'm really sorry."

"What else did she take? My wallet and what else?"

"Money in the desk drawer. All the prescription drugs in your bathroom. I think that's it."

He kept more than five thousand dollars in the desk drawer. His emergency fund, in case of a bird flu–like disaster that would temporarily close down banks and ATMs. The medicines he didn't care about, except Lomotil, which he always took on trips overseas, for diarrhea. He couldn't imagine why a druggie would want it. The Percocet he'd gotten for his knee injury last year, the samples of Vicodin for a toothache a few months ago, the Ativan he took for occasional anxiety and sleep: all of those made sense, but Lomotil? Dammit. Now he'd have to pick up Imodium at the airport. Another thing to do, and time was short already.

"I made her leave your driver's license," the kid said, pointing at the end table.

"How thoughtful," Matthew snapped, though he was relieved to see it lying there. He absolutely had to have that and his passport, or he'd miss his plane.

As he walked into his bedroom to get his keys and watch and cell phone charger, he yelled to the kid that everyone had to go now.

"I'm leaving and you and your sister are, too. Sorry, but this isn't a shelter. I have to go to Japan and you'll have to go back to wherever the hell you came from."

"How long will you be gone?" the kid said, following him.

Matthew spun around. "Why?"

"Just wondering."

"This building has the most advanced security system in the city. If you're thinking you'll sneak in after I'm gone, give it up." He snapped the band on his Rolex to emphasize his point, and forced himself not to wince. "The one and only reason I'm not calling the police right now is I don't have time."

"That's nice," the kid said sarcastically.

"Why aren't you waking up your sister?" He had the charger in his briefcase, along with his tablet laptop and the second corporate Amex he was supposed to use only in emergencies, but now he couldn't find his goddamn cell. It was in his pants when he fell asleep, wasn't it? Had it fallen on the floor? He knelt down to look and said, "I told you to get out. If you don't, I'm calling the security guard to throw you out."

The boy watched him as he looked around the bedside table, under the bed, everywhere he could think of. Then he said, "Have you ever brought kids back here before?"

"You know I haven't," Matthew said, because he was suddenly sure this kid did know. This boy's eyes were cunning, suspicious, nothing like the innocent child he'd seen the night before. Fucking E. He'd never take it again as long as he lived, if he could just get through this morning and on the plane.

"I don't think you want to call the security guard."

"Oh, really?" Matthew stomped over to his bedroom phone and picked up the receiver. "We'll see about that."

"I mean," the kid said quickly, "how will it look when I tell him that you brought me back here for sex?"

"What?" he said, though he'd heard the kid perfectly. "You scheming little—"

"I won't hurt any of your stuff. I swear. It's just, I have to let Isabelle sleep. Even with all your yelling, she hasn't woken up because she's really sick. I can't take her out yet or she might die."

"Boo hoo hoo. And how is that my problem again?"

"It isn't your problem. I know. But I have to protect my sister."

Matthew was still holding the receiver, but his finger was hesitating on the 7, the number for security. He didn't know the security guard beyond awkward hellos in the hall and the less awkward giving of frequent tips, including five hundred dollars last Christmas. What if the man was some kind of kiddie advocate? What if he'd been abused by his father or his priest? The world was full of whiners, crying about what happened to them in their childhood. Unfortunately, even a 275-pound security guard might turn out to be one of them.

The boy stood with his arms crossed, watching Matthew. Matthew was watching him, too, and suddenly he remembered the kid's name. He'd introduced himself last night in the elevator. His manner had been surprisingly formal. "I'm Danny, sir. Thank you so much for helping us."

Matthew smiled as it hit him that the kid was bluffing. He told him so, looking straight into his eyes. "You won't do it because you want to be better than your mother. She's the liar, not you."

"Whatever you say," Danny said, smirking like a monkey. A clever monkey; Matthew had to give him that. "But I'm gonna do whatever I have to do for Isabelle. If that means putting you in jail until they can prove you didn't have sex with me? Guess you'd miss your plane and all, but if you don't care about that, then—"

"All right, all right, Jesus Christ!" Matthew banged down the receiver. It was 6:49; he had to go. "But you better get out of here before I get on that plane or—"

"I swear we'll leave as soon as she has a chance to sleep. Just tell me how to lock the door."

"It locks automatically. All you have to do is shut it when you get the hell out." As he walked back into the main room, he was still yelling, "Because once I'm on the plane, I'm calling security. I'll tell them the whole story and you can try your sex lie; be my guest. I'm sure they'll realize you're a little shit long before I'm back in the country."

He glanced at the baby girl as he walked to the closet for his coat. She did look so peaceful lying there, and she had a beautiful face, just as he remembered. For a split second, he felt sorry for her and her lying brother, but then he realized he still hadn't found his phone. When he asked Danny if his mother had taken that, too, the kid sighed and nodded.

"I really am sorry, mister."

"Not as sorry as I am," Matthew said, walking to the door. "And not half as sorry as you're going to be if you aren't gone before the police arrive."

Of course he was furious; he had too many problems to deal with this mess. And he didn't want homeless people in his house, but as he reminded himself as he stepped on the elevator, who would?

CHAPTER TWO

A Knight's Tale

The boy who'd called himself Danny never used his real name. He hated his real name, and he couldn't use it anyway, since it didn't work as well. "Timmy," he'd discovered, was best for old people; "Jacob," for women, but also sympathetic-looking men; and his personal favorite, "Danny," for rich men and teenage girls. (Nothing he'd tried so far worked with teenage boys, and he usually ran away from them.) His mother said she wished she'd named him Daniel, since he loved that name so much. "Or maybe Richard," she said, smiling. She had the softest blue eyes. "Because he had a lion's heart, just like my son."

This was the way his mother talked whenever she wasn't sick.

He used to fall in love with her all over again within hours after she got her medicine. He was a little boy then; he thought her medicine came from doctors, like the pink stuff he had to take whenever he had an ear infection. This was back when her habit wasn't as strong and she could work hard and still afford three weeks of drugs and their one-bedroom apartment. But the fourth week, she was always sick with what she called the flu. Sometimes she would get fired during that week, but she always got another job once she got better. He was able to go to kindergarten and first grade like a normal kid. Mrs. Greenly, his first-grade teacher, told him he was smart, but she told everybody that. He hoped it was true, so he could eventually figure out a way to teach Isabelle to read and print and do basic arithmetic. You couldn't get by in the world without reading street signs and counting the quarters and nickels and dimes people gave you. You had to know how much you could buy with $3.12, which meant figuring taxes, unless you could find a clerk who would cut you a break, but those people were few and far between. You couldn't rely on them. You couldn't rely on anyone but yourself.

Danny wasn't afraid of being without a roof over his head—that was the way knights had always lived. He wasn't afraid of rain or snow or sun so hot it burned his cheeks and chin. Most of all, he wasn't afraid of the dark, because the dark meant fewer people, and people were the one thing that still frightened him. Most of them were mean and in a hurry and disgusted with poor people, if not downright cruel. And then there were cops and social workers and intake clerks at rehab who were always threatening to take Danny and Isabelle away from their mother, which Danny feared more than anything, because then they would take his sister away from him.

He'd met all kinds of foster kids, and they were almost never with their sisters or brothers. Not if there was a big difference in their ages. Not if they were of different races. And there was no chance at all if one of the kids was normal and the other could barely walk or speak at three years old.

Danny considered himself lucky to have been born before his mother started on drugs. He was wrong about this; she'd started when she was only seventeen years old, though of course she didn't admit that to him. She didn't admit anything about the drugs until after Isabelle was born, when he knew something was wrong with his sister. Her tiny arms and legs shook all the time. His mom's legs shook only when they were out of money again. The needles made his mom's legs stop shaking. Somehow, his mom's needles had done this to his sister; he was sure of it.

When she finally confessed that it was true, he realized he wasn't going to fall in love with his mother anymore. He would love her, because he couldn't help that, but he wouldn't be taken in by all her smiles and laughs and beautiful stories about the past and the future. Even as his mom cried and begged God to forgive her for hurting the baby, Danny was promising himself that he would never forgive her for this, not as long as he lived.

He was seven years old then, living in an abandoned car by the train tracks. He'd dropped out of second grade when they lost the tiny apartment, but he didn't mind the car. Every day his mother would leave him with Isabelle, but only after his sister's morning feeding, so he wouldn't have to light the propane burner to heat up a bottle of formula. As he watched his mother walk away, he would pick up little Isabelle and hold her tightly to his chest so she could feel his heart beat, hoping it would calm her like the tick of the alarm clock had calmed the kitten they'd had for a few weeks when they lived in the apartment. If that didn't work, he would rock her and sing song after song, all the ones his mother had taught him over the years. His mother had such a sweet, clear voice that he almost believed her when she told him her favorite story from the past, the one where she'd come close to becoming a famous singer. Sometimes when he sang to Isabelle, he would change the song's words, like his mom always did, but instead of "Momma gonna buy you a mockingbird," he would sing, "Danny's gonna buy you a parakeet." He didn't know what a mockingbird was, but it sounded mean.

His mother always came back before it was time for the second feeding, even if all she'd managed to scrounge was some food or another layer of clothing from Goodwill. She didn't want to be away from Isabelle for too long, fearing what would happen to the sick newborn. They even stayed in shelters when it got cold, which normally Danny's mom hated because there were all kinds of rules to follow and, she said, the people who worked there looked down on her for being an addict. "Of course none of them can tell me how to quit," she said. "None of them are offering me a place to go where I can really get clean."

This was the one thing Danny knew about his mother—she did want to quit using drugs. This was why he knew he'd never be able to hate her: because he'd seen her try again and again to stop. She'd tried cold turkey hundreds of times, usually when she ran out, but sometimes when she just decided to give it up. Danny would wake in the morning and find her with her eyes watering and her nose running, always the first signs that she was getting sick. "I threw it all away. I have to get you and your sister out of this mess. I'm going to get a job and an apartment so you can go back to school. Wouldn't you like that, honey? You could meet some friends."

Part of him knew it would never happen, but another part of him, deep in his chest, felt lighter, like a hand had just reached inside him to hold up the weight of his heart. Each and every stupid time. He always felt like a fool when his mother inevitably failed again, usually within hours of the nausea starting. Even the detox places couldn't help because the free ones were always seventy-two hours, and seventy-two hours wasn't enough to make his mom get better. She'd come out still throwing up, sometimes as often as every fifteen minutes. When she tried to go back in, the detox place said there wasn't an open bed; she'd have to go to the ER. The ER was out; his mom had been arrested the last time she went there, and Danny had barely managed to escape with Isabelle before the cops took them away, too. By the time his mom finally broke down and got more drugs, she would be so dehydrated she'd have trouble finding a vein and have to sniff the stuff until she could hold down Gatorade. Yeah, he knew about Gatorade for dehydration, and he knew about Emetrol, too. His mom had tried everything to stop vomiting, but nothing seemed to work except the stuff in the needles.

The winter after Isabelle was born, his mom stopped being pretty. She'd lost too much weight and she was always dirty, refusing to wash when the rain bucket was full, saying it was too cold, or even to clean up when Danny offered her one of Isabelle's precious baby wipes. She looked like a homeless person, which just made it harder, since no one would believe her when she said she needed money for food or diapers, even when it was true. By the time Isabelle was a year old, all the begging fell to Danny, but, luckily, he knew that providing for the weak was part of a knight's job. Of course a knight had to be dignified about it, too. He couldn't just come right out and beg for food. That was beneath him; plus, it wasn't smart. Danny could tell it made people nervous, knowing they were looking at someone too poor to eat, at least if that someone was an eight-year-old kid holding a one-year-old. After a few hungry days, he discovered that what he really needed to ask for wasn't food or diapers or even money, but train fare.

Over the next month or so, he developed an elaborate story about his mom taking him and his sister shopping at the Gallery, but then losing sight of her. "It was all my fault," he'd say, sniffing like he was holding back tears. "She told me to stand right by the fountain, but I saw this toy car and I walked away with Isabelle. When I got back, I couldn't find her anywhere." Before the person could say a word, he would stand up straighter, square his skinny shoulders, and add, "But my dad taught me what to do if this ever happened. You know, like in a 9/11 attack or something. Dad said to go to the train station and buy tickets for Isabelle and me on the R5 and then get off at Ardmore Station. Our house is only a block from there. I know how to walk home, too, 'cause Dad taught me."

So far, so good, as long as he and Isabelle were reasonably clean (face and hands washed, no heavy body odor) and he was in the vicinity of Suburban Station, where he liked to be anyway, since the big companies with lots of employees were around there. He'd learned how to pick out people who were comfortable in the city, people who knew that kids rode trains all the time, even if most of those kids were older than Danny. He'd learned not to be too close to the Gallery, or some lady might try to force him back to the mall, thinking they could just have a security guard page his missing mom. He'd also learned that it had to be his dad's advice to take the train, since when he used Mom instead people mumbled that his mom was harsh and suggested calling either his parents or the police—in which case he said no thanks and took off. The house in Ardmore was trial and error, discovered after a bunch of other towns didn't work. He wasn't sure why; maybe because they didn't have houses a block from the train station. The 9/11 part he never would have thought of, but it was handed to him by a stooped old guy who said, "I bet your dad taught you that in case of another terrorist stunt like 9/11. You can never be too prepared. Your dad is one smart fellow."

The final touch was all his own idea, and it was the best part. He would take a toy car out of his pocket and force out the tears, sputtering, "But now I can't do what Dad told me, because I spent the emergency train fare he gave me on this." Almost everyone who'd stayed with him this far—and Danny told the whole story very quickly, knowing most people can walk away from pleas for help without a second thought—would hand over the train fare. Sometimes they gave him ten or even twenty dollars extra, "just in case."

The toy car was back in his pocket before anyone could get a good look at it, but that just made it seem like Danny didn't care about the dumb old car anymore, which happened to be true. He hated that car because he'd stolen it. This was before he'd sworn himself in as a knight, but it was still embarrassing to him. The code was to steal only when absolutely necessary, meaning food, clothing, shelter, or medicine. Since his story was a lie, his begging was stealing, too, and he knew it, but it was okay as long as he used the money only for necessities. The only toy he had ever let himself buy with the train fare money was Isabelle's stuffed elephant. He bought it because she wouldn't let go of it, but also because it had a string on its back that you could pull and make it say things. He figured she'd learn some words that way. He was wrong, but even his mom said it was a good idea. Somehow Isabelle had to learn to talk.

Of course Danny wanted all kinds of things for himself, but most of them he could put out of his mind by reminding himself that toys were for kids. It helped that he didn't really feel like a kid anymore, partly because he had to work so hard to get money for his mom and his sister, but mainly because he was the only person in the house who tried to clean the toilet and bathtub or even dumped the trash can before it overflowed.

Isabelle was fourteen months old when his mom suddenly found a place for them to live. "And it's free," she said. "All we have to do is walk over there and move right in." Danny was glad to get out of the abandoned car, but he wondered what kind of house could cost nothing. He found out when they got there. The tiny yard had junk all over it, half the windows were boarded up, and the front door was split at the bottom, like someone had tried to kick it in. But Danny was relieved, figuring his mom might have lucked out and really found a house no one else wanted. Too bad it wasn't true. The house already had lots of people living there—so many that Danny never learned half of their names. It didn't help that new people were always moving in just as people he'd gotten used to decided to leave, or "split," as they called it. Almost everyone who lived there used needles like his mom; the only ones who didn't were babies and kids. Danny was terrified of these people and he begged his mom to move back to the car, even though it was October and already getting cold again, but she said it had been towed. When he walked over a few days later, he was surprised to discover that she wasn't lying; the car was gone.

So they weren't homeless anymore and, really, the house wasn't as bad as it looked on the outside. It didn't have much heat, but it did have running water and flushing toilets and a microwave oven someone brought and an old TV, though no refrigerator or stove. The lights were off a lot, but when they had power, it was like a party and everyone made bags of popcorn in the microwave and sat on the floor, huddling around the space heaters, watching the one channel they could get on the TV, the one with *Eyewitness News*, which Danny liked because it taught him so many useful things about the city. For example, though he'd already been to most sections of Center City—Society Hill, Queen Village, Old City, Northern Liberties, the Art Museum area, Rittenhouse Square—*Eyewitness News* taught him that West Philadelphia wasn't a slum, like his mom always said, but a place with the richest college in town, the University of Pennsylvania. He wouldn't have been on the Walnut Street Bridge that night if he hadn't known this. His plan was to find a rich college student coming back late to the dorms. He was going to tell this college student the truth: that his sister was sick and he needed money for a cheap hotel, just for a day or two. The power was off again at the house, and even though he'd managed to find enough branches to keep a fire going in the fireplace, it was still way too cold there for Isabelle to get well.

His mom had insisted on coming with them because it was so late, even though she was out of drugs. Everyone in the house seemed to be out of drugs that week; Danny wasn't sure why, but he knew all that sickness had to be bad for his sister. That was the other reason he was determined to get her out of there. Someone was always in the bathroom, and he couldn't even get in to wash the vomit off Isabelle's face and hands.

When the rich man offered to help them, Danny was stunned. He was almost sure the guy was on something, but it still didn't make sense because, from everything he'd seen, being on drugs didn't make a person more likely to help anyone. Before the man passed out, Danny's plan was to take the Emetrol and Gatorade and then ask him for the hotel money, which he was pretty sure the guy would have given him. He would never have dreamed of asking to spend the night in the man's apartment. Even the most sympathetic people wouldn't offer to let Danny and Isabelle stay in their house, not for a night, not even for an hour.

He was still planning to ask for hotel money in the morning, when the man woke up, but by then his mother had changed everything by stealing from him. Isabelle was sleeping so peacefully, but he still would have picked her up and left with his mom if only she'd given him enough of the stolen cash to pay for a hotel. When she wouldn't give it to him, he told her she'd have to leave without them. She cried and said he didn't trust her. "What has happened to you? I'm your mom. With all this money, I can find us an apartment. I have enough here for a down payment and the rent for months!"

They argued for a while, but he wouldn't budge and finally she left, saying she'd be back in the morning and prove he was wrong; she'd come by and get them and take them to their new home. He didn't believe any of it. He blamed himself for bringing his mom along in the first place. He'd been worried that she'd just lie on the riverbank and freeze to death, but he had to learn to harden his heart to her, somehow, if he was ever going to protect Isabelle. What if the man really had called the security guard and the police? His sister might have ended up in some home for retarded kids where no one cared for her, and no one even saw how special she was. And Isabelle wasn't retarded anyway; he always wanted to punch kids who called her that. She was slow in some ways, but she was thinking a lot, he was sure. She laughed at jokes and even tried to make some herself, without words. Even his mom said Isabelle was "funny as all get-out," which was one of her phrases from child-hood. She'd grown up in the South: a small town outside of Memphis. Danny wasn't sure why "all get-out" would be funny, but he knew what his mom meant.

If it weren't for *Eyewitness News*, he wouldn't have known that some grown-ups like to have sex with kids, and he wouldn't have known how horrible everyone thought grown-ups like that were. He felt like a creep using that to threaten the guy, but he knew he didn't have a choice. Even if the man would have given him the money for a hotel at that point, just to get rid of them, there was no money left because his mom had taken it all. There was no time to go to an ATM, either, because he was going to Japan, which Danny knew was a long way from here, but still, he planned on keeping his word. As soon as Isabelle woke up, they would leave. She was obviously feeling better because she hadn't vomited all night; the Emetrol must have done the trick. He'd find some food in the kitchen, and then he'd walk out of there forever. They'd go back to the house, where they'd probably find that his mom had blown all the cash she stole getting drugs for everyone. She was always generous like that.

In the meantime, he figured it wouldn't hurt to tiptoe around and take in all the wonders of this place, the most beautiful house he'd ever seen, better than any TV apartment, so large it was like the inside of a castle. There was an entire wall of enormous windows. A ceiling that went up so high, it was like some giant lived here. A bathroom large enough for a giant, larger than the room where he and Isabelle and his mom slept with six or seven other people. An enormous tub and, across from it, a shower in a box all by itself, made of glass that was so clean you could see the on/off handles sparkling without even opening the door. If there was a door—Danny didn't see one, and he wondered how you got in the box. Maybe there was a button that made one of the glass walls evaporate. Anything could happen in a place as fantastic as this.

In the kitchen, he looked up to see dozens of gleaming pans hanging from the ceiling. A case of knives that all looked serious enough to stab someone, though he figured they were just for cutting thick food. Dozens and dozens of white electric gadgets; Danny didn't know what most of them did. He gently opened the cabinets, looking for food, but there wasn't as much as he expected. He did find a box of Premium crackers, which he knew would be good for Isabelle since she'd been sick. Then he kept looking until he found a drawer with a loaf of bread. He took out two slices, hoping to make himself a sandwich, but the refrigerator didn't have any meat slices or cheese. He couldn't even find any peanut butter, so he ended up eating the bread by itself—an "air sandwich," as his mom called it. He also found some fancy cookies that tasted like ginger and ate about a dozen of them.

The desk where his mom found all the money was right out in the open, in what the man had called the "loft area" but his mom called the living room. Probably because the desk was too big to fit anywhere else in the place. The top was as big as the double doors that led to the kitchen. The chair was big, too, but not big enough to let the man reach the far side of the desk, where a bunch of magazines were stacked up, all with weird names. Danny had a library card and he read at night when Isabelle was asleep, whenever he had batteries for his flashlight, but he had no idea what a lot of these words meant.

When Danny sat down in the chair, he was just planning to watch the big screen change pictures while he waited for Isabelle. He knew this was called a computer monitor, and the thin gray thing attached to it was a computer. It was the man's second computer, actually; Danny had noticed another one peeking out of the top of his black bag before he zipped it up and left. To most people the pictures on this screen might have been boring, but to Danny, just watching them shift and change was interesting enough to keep him sitting quietly for ten minutes. He loved watching the word *Research* dissolve and be replaced by *Innovation*, even if he didn't know what Innovation was. He wasn't sure about Integrity, either, but he knew it was all some kind of math when he saw the big orange block containing an equal sign. He waited through several more pictures before the screen finally put it all together: ASTOR-DENNING. RESEARCH + INNOVATION + INTEGRITY = ENHANCING HEALTH, SAVING LIVES.

He'd been very good at math in first grade, but they hadn't gotten around to how you add words together. He smiled at how cool the idea was. Everything here was so cool that he thought the man was the luckiest guy on the planet. He even liked him more because he had all this great stuff and because Danny had a hunch he'd gotten all this from that weird equation. Maybe the guy was even saving lives, which would mean he deserved to have a palace, like any good king. No wonder he had to protect this place from strangers. Danny was relieved his mom hadn't thought to take the computer.

She would have pawned it without even knowing it contained the equation, and maybe been responsible for killing someone.

After Danny finally grew tired of the pictures on the screen, he noticed something else hanging off the side of the gray computer. He couldn't believe it had taken him so long to see this beautiful thing. It was the one thing in the world that was absolutely irresistible to him.

He'd thought about it for months, wanting one so bad, even though he knew it was as unnecessary as a toy. He'd reminded himself over and over that he couldn't steal one, no matter how easy it would be. And it would be so easy—that was the hardest part. Though it cost hundreds of dollars, it was so small he could drop it in his pocket and run before whoever he'd taken it from even noticed it was gone. And people treated theirs so casually. Every day, he saw these treasures hanging out of backpacks and purses; once, he even spotted one sitting all alone on the bottom step of a fire escape. That one he would have taken if its owner hadn't remembered to come back for it right as Danny made up his mind that it didn't belong to anyone now, so it wasn't stealing.

Obsessing about this stupid thing had made him so miserable that he wished he'd never discovered it. If only he hadn't let that teenage girl talk him into listening to it. The girl had just given him thirty-two dollars, though she said she didn't believe his train fare story. Probably because he didn't have Isabelle with him; it never worked as well when his sister wasn't there. That day she had a doctor's appointment, and his mom had promised she'd take his sister to the clinic for all her shots. His mom wasn't sick, so he knew she'd do it.

"But hey," the girl said, smiling, "I know you need money and I don't; my parents are loaded. So here, I'll give you whatever I have."

She had long golden hair, just like a princess. He thought she was the most beautiful girl he'd ever seen, even if she did talk too loud. He must have stepped back from her voice because she laughed and said, "Sorry. I'm shouting over Radiohead. God, I love that band. Ever heard them?"

"No."

She pulled tiny white plugs from her ears and handed them to him. "Check it out."

"I better not." He wasn't sure how to work the plugs. The only headphones he'd seen people use were much bigger, probably because this kind was too small to notice unless you stared at someone, which Danny never did. It put people off to be stared at.

"Come on, don't be scared. I'm not going to bite you, even though I am a girl."

"I'm not scared," he said, lifting his chin. "I just don't want to bother you."

"It won't bother me, it will make me happy." She smiled her radiant, straight-teeth smile. "Knowing I taught a little kid about the best band in the world." When he still hesitated, she said, "Consider it your way of repaying me, okay?"

He couldn't let her put the white plugs in for him; he didn't want her to see how dirty his ears were. He figured out how to use the earphones easily enough, and when he was finished listening, he remembered to wipe the plugs on his jacket sleeve to remove any wax. He didn't want to be disgusting to this girl. For some reason, his usual knight's excuse of spending too much time traveling outdoors, without access to daily baths and other civilized things, didn't comfort him the way it always had before. Standing with this perfect girl, none of that even seemed real.

The total time he'd listened to the music was probably no more than a minute. One of the girl's friends had come along and told her that it was time to go back in, lunch was over. They were students at a school near Suburban Station called Friends Select, where Danny loved to hang out. Most of the kids were really nice, even those who didn't give him any money.

One minute, but it was enough. He couldn't get his mind off that white music-making box. Before the end of the day, he knew what it was called. He'd even seen it in a commercial with people dancing, but he hadn't paid attention then. Now it was a word he noticed everywhere, a word he loved as much as he'd ever loved crown and sword and knights and honor. iPod.

He wanted one more than he'd ever wanted a home. If only he had an iPod, he wouldn't have to listen to the people in their house cry and moan when they ran out of drugs. He wouldn't have to listen to the screaming all around the neighborhood. He wouldn't even have to listen to people who didn't believe him and yelled that he was supposed to be in school, not panhandling on the street. "I got my own kids to feed. Tell your mom and dad to get off their lazy asses and get a job, like everybody else."

The iPod would fill the whole world with music, and everything in his life would be different. Maybe he would make it play sad music to get him in the mood for tears, when necessary. Or he could have it play happy music when he was trudging home and Isabelle seemed so heavy. He could even play Big music when he was looking at the whole city from 30th Street Station, and the Big music would remind him he could do anything, just like it did for the boxer in the only movie he could remember seeing, a movie set in Philly called *Rocky* that they'd shown every night in the homeless shelter. His mom said *Rocky* was supposed to inspire them to get off the streets and find work.

Naturally, the man had an iPod; he had everything. When Danny picked up the white beauty, connected by a cord to the computer, his only conscious thought was to listen to it until Isabelle woke up. He'd already heard her stirring, so he knew it wouldn't be long. He had to take this chance now, while he still could.

He hoped he wasn't about to steal the man's iPod, but he couldn't be sure. If the iPod hadn't lit up when he touched it and told him DO NOT DISCONNECT, he might have figured out how to get the wire off, he might have slipped it in his pocket. Instead, he let go immediately, afraid an alarm was about to go off. Then he jumped in his seat as the computer screen suddenly came to life. The shifting pictures were gone, and in their place was a box with hundreds and hundreds of numbers. Above the box it said Microsoft Excel. Next to it was another, smaller box that repeated the warning not to disconnect the iPod. But most noticeable of all was that the computer had started talking to him.

He understood the first word, *hello*, but after that it was all gibberish except the word *hola*, which some of his mom's friends used. After a minute or two, he heard another regular English sentence, "How are you? I'm fine, thank you," followed by more gibberish. The pattern continued, English, gibberish, until he figured out that *all* the gibberish must be words in other languages. The clue was that each gibberish sentence had a different accent. He recognized the Italian accent from the *Rocky* movie. He recognized the Spanish accent from a woman his mom knew. Why he recognized the Japanese he wasn't sure, but that made him guess the man had been listening to this to learn how to say things on his trips.

He was just deciding that the guy might not be all that smart—his mom knew lots of Spanish, just from having friends; shouldn't the man already know *hello* in Japanese if he was flying there?—when he heard a sound that made him spin around so fast he hit his shin on the leg of the desk. It was Isabelle's voice, and it was so loud that he thought she'd fallen off the couch. But no, she was sitting up, looking at him, making the same loud sound over and over. "Chow! Chow! Chow!"

He knew she didn't mean food, but he had to wait for the whole thing to start from the beginning again before he could figure out what the word meant. It was her first word other than constant *nos* and the rare *yes*, and of course he was thrilled. Even if it was in Italian, it was still hello. And she was smiling at him like she meant it.

During the next hour, while he was feeding her crackers and giving her sips of Gatorade, the tape kept playing. Danny wasn't sure how to stop it, and he was glad he didn't because Isabelle got two more words before she put her hand out, meaning she was full. One of the words was from the middle of a sentence and Danny couldn't tell what it meant or even what language it was, but the other one was *you*. And she said it over and over, pointing at him all the while.

He wasn't surprised she knew what it meant; she'd understood language for a long time. But that she could talk, well, that was a miracle. It had to be, because a mean nurse at the clinic had told his mom, "It will take a miracle for your daughter to suddenly start speaking."

That this miracle came from the computer with the equation made the little hairs on Danny's arms stand up as he wondered what else this computer could do. How could he leave before he found out how many more words Isabelle could learn? And what about the other things in this apartment? What if this magical place even held the key to fixing his sister?

Of course the security guard was still a problem. For all he knew, the man was calling him right now. Somehow, Danny needed a way to stay here without anybody finding them. He thought for a moment, until he remembered the guy's bedroom. As he was wandering around the apartment, he'd noticed something in that room. He picked up Isabelle and headed in that direction, squinting his eyes the way he always did when he was hoping hard that this time, something good would actually work out.

CHAPTER THREE

Matthew's No-Good, Very Bad Day

While Danny was examining Matthew's bedroom, Matthew himself was on a plane to Chicago—where he had a short layover before he boarded the flight to Tokyo—drinking his second cup of bad airplane coffee, trying to decipher a cryptic but clearly panicked email from his assistant, Cassie. He'd tried to call her from the pay-as-you-go-phone he'd picked up in the Philly airport, but he never got through. He suspected that she was frantically dialing his cell, wondering why he wasn't answering since he always answered her calls unless he was in the air or with a client, and she knew his schedule perfectly so she knew that until

8:27 that morning, neither of those was true. Takeoff at 8:37 meant cell phones off at 8:27, which always annoyed Matthew since he thought the evidence that cell phones caused navigation problems at any point during a flight was unconvincing and probably paid for by the maker of those overpriced, ugly, seat-back-mounted phones. Which of course he still tried to use, repeatedly, to reach Cassie or Cassie's assistant, Geoff, or any of the managers in his division, but no one was answering—if the piece of shit was even dialing his office, which he couldn't be sure of since the calls just rang and rang rather than switching over to voice mail.

Writing cryptic emails was part of Cassie's job, to avoid creating an audit trail for anything beyond the mundane. But obviously the point was to make the meaning indecipherable to everyone *except* Matthew.

"Hello, Dr. Connelly. I've heard Tokyo may be having bad weather. Perhaps you should reschedule your trip. I'll be in at 6:30 to discuss alternate flight plans. If you like, I can schedule you for a lunch today at Bookbinders. The email server keeps going down, so it would be best to call me directly about this. Cassie."

She always called him Matthew, but he insisted on Dr. Connelly for emails to hide how closely they worked together, in case he was ever in trouble, so she wouldn't go down with him. Bad weather in Tokyo was obviously a problem in Japan, but a problem wouldn't mean rescheduling the trip, but rather going there immediately, as Matthew already was. The email server lie was fairly standard procedure, but it did mean that the problem was too delicate to discuss in even the most cryptic of emails. The six-thirty arrival was the real sign that she was panicking, as Cassie had kids (two or three, he wasn't sure), and she wouldn't come in at that hour unless something was seriously wrong. The other sign was the Bookbinders lunch date, which was code that his boss, Walter Healy, wanted to meet with him—but that had to be Cassie going over the edge and forgetting what lunch at Bookbinders meant. Everyone on his staff knew that Walter was in Paris, where he was the keynote speaker at a European Union conference.

His second cup of crap coffee finished, he found himself worrying what could be so wrong in Tokyo that Cassie had decided he shouldn't make the trip. That idiotic TV show had been shown on every channel in the country? Picked up by all the newspapers and radio stations? The Japanese government had decided to hold emergency hearings? Even so, Matthew would have gone there to protect his billion-dollar baby. He had nothing to worry about; all the Galvenar safety data in his PowerPoint presentation had been extensively verified by statisticians, not to mention by the "geniuses" at the FDA.

His mind wandered to Ben and Amelia then, and before long he'd fallen asleep, waking up only when the plane landed. Waiting for him at his gate was the PR rep, Dorothy Hilton, an older gal (really older, not older like forty) known for her immensely reassuring presence, her knowledge of Japanese and several other languages, and her endless ability to sling intelligent-sounding bullshit. Her firm was the top of the line for pharmaceutical PR, and Matthew was glad to see her smiling. Dorothy Hilton would not be grinning if there were a problem in Tokyo. "Nothing new," she said, and showed him a thick file of downloaded Japanese newspapers. No news is good news, as she said.

Meaning Cassie knew something about Japan that this PR expert didn't? Highly unlikely. So what was she talking about? Jesus, why couldn't he get through to anyone? Was Astor-Denning on fire? He finally decided to call the company's main number and asked the receptionist to connect him with anybody on the third floor, building B.

"Could you be more specific, sir? We have more than a hundred people on that floor."

"I'm aware of that. And any one of them will know who I am, so just put me through to someone you know is in today. The higher up the better."

"Fine," she said snippily. Maybe he had sounded a little pissed off. He was about to apologize, but then he found himself transferred, and the phone was ringing. When he heard the click to voice mail he was relieved, but then he heard his own voice. The receptionist had put him through to himself. Fuck.

Dorothy had gotten him a latte and a bagel at Starbucks, accepting without question the strange fact that he didn't have any cash or his ATM card. She sat down and repeated her reassurance that the receptionist's busy signal when he tried to call again (and again and again) wasn't worrying. "Our trip is going to be a dazzling success. It's all good."

He tore off a chunk of the bagel and wondered why PR people always repeated themselves, like good kindergarten teachers making sure everyone understood. For instance, "It's all good," which had been repeated so often it was an annoying cliché. *All* good? Then how come I'm sitting on an ugly blue plastic bolted-to-the-ground chair in Chicago, about to board a fourteen-hour flight? How come I feel like I've just been run over by a bus? How come I can't get through to my assistant, or her assistant, or anybody in my department? How come I couldn't think fast enough last night to get out of doing an illegal drug that caused me to get robbed? How come I let homeless people take over the only place I can really relax, my citadel against all the slings and arrows, my personal little castle complete with security system moat, my home sweet home?

Of course the scheming boy and the sick girl he'd left in his apartment had been bugging him all morning. His plan had been to explain what happened to Cassie—all of it, including the E—and then get her to deal with the security guard and social services or whoever would get them out of his house. In the cold fluorescent light of the airport, it was abundantly obvious that no sane person would believe he'd let two homeless kids in just to be *nice*. Hell, he wouldn't believe it himself if he hadn't done it. So calling the security guard, knowing the boy would bring up the sex allegation, was out of the question. He could imagine the headline: ASTOR-DENNING VICE PRESIDENT A PEDOPHILE? Better to have his entire place ransacked by the addict mom and all her addict friends than risk that nuclear-sized disaster.

He hoped that the kid wasn't lying and they were already gone. It was possible, if unlikely. If only he had some way to find out. Too bad he hadn't gone to any of the building parties and had ignored all his neighbors' attempts to be friends. Too bad he didn't have a wife or at least a live-in girlfriend. The girlfriend could handle all this for him, not to mention that the pedophile story wouldn't be as compelling if he wasn't a forty-year-old man, living alone, never married. It sounded bad even to him. In his thirties, he had been considered a player, but suddenly, at forty, he found himself nailing the profile of a sicko who hit on little kids. The march of time: inevitable, inexorable, inescapable—whatever word you used, it really sucked.

He'd always thought he would be married someday, but later, when he had time to think about finding someone who wasn't the beautiful-but-dumb type he always found himself in bed with. Marrying one of those women was out of the question; he couldn't even stand them after a few weeks (or, more often, after one night), when he realized they had no idea what he was talking about. The only woman he'd ever lived with and thought he loved was Amelia. She wasn't traditionally beautiful, but she was beautiful to him and incredibly smart—and look how well that worked out. She not only hated his guts, but she'd used every opportunity to make his life miserable *for years*. Everyone in his office was afraid of the woman, and no wonder: she was considered one of the most vocal critics of

American pharmaceutical companies. Even Walter, a soft-spoken southern gentleman, had called Amelia Johannsen a "vicious bitch" and some other things that Matthew himself, no gentleman at all, really, was too much of a gentleman to repeat.

But Walter had forgiven Miss Johannsen for all her numerous affronts against Astor-Denning when an entire year and then another passed without one peep out of her about Galvenar. Of course she kept up her diatribes against Big Pharma in general and AD specifically, but she never said one public word about their baby, which was an unprecedented stroke of something—could it be luck? Walter even asked Matthew if he was sleeping with her, which would have been funny if Matthew hadn't already tried that a few years ago and found it most definitely did not work. If anything, trying to get back together with Amelia was the stupidest thing he'd ever done, but he'd learned his lesson from that fiasco. This time around, he'd come up with something much more effective.

The plan had taken over a year to execute, but it had turned out exactly as he had envisioned. Even better, actually, as he never expected Amelia to say she was ready to put the past behind them. Yet she'd said those exact words, last weekend in the Caymans. Of course she was madly in love with one of the most famously ethical scientists in the world, which probably made her see things through a softer lens. Give her enough time and Matthew was sure she'd return to her old tired way of separating everything and everyone into Do Right or Do Wrong. Matthew also knew on which side of the black and white line he would inevitably fall, because he knew Amelia. This was why he'd never once believed that Galvenar would go unnoticed by her forever. The very idea was laughable.

"I hear congratulations are in order," Dorothy said. They were standing in line, getting ready to board the plane. She'd been talking nonstop and Matthew wished again that he'd remembered to bring his iPod. "Paris appears to be off to a fabulous start."

Matthew nodded. Though the EU conference hadn't officially begun yet, AD was already enjoying a big public relations boost for aligning itself with the World Health Organization as sponsors of this "humanitarian" event. Matthew wasn't surprised it was going well, despite the stupid fears of some of the company's old guard, who'd worried that paying for a conference to examine the issue of drugs in the third world might confuse stockholders and make them think AD was becoming dangerously soft on profit. He expected the news would be even better after Walter's excellent keynote speech.

"We'll have dozens of our own articles tomorrow on access to quality-of-life medicines," Dorothy added. "Reprints of 'Chronic Heartbreak,' too. It's all good."

"Chronic Heartbreak" was a first-person account of what it was like to live with severe, untreated pain from MS. For the last two years, it had been widely circulated by members of the grassroots organization Pain Matters, as part of their vigorous and relentless lobbying campaign to force doctors and medical schools around the world to take pain as seriously as any other disease because pain kills.

It's true; pain does kill. Chronic pain patients commit suicide when their pain goes untreated, not to mention the demonstrated effect of pain on the heart and immune system. But Pain Matters was not really a grassroots organization, but the creation of Dorothy Hilton's PR firm, when Matthew first hired them to help him launch Galvenar. This particular PR stunt, cleverly named *astroturfing*, was so common in corporate and political marketing campaigns that Matthew had never given it a second thought. Since pain does matter, why shouldn't they say so as often and loudly as they wanted?

The articles and reprints about pain (and, of course, Galvenar) were part of Astor-Denning's other, more complicated reason for sponsoring the conference. Which was yet another reason to be glad it was going well so far. Matthew had all the problems he could handle right now, or so he stupidly thought.

He was on the plane, sitting in his first-class, cubicle-like pod, ignoring yet another pep talk from Dorothy. She was kneeling in the aisle, at his elbow, rather than sitting across the aisle in her own personal pod, while he thumbed through the *Wall Street Journal*, hoping she would get the message and go away. All of a sudden, he knew exactly why Cassie was so upset. There it was, right on the second page of *WSJ*'s Marketplace section: the short, simple, and hideous news that there had been a "late addition" to the EU conference roster—bioethicist Amelia Johannsen. A "surprising development," they said, which Matthew considered the understatement of the year.

At least it was obvious now what Cassie had been trying to tell him. Bookbinders had meant that he needed to see Walter immediately, not in Philadelphia, but in France. This was why she'd used the phrase "alternate flight plans." She was trying to let him know that he needed to go directly to Paris. She was probably too panicked to figure out a sensible way to say that bad weather in Paris meant he shouldn't go to Japan, if a sensible way to say such a geographically ridiculous thing existed. He couldn't think of one at that moment, though he was telling himself that this new development was nothing to panic about because he knew how to manage the problem.

True, he hadn't expected it to happen so soon—that lying bitch! Put the past behind them, what a crock!—but that it would happen someday, he was positive. And he was ready. All he had to do was use the international first-class personal phone at his elbow, and he could make this go away. No need to fly to Paris, though of course he would since Walter wanted him to, as soon as he did the bare minimum to settle Japan. He'd send Cassie there immediately to calm the boss's understandable fears.

He had no problem getting through to her this time; Cassie said she didn't know why his calls hadn't come through earlier. Maybe a computer glitch in the phone system? Whatever, there was no time to discuss it now. This day was obviously screwed.

Though Matthew had not been in charge of putting together the conference participant list, he had signed off on the final version: mostly scientists and doctors, a few ethicists and policy-makers—and, most important, all with personal or institutional ties to Astor-Denning. The only person on the list who was known to be above taking any dollars from Big Pharma was no threat to them, Matthew was sure. But Ben's soul mate, as he kept calling Amelia—nauseatingly enough—was another story entirely. How she managed to get herself added to this list, the *day* before the conference started, would be the first thing Walter would ask, no doubt screaming and cursing as though he blamed Matthew, though of course he really didn't. He never had any idea that the Amelia problem was, in fact, Matthew's fault, in the past and (fuck it all!) this time, too.

Why hadn't he thought of this hideous possibility? He knew full well that only Ben had the clout to get anyone added without approval from the sponsors. That only Ben could just call up the WHO organizers, sure that whoever answered would be so im-pressed just hearing his name that they would agree to whatever he wanted.

Of course the bitch must have put him up to it. Ben was too busy inventing cures for the world's poor to devote even one per-cent of his enormous brainpower to the topic of why Amelia had asked him to get her on the bioethics panel. And Ben was too in-nocent to go beyond the obvious thought that since Amelia was in Paris with him anyway, why not?

Predictably, the *WSJ* report caused AD stock to start fluctuating as brokers tried to decide what it meant: Nothing? (hold) Galvenar was about to take a serious hit? (sell) The incorruptible Amelia had finally accepted a payday? (buy) It went down; it went up; it went back down; Cassie's assistant, Geoff, kept watch until the final bell rang. Net result: a loss of almost two percent. Bad, yes, but not that bad until you factored in that the stock had been on the increase for months, and then it was very, very bad. Walter had left Matthew several voice mails (fourteen at last count) to make sure he was aware of that.

All day, Matthew had been calling Geoff every twenty minutes or so for updates. Cassie had quickly left for Paris. At some point, Matthew remembered to ask Geoff to overnight another Motorola international cell and cancel his phone number and credit cards. He explained that he'd been mugged, but gave no details.

He'd been on the plane for seven hours; Dorothy was asleep in her own personal pod and he was exhausted, too. It was time to do the deed, despite how much he was dreading it. Benjamin had always been an early-to-bed, early-to-rise guy, and it was already 10:35 in Paris. Matthew had Ben's cell number programmed into his phone, but that was just for speed dialing. He knew Ben's number as well as he knew Cassie's. Of course he did. Ben was his oldest, closest friend.

CHAPTER FOUR

The Logic of Amelia's Life

When Amelia was a little girl, her grandmother gave her an adopted child for Christmas. The girl's name was Esteysi Mariela and she was seven years old, just like Amelia, and she lived in Guatemala, which started with a G, just like Greenwich, where Amelia lived. There the similarities ended, however. Grandma told her that Guatemala was nothing like Greenwich, Connecticut, and Esteysi was so poor that she didn't have any clothes (other than the pink dress she was wearing in the picture) or a school or a dentist or even a doctor to make her better when she was sick. But now that Amelia had adopted her, Esteysi would have all of this. All Amelia had to do was write to Esteysi once a month, like a pen pal. But she mustn't forget about Esteysi, because Esteysi was counting on her. Grandma would send the monthly checks, but Amelia would be the real sponsor of this child. She would be the one saving Esteysi's life.

Amelia thought it was the best Christmas present she'd ever received. She loved little Esteysi and the child Grandma added the next year, an eight-year-old boy named Pablo who lived in Venezuela, and Astrid from Chile, who was nine when Amelia was nine, and ten-year-old Maria from the Philippines, and so on and so on, until Grandma died when Amelia was fifteen. Amelia's parents thought sponsoring nine needy children was more than enough, and they were glad these children would all turn eighteen around the time Amelia did so she could go to college free of the responsibility of writing all those letters and sending the money, too, now that Grandma wasn't around. Honestly, Amelia's parents thought Grandma was something of a crackpot, and they wished she hadn't gotten Amelia started on what had become an obsession with righting all of society's wrongs. Other kids wanted cars for their sixteenth birthdays; Amelia wanted a donation to a New York homeless shelter. When would she get over this?

Amelia entered college hoping her professors could answer the question that had bothered her since Grandma had introduced her to poor Esteysi: Why do such bad things happen to innocent people? In her first philosophy class, she learned an answer that was short, if nothing like sweet: Bad things happen to all people. All people includes innocent people. Therefore, bad things happen to innocent people. QED.

The only part of this answer Amelia liked was QED, the abbreviation of the Latin phrase *quod erat demonstrandum*, meaning "which was to be demonstrated" or, in simpler terms, "it is proved." It wasn't much of a proof, Amelia thought, though she knew her professor was right that the logic was irrefutable if you accept the first sentence, which philosophers call the premise. But when she asked her prof the bigger question, "Why do bad things happen to all people?" he had no answer other than to wave his arms around and say, "This is the world we find ourselves in." She decided he'd given up, and she stopped caring what he thought. She was premed; once she was a doctor, she would do *something* to change this.

But Amelia didn't end up going to medical school. She decided on a different career after her dean broke the news, at the beginning of senior year, that she wouldn't be going to Hopkins. The dean emphasized that there were other very good schools, but Hopkins had been Amelia's dream since she was a freshman: it was the next step in her life plan, the place her parents and all her friends expected her to go. The premeds at her college were all aware that only two students would have their applications supported for Hopkins; they'd even made bets on who would be the second one chosen—since the first one, everybody knew, would be Ben Watkins, a scarily brilliant guy who'd never had a date and was jokingly rumored to be working on a nuclear weapon to express his frustration. Amelia had been the hands-down favorite: she had the grades, the recommendations, and an amazing record of volunteer work that was tiring just to read. Everyone assumed she would do well on the MCAT, and she did; yet her score seemed only average compared to the unheard-of perfect performance by another student, a guy who nobody had picked to win, not even himself. Since Ben had refused to answer three of the multiple-choice questions, saying none of the answers were really correct, Matthew beat out even him.

Of course it galled Amelia that pretty-boy Matthew, a smart-ass who didn't seem to care about medicine or anything else, had taken her spot at Hopkins. He was an English major who could talk circles around everyone else in the premed group, but she'd never said one word to him. His perfect MCAT score did not change her opinion that he was "obviously" shallow.

How odd that Matthew Connelly would prove to be the logic of her life. It was because of him that she went to graduate school in philosophy instead of becoming a doctor. She did end up at Hopkins, after all, because they had a concentration in the history of science. She convinced herself that it was a better fit anyway, since she'd always loved thinking about the moral issues of medicine more than the gritty, icky details of the body. When Matthew heard that she was moving to Baltimore, he sought her out to tell her about a great apartment building where he and Ben were going to be sharing a place. She didn't even realize he knew Ben, and she couldn't imagine the two of them as roommates. But the building was perfect and she moved there, too, five floors above Matthew and Ben's apartment. Whenever Matthew saw her, in the elevator or in the hall by the mailboxes, he would insist that she come over and have dinner with them. After months of this, she finally broke down, and they became friends.

Amelia considered herself shy, and Ben acted like it caused him physical pain to make small talk; yet somehow Matthew held them all together. He cooked wonderful meals his mother had taught him to make—spaghetti and meatballs, mushroom quiche, chicken fajitas—and he invented weird games like What If. What if you must choose between strangling a kitten and having ten thousand acres of the rain forest pulverized? What if you're given a chance to meet Shakespeare, but only with your clothes off? What if you could discover a cure for cancer, but you can make it public only if you agree to blow Oliver North? What if you were in Damien's shoes in *Omen II*—would you kill yourself after discovering you were the Antichrist, or go ahead and use your evil powers to take control of the earth?

Amelia wasn't sure when she fell in love with him, but she remembered their first kiss. She'd lived in Baltimore for three years; he was upstairs at her place. She'd called him, crying, after she'd tried to light her oven and caught her hair on fire. He said it wasn't that dumb, especially if you didn't know about pilot lights. Then he examined her hair and said it was only singed at the ends. "Don't worry," he said, "you can still be the little red-haired girl." He'd been calling her "little red-haired girl" since he found out she loved Peanuts, but this time she leaned over and kissed him, and he kissed her back. Before long they were sleeping together, but not every night because Matthew didn't want to leave Ben all by himself, since Ben didn't have a girlfriend.

When Matthew dropped out of the program at the end of the fourth year—with an MD his adviser said would be worthless without a residency—Amelia certainly didn't understand the decision, but she was thrilled when he asked her to come live with him in Philadelphia. He told her the reason for leaving was simple: he was sick of not having any money. She thought, as did his professors, that he was being extremely shortsighted, but she also knew she might feel the same way if she were in his shoes. Though she hadn't known it at the time, she'd discovered that he and Ben had been the only two "scholarship" students in the premed program. She wasn't sure about Ben's circumstances, but she knew Matthew's father had died of liver problems when Matthew was twelve and his mom had died of ovarian cancer right before he started college. He was an *orphan*, while she had two successful parents and a trust fund from her grandmother. How could she begin to understand what money meant to him?

She admired his stance of refusing to take money from her, even when he'd had to steal food from the hospital cafeteria. This proved he had to be kidding when he always said an ethical position was like a yacht: "I'll let you know when I can afford to think about buying either of them."

Still, she was positive he was making a huge mistake taking a job at Astor-Denning, even if he did have more than a hundred thousand dollars in student loans to pay. She'd followed all the news about big pharmaceutical companies fighting to keep Congress from mandating lower prices for poor people, even though pharmaceutical profits had been skyrocketing since the eighties. She told Matthew it sounded like a creepy place to work, but she assumed it would be temporary, and it wasn't really a problem. While he worked at Astor-Denning, she sat in their adorable little rental house in the suburbs, writing her dissertation about the moral issues of medical research. At night when he got home, he would cook and listen to what she'd written all day. After they did the dishes together, they would sit on the couch and watch a video or, more often, argue about everything she'd just read to him.

The arguments were real, but also, admittedly, a lot of fun. Like any philosophy grad student, she was always up for a take-no-prisoners argument; then too, Matthew usually rubbed her feet while he told her she was "out of touch with the reality of modern medicine" and "touchingly naïve." They made up at night when they went to bed, and that was a big part of the fun, too. Matthew was such a hot guy back then (and still was, if she was being honest): six-foot-three with thick brown hair and the most piercing blue eyes, not to mention that perfect body, which he never seemed to notice and never lifted a finger to maintain. Every morning, when she got up at five-thirty, to run in the dark around their little neighborhood, Matthew slept on, oblivious to the work being thin required of her (and almost everyone but him). One Saturday, when she confessed how much she hated running, he said, "Stop it, then." When she said her ass would spread like the wings on a butterfly, he said, "Your simile sucks, but I like the image of you with a fat ass." Then he grinned that irresistible grin. "Let's try it. More Amelia to love."

Of course she was in love with him: he was witty and smart and obviously in love with her, though she wasn't sure why. Her own mother said Amelia was extremely lucky to have "snagged" a guy like Matthew. "Like in *Funny Girl*," her mother said, referring to a Barbra Streisand musical. Amelia knew what her mother meant. That damned "groom was prettier than the bride" song had been stuck in her head for months when she'd first moved in with Matthew.

But still, he'd chosen her, and that simple fact made her feel even luckier than she had felt as a little girl, comparing herself with the kids in Guatemala. She and Matthew were twenty-six years old; they'd lived together for only a year and they were already talking about marriage and children with a confidence that of course they would do all that, as soon as she finished her dissertation and his student loans were paid off. They would buy a house in their cute little neighborhood—a starter house, Matthew said. They could get a bigger one once they had their 2.5 kids.

Looking back on that time, what always surprised her was just how happy she and Matthew had been. Even years later, when she completely and truly hated his evil guts, she would catch herself remembering those mornings after her runs, when she watched him as he slept. He slept on his left side, with his hands curled up like a child's. In the early morning sunlight, she could see the beautiful blond hairs on his arm, and sometimes she reached out and touched them, lightly, just enough to make him smile in his sleep. She wondered what he dreamed about; he never talked about his dreams. She talked about hers all the time and he acted like they were interesting, even when they were plotless and pointless, held together only by her emotions, often fear, usually fear of losing him. If she woke up having one of these nightmares, he always said, "I'm right here," and collected her in his strong arms, pulling her head against his chest. She remembered the comfort of his heart beating in her ear. She remembered his smell and the way his skin tasted. As much as she wanted to, she would never forget the simple facts of loving him.

During the spring when everything started to change, they were all twenty-seven: Matthew, Ben, and Amelia. The main thing she remembered was that Ben was calling Matthew constantly back then. He'd finished his MD and his PhD in biochemistry and was about to finish his internship (all in only six years—he really was a genius) and he wanted Matthew's help because he was being courted by dozens of labs after publishing the first article based on his research in the incredibly prestigious journal *Cell*. Why Ben had to ask Matthew's advice about everything he did was something Amelia could never understand. Matthew told her to think of them as brothers, and she tried to, especially when Matthew went to Boston at the end of May, using a full week of their precious vacation time to help Ben move into an apartment. But that summer, after Ben was settled in at a great lab working on infectious diseases, he still kept calling, sometimes in the middle of the night. "He's having some problems," Matthew said by way of explanation, but of course this didn't explain anything. It certainly didn't explain why Matthew himself was becoming so taciturn, unless it was sleep deprivation. Half the time now, when he got home from work, he didn't want to cook or talk or do anything but sit and stare at the television. When she asked him what was wrong, over pizza or Chinese (since Amelia herself had never learned to cook), he said, "Tired." When she suggested he go to bed, he said, "I will. Don't worry."

A few months later, Matthew got a promotion and enrolled in an executive MBA program that his boss said would be crucial if he wanted to keep advancing. It was no surprise that he was even more unwilling to talk after spending all evening in some stupid marketing or finance class. Amelia herself was getting ready to go on the job market, now that she'd finally finished her dissertation. Maybe they were both changing, though it felt like it was only Matthew, and he seemed to be changing so fast she kept thinking she had to be imagining it. She was dying to argue with him like they used to, really work out whatever was going on, but he was always too exhausted. When she tried to get him started by saying the same inflammatory things she had always said before, he either shrugged them off or asked her, in an ominous voice, if she was looking for a fight.

By January, the answer was yes. Even a fight was preferable to this strange nothingness between them. At least, that's how she saw it. Once she asked for a fight, she got one—many of them, actually—and that was how she discovered that Matthew had moved into a completely different world.

She was shocked at how angry he was that she'd consistently refused to set foot into Astor-Denning. He'd asked her to come for lunch many times, but she'd always said it had to be somewhere away from the "evil corporate monster." She'd always called AD that, but now he said he was sick of it.

"You wouldn't even come to the Christmas party. How do you think I felt, the only guy in the room without the person I love? The woman who says she loves me, but won't come on any of my trips, just because I'm traveling for my company?"

He used to call it Astor-Denning or AD. Now it was "my company." She said the first word that crossed her mind. "Yuck."

"Brilliant comeback." They were having a Sunday dinner of sorts, eating lasagna, the frozen kind, now that they had a microwave. He threw down his fork. "Next time, maybe you'll try two syllables."

"You work for the devil. How is that my fault?"

"It isn't, but it certainly is your fault, as you so childishly put it, that you reap the benefits of my so-called pact with Satan every day. Look at this house. In the last year, you've bought more than thirty thousand dollars' worth of furniture, to make it—and I quote—'livable.' You bought an eight-hundred-dollar dress for an interview at a public policy think tank working on health care for the poor. I hope the irony wasn't lost on you."

"I have my own money. I didn't think you—"

"Mind that you give it away to your charities? I don't. I love supporting you, but I want you to admit that's what's happening here. I'm supporting you, and you won't support me in the most trivial of ways."

"Meaning the Christmas party. Look, I didn't know that—"

"I had this elaborate plan." He looked away from her, and she followed his gaze to the window. It was snowing again, big soft flakes that made her think of the smell of snow, the feel of it on her face. "After the party, I was going to take you up to my new office and ask you to marry me. I thought it would change that place forever, mark it with you and me and our future, which is what I'm doing there. Giving us one."

Amelia knew that most women wouldn't find an office proposal romantic, but she remembered telling Matthew a long time ago that she loved the idea of a man asking a woman to marry him in a place that was special in his daily life, rather than the "ordinary" special of fancy restaurants or even Paris. She was surprised and very touched, but then she became angry at the way he was rewriting history, changing his job into something good and necessary for them, when it was neither. "You're lying to yourself, Matthew. You know if you quit tomorrow, we could live off my trust fund and the job I'm going to get in a few months and we'd be absolutely fine. We wouldn't be rich, but that's a good thing. I don't want to be rich."

He laughed. "Of course you don't. You are and always have been."

"You didn't address my point."

"Let's see if I can do it justice. You want me to quit my job and trust in your charitable instincts. What exactly do I do in this scenario? Have sex with you more often? Cook and clean while you establish your philosophy career?"

"What's wrong with that?" She honestly didn't know. "Of course you wouldn't have to clean, but you like cooking and gardening and staying home. You were happier when you didn't have to work day and night for them."

"You may be right, but let's just say I don't trust you enough to do that. Certainly not now, when you won't help me with anything."

"But what do you want help with?" She put her hand out to touch him, but at the last minute she changed direction, wrapping her arm around herself instead. "I really had no idea that you needed my help."

"This new job is difficult." He rubbed his eyes. "Doing the MBA work on top of it is extremely difficult. In case you haven't noticed, I come home nearly every night beaten to shit. I'd like you—just once—to act like you care. Because even though you hate AD, you love me. And that's where I work. Accept it or don't, but make up your mind."

He was right, she still hadn't accepted it. When her friends asked what Matthew was doing, she said he was temporarily consulting for a small pharmaceutical company before starting his residency. Last week at the think tank interview, she'd said her boyfriend was trying to find a cure for cancer. If only it were true. Matthew had never done one moment of research at AD. No one seemed to, at least no one he worked with.

"I think you have a point," she said slowly. "I'll have to figure out a way to support you while still loathing that—"

"Jesus Christ, you can't even mention my job without pointing out for the millionth time that you hate it." He stomped away, muttering, "Redundancy R us."

He watched some stupid horror movie on television and then went to bed. At eight-thirty. She thought maybe they could make up the old-fashioned way, but no, he was sound asleep by the time she brushed her teeth and took off her clothes. When she nuzzled up against him, he said, "Love you," in that sleepy unconscious way that made it impossible to doubt he meant it. She started crying then, but softly, so she wouldn't wake him. It was the least she could do, given how tired he was. Even if he was working for the devil.

The core problem would have fascinated her if she hadn't been in the middle of it. How do you make peace with the fact that the man you love is doing something you can't respect? Being on the job market made her very aware of her own values. Astor-Denning was being investigated for offering bribes to doctors; yet she had turned down the think tank job because part of their funding came from a giant HMO. Did that make her a better person than him? Yes and no. If everyone compromises his or her ethics to make money, you have a world run by greed. But goodness is personal, too, and in some essential way, Matthew was better to her than she was to him. He rarely judged her, and he always supported her work; he'd even brought home expensive champagne when she published her first anti–corporate science article. It was almost as if he believed the world was the two of them and the rest was just a silly game they played. But it wasn't a game. It was what their lives would mean and be, ten years from now, twenty years, when they were old and looked back on what they'd lived for and believed.

After a few more pointless fights, she thought of a new tactic. It was a Saturday afternoon. He was sitting in the living room, taking notes from a statistics book. He had his David Bowie CD set on repeat, and he'd been listening to "Space Oddity" over and over—a clear sign that he was stressed. In Baltimore, he and Ben used to play that song whenever they were studying for a big exam; she would go down to their apartment and it would be blasting through the door. They even invented this goofy code where Ben called Matthew "Ground Control" and Matthew called Ben "Major Tom." Amelia never understood most of the code, but the whole thing annoyed her. When one of them said, "Planet Earth is blue," the other inevitably responded, "And there's nothing I can do." They were young and under a lot of pressure, but it still seemed so stupid.

She walked to the stereo and turned the volume down. She ignored Matthew's protest and asked him what his "brother" thought of what he was doing at Astor-Denning.

"Why are you bringing that up?"

"I'm just wondering if the two of you have ever talked about it."

"No, Amelia." His voice was dripping with sarcasm. "We never talked about it."

"All right, then what did Ben say?"

"Ben is a real scientist. He wishes I was in there with him, trying to discover—"

"Why aren't you? You're smart, too. You could be anything you wanted."

"How would you know? Because I got into Hopkins and you didn't?"

"I didn't apply," she said stiffly. "But no, because you did well there. Because your professors said you could do any residency you wanted."

"I'm doing what I want." He smirked. "Can't you tell how much I love the MBA program?"

"I can't believe you feel sorry for yourself. You're young, and you have no responsibilities. It's not like you're stuck working on the assembly line at Ford."

The last part just slipped out, but she didn't regret saying it. If anything, she thought it was an important insight. Matthew's father had worked on the Ford assembly line and hated it so much that Matthew blamed the job for his father's alcoholism. Maybe Matthew was living against that history, rather than choosing what he wanted for his own life.

Her important insight was met with a sneer. Then he turned the volume back up, louder than before. "This is Ground Control to Major Tom," screamed from the stereo.

She was desperate. "I'm going to call Ben," she shouted. "See if he can get through to you."

He was up and walking to the kitchen before she finished the sentence. When she got there, he had his big hand on the phone. "Don't you even think of involving him in our shit."

"He cares about you. I'd think he'd want to help." When Matthew didn't reply or move his hand, she said, "Oh, the precious Ben. He can call you in the middle of the night, but you can't call him for anything. He's too important. He can't think about anything but science."

She'd said "science" in a stupidly bratty voice—and Matthew called her on it. He walked around the kitchen, ranting that science was important, the only truly important part of both of their careers. "If you don't care about science, then you don't deserve to be talking about how it's funded. You have no business talking about any of this."

"And I suppose you do care about science? That's why you gave up your medical career?"

He looked away, but she could tell he knew the answer and was just trying to decide whether to share it with her. Which made her feel like she absolutely had to know why he'd left Hopkins. The money was only part of it, as she'd suspected all along. The rest she felt sure he'd told no one but Ben. At that moment, she hated Ben in the same way she'd hated her own brother, for being born, for taking her mom's attention, for growing up to be a stockbroker, the kind of person she could never understand. She remembered back in Baltimore, all those nights when Matthew had gotten out of her bed to go back to his apartment because he didn't want to leave poor Ben alone. And the times when he couldn't see her at all because he and Ben were studying together or just talking about something "fascinating." It was almost like a love affair, and she realized she'd always been painfully jealous of that stupid, brilliant guy.

"I wasn't interested in clinical practice," Matthew said. "For a variety of reasons, but the main one was that the practice of medicine was being taken over by insurance companies. They decided who we could admit to the hospital, and even what tests we could use to diagnose. Everything had to be solved as quickly as possible, usually with the administration of the right drug."

"I know all this. What does it have—"

"At some point, Ben told me the future of medicine would be determined by technology like diagnostic software and especially the quality of available drugs."

She waited a moment. "That's it?"

"That's it." He shrugged. "I decided he was right."

"But it makes no sense! Ben didn't quit medicine. Ben didn't go to work for a company that dumps untested drugs in the market just to make a profit. Ben didn't—"

"The drugs are not 'untested.' Ever heard of clinical trials? Christ, if you want to be Ralph Nader, you're going to have to work a hell of a lot harder."

The phone rang then, Amelia's father, calling to see how her job hunt was going. Matthew walked out the back door, without his coat or gloves, even though it was no more than 20 degrees. She saw him pacing around the backyard while she told her dad that she'd been offered a wonderful position at a university in Chicago. It was tenure track; their philosophy department was planning a new major in ethics and policy, and they wanted her to help create it.

"What about Matthew?" her dad said. When she didn't answer, he said, "Are you sure you're doing the right thing, honey? If you love this man, you might regret—"

"Please be happy for me, Dad. I've worked hard for this."

"Of course you have. And we'll be proud of you no matter what you decide."

When Matthew came back in, his cheeks were bright red and he was rubbing his hands together. His timing was perfect, though, as if he'd gone outside so he didn't have to hear her talking about the Chicago job. He'd already told her he would understand if she took the position, but when she asked what would happen to them, he threw the question back at her. "What do you want to happen?"

The answer was always the same: she wanted him to come with her, to quit his stupid job and be like he used to be, but he refused to even consider that. She felt like they were reaching the breaking point, but still, she kept fighting with him. They fought constantly through February and the first two weeks of March. The last big argument was right before Matthew left for an AD corporate conference in Palm Beach, Florida. She knew he was mad that she'd refused to budge on going with him, even though the resort had a great pool and he'd been booked into a suite with a Jacuzzi. He was also extremely stressed because he had to give a big speech about the future of some chemical that might turn into a good drug, somewhere down the line, ten or twelve years from now. If they spent millions of dollars developing it. If his speech was good enough to convince the company officers to invest in it. Blah, blah, blah.

She'd asked him if the drug would really cure anything, or if it was just another thing they could make money on. He'd said she was guilty of a logical fallacy: the false dichotomy. If it cured something, of course they would make money on it.

He was packing to leave when she begged him to play the What If game with her. He shot her a look like she'd lost her mind, but she pressed on. "Just a few questions." She was sitting on the bed, watching him hang suits in his garment bag. "Only really important ones. I'll do all the asking."

"Fine." He exhaled loudly. "But I can't imagine why we have to do this now."

"What if you were asked to lie for Astor-Denning?"

"Oh, Christ. But all right, I'll answer. Yes, I'd lie for them."

"What if the lie would hurt someone?"

"I'd have to think about the circumstances. Every decision has risks and benefits. That's the first thing you learn in medical school. If you do treat, you can kill someone. If you don't treat, you can also kill them. It's all about the probabilities. Making the best decision you can, given the available information."

"What if you found out that one of your biggest-selling drugs was killing people?"

"I already know that some of our biggest-selling drugs have killed people. Chemotherapy drugs, to give just one example. They all present a risk of leukopenia, which can be fatal. But what choice does the doctor have if the patient will die from cancer?" He zipped the garment bag closed and sat down on the bed, several feet away. "Why are you asking me all this?"

"Because I realized I really don't know what you're doing there. And I need to know before I—"

"Decide to leave? Here's a question I should be answering: What if Amelia decides I'm not up to her Little Miss Perfect standards?"

She ignored that, but waited a moment. "What if you had to be a whistle-blower? Like you found data that showed a drug was bad for everyone?"

"You mean if one of our medicines is really a poison? I doubt I'd be the one breaking that news to our scientists, but sure, I'd do it." He jerked his hand up in exaggerated salute. "The human race will not become extinct on my watch."

"Why turn the question into a joke?"

"Because it is a joke. It's also beneath you. You write articles that make the subtlest moral distinctions. Is it that you don't think I'm capable of doing that myself? Or that I'm unwilling? Or both?"

"I don't know— I'm trying—"

"What exactly is it about me that makes me so eminently worthy of your contempt? Because to tell you the truth, I'm getting really fucking sick of it."

"I don't have contempt for you," she said slowly. "I have contempt for what you do for a living, and the place you—"

"Yes, yes, I know. But unfortunately, I think separating the two is becoming increasingly impossible for us both. I don't care anymore. I just want to end these arguments."

She felt a lightness in her stomach that she recognized as fear, but she pushed on. "I need to know that if you were ever forced to choose between the company and the right thing that you would do the right thing. I know you always say, 'What is right? Who knows? We live in a complicated world. Postmodernism is a bitch. Relativism sucks.' On and on, one clever comeback after another, but deep down, you have to know what I mean. What if a young child had a disease? And you could either save her and ruin Astor-Denning or—"

"If only it were that simple. Let's say I ruined AD for this kid. Do you think another company could instantly re-create our manufacturing process? What about all the other kids who would die when every one of our medicines disappeared from the market?"

"What if it wasn't a child, but your mother? Are you saying you would have saved AD and let your own mother die?"

"Enough," he hissed, and grabbed his bags and went down the stairs. She heard the door slam downstairs and then the sound of his Honda as he sped out of the driveway and down the street. A few minutes later, she broke down sobbing because she realized how cruel that last question had been. Why had she done this to Matthew? It was as though she couldn't even see him anymore.

She spent the rest of the day in a panic, afraid she'd never have a chance to make it up to him. What if he died in a plane crash? What if he died in a taxi in Palm Beach? What if he just didn't come home? She felt even worse when she found something in his underwear drawer. She wasn't snooping; she wanted to wear his flannel boxers and one of his old T-shirts to bed so she could pretend she was close to him. Crammed into the back of the drawer was a Hallmark greeting card: green background with yellow streamers and the word *Congratulations* on the front. Inside he'd written, "Since you're going to be doing all your thinking in a tank soon, why not come to Palm Beach first for a mindless week? You, me, and all the hot bubbling water we want? How can we go wrong?"

He'd obviously bought the card when he thought she was going to accept the think tank job, which was in downtown Philly. It made her sad that he'd shoved it in the drawer when she finally admitted she'd turned them down, but what really got to her was the bubbling water comment. They never had enough hot water in the house. She was always complaining that she could barely take a bath. Now she knew why he'd mentioned that his suite had a Jacuzzi. He wasn't bragging about the perks of his gig; he was saying she might like to be there, with him.

The next morning, she decided to go to Palm Beach. It was the most impulsive decision she'd ever made, and she felt proud of herself, that she could be so spontaneous. By the time she got a flight and arrived it was after six, but that was fine since Matthew's speech was scheduled for 9:15, after a formal dinner held in the ballroom. She'd brought along the dressiest clothes she owned: her interview dress and black pumps and a little black jacket she hoped would make the outfit formal enough. This was before everyone had cell phones, though Matthew had one, an enormous thing that was always losing its charge. She thought about calling that number or his room number, but she was afraid it might rattle him somehow and ruin the speech. Maybe a little part of her was excited at the idea of spying on Astor-Denning.

It wasn't hard to get into the ballroom, which surprised her since she knew Matthew's speech, like everything he did, involved proprietary information. They had security guards at the main door but the others were unlocked, probably so people could quickly go to the bathroom. Amelia was able to slip in unnoticed and sit near the wall, where it was dark enough that she knew Matthew wouldn't see her, especially when he was up on the stage, surrounded by lights. She swallowed hard as she watched him walk out: so gorgeous in his best suit, the most beautiful man she would ever be with for the rest of her life; she already knew that. When they introduced him as an MD from Hopkins who had already achieved the impossible, a perfect MCAT score, the crowd let out a collective gasp before they clapped and laughed with appreciation. She felt proud that the guy she lived with could amaze all these corporate big shots.

He turned out to be a wonderful speaker, looking around the room, projecting his voice, pausing at the best moments—she wondered where he'd learned to do this. What really amazed her was what he said. She'd never heard him talk about the principles of the company's founders and his personal commitment to integrity. She'd never heard him say that the most troubling thing to him in medical school was intractable patient pain. As he presented the information about AD-7219, the NCE or "new chemical entity" they had in development, he sounded as brilliant as Ben, but a lot less confusing. Matthew really cared about this NCE, and that was what surprised Amelia the most. He wasn't playing a game; he truly believed that this untested thing, represented only by a slide with a sketch of a molecule, might someday change the way pain was treated around the globe.

Sitting in her dark corner, watching the man she'd lived with for two and a half years and known since college, she was amazed that she was still learning new things about him and filled with ideas of the work they could do together now. He could study his molecule and she could write about modern pain treatment, which she knew was in horrible shape, largely because of the stupid War on Drugs. Her grandmother had suffered so much in her last days, but the doctor wouldn't give her stronger painkillers because they were addictive. Pablo, her sponsored child from Venezuela, had a bone disease that caused him pain whenever he walked without his crutches. So many people suffered all over the world. Maybe her very own boyfriend would be the one to change this.

When the speech was over, the crowd was on its feet, cheering for her hero. Someone else went up to shake his hand, an older guy, a little sleazy-looking, more like a traditional pharmaceutical executive. Well, there had to be some of those, too. Amelia knew that as well as anyone. Capitalism had its demands, but like Matthew told her, it was a false dichotomy to think a drug couldn't be good for people and make money.

She slipped out the door and went back up to her room. She had to get out of her pumps, and she could tell Matthew was going to be stuck in the ballroom for a while. After she took off her expensive dress, she put on what Matthew called her sexy jeans and a silk shirt. Then she turned on the TV and watched two PBS *Frontline* repeats before she decided it was time to try his room. It was on the top floor; she wondered if the view would be romantic. Maybe there would be a balcony. They could order room service and sip champagne and toast the NCE, the future cure for pain.

His room number was 1230. She'd written it on her hand, knowing she always doubted herself about numbers unless they were written down. When she knocked and he didn't answer, she figured he was probably still downstairs. Unless he was asleep. It was after midnight, and he'd probably been running around all day.

She hated to wake him, but she knocked again, harder, because she wanted him to know she'd come to Palm Beach after all. She'd heard his glorious speech.

This time, he did answer. He opened the door a crack, wearing only a towel. That's when she remembered the Jacuzzi tub and broke into a smile. She was still smiling like an idiot when she heard a woman say, "What is it?"

She knew this kind of thing happened all the time; she'd even read a statistic that said 60 percent of men were unfaithful, but that was precisely why she didn't think it could happen to her. It was so ordinary, and Matthew wasn't ordinary.

His face begged her not to come in, but she pushed past him anyway. She had to see the woman, even though she already knew she'd bitterly regret that decision. The woman was tall, with long legs and a stomach so flat Matthew could have eaten off it. Not to mention that her face looked like some model's. Amelia noticed the face last because as soon as she'd forced her way inside, the woman had jumped up out of the Jacuzzi, shockingly naked, and run across the room, grabbing her clothes off the floor and taking them into the bathroom. Later, Amelia realized who she'd looked like: Christy something-or-other, that supermodel in billboard ads who said she'd rather go naked than wear fur.

Matthew had thrown on a pair of jeans and a T-shirt. The woman was dressed and gone, but he and Amelia were still just standing in the middle of the room, looking at each other. Finally, he said, "I've never done this before. I hope you can believe that."

She did believe it, but there was something she had to know. "Where did you meet her?"

"Why does it matter?"

"Just tell me."

"Why?"

"Please, Matthew. Answer the question."

64

He waited for another minute. "You think she works for Astor-Denning. Oh, Jesus, that's it, isn't it?"

"No," she said, though it was. She thought the woman was probably his new assistant who he'd raved about last week, and that he'd been lying when he'd described Cassie as an Ivy League grad—and a black woman. "I know she doesn't work at AD, but I think they provided her to you. Like some kind of disgusting bonus for the speech you wrote."

Amelia was about to add that she'd been in the ballroom and heard how great the speech was when he said, "You are so way off it's hilarious." He shook his head. "I know you've never had a job, so let me explain how it works. When a company is deciding whether to spend upwards of eight hundred million to develop a product that may never make it through the rats and dogs, much less Phase 1 trials, guess what? They don't hand over the responsibility to some middle-management guy in the marketing department. The speech I gave was written by a committee of scientists and executives. It was still being revised until Thursday night, when my boss's boss turned it over to us. My guess is they picked me to deliver it because they wanted to put a young face with the product, and because of the Hopkins doctor, MCAT crap. I don't know. I'm not privy to the process of making those decisions."

She felt like a complete and utter fool, though she didn't intend to say so, wasn't even aware she had until she heard his response.

"You're not a fool, but for god's sake, don't you think it's time you grew up? Every shitty thing in the world is not the fault of some spooky corporation. It's not the good, innocent people versus the big, bad businesses."

"But that woman?"

"The company had nothing to do with her. I'm the bad guy here. Just me."

"But where did you even meet someone like that?"

"You can't be serious. Christ, Amelia, I've run into women like her all over the country. They don't give a shit if the guy says he has a girlfriend. They don't think about whether it's right or wrong, they just want . . ."

He stopped midsentence, but it was too late; she finally understood—and he did, too. She watched as his expression moved from the panicked realization that there was no way back from what he'd just admitted to the depressed conclusion that it was over between them, before finally settling on a calm acceptance that was unmistakably tender, clearly sorry for her. And then, because he was right, because she really hadn't grown up yet, she let him fold her in his arms. She let him walk her back to her room and help her pack; she even let him drive her to the airport in his rental car. And god did she cry: she wet his shirt and used the entire box of Kleenex in the hotel room while she went on about how heartbroken she was that he'd betrayed her over and over again, all over the country, on his trips.

If only he'd said something, anything, one word of defense or justification or explanation, she would have realized how pathetic she was, pouring her heart out about this to him. Instead, he just kept listening, his eyes full of pity for her. This pity was the one thing she still blamed him for, even after she'd grown up and realized that everything else had been at least partially her fault. But his pity had encouraged her to behave that night in a way that would still embarrass her years later, despite all her accomplishments. For that, she would never forgive him.

The one good thing that came out of that night was her reaction to Matthew's speech, which made her realize, just as Ben and Matthew had, that the future of medicine was all about drugs. She turned down the job in Chicago and took a riskier career step, starting her own think tank to study the ethics of drug development and the practices of pharmaceutical companies worldwide. She found the topic fascinating, and yes, maybe some part of her was still fighting with Matthew, still trying to prove that he was wrong about Astor-Denning.

She never lost interest in the NCE that his speech had made her care about, even if he hadn't meant a word he said. She followed it closely as it made its way through the AD pipeline, read about the clinical trials, talked to the FDA about its safety record and approval. As she watched this drug go out into the world, she hoped Galvenar really was a miracle drug for pain, but she was ready to accept whatever she found out, as long as it was that precious thing, the real orphan of the twenty-first century, neglected by almost everyone, even most of the good guys: the truth.

CHAPTER FIVE

A Real Kid

In all the stories Danny read, once the knight slays the fire-breathing dragon, he comes back to civilization and is welcomed as a hero. The drawings in the books were always the same: the brave knight riding in on his trusty horse, everyone in town cheering and throwing flowers and, sometimes, on the far right corner of the page, the king, who was waiting to give his personal thanks. This always happened on the last page of the story. It was the happy ending.

That was what Danny had always thought, anyway—until he spent a few days in the man's house. Then he'd discovered that the stuff these books left out, after the parade into town, after the king's welcome, was the *really* happy part. When the knight climbed into his first hot bath and stayed there as long as he liked, soaking until he was clean from his greasy hair to his filthy black feet. The huge meals the knight got to eat whenever he wanted: beef and chicken and fish and caldrons of soup. All the daydreaming the knight got to do, sitting around strumming his lute or just looking out the castle window, relaxed, knowing that there was no dragon to fear anymore, the town was secure.

Not that it was exactly like that for Danny. The first day, he couldn't relax for a minute because he didn't know when the security guard would show up. He'd come up with a plan, but for the plan to work the apartment had to look like no one was there. He kept everything clean, but unfortunately Isabelle had found the garbage bag Danny brought with them and had taken out her three favorite things: the talking stuffed elephant Danny had bought her, the pink baby shoe with the puppy pattern she'd found on the sidewalk, and the Barbie doll she'd gotten in a Happy Meal. As she crawled around the apartment, he ran after her, picking up whatever she'd dropped and sticking it in the closet, knowing it would be right back out a minute later, when Isabelle crawled into the same closet and found it again. At least his sister was getting used to the closet as "their" part of the house, though he told her she couldn't touch any of the boxes of papers the man kept in there, figuring they had to be important or the guy wouldn't have put a dead bolt on the closet door.

Danny had noticed the dead bolt when he was walking around in the man's bedroom while Isabelle was still asleep. The man had a clothes closet, too, which was normal except for the size, so big that three lights were needed to see all the shirts and ties and suits and shoes. The closet with the dead bolt was smaller, but still big enough that he and Isabelle would be comfortable in there. And of course they could lock the door from the inside, which would make it look like the man had left it that way. That was the point, and the reason Danny had spent almost a half hour picking that dead bolt in the first place.

He'd learned how to pick a dead bolt because someone at their house was always locking him out. His mom wouldn't give him the key since she insisted she was always home to let them in. It was true that she was home, but it wasn't true that she let them in. Half the time when he pounded on the door, his mom didn't answer, and nobody else did, either.

After several cold evenings waiting on the front step and a broken window that everybody was mad about, Danny asked another kid in the house if he knew anything about picking locks. The boy was younger than Danny, but he was always coming home with expensive toys Danny knew had to be stolen. He told Danny the basics, and Danny spent the next day scrounging for the two tools he'd need: a bent nail and a bristle from a street sweeper. He hammered the nail flat and put it in the bottom of the lock, like a key. He turned it just a little bit and held it. Then he was ready to use the bristle, which was skinny enough to fit in the top of the keyhole and was the real "pick," according to the other boy. The easiest way was to push on the street-sweeper bristle, then pull it out, then put it in the keyhole again, and out. Over and over again, all the while turning the nail key just a little. The more pins had moved to their right place inside the lock, the more the key would turn. All he had to do was be patient until every pin was in place and the key would turn all the way and the door would open.

His mother was amazed that he'd learned such a useful skill. After that, she never worried if she wanted to go out when he and Isabelle might be on their way home. "You can just pick your way in, my little genius," she said—ignoring how frustrating it was for him to have to spend at least ten minutes just to get into the house.

If his mother hadn't been so upset she would have remembered

Danny's skill and known where he and Isabelle were when the se-curity guard let her into the man's apartment. It was almost nine o'clock in the morning on the second day; Danny was exhausted from keeping watch all night, waiting to see who would try to make them leave this place. When Danny heard someone knocking, he grabbed his sister and her Barbie and ran into the special closet, locking the door behind them. Then he told Isabelle, "Cops," which she knew meant she had to be absolutely quiet, not one sound. Even if she heard their mother, which they usually did when they were hiding from the cops. Their mother wasn't the problem; Isabelle instinctively understood that. The other voice was the one they had to hide from.

Except in this case, it was really the opposite. The security guard didn't want to find them; he didn't even want to be in the man's apartment. He kept saying, "I'm not supposed to do this," but their mom kept hysterically insisting that this man had "stolen" her chil-dren.

Danny was stunned that his mom had managed to talk this secu-rity guard into letting her in. She didn't seem sick, but he couldn't really tell since he couldn't see her. He kept his ear to the door. He heard the guard say, "You can look around, but don't touch any-thing." He felt his heart pounding as he wondered if he'd left any signs. The computer was still talking, but the security guard told his mom that happened with computers; it didn't mean anybody was home. (Actually, Danny was responsible for that. Every hour or so, the computer stopped speaking and the changing screen with the equation came back, but Danny discovered all he had to do was shake the desk a little and it started again.) The trash was all thrown away. They still hadn't found any food other than crack-ers and bread, which he knew hadn't smelled up the place. He'd flushed both toilets. He'd put the man's toothbrush back where it belonged, after he'd used it to brush his teeth and his sister's.

He could hear people moving around, and then the sound of his mom crying. "I'm telling you, they were here! It was Monday night. I left for just a minute and this man took them from me."

Danny felt sorry for her, but the "just a minute" part reminded him that he couldn't trust her. She'd left them for a whole day. Anything could have happened while she was gone. If the man hadn't been in a hurry, Isabelle might be in some horrible foster home right now.

"Look," the guard said, "I only let you in here because my brother has a habit, and I felt sorry for you." He sounded both annoyed and bored. "I'm telling you, the guy who lives here, Doctor Connelly, is never home. He's probably in Germany, somewhere like that. He travels all the time, works for a big drug company. He may not be back here for a month."

"But where did they go, then?" Danny could hear her coming closer. Now she was standing in the man's bedroom, maybe looking right at the closet. "What did he do with them before he left?"

"I told you, I didn't see any kids here. Not Monday night, not that I remember. And I was here then, too. Me and the maintenance guy, we live on-site."

Danny thought about this. He'd seen the security guard when the rich man brought them into the building. The guard had been on the phone, but he'd looked in their direction. The rich guy had waved hello. Was it possible the guard really hadn't seen them? Most people didn't; Danny knew that. This was why he'd yelled and screamed so the man would notice them on the bridge.

His mom cried harder. "Does this mean you won't help me?"

"Hey, I risked my job to let you in here, lady. We're never supposed to use the master key unless there's a plumbing problem or a fire or the police have a warrant." He paused. "Maybe you should call the police. Tell them your story."

The guard obviously didn't believe his mom, which wasn't surprising. Nobody seemed to believe her, even when she was telling the truth. Of course his mom wouldn't really call the police, but it took Danny a few minutes to realize the best part of all. Now, when the rich guy finally did call the security guard to throw them out, the guard would already know it wasn't necessary. He'd either tell the guy he'd checked the place recently or, more likely, considering he wasn't supposed to be up here, wait a few minutes, pretend he was checking, and then tell the man that nobody was there, that everything was fine.

It was an amazing stroke of luck, and all thanks to his mom.

He heard her ask the guard if she could stay here and wait, in case her children came back. When the guard said that would never happen—they couldn't get in without a building pass—she broke down completely. Danny looked at Isabelle, who was sucking on the strings of the puppy shoe. It was hard to hear their mom sobbing, but they were used to it. She did it all the time with real cops, to get them to let her go.

He heard more movement and the voices got farther away. His mom asked the guard to call the man's work so she could ask about her kids, but the guard said no way. "I'm not gonna bother Doctor Connelly with this. I'll end up fired." A few minutes later, Danny heard them leaving. "You're gonna have to figure out where your kids are. I did you a favor, but that's it."

The front door closed, but Danny still waited several minutes before he took Isabelle and her toys back into the living room. She was back to crawling around, putting the Barbie in the shoe, playing with the edge of the man's rug. Danny was looking out the big window, watching his mom grow smaller and smaller as she walked back to the bridge.

His plan had been to hide from whoever the man sent to throw them out, not from his own mom. But his mom wanted them thrown out, too, even if her reasons were different. She wanted them back in the ugly, freezing house where Isabelle couldn't crawl without getting splinters in her hands. Where there wasn't a computer to teach his sister to talk. Where it was so loud that Isabelle never slept all the way through the night the way she had last night in the guest room bed. And, worst of all, where his sister had thrown up so much he'd been afraid she was dying and his mom hadn't done a thing to help. She'd even refused to give Danny any of the stolen cash for a hotel, though he'd begged and pleaded with her to put Isabelle first for once in her life.

He had to learn to harden his heart. He had to tell himself that it wasn't his mom walking away, so pitifully alone and scared—it was the dragon. And now that the dragon was gone, the town was safe. He could rest in this castle until the man came back, which, from what the guard said, could be a very long time.

It was time to relax, and the first thing he did was take a long hot bath while Isabelle sat on the bathroom rug, unwrapping bars of soap. When the water got cool, he just turned on the tap; somehow, amazingly, there was always more hot. He washed his hair and stayed in until his skin was all shriveled and pink; then he let out the dirty water, got dressed, and gave Isabelle her bath. She loved the way the soap smelled; she kept sticking it on her nose and saying her newest word, "Good!" Later in the week, she also said, "Three," the number of washcloths she wanted in the tub with her: two she liked to wrap around her feet and one she put flat on her tummy. It didn't matter because the man had tons of thick washcloths; Danny found a huge stack of them next to the towels on some shelves by the shower, the same shelves where Isabelle had found all the great-smelling soap.

Now that they were clean, he had to tackle the serious problem of food. He rummaged through every cabinet and every drawer in the refrigerator: all empty. By nightfall, they'd finished the loaf of bread and the crackers and the cookies, but Isabelle was still hungry.

He was just wondering if they would have to leave this wonderful place when he got lucky again. He saw one place he hadn't tried, a silver box in the corner, across from the cabinets. That silver box turned out to be the jackpot. Inside were dozens and dozens of frozen meals, a weird brand he'd never seen in any grocery store, probably made especially for the rich man. The food had weird names, too, like "herbed cod" and "bison chili," but the instructions were right on the package, just like any frozen dinner, though you didn't cook them in the microwave, but in a pan of water on the stove. It took Danny a minute to figure out the fancy stove, but then he dropped the packages in the water, and fifteen minutes later they were ready. Isabelle's favorite was cranberry-stuffed chicken. Her least favorite was veal stew, which Danny made later in the week, for himself, but he was glad he gave her a taste because she said her first two-word phrase: "Don't wike!"

Danny liked everything but the vegetables, and even they were decent, except the asparagus, which he flushed down the toilet so it wouldn't smell up the trash. And he loved the man's plates, his heavy forks and spoons, the dark wood table where he and Isabelle ate their meals. His sister loved sitting on her phone books, holding a spoon, and feeding herself with her fingers, no matter how messy the dish. Danny put a garbage bag under the phone books and another one under her chair, but inevitably some food would miss the bags and end up on the floor or, once or twice, on the walls. Luckily, everything washed up easily, even the walls. He didn't want to harm this place.

By the fourth day they were so well fed that Danny almost forgot what it was like to be hungry. They were clean all the time, too. Even their clothes didn't smell now that Danny had discovered the coolest black washer and dryer in a room right off the kitchen. And they were celebrating, just like the knights did when they returned from their battles.

Celebrating in the man's castle was obviously different from the olden days. Then it was probably all parties and singing and merriment. Now it was the huge television hanging on the man's bedroom wall, flat as a painting, with hundreds of channels, including a whole channel just to tell him what was on the other ones.

It hadn't taken Danny long to discover how to work the remote control. Now Isabelle was learning word after word, in English, since he'd let the computer stop talking so she could watch cartoons and *Sesame Street*. On the fifth day he came into the bedroom and saw his sister perform another miracle. She was in the middle of the room, standing up, and then he saw her taking steps, walking over to the dresser, where her elephant was. Until then, she'd been able to walk only if he stood her up and held on tightly to her hands. The furniture had made the difference, and Danny felt stupid that he'd never thought of it before. How could she learn to walk by herself without something to pull herself up on? Their house had no furniture other than mattresses lying on the floor. Here she had regular beds and end tables and couches. She had thick rugs beneath her, so she wouldn't be hurt if she stumbled and fell. She had a real house, and she could become a real kid.

Even if the guy came back tomorrow, Danny would never regret breaking his promise to leave this castle. Of course he'd have to run like hell with Isabelle before the man called the guard, but he could do that. He'd pick up his sister and take off, even though he knew she'd protest all the way. After their first day here, she'd decided she hated being carried, and now she told him so, repeatedly, even if he picked her up for a good reason. "I do!" she said, and he said okay, unless it was the tub, which was too big and too dangerous to let her get into by herself.

As she struggled to climb into the guest bed that night, he didn't try to rush her, even though he was looking forward to her bedtime, as always, so he could do whatever he wanted. He watched a lot of

TV himself: a show about penguins he really liked, a movie about kids with superpowers, the History Channel, where he learned that the bad things that had happened to his family were really nothing compared to World War II and the Holocaust. The one show he wouldn't watch, no matter how many channels it was on, was *Law & Order*. He watched it once, that was all, but it was enough to make him understand the way people saw his mother. The cops on the show talked about drug addicts like they were garbage. It was hard enough thinking of his mother as a dragon; he hated that anyone would think of her as trash. And it just wasn't true, not about his mom, not even about the other addicts who lived in his house. They annoyed him all the time, and they scared him, too, but they were still real people who made popcorn and laughed and talked about whether it would snow. Most of them wanted to change; Danny heard them telling one another this constantly. Most of them were afraid that if they didn't change soon, they wouldn't "make it." Danny had never known what that meant until he saw *Law & Order*, but now he did. They were afraid they were going to die.

When he wasn't watching TV, he wandered around the loft area or cooked himself another frozen meal or sat on the big leather couch, looking at the city lights, wondering what it would be like if he really lived here, if he were the man the security guard was afraid to bother at work: Dr. Connelly. He wasn't surprised the guy was a doctor; no wonder he had the equation. He knew what Astor-Denning was, too; he'd seen it on a TV commercial. It was the drug company where the doctor worked, and the commercial helped Danny figure out that what they mainly did was research, which meant finding cures for sick people. He liked thinking that Dr. Connelly might have found a lot of cures himself.

On Monday morning, the sixth day, Isabelle insisted on walking to the potty, too. She'd been trained to use it last summer, not by him but by his mom, who'd said she couldn't wait any longer because it was too expensive to keep buying diapers. His mom had taught Isabelle to make this squeaky noise and point whenever she had to go; then someone, usually Danny, carried her into the bathroom and held her on the toilet. At home, that is. When they were out begging for train fare, Danny kept her in toddler Pampers so he wouldn't have to deal with stopping every hour to find a bathroom. He had only one large pack of Pampers left in the garbage bag, but he still made Isabelle wear a diaper during every nap and at night because he didn't want to risk her wetting the guest bed. He didn't want her crawling up on the hard ceramic potty, either, but he couldn't talk her out of it. She held on to his arm so she wouldn't fall in, and she let him wipe her, but otherwise she did it all by herself.

She wanted to do everything by herself. It was hard for Danny to get used to. He'd been carrying her around for three years, talking to her, but she'd never talked back. Now she not only talked, she got mad if she didn't get what she wanted. If he tried to put her toys away in the garbage bag, she yelled at him, and sometimes threw herself on the floor. Danny tried to ignore her, but that afternoon, when it was time for her nap, she screamed no, and when he picked her up to carry her there anyway, she hit him in the nose.

It hurt—a lot—but he was still surprised when he discovered that the wetness on his face was blood. He had to let Isabelle down so he could get some toilet paper and keep his nose from bleeding onto the floor. While he was in the bathroom he looked at himself, like he always did. There wasn't a mirror in their house, and he kept being surprised at his own reflection. His brown hair was a mess; it wouldn't stay down no matter how often he combed it, probably because his mom had cut it off too quickly when she was sick. He was so short he didn't come even halfway up the glass. He was still a lot skinnier than the regular kids who went to school. But what bothered him most was how young he seemed in that mirror. He didn't look like a grown-up or a knight. He looked like a little kid.

A little kid with a bloody nose, no less, which made him start to cry. It was the stupidest thing to cry about, that a three-year-old had hit him. He wished someone were there to tell him to stop feeling sorry for himself, but nobody was. He felt really alone for the first time since they'd been in this place. He wanted his mom.

He sat down on the floor, still holding the toilet paper against his nose, still crying. He called himself dumb over and over, but now that the tears had come, he couldn't seem to make them go away. He didn't notice that Isabelle had walked into the bathroom, too, but he felt her hand on his head. He shook her off, not because she'd hit him but because he was embarrassed. He didn't want her to see him bawling like a baby.

She walked around in front of him; he saw her pink and yellow striped shirt that didn't quite cover her tummy, and the stretchy blue pants that he'd safety-pinned on her that morning because they were way too big. He wanted to look up at her and say it was all right, but he just couldn't do it. Nothing was all right; that was the problem. It was like the punch to the nose made him realize that he didn't belong here, but he didn't belong anywhere else, either. His mom would never stop using drugs. His mom might die.

He felt Isabelle put her arms around him. Then he heard her voice. "Danny."

He sniffed hard and looked at her. She'd never said his name before, and he didn't think she knew it—half the time, his mom called him by his real name, forgetting that he hated it, and everyone else called him whatever name he gave them. And since his sister had started using words, no one had called him anything, of course, because no one was around. He was just wondering if he'd imagined it when Isabelle said "Danny" again and broke out in a big smile. He smiled, too, when she pointed at herself and giggled.

After a moment he stood up, threw away the toilet paper, and washed off his eyes. He watched Isabelle moving bars of soap around the bathroom for several minutes before he reminded her that it was naptime. "Will you go sleepy-bye now?"

She held out her arms. "Up."

Maybe she was just tired, but he felt like she was still trying to make him feel better. He waved his hand in the direction of the guest bedroom. "Go ahead. You can do it yourself."

She started off in that direction, but halfway down the hall, she turned around to look for him.

"I'm here," he said, walking toward her. "It's all right."

CHAPTER SIX

Ben and Amelia in Paris, or Strangling the Kitten

The year before, in November, when Matthew had called Amelia to ask her to lunch, she was about to tell him no, absolutely not, but then he said he was going to divulge an important secret that was decades old. Big Pharma was having a terrible year: there were so many lawsuits and scandals and government fines that her staff was having trouble keeping up with it all. Astor-Denning, in particular, was facing a public relations nightmare after downplaying a serious side effect of their newest bipolar drug and giving psychiatrists frequent flyer miles as an "incentive" to prescribe it. But still, the thought that Matthew was about to blow the whistle on that creepy company was irresistible, and she agreed to the lunch. She also brought along her tape recorder. They met in a restaurant in Hell's Kitchen, her choice, a funky little place that served New Orleans cuisine. A poignant reminder of the flood—at least that's what she hoped it would be to Matthew. She'd just written an article about the shocking lack of prescription access for the Katrina refugees: some who'd lost their insurance cards, many who'd never had insurance in the first place.

He was on time, dressed in an outrageously expensive, tailor-made suit, and charming to the hostess, the busboy, the waitress. He told Amelia, "You're looking well," which was innocent enough. She'd already decided to walk out if he even alluded to the last time they'd seen each other, that February night in Aspen, Colorado, three years earlier, when they'd hotly debated direct-to-consumer ads in front of hundreds of physicians, and afterward he'd somehow managed—against all her instincts, against every ounce of her better judgment—to get her into the hotel bar and, a few hours later, into his bed. The morning after was unbelievably awkward: he claimed it meant they should get back together; she thought it was a one-night stand, which was, after all, his specialty. She said some cruel things and he fought back, but in that clever, smart-ass way that reminded her of everything she detested about him. Eventually, he shouted that he hated her, too. So they hated each other, but they'd had great sex. A night in every way worth forgetting.

After she ordered shrimp gumbo, Matthew ordered a Diet Coke, apologizing to her and the waitress, claiming his stomach was a little off. Amelia suspected he was watching his weight, which was funny but also annoying; he was still in great shape, as thin as he'd been in college, and why suggest having lunch if he wasn't going to eat? While she was munching on corn bread, he did divulge a secret, but it wasn't anything she needed to put on tape. It was decades old; he hadn't lied to her about that. Unless he was lying about the whole thing, which was possible, though what he said made a surprising amount of sense.

"Remember in Baltimore, when I kept inviting you to our apartment? I know it sounds strange, but I was doing that for Ben." Matthew paused. "He had this huge crush on you. It started way back, freshman year in college, when he sat next to you in bio. It was his idea to tell you about our apartment. He hoped that if you moved to that building, eventually you might agree to go out with him."

Before she could stop herself, she said, "So you didn't want me to move there?"

"Of course I did, but at the time, I really couldn't think about you as anything other than Ben's future girlfriend. Because Ben was my best friend; I couldn't get in his way."

She kept her mouth shut, but she was wondering when this changed, if she herself had changed it that day in her apartment when she'd kissed him. What if she hadn't done that? Would her whole life have been different?

When the waitress brought her bowl of steaming gumbo, Matthew discreetly swallowed two pills, which made Amelia wonder if he really was feeling sick or, more likely, nervous. He never drank, but he used all kinds of prescription drugs, including one for anxiety. She'd seen the pill bottles on his nightstand in Aspen; he'd laughed and said it just proved he believed in the safety of his products.

She took a few bites of the delicious gumbo. "Why are you telling me this now? Are you trying to give me something else to regret, that I picked a man who turned out to be a corporate sleazebag over a good man who will probably win the Nobel?"

"Thank you, but no, I'm telling you because it's still true. Ben has been in love with you all these years. He's followed your career; he reads your blog every day; he reads your articles. He tells me all about it, even if by some miracle AD isn't your target."

She was flattered, but she said, "What's wrong with him?"

"Jesus, Amelia, that's cold. It's hard to meet the right person, and Ben is so shy—"

"No, I mean, why is he still friends with you?"

"You can hardly hold that against him. You of all people." Matthew grinned. "Why not think of it as something you have in common? The way you both had an odd affection for Damien in *Omen II*."

"It's not something we have in common anymore."

"I wouldn't be so sure." He was still grinning. "We'll always have Aspen."

She pushed her chair back, but before she could stand up he said, "All right, I'm sorry, I shouldn't have said that. Look, Ben doesn't have your experience with me. We met when we were eighteen. He's like my brother. I've helped him move. I've given him money, and he—"

"Are you saying you've been funding Ben? Because I will make that public."

"Not Astor-Denning money. You know how Ben is; he wouldn't take a chance on tainting his research. I mean from me personally, mainly when we were in college. And he's an innocent guy in a lot of ways, but look at what he's accomplished. And he really does have this thing for you. That's the point here."

"Where did you get the money to give Ben?"

"Who cares? It's not like I ran a prostitution ring outside the dean's office. And even if I did, Ben didn't know about it, so what—"

"Tell me or I'm leaving."

"Sit still. You already know this. I told you a long time ago. I had that job downtown, number crunching for a financial software company, Tuesday through Saturday from four to midnight. That's why you never saw me on campus except at the premed meetings. Your theory, if I remember correctly, was that I was off doing shallow things like watching football."

"Does he take money from you now?"

"Haven't you seen him on CNN?"

She hadn't, though she'd seen pictures of Ben, most recently on the cover of *Newsweek*: CURING THE INCURABLE: A RENEGADE DOCTOR, HIS VACCINE, AND THE END OF MALARIA. She barely watched TV anymore. She got all the news she could handle online.

"You must have noticed that, in addition to blinking and freaking out like the camera just woke him up, he's always dressed in some cheap department store crap."

"Has he taken any money from you in the last ten years? A simple yes or no."

"What is this, a DOJ hearing?"

"Are you testifying with them? Which complaint?" Amelia knew the Department of Justice was investigating AD not only for their marketing of the bipolar drug, but also for making false claims about their epilepsy medicine and for overcharging the federal government by setting higher prices for Medicaid. Maybe there was even something new she hadn't heard about.

"No, I'm not. And no to the other question, too. Now, can we please get back to the topic?" Matthew took a drink of his Diet Coke. "You know, you and Ben really do have a lot in common. It's true now, and it was true in Baltimore. Recall, I was the only one strangling the kitten."

The What If game. Matthew had strangled the kitten; she and Ben had said they couldn't do it, not even to save ten thousand acres of the rain forest. Come to think of it, she and Ben had always been on the same side of those questions. It struck her now that Matthew had probably invented that game to help Ben win her over. Too bad it hadn't worked.

She'd eaten only half her lunch, but she let the waitress take her bowl and said she didn't want coffee. "I don't know what you think you're getting out of this, but I'm not—"

"I'm just trying to help a friend."

"And involve me in something that looks like a conflict of interest." She opened her purse and took out a twenty, more than enough for her share of the meal. "You know I won't take your company's 'grants,' so instead you try this stunt."

"It's not a stunt, and I knew you wouldn't want me involved. I gave Ben your number and told him to call you himself, but he just can't do it. He's afraid you still have feelings for someone else. Understandably."

She snorted and placed the twenty on the table.

"Look, he's going to be here next Tuesday. He's giving a speech. You could go and just say hello afterward. That's all the encouragement he needs."

Amelia knew about the speech. She'd read about it that very morning in *The New York Times*. She'd even thought of going to listen to her former friend who'd become such an amazing scientist, but she was afraid Matthew might be there and that had been enough to make her table the idea.

"I have to get back to work," she said. "I have a lot to do."

"One thing—if you do see him, please don't tell him I told you all this. He made me promise I wouldn't way back in Baltimore."

"It's not going to happen." She stood up. "But I want you to know this: even if by some crazy chance I did end up dating some friend of yours, even if I fell in love with him, it wouldn't change anything about my positions on Astor-Denning. If you think you're pulling something over on me, think again."

He stood up, too, and held his hands out, palms up. All innocence, except that grin. "Why do you always think the worst of me, Amelia?"

She spent the next week wondering what he was up to. He hadn't taken a train from Philly to New York, in the middle of a workday, just to be nice to a friend. And why do it now? Even as she took a cab to listen to Ben's speech, she was hoping to discover why Matthew wanted her to go. She planned to talk to Ben and try to uncover what he knew about Matthew's current situation—maybe he *was* dealing with the DOJ; maybe he was even facing criminal charges. Somehow having Amelia distracted would help his case? There had to be an ulterior motive.

True, she was without a boyfriend again, after she'd broken up over the summer with a history professor who didn't want children because he had already had two poorly behaved teenagers. But the unfortunate reality was she'd never been attracted to Ben, no matter how perfect he was for her in an abstract sense or how flattered she was that Ben had feelings for her. Even the way Matthew talked about Ben turned her off, like Ben was incapable of having a conversation or even dressing himself before an interview.

That the real Ben turned out to be nothing like she remembered wouldn't have been such a surprise—after all, it had been almost fifteen years—but that Ben was also nothing like Matthew had described, well, that stupidly confused her. The auditorium was a mob scene: every seat taken, people standing in the aisles and the doorway, and at least two hundred more who couldn't be accommodated and were forced to watch the speech on a monitor in another lecture hall. Amelia was in the latter group, since it had never occurred to her that a speech about "parasitic diseases and the future of vaccinology" could generate this kind of crowd. She was in the back of the room, and she didn't have her glasses, so she couldn't see the monitor that well. She also didn't understand most of what Ben was saying, though she couldn't miss the standing ovation at the end, complete with cheers and whistles, confirming again that Ben was a rock star of science. Afterward, hundreds of people waited in line to meet the famous man, and Amelia took her place in the line, even though she was unaccountably nervous. When it was finally her turn, her voice shook a little as she said, "Ben, hi. It's me, Amelia." She felt stupid after the second sentence, but what if he hadn't recognized her?

He reached out and took her hand in both of his. "Amelia." His voice was warm and kind, and so was his expression. "What a surprise."

Back in Baltimore, he'd been cute enough, in a nerdy way—a sweet face, big brown eyes, lots of curly black hair that tended to sprout horns whenever he leaned his head back—but the years had transformed him into an undeniably attractive man. And it wasn't just his presence and authority. He had a two- or three-day stubble that made him look ruggedly handsome, the same curly hair but neatly trimmed, and soft lines around his eyes that seemed to emphasize his intelligence and compassion. Even his clothes were perfect: not department store crap at all, but thick corduroy pants, a blue button-down shirt, and a plaid jacket that was a little grunge, but that was fine by Amelia, who'd loved the Seattle sound in the early nineties and still loved the slightly sloppy grunge style on men. Perfect grooming was an obvious sign that a man wasn't her type. Ben was so exactly her type, right down to his Doc Martens, that she wondered how she was still standing, since her knees were gone.

"It's great to see you," he said, dropping her hand. "Are you living in New York?"

"Yes," she said. "I've been here for more than ten years." The person behind her was inching closer, rattling her. She swallowed, knowing she had only a few more seconds to get out her question. "I was wondering if you'd like to go out for coffee? When you're finished here, I mean. I don't mind waiting. It would be fun to catch up."

"I'd love to, but unfortunately I've already committed to a late dinner with my hosts and some of their postdocs. My schedule for the next three days is jam-packed. I won't be able to breathe until Saturday, when I fly to Brazil."

"Oh." She could feel her face burning. Why had she believed that Ben had any interest in her? "Well, congratulations. On the speech, everything." She stood up straighter and forced a smile. "I can always say I knew him when."

Ben was nodding to somebody back in the line who'd just yelled his name. As Amelia was about to walk away, he said, "I might be able to find some time on Thursday."

"Great. Just let me know."

"Can I call you tomorrow about it?"

She nodded and turned around to leave, when Ben said, "Amelia?"

"Yes?"

"I don't have your phone number."

Naturally, Matthew had lied about giving him the number, too.

After she handed Ben her card, he said, "Yes, I'd heard you were writing about bioethics. Who told me that?" He squinted, clearly thinking. "Of course, Matthew. Our mutual friend. Very important field. Glad to hear good people like you are in it."

She managed to say "Thanks" before she gratefully made her escape. When she was outside in the night air, her cheeks still on fire, her phone started ringing. She was horrified that she hadn't turned it off before the speech and quickly answered without looking to see who it was.

As soon as she heard his voice, she hissed, "How did you get my cell number?"

"I had AD security obtain your Verizon bill." Her gasp was, unfortunately, audible, because he laughed. "You gave it to me, silly. Last week, in case I couldn't find the restaurant." He paused, still chuckling. "He looks a lot better in person, doesn't he? His girlfriends have cleaned him up, especially Karen, the woman he lived with until a few months ago. I bet you're meeting up with him while he's in New York, aren't you? Probably already thinking about what you'll wear on your very first date. How sweet."

She was so angry she forgot to look and stepped into the street as a cab was coming around the corner. The driver slammed on the brakes and screamed curses at her.

"It's all right," Matthew said, "you don't have to thank me yet. Let's see how it goes. One small piece of advice, though. Don't spend all your time listening to him talk about what it's like to be the top story in every science journal in the world. Be sure to tell him all about your own famous work, especially the latest blog post."

He hung up before she could hang up on him. She threw her phone in her purse, yelling curses at the sky.

By the time she got home, she felt better enough to remember that this was all part of some strategy. Of course he wanted her to feel insignificant; then her criticisms of his company were insignificant, too. He obviously didn't believe it, or he wouldn't be trying to do whatever he was trying to do here. If only she knew what that was.

She wasn't sure if Ben would call, but he did, the next day. It turned out that he had all evening free on Thursday; would she like to have dinner? She spent hours getting ready and, yes, thinking about what to wear. She finally decided on her suede skirt and a beige sweater, with low-heeled boots. In case Ben wanted to take a walk—and also because he wasn't that tall: 5'8" or so. She was 5'4"; low heels would be perfect.

They met at a little Italian restaurant in Brooklyn, near her apartment, where she knew it would be quiet. When she got there, Ben was already sitting in the waiting area. He was hunched forward, trying to read, despite how dark it was in the restaurant, which was lit only by candles. She said "Now there's a hard worker" before she noticed what it was he was trying to read: a printout of the main page of her blog.

He stood up and smiled, but she was distracted. After the hostess seated them, before he could open his menu, she said, "Where did you find out about my blog?"

He put his menu down. His eyes were confused, but she said, "Just tell me."

"I googled you." His voice was clearly embarrassed. "This morning, in my hotel."

When the waitress asked if they wanted to order drinks, Ben said to Amelia, "What would you like?"

She leaned forward. "Are you saying you haven't talked to Matthew recently?"

"I didn't say that." He seemed surprised. "I talked to him yesterday."

"Before or after you called me?"

"Before." He turned to the waitress. "Better give us a minute."

Amelia didn't look away from Ben's face. "What did you talk to him about?"

She was suddenly sure that Matthew was orchestrating all of this. He'd told Ben to call her, and he'd told Ben to read her blog—just so he could laugh when she was pleased about it. Maybe he'd even claimed that Amelia had a crush on Ben after hearing his speech, or even back in college. Who knows what he said, but he wasn't going to get away with it. She would not let Matthew treat them like they were puppets in some sick game.

"What did you talk to him about?" she repeated.

"I'd rather not discuss it."

"I'm sorry, but I have to know."

Ben sat back in his chair, but Amelia persisted. "Look, I knew he would call you. I just don't know what he said, though I can imagine."

"I called him."

"Why?"

"To ask how he felt."

"About what?"

"This. Tonight."

"How is it any of Matthew's business?"

"I felt like it was the right thing to do. Since you and he . . ." Ben ran his hand through his hair. "He told me he had no problem with us having dinner, but I confess I'm a little baffled at your reaction. If there's something going on between the two of you, and I've walked into the middle of it . . ." He sat up straight. "I'm sorry, I'm in over my head here. I think I'd better go."

His expression was clearly confused, and utterly miserable. She was very confused herself, but she knew she'd just been horribly rude.

"Wait." She leaned forward, willing him not to bolt before she explained. "I'm the one who needs to apologize. In my work, I have to talk to lots of people who are evasive, but that doesn't give me an excuse to treat you this way." When he still looked unsure, she impulsively reached for his hand. "Please, Ben. I promise, I won't do it anymore."

He finally relented, and she let go of his hand, feeling mortified that she'd grabbed it in the first place. She'd never done any of this with a man she was attracted to. Was she trying to screw this up? Is that what Matthew wanted, to make her feel bad?

She vowed to avoid any talk of the past for the rest of the evening. Ben cleared his throat and suggested they order a bottle of wine. They agreed on Chianti and then sat in silence, studying the menu, or pretending to, until the bottle arrived a few minutes later. After Ben finished half his glass in one gulp, he said, "I hate evasiveness myself. Manipulation of any kind seems like a pointless waste of mental energy." He took another drink and finally smiled. "I sense you're very good at what you do."

"I've been called a bulldog, and worse."

"I read several of your articles this morning. I was impressed. Work like yours is what keeps science honest."

She knew she was blushing; she hoped it was so dark he couldn't see. She was so nervous now; maybe he was, too. Maybe that's why they said fine to everything the waitress suggested: bread and cheese, linguine with red clam sauce, scampi, rolled veal, mushroom ravioli. When the food arrived, the table was covered with plates, but it wasn't awkward. Ben's suggestion that they just share everything charmed her. She'd met so many germ-phobic men lately, but of course this medical genius wasn't one of them.

While they ate, they talked about what it had been like for him, becoming suddenly famous for his vaccine. He'd been in London for years working on it; he told her a lot about his experimental process, which sounded shockingly difficult, requiring a patience for repeated failure she knew she'd never have. He was patient about answering her questions, too, even though he'd probably heard them all a hundred times, and some, embarrassingly, were basic biochemistry she'd forgotten since college. He also told her about the last few months: all the traveling and interviews, speeches around the world, photos and TV, being called the "new Jonas Salk," and so on. "I wish I could clone another me to do this part. Let this me get back to working. I miss my lab. I even miss the mosquitoes."

She laughed. "I'm sure the mosquitoes miss you, too."

Ben laughed with her. "If they had any sense, they'd thank me for going after the parasites and saving their species from DDT."

Amelia felt shy as it struck her that she was sitting with the first person in the history of the world to discover a vaccine against a parasitic disease. "Even if the mosquitoes don't understand," she said softly, "humanity does. Humanity thanks you."

"Humanity doesn't need to thank me." He exhaled. "This has been so surreal, knowing millions of strangers suddenly believe I'm more than I am." He took a bite of linguine. "I think that's one of the reasons I was looking forward to tonight. You're part of my past, before all this happened."

Naturally, her vow to avoid talking about the past went out the window then. They were talking about college, and Ben had had three glasses of wine; maybe that's why he felt comfortable enough to tell her he'd had a crush on her freshman year. "We sat next to each other in bio. Most of the students hated that course because Hauser made no secret that he felt premeds were 'money-grubbers with no interest in the topic.' Remember?"

"Definitely." She laughed. "Hell Hauser." Though even Professor Hauser had respected Ben; he'd made a point of telling the whole class that Ben was the only one of them who would ever be a true scientist. It was a cruel thing to do, since Ben was already unpopular, but maybe Hauser had been right. Judging from her and Matthew, he certainly was. After a minute, she said, "Did you ever tell Matthew about this crush?"

"Sure. We lived on the same dorm floor; we talked about you all the time. He was openly competitive—you know how Matt is. Even though I met you first, he said he was more 'driven.' A week before homecoming, he wanted to bet who would end up taking you, him or me. I pointed out that it wouldn't be either of us since we hadn't even managed to talk to you yet. 'A minor detail,' Matt said, 'statistically insignificant.'" Ben laughed. "I know we sound like science nerds, because that's what we were. Neither of us had really had a girlfriend in high school. You were our female ideal: a pretty girl who was also serious and smart."

She flushed with pleasure, though she knew Ben was wrong about Matthew. Even in high school, he'd had girlfriends. He was never a science nerd. A science slut, maybe.

"Since you know Matt," Ben said, "you won't be surprised to learn that when the two of you got involved—what? seven years later?—he still had to remind me he won."

When Ben laughed again, she did, too. She even said, trying to get into the spirit of this, "And I'm sure he didn't take it back when we broke up."

Wrong move. "Matt was devastated about that for a long time." Ben's voice was quieter, a little sad. "I know he tried to get back together with you; this was a few years ago. He didn't tell me what happened, just that it didn't go as he'd hoped."

"It wasn't serious. We were thrown together at a conference. A stupid mistake."

"I'm sure you're right, but Matt was a mess for months afterward. Quite honestly, when I talked to him yesterday, I was afraid he still had feelings for you, but he insisted he'd moved on. He also said if I held back from this on his account, he would come to New York and force me to play racquetball." Ben shook his head. "He knows how I feel about that. He always slams the ball so hard, I'm sure one of us will end up in the ER."

"It's completely over between us," she said, lightly but firmly. "You might even say we're enemies now, since part of my work is uncovering his company's unethical practices."

"I noticed. The first Google hit was your editorial about Astor-Denning's profit last quarter and their declining budget for R&D. I'm sure Matt read that, too. I wouldn't be surprised if he's read everything you've written. He probably sees it as a challenge, trying to outwit you, but I know he doesn't think of you as an enemy. Matt would never hurt you, but you should hear the stories he's told me about rivals at work. He's ruthless with his enemies, but he can't help it. Playing to win seems to be coded in his DNA."

Ben's tone when he talked about Matthew was so obviously affectionate—even the way he called him "Matt," which no one else ever did. It was all so strange, but oddly appealing, like the candles flickering on the tables, making everything look softer.

They'd already moved their chairs together. Now he took her hand and held it securely in his while they waited for coffee. She didn't want to push him to see Matthew the way she did, but she couldn't help asking one more question.

"I read an article about ethics and your vaccine. You were so careful, choosing a company in India to do the manufacturing, refusing all the Big Pharma offers to buy the patent, even though you could have made millions." She paused. "You and Matthew are leading such different lives. I wonder how you've stayed friends."

"Matt works in a corrupt industry, but a lot of good scientists work in pharmaceuticals. They're not the problem. Certainly not Matt."

"You sound very sure."

"Remember sophomore year, in genetics, when the prof decided we were all mature enough to follow the honor code and have take-home tests? The first test, I was approached by more than half the students in the class. They all wanted me to let them copy my answers, and they were willing to pay from fifty dollars to five hundred. But two people who didn't try to use me to cheat were you and Matt."

"I never cheated on anything."

He smiled. "Somehow I knew that. But Matt impressed me, too. He was the only guy in our dorm with a full-time job. He had to do all his studying when he got home from work, in the middle of the night. The poor guy took cold showers to wake up and still had to pinch himself repeatedly to stay alert in morning classes. But he wouldn't cheat."

"Perhaps he's changed," she said, as evenly as she could manage.

"I've known him for twenty-one years. I know how ambitious he is, and I hope he does become CEO. I'd love to have at least one pharmaceutical company run by someone who will do the right thing."

The coffee arrived, but Ben didn't let go of her hand as he told her about his schedule for the next day. His first appointment was at 7:45; he'd agreed to do an interview at NBC. Every hour after was booked, until a speech at 7:30 with Bill Clinton.

"*The* Bill Clinton?" she said.

"I know. It's a tremendous honor, but I still wish I could get out of it. The problem is that all these appearances are generating huge contributions for the foundation. I have to do as many of them as I can."

The foundation was brand-new, but Amelia knew it had been set up by a medical charity with a spotless reputation and given Ben's name. Their mission was nothing less than the worldwide eradication of a scourge that killed millions of people a year and left children blind and brain-damaged. Amelia had seen the horrible pictures of toddlers with malaria. She'd donated to the foundation herself after she read that it would take at least $3 billion to vaccinate every at-risk child—an enormous challenge.

She was even more impressed with Ben, but a little disappointed because she assumed he was telling her about his schedule to explain why he had to get back to the hotel. She was wrong about that, but she'd been wrong about so many things that night and in the last week that she gave up trying to predict what was happening to her. When Ben suggested walking her home, and then came upstairs without any prompting, she forgot all about Matthew. But the next morning, when he left with only a vague promise to see her again, she felt awful, sure she'd done something wrong but unable to figure out exactly what. It was a week and a half before he called, from the airport; he was just back from Brazil, on the way to London, with one night between—could he come over? Again, they spent a wonderful night together; again, he left without saying when he'd be back. It went on like this for months: a day or two with her, a week or more away. She wondered if Matthew had known this would happen, and if that was why he got them together, hoping if Amelia's self-esteem suffered, her work would, too.

She worked harder than ever, though it was true that her confidence had never been lower. She felt like they were perfect for each other, but he never said he loved her, never talked about the future beyond his work. She reminded herself that he was a cautious person, as patient with his life as with his science, and that he was going through such a crazy time, trying to deal with fame, cut off from doing the experiments that really mattered to him. But she was thirty-nine years old. She still dreamed of being a mother. She worried that this would never change. She didn't understand why he didn't want to be with her all the time.

When he finally told her he did, the first week of July when he came back from Toronto, she couldn't help it; she began to cry. "Of course I want you with me." Ben was holding her in his arms, kissing her hair. "You're my soul mate."

The months after that were the happiest in Amelia's life, as she crisscrossed the world with this amazing man. She didn't even hate Matthew anymore: How could she, when the man she adored was so clearly fond of the guy? She could always tell when Ben was on the phone with him because his voice was relaxed and he laughed so often. When she asked what was so funny, Ben often said, "I don't remember." Matthew himself just seemed to crack him up.

Ben thought it was obvious that Matthew had played match-maker because he cared about them. "He knew what I was going through after Karen and I broke up, alone, facing all that publicity. He called you to give me hope." He smiled. "It worked, too."

Amelia believed this, but she could never quite believe that Matthew was trying to be nice to her, though Ben made a strong case for his view that Matt wasn't her enemy. "If he wanted to hurt you, it would have been so easy. He could have destroyed your career before it got started if he'd gone public with the fact that you'd lived with him right up until you started the think tank. To this day, if he let anyone in the media know about your former relationship, it could seriously damage your credibility."

This was so obvious, it stunned her that she'd never thought of it before. Especially if Matthew released the details of Palm Beach, every article she'd written about Astor-Denning could be spun as meaningless, just the ravings of a scorned, jealous woman.

"But Matt has been extremely careful both outside and inside his company to make sure no one knows about your past. He feels strongly that he will never let you be punished for being with him."

This certainly didn't sound like the Matthew she knew, but whoever he was didn't really matter anymore. As she told him the first night on Grand Cayman, she was ready to put the past behind them. It was true; her focus was the future, now that she had her secret news. She hadn't intended to keep it a secret from Ben, but she kept waiting for the best time to tell him, and they were so busy that the best time kept eluding her. She planned to tell him on their vacation to the Caymans, but this was before they arrived at the hotel and discovered that Matthew was there, too. Ben was as surprised as she was, though he blamed himself, saying he must have misunderstood what Matthew had in mind when he suggested that *they* spend the weekend on the island.

Amelia didn't know that Ben and Matthew had been there before, scuba diving. When she told Ben she'd never gone diving and had no interest in learning, he said he wouldn't dive, either. They still had to hang out with Matthew, though. But it wasn't that bad. If anything, Amelia was surprised by how hard he tried to make sure they had a good time. He took over driving the rental car since both she and Ben found it stressful driving British style, on the "wrong" side of the road. He made all the reservations at the best restaurants, where they ate delicious local favorites like conch fritters and mahi-mahi while looking out on the most gorgeous beaches she'd ever seen in her life. He took them to see George Town and Hell rock formations and her personal favorite, the lovely Butterfly Farm. On Saturday night, when Ben was a little tipsy, he told Amelia that Matthew was always like this. "He's my big brother. He looks out for me."

Matthew was sitting across from them, and he raised his eyebrows. "Big brother? You're four months older than I am, not to mention that I look younger, am in better shape, and can still beat you at arm wrestling."

Amelia was a little embarrassed when Ben insisted on arm wrestling right then, in the hotel bar, but she knew that boys will be boys and men will be boys, too, occasionally. That was the other reason she didn't tell Ben her secret while they were on Grand Cayman: he did seem weirdly younger and less mature when he was around Matthew. He always had, but it didn't bother her because she knew he'd change back as soon as they were on the plane.

She ended up blurting out that she was pregnant on the flight to Paris. His reaction to the news was to cry, which touched her more than anything he could have said, because she'd reacted the same way.

It had been almost ten years since Amelia's gynecologist had informed her that the irregular periods she'd had since she was in grad school meant she didn't ovulate like other women. Though it wasn't impossible for her to get pregnant, she'd have to take fertility drugs and even then, it might never happen. Yet here she was, pregnant without even trying. It felt like a gift or even a miracle; certainly the only thing she hadn't had to struggle for in a very long time.

They spent most of the flight discussing the changes they would make to get ready. They would stay in the States for at least a few years. Ben said he was already talking to several university labs and the NIH; obviously, he'd have his choice of positions. He was dying to stop traveling anyway, and his foundation could get along without him for a while, though of course he would still have to do some appearances, like the EU conference. The topic, medical care in the third world, was obviously important to him, and the sponsor, Astor-Denning, was important to Amelia, especially after they'd consistently refused her application to be on the bioethics panel. But now that Ben had gotten her added to the roster, she would force AD to be honest about their real agenda here: to push Galvenar onto the World Health Organization's list of "essential medicines." Her staff had been working for two years on this investigation, and now they knew the truth about the "grassroots group" Pain Matters, which had more than ten thousand members and was the most vocal proponent for AD's "miracle drug," both in the United States and around the world. She felt a little bad for Matthew, for Ben's Matt anyway, but he had to understand that if AD wanted to sponsor a "hippie-dippy, crunchy-granola, do-gooders' conference"—as he called it, even to Ben, who found it funny—then they had to deal with at least some crunching noises from the do-gooders.

In Paris, she and Ben decided to celebrate her pregnancy by staying at the Ritz, Amelia's favorite hotel. It was Monday night; she was taking a bath in the lovely white marble and gold bathroom, humming, while Ben was talking to someone on the phone. When she came out in her peach robe, he'd just hung up and was standing by the desk. She walked over to hug him, but before she could, he asked her what she was planning to talk about at the panel.

"Wouldn't you like to know?" she said, kissing him on the nose. Ben himself had told her several times that she should never discuss her work with him or anyone outside of her staff until it was made public. He said her ethical positions were like his research, and she had to be very careful not to do anything that could skew the results.

When he didn't laugh or move, she said, "Anyway, it's a response panel. I can't be sure until I hear the final talks tomorrow and Wednesday morning."

"Amelia, please. I know you're breaking something. You always do." He was running his left hand through his hair, the way he did when he was worried, but when she asked him what was wrong, he said he was overreacting. "I'm sorry, I know I shouldn't have asked what you're going to say. I just need you to tell me that it doesn't have anything to do with a specific drug. I can't imagine why it would. Tegabadol has nothing to do with this conference."

"Of course it does." Tegabadol was the generic name for Galvenar. She was so surprised, she was sputtering. "It's the real reason they sponsored this."

He shook his head. "It's not on the WHO essential medicine list. There's no connection."

She didn't blame him for not knowing about the rest of the schedule; he'd been insanely busy with his own appearances and interviews. But she still knew he was wrong, and her voice was patient but firm. "They've already had four panels discussing 'quality-of-life medicines in the developing world.' They claim it's an issue of 'access' to 'state-of-the-art' medicines. They want ministries of health and charities to earmark funds to pay for Galvenar."

He walked across the room and back, twice, before he mumbled, "Shit."

"What is it?" Ben never cursed, and she was suddenly very nervous. "Who were you just talking to?"

She'd seen *The Constant Gardener* on DVD a few weeks earlier. Ben had been in bed next to her, engrossed in the latest issue of *JBC* (*The Journal of Biological Chemistry*). He never watched movies or television; he just didn't find them interesting enough. But this one must have interested him at least a little because when it was over he said that the movie was "based on a misperception about current science." The drug company was supposedly working to get the TB formula right, but Ben said no amount of tweaking the formula would change it from a killer to a real cure; you can't just switch out an atom or two and make a drug work; if only it were that easy. Amelia believed him, but what fascinated her was the drug company killing people to shut them up. She knew that didn't really happen, either—right?

The woman in the movie had gotten pregnant, too. It was an eerie connection. Amelia was seconds from panicking, sure AD had some thug call to threaten her, when Ben said it was Matthew.

Matthew. Of course. He'd called Ben almost every night since they'd been in Paris. She felt very relieved, if a little silly.

"Honey, I know he's your best friend." She put her arm around his waist. "But you know that can't make any difference to my work." When he didn't respond, she said, "Matthew told you it was his drug, didn't he? It's not true; he just says that. It started in Palm Beach, when he—"

"You're wrong. Matt's in charge of it. He has been since the trials."

She was surprised, but she said, "So?"

"You can't talk about tegabadol. You really can't."

"Do you realize what you're asking me to do?" She put her hands on his cheeks and forced him to look at her. "I know Matthew's career could suffer, but this is a principle. This is about what we believe, everything we stand for, everything we've—"

"I know." He was blinking; he wouldn't meet her eyes. "If it was just about Matt's career, it would be different."

"What is it about, then? Who else will it hurt other than that stupid company?"

He turned away from her.

"Who?"

"I'm so sorry to put you in this position." She heard him take a breath. "But my reputation—the foundation—I don't know how bad it would get before it was finished." He turned around and looked at her then. His sweet face was so pained she felt tears spring to her eyes. "It's me, Amelia." His tone was surprised, as if he couldn't understand how this could have happened to them. "It will hurt me."

CHAPTER SEVEN

Me, Too!

Matthew wasn't gloating as he flew back to Philadelphia. He loved a good gloat as much as the next guy, but he just couldn't muster the energy.

As expected, Tokyo had been easy to resolve. After his massive display of safety data had put the entire room into a PowerPoint coma, Dorothy Hilton had quickly finished them off while he excused himself to take an urgent call about a problem with the post-market Galvenar trial in Jakarta. Walter agreed that Matthew had to deal with this immediately, and off he went to Indonesia, where he spent his days helping the AD statisticians untangle a screwup in the sample selection process and his nights partying with a bunch of locals and American expats. Jakarta was Matthew's favorite city in Asia, but when he left on Saturday for Paris he was already tired and having trouble sleeping because he didn't have his Ativan. He was in no mood for any problems in Paris, and he was very concerned that Ben had kept putting off *the talk*.

Luckily, Paris had been an unqualified success. On Tuesday evening, the CEO himself called Matthew to thank him for doing an outstanding job. Walter had obviously been talking up Matthew because the (normally clueless) CEO was aware of Matthew's excellent performance in Tokyo and Jakarta, as well as his management of several situations in Paris, including Monday afternoon, when a mob of protestors showed up outside Le Palais des Congrès determined to attract the attention of American journalists, and Matthew quickly arranged a private press conference for the journalists with the three top scientists at the conference (including the almighty Ben), after which the number of protestors dwindled to a handful. And while the CEO didn't mention Amelia's "sudden, unexpected" announcement on Tuesday morning that she was withdrawing from the bioethics panel, Matthew knew Walter had given him credit for that as well. Walter called it a major coup and bragged that Matthew could walk on water, ignoring all Matthew's humble protests that he just knew where to buy the best boat.

Despite all this, he still spent his nights in Paris tossing in jet lag hell, wondering if he should just pay the concierge to bring up a frying pan and bash him over the head. The only sleeping pills he'd been able to get his hands on were the new-generation variety, and he tried them all, including the much-hyped AD drug Restrien, but even at ten times the normal dose the only effect was an annoying hallucination that the message light on his phone was blinking. He answered the phone over and over before he realized it wasn't real. He wanted to curse Restrien, but he knew those seven-day coupon ads had resulted in millions of prescriptions and hundreds of millions in profit. Consumers—sorry, *patients*—love Restrien, he thought, while flushing the pills down the toilet. Patients are never wrong. Then he laughed a hysterical laugh, which made him worry that he was on the edge of insomnia-induced psychosis.

By the time he got on the plane to Philly, his internal clock was so screwed up that nothing made him drift off, not the almost-comfortable first-class bed, not stuffing himself with tasteless airplane food, not even the uniformly bad movies. But, as he kept reminding himself, the trip had been well worth it. Right before he boarded the plane, he'd gone online to read that day's *WSJ* and discovered the very good news that Astor-Denning's stock was once again on the rise, the only pharmaceutical company to have gained in value that quarter. The rise was attributed to several factors, not the least of which was the company's "dazzling success" at the EU conference, where AD had managed to reposition itself as a "socially responsible citizen" of the global health community.

Since it was the Wednesday before Thanksgiving, Matthew had already decided to skip going into the office when he got back to Philadelphia. His plane touched down a little ahead of schedule, at 1:45 P.M., meaning he would get home long before the going-to-grandmas crowd snarled traffic. He turned on his cell phone and dialed voice mail. Thirty-seven messages. Not bad. He could quickly review them on the cab ride home. Deal with the bare minimum, delete the rest, and then sleep for the next four days.

When the phone rang, the caller ID didn't show a number, but he assumed it was Cassie. She'd said she would check in when he arrived.

"What did you do to him?" Amelia. Oh, no. Not now. "Make him sign on to one of your Galvenar clinical trials? Use your relationship with him to confuse him into something he never meant to do? God, you are evil. I will find out what it is. Ben feels he can't tell me. Fine. I trust him completely. I dropped out of the panel because he told me it would hurt him. That was enough. But you are another story, and I will find out what your hold on him is. I'll find out if I have to spend the rest of my life."

He had to hold the phone away from his ear because she was shouting. He should have expected this; of course she was angry, but Ben wasn't. That was the important point, as Matthew reminded himself now. Ben was still feeling grateful to Matthew for paying for the trip to the Caymans, and he'd been glad to go out for coffee with him on Tuesday afternoon, at a café on Rue de Miromesnil, hours after Amelia announced her withdrawal. Unfortunately, Ben didn't know what Amelia had planned to say about Galvenar because he didn't ask her. But they talked about the general situation, and Ben seemed to feel better. He even shared the stunning news that Amelia was pregnant.

Her condition hadn't changed her one bit. The moment Matthew heard her voice his briefcase had gained fifty pounds, and now he was rubbing his shoulder on the long walk to the escalator.

"From now on, I'm going to take a very hard look at every damn thing you do. Every place you go, every place you send your people, every article about AD in every paper. I'll call the journalist personally and ask if they were contacted by a source. And as soon I get home, I'm going to write an article just about you. Your career, the way you use your unfinished medical training and MCAT score from twenty years ago. I'm going to reveal how Astor-Denning picked you, a pretty-face nonscientist, to woo scientists into compromising positions. When I'm finished, it'll be crystal clear that Matthew Connelly, MD, MBA, is no different from the cheerleader types your company uses to hand out pens to horny doctors in Kansas. That should help your alliances!"

"Amelia, please, I'm really not up to—"

"I'm not worried that you'll out me. You can tell Ben that you're being kind and he believes you, but I saw the headline that AD

108

stock went up after I canceled. You don't want your boss to know that you used to live with me. You don't want anyone to know that, thanks to you, I was in the audience at Palm Beach, where all your lying spin about Galvenar started."

Matthew felt a migraine coming on—he didn't have migraines, but this headache was way too painful to be ordinary—and he slumped against the wall outside baggage claim. It had never occurred to him that Amelia had been in the ballroom when he gave that speech. How did she get past security? And how did she know that NCE turned out to be Galvenar, unless she'd been scrutinizing their pipeline for years? Jesus, no wonder she was a threat to his baby. In her mind, it was all connected: Galvenar, that night in his hotel room, his infidelity, the end of what they had both hoped (yes, he really had, though he would never admit it to her now) would be a lifelong relationship.

She was still ranting, but he was thinking about how to handle this new problem. He could call Ben again, but if he did, he was in danger of Ben confessing the whole thing. Then he'd not only lose control of the situation, but Amelia would come after him like the wrath of God for ruining her paradise.

"Wait, Amelia. Please. You really have me all wrong." He forced his voice to sound contrite. "I've done bad things in the past, no question, but I've changed in the last year." He gulped. "Maybe it's turning forty, but—"

"Yes, Ben told me about this. Supposedly you're starting a family, too. He said you told him, 'I want to be the kind of person my children can respect.' Mmm, I wonder why you didn't mention a word of this in Grand Cayman, and why you were so vague with Ben about the details? He thinks you didn't mention the woman's name for fear of jinxing it. Poor Matt, he's been lonely for so long. Ha! I think it's time we call your bluff. Let Ben see exactly who you really are. As it happens, we're going to be in South Jersey tomorrow, at his cousin's house for Thanksgiving. You bring your girlfriend and I'll bring the EPT."

His head was pounding, but he managed to say, "I wish we could, but we're having dinner at our house."

"Okay, we'll drop by there. Eight o'clock," she said, and hung up.

He pushed his palm against his left eye, which was throbbing like it was about to pop out of his skull. When he'd told Ben that bullshit about starting his own family, it was Tuesday afternoon, when he was already losing it from lack of sleep, but he'd tried to be careful. He'd made Ben promise not to share this information with anyone—and *specifically* not with Amelia.

He knew full well the risk he was running here. Just a few months earlier, when he brought in a psychologist to run a training seminar for new people in his alliances group on "Winning the Trust of Skeptics"—e.g., med school professors, who were the very definition of skeptical, at least in their own minds—one of the first things the psychologist mentioned was avoiding the human tendency of "me, too." The staff had laughed at the phrase, and Matthew had explained to her that "me, too" was an expression their industry used for a new drug that was structurally similar to another company's blockbuster. "I gather it's derogatory then," she said crisply. "That's good. It will be easier to remember in this new context."

She wrote on the whiteboard:

Oh, you love golf? Me, too.

You just saw The Da Vinci Code? *Me, too.*

Innocent-seeming responses, the psychologist said, yet both risk losing the respect of your contact. What if the doctor invites you to play golf with him? What if the professor asks what you thought of the scene where Tom Hanks chokes on a bite of sushi? In the first case, your unwillingness to meet him for golf, no matter how creative your excuses, will make him suspect you're a liar. In the second, if you say anything about the scene, even "It was interesting," he'll know you're a liar because there wasn't a sushi scene in the movie. The client was trying to expose you, and you played right into his hand. While "me, too" happens every day in social situations, you have to train yourself not to do it with contacts. The friendlier you are with the client, the harder you will have to work to resist this natural tendency. Now, if you do play a good game of golf, fine. Or you can claim you love rare steak, too, as long as you manage to choke down the bloody meat during your client dinner. Both truth and lies are perfectly acceptable, as long as you avoid the provably false.

Again, laughter from the staff, but the psychologist didn't ask for an explanation. She was busy filling the whiteboard with examples of how the truth can also be provably false, because what is "true" depends heavily on the client's perceptions. Matthew went back to his office knowing his people were in good hands. He didn't need to hear this. He could teach this course, if he wasn't so busy living it.

Yet here he was now, facing exactly the kind of disaster the psychologist had warned them about.

Hey, buddy, you and Amelia are starting a family? Me, too!

Of course he knew that at some point he'd have to tell Ben it hadn't worked out. His plan was to hint at a miscarriage, knowing Ben wouldn't care enough to ask about the details. Ben hadn't even asked who the woman was, primarily because, though he obviously hadn't shared *this* part with Amelia, he'd been in the middle of his own freak-out. They were at the café and Ben was confessing that he wished Amelia hadn't gotten pregnant, which hadn't surprised Matthew one bit. Ben had been saying for years that he never wanted to have children because they would take too much time away from his research.

Meaning that Matthew obviously hadn't done his "me, too"

Lisa Tucker

for the usual reason of making a connection with Ben. If he'd just wanted a connection, he would have used something much simpler and absolutely true: "You wish you could have sex without ever worrying about pregnancy? Hell, yeah! Me, too!" What Matthew was trying to do was far more complicated. Admittedly, he was attempting to soothe his own guilty conscience and, as always, he was interested in protecting his billion-dollar baby, but he was also trying to—

Oh, what the hell. There was no point in trying to justify this. It was a stupid move, and he deserved to be sitting in the airport with his nonexistent family stabbing him in the left eye.

If he refused Amelia's demand, which, after all, was the reasonable response, the bitch would keep working on Ben until she convinced him it was all a lie. Losing Ben's trust right now was absolutely out of the question. He would just have to engage his exhausted brain and think of a way to make this bullshit ring true.

He took his bag from the carousel and headed to the taxis. After he gave the cabdriver his address, he called Cassie and asked if she was, by any chance, pregnant. When she didn't laugh, even after he shared all the basics (leaving out the name of the scientist and his meddling girlfriend), he told her she was getting a raise. Unfortunately, she had nothing to offer for the obvious reason that there was no rational way out of this. Even if one of the women he dated would agree to play the part of his pregnant girlfriend, such a ruse would make him forever indebted to the woman, which he certainly couldn't allow.

The cab was racing down the Schuylkill Expressway, but it no longer made Matthew happy to be avoiding traffic. The holiday was still coming tomorrow, and no matter how many cholesterol-lowering prescriptions it generated (Walter called the whole season "Statin Claus"), Amelia would be coming to his house, too, hating his guts more than ever, waving a pregnancy test in his face.

112

"You never actually told this scientist you had a girlfriend," Cassie pointed out. "You said you were starting a family. Perhaps there's a way to tease out that distinction to maintain credibility?"

Ah, Cassie. Why hadn't he married her? True, she was already married when she came to AD, and true, they didn't love each other, but those were minor matters compared to their complete compatibility when trying to solve a messy problem. They were the real soul mates, not Ben and Bitchface. They'd certainly been together a hell of a lot longer.

He praised Cassie for her creative approach before admitting he doubted it would work. "I'll have to keep thinking about it." The cab had just pulled off on South Street. Almost home, but no chance of jumping into his own bed and falling asleep to CNBC's comforting market talk and the pleasing green arrows for Astor-Denning on the simulated ticker tape.

Cassie said she'd keep thinking about it, too, even though she had to leave the office early because her kids were home. He thanked her again for handling Paris while he was in Japan and Jakarta and for dealing with the homeless-people robbery mess in the middle of everything.

"All I did was call the guard at your building. He assured me that everything was secured. Nothing to do."

As Matthew flashed his security card and the lobby door opened, he gave thanks that he still had his apartment. At least he could take a nice long shit, which he'd needed to do since he'd arrived at Charles de Gaulle.

He was in the elevator when it occurred to him that asking an employee if she was pregnant, even in jest, might be considered a sexual harassment violation by the gestapo in HR. It made him nervous; not that Cassie would tell on him, of course, but that he was just realizing this. He prided himself on being aware of any rules he was about to break *before* he broke them. Which left only one conclusion: this sleep deprivation had turned him into a blithering idiot.

He opened the door to his apartment and came face-to-face with another problem. There they were (still!), the homeless kid and his sister, sitting at his dining room table, eating what looked to be his pasta puttanesca—the boy—and his Peking duck with dumplings—the little girl. He dropped his briefcase on the floor next to his suitcase, walked over, crossed his arms, and stared at them.

"Having a late lunch?" he said, and laughed because it struck him as just hilarious that all those tips to the security guard hadn't done one bit of good.

The boy was tripping over himself to get up, but Matthew told him to sit still, and when he didn't listen, Matthew put his hand on his shoulder and said, "Stay." He wasn't about to let them leave until he'd done a thorough search of his apartment.

"What are you going to do to us?"

"I don't know." Matthew's legs were shaky; he had to sit down. He took the seat farthest away from the boy.

"Throw us out?" the kid said hopefully.

"That's one idea. My other thought was to wring your lying little neck."

"Ring," the little girl said.

Matthew looked at her. "So she can talk."

"She learned from your computer."

"If you tell me you touched any of the data in my computer, I will kill you. I won't go to jail, either. You see, I haven't slept for seventy-two hours and I'll just have my lawyers say I had a psychotic break." He paused and gave the boy a mean smile. "I have very good lawyers."

"I didn't touch the computer," the kid said, though he didn't seem afraid. Why wasn't he? Had Matthew's ability to intimidate gone the way of his ability to think? The boy glanced at the computer. "It just started talking when I touched the desk."

"That's a language program. I planned to listen to it on my iPod, but then I forgot my iPod because your mother had stolen my wallet and— But of course you know all this. You were here *eight days ago* when I left."

"I was going to leave, really, but then the computer was teaching Isabelle all these words and she even learned to walk by herself using your furniture. I'm sorry, Doctor Connelly."

Matthew wondered how the kid knew his name, but he didn't care enough to ask. He felt sleepy just watching them eat. Something about them looked different from last week, and then he realized what it was. The dirty boy wasn't dirty anymore. The little girl looked even more beautiful now that she'd lost her chapped hands and cheeks. Even their clothes looked brighter, although in the boy's case, this was yet another reason to be annoyed. The kid was wearing one of the Hopkins sweatshirts that Matthew wore when he went running. The sleeves were rolled up, and it hung down past his knees. There was also a red stain on the elbow, probably from the pasta he was eating.

"Made yourself quite at home, did you? Found my sweatshirt? Found the washer and dryer, too?"

The kid nodded.

"Treated *my* apartment exactly like you lived here?"

The boy nodded again, but he looked almost comically miserable.

"Live here," Isabelle said, but her mouth was full of half-chewed dumplings and Matthew quickly turned away before he retched.

Live here, he thought. As if. But then he heard Cassie's voice cutting through his angry fog: "You never actually told this scientist you had a girlfriend. You said you were starting a family."

"No way," he said aloud. "I'd rather throw myself in front of a bus."

The boy said, "What?"

"Please," Matthew said, "I'm having a private conversation with my assistant."

The kid finally looked scared then, but Matthew ignored him.

"But," Cassie reminded him, "we haven't come up with any other options, and Thanksgiving is tomorrow."

True, he thought, or said—he wasn't sure. He stared at the wall for a minute, then he sighed and told Cassie, "Well, Amelia has always had this thing about orphans."

"Me-la," the little girl said.

"Cute," Matthew said. He wasn't being sarcastic; he was assessing the situation. They were cute as far as kids go, even the boy. Certainly a thousand times cuter than he'd been on the bridge.

His eyes were so heavy that he kept seeing double—four kids, which would suck a lot more than these two. Danny, the boy, had even managed to keep the place relatively clean. The girl dropped half the food before it reached her mouth, but the drops hit a carefully placed garbage bag on the floor. Which struck Matthew as a rather ingenious solution, but maybe it only seemed ingenious in his current state.

He heard himself talking. "What if I told you that you could stay here tonight and tomorrow? I assume you'd agree to that."

"Why would you let us stay?" the kid said, narrowing his eyes.

"Because I'm having people over tomorrow and I'm in the absurd position of needing to convince them I'm starting a family. You two could play the role of my about-to-be adopted children."

"So you need us to lie for you," the kid said. "What would we get out of the deal?"

"Other than avoiding being arrested? Other than not being thrown on the street?"

116

"Yeah," the kid said. "What else?"

The boy had nerve. Matthew enjoyed negotiations, but this seemed ridiculous. "What do you want? Some toy? Money?"

"I want to have one of the Astor-Denning cures. You know, from the commercial."

"The one that ends with 'Expect your next miracle from Astor-Denning'?"

"Yeah."

Matthew smiled. "I was on the approval committee for that. In fact, I had to fight for it inside my company even though the ad agency clearly believed it was the best candidate. But why listen to the ad people? We only pay them millions for their expertise." Most of the other people on the committee had been nervous old-school types who worried obsessively about liability. They'd spent an infuriating hour just discussing the word *expect*.

"Okay." The boy coughed. "So, can my mom have the next miracle?"

His exhaustion must have drastically lowered his serotonin level. How else to explain that the kid's request made him drop his head on the table in despair?

Finally, and with difficulty, he lifted his throbbing head and looked at the boy. "The only thing you want—the only thing in the world—is help for your mom?"

He nodded.

"Aren't you forgetting that she left you and your sister here and never came back? What if I'd really been a pervert or a serial killer? What if I was about to get out the knives and torture you both right now?"

Still no fear from the kid, and then it hit Matthew why. Dr. Connelly. Everyone trusts a doctor. He'd used this fact a thousand times, but it never stopped surprising him. Even a street kid would think he was perfectly safe in a doctor's house.

"I want my mom to have a cure."

"We don't have a cure for addiction. Sorry."

The boy thought for a minute. "You can send her to Changes, then."

"How the hell do you know about Changes?" It was an upscale rehab in Florida; Matthew knew the director very well. In the last year alone, Changes had received more than a million dollars from AD's community outreach program. The place had an excellent reputation; Matthew had sent one of the Galvenar investigators there after the guy was caught stealing morphine. That guy was a disaster at running a clinical trial, but a very well-known neurologist, and very cooperative. He'd signed on to the results paper sight unseen, and the weight of his name got the paper accepted by one of the most prestigious medical journals in the country.

"My mom and her friends always talk about it. I wasn't sure if it was real, but it is, right? And they keep you for thirty days? It really works?"

"It can. If you have forty thousand dollars." Matthew wasn't sure how much it cost, but this sounded about right. Jerome Drossman, the director, had handled the Galvenar investigator off the books, as a personal favor.

"Oh." The kid fell silent and Matthew fell into a stupor. What seemed like a year later, the boy said, "Isabelle has to go to the bathroom."

"That's why she's kicking my table leg? Fine, go before she has an accident."

The kid lifted her off the phone books and started to carry her off, but the little girl went nuts. "Down, Danny. Down!" He put her down and she toddled in the direction of the guest room, but she didn't pee on the floor and she didn't touch any furniture, thank god. Her hands were covered in duck sauce.

While they were in the bathroom, Cassie, the real Cassie, called

to say she had an idea. "I've just been googling international adoption. I think we could put together convincing-looking documents
to show that you're in the process of getting approved for one or
more children from Africa. It's a very hot thing to do right now,
despite the Madonna situation."

"Very good thinking," he said, "but unfortunately the meddling
girlfriend in this case has some big moral objection to removing
children from their native environment."

No doubt if Amelia didn't have this attitude, she would have already adopted a pack of third-world kids for herself. She'd wanted
to be a mother for a very long time. Back when they'd lived together, she couldn't take the Pill and her period was so erratic
that they'd had to worry every few months about pregnancy; or,
to be precise, he'd worried, while she'd positively glowed at the
thought. Of course he'd told her that he was ready and even happy
about it, but when her period started and she got over the tears,
he convinced her that they should keep using the diaphragm
and wait a little longer. At least get married first, so their baby
would have all the benefits of having a dad with a good job and
insurance.

It struck him that Ben hadn't said a word about marrying Amelia, but it had to have been an oversight. True, Ben had refused to
marry Karen or any of the others—even when they dumped him
over the issue—but this was different. Amelia was having his kid.

"I think I'm getting a migraine," he said to Cassie, and then described the hideous pain on the left side of his face that hadn't been
touched by any of the over-the-counter meds he'd tried. The kids
were out of the bathroom. Isabelle was stumbling around like a tiny
astronaut; Danny was just standing near the wall, clearly depressed.
"Is it possible when I've never had one before?"

Cassie had migraines. She said it was possible; she also didn't say
a word about him being the one who went to medical school. "Do

you want me to bring over some Imitrex? If it's a migraine, that's probably the only thing that will work."

"What about your kids?"

"Gerald is home now, too. I don't mind. We could brainstorm about the problem."

Gerald? Oh, right, her husband. Normally, Matthew would have said thanks, but no. He was always careful not to take advantage of Cassie's unwavering loyalty. But in this case, he saw a distinct benefit to getting a second opinion before he proceeded. It was such a crazy scheme—and so entirely unlike him—that he had to make sure his stupidity wasn't leading him to do something that was, well, stupid.

When he hung up, he decided to go to the bathroom (finally!) and then lie down for a while. Cassie lived way out in the suburbs near AD; it would be at least an hour before she arrived.

He was looking around his desk for something to read when he noticed that the boy was packing up his garbage bag. And he'd replaced Matthew's sweatshirt with one of his own raggedy shirts.

"Where do you think you're going?"

"Home."

"You don't have a home." Matthew paused. "Do you?"

"Not like this, but yeah."

"Not like this meaning what? No heat, no water, no lights? A crack house?"

"Yeah, I guess."

"Why would you want to go to a place like that when I just told you I'm thinking of letting you stay here?"

"But you won't help my mom."

"Fuck your mom, what about her?" He pointed at the little girl, who was grinning at something invisible on the floor. A speck of dust? "She's happy here."

Danny didn't answer, but Matthew suspected that the kid was

afraid his mom was shooting up all the money she'd stolen and that somehow if he was there, he could stop her, or at least slow her down. It was stupid, but not surprising. He'd thought the same thing about his dad's drinking.

"Look, what if I say I'll consider sending your mom to Changes?"

"For real?" the kid said.

"Yes," Matthew said. He didn't mean it, but he really needed to get to the bathroom. He grabbed the first journal on the stack, *Current Enzyme Inhibition*, which was so reliably dull he just might fall asleep on the toilet. "Stay put until Cassie gets here. It shouldn't be more than an hour or so. Let me do a few things."

"Sure," the boy said happily. "We can wait that long, I guess."

"How nice," Matthew muttered, but he kept himself from cursing about the unfairness of it all, that they'd lived in his house for eight days and now he had to negotiate with this kid for an additional hour.

The bathroom was fairly clean, with the notable exception of his soap. At least twenty bars were unwrapped and strewn around the room. Just being kids, he thought, like he actually knew why kids would do something so pointless. He'd have to ask Cassie about that, too.

CHAPTER EIGHT

Lucky Trash

When the woman knocked on the door, Dr. Connelly had been shut up in his bedroom for a long time, more than an hour. Danny figured he'd fallen asleep, since he'd kept saying how tired he was—and he looked it, too, like his trip had turned him into a zombie. The knock was soft, but the man heard it somehow because he was out of the bedroom and moving to the door so quickly that Isabelle fell over. She wasn't hurt; she clapped her hands like something exciting was about to happen. Danny felt sorry for her when the woman, Cassie, walked in without even noticing Isabelle's enormous welcome grin. Cassie didn't say hello to Danny, either, but he didn't care.

He just wanted to listen and find out if they were going to help his mom.

He'd threatened to leave so the guy would take him seriously, but while Dr. Connelly was in the bedroom, he'd realized that he was ready to go home. He was worried about his mom; he had to be sure she was all right. It would be hard to take Isabelle away from here, but it was going to happen in a few days either way.

For several minutes Dr. Connelly and Cassie talked about the failure of the security guard to throw them out last week. Cassie blamed herself, but Dr. Connelly said it wasn't her fault; she couldn't have known the guard was a slacker. "But I should have followed up," Cassie said. "I feel terrible that you came home to this."

Danny couldn't tell how old Cassie was. She looked a lot older than Dr. Connelly, but maybe it was because she was sitting up so straight and her face didn't give away any emotion. Dr. Connelly, on the other hand, looked freaked-out. He'd taken off his tie and un-tucked his shirt in the bedroom and now he was pacing around the apartment in his socks. Isabelle was hugging her elephant, watching him. Danny was standing near the window, a few feet down from the table where Cassie was sitting. She'd just opened her purse and taken out a pill bottle.

"Thanks." Dr. Connelly took the pill she handed him and swallowed it without water. "The pain is hideous. The worst headache I've ever had."

"Isn't that something you should have checked out?"

He shrugged. "It's an early symptom of a brain aneurysm, but in my case, I think it's from insomnia. I haven't slept since Jakarta."

"At all?"

"I ran out of Ativan, thanks to their thieving mother. At this point, I think I've gone over some kind of threshold. I couldn't even sleep on the plane or while I was waiting for you."

"The stress of the problem can't be helping." She paused. "Are you thinking these two could be of some use for that?"

He was over by the front door, and he turned to look at her. "I know it sounds ludicrous, but it crossed my mind. What do you think of the idea?"

"I'm concerned about possible legal ramifications. Where is the mother now?"

"She lives in a crack house, apparently. At this moment, she's probably sitting in her own shit after partying all week with my five grand."

"We could still press charges. I could connect with the people we used last year to get Herdrich's DUI dismissed."

Danny was scared then. "My mom didn't mean to—"

Dr. Connelly shook his head. "Let's say the mother agreed to let them stay. It shouldn't be hard to convince her. Fifty dollars should do it. Hell, she'd probably sell them outright for a few hundred."

"I don't think paying her is the best way to handle this."

"Judiciously put," Dr. Connelly said, and he walked over to the couch, near Danny's sister. He leaned down to Isabelle and smiled. "If I pay for you, I'll look like what your brother calls a perv. Then your dope fiend mother can blackmail me. We don't want that, do we?"

"No!" Isabelle said, laughing.

Danny said, "Don't talk to my sister."

"Why shouldn't I?" Dr. Connelly said. "She lives with me in this scheme, remember? So do you." Then he said, "Luke, I am your father," in a really weird voice, and Cassie laughed; Danny wasn't sure why.

After a while the man sat down, resting his hand on the left side of his face, and said to her, "Is this as stupid as I think it is?"

Cassie waited a moment. "Perhaps you could just confess to this scientist that you stretched the truth. If you had—"

"No. Absolutely out of the question."

"Even if you gave him a compelling emotional reason? You said he's having a child and is obviously very involved with his girl-friend. If he doesn't know you very well, he might be able to believe that you were momentarily jealous."

Dr. Connelly put his other hand on his face, too, and sat there like that for so long that Cassie finally coughed.

"Sorry," he said. "I keep going into these trances. Good thinking, but unfortunately the scientist does know me."

"Oh," Cassie said. "That won't work then."

Danny was getting worried. It had been dusk when the woman arrived, and now it was dark. If he was walking home, he wanted to get out there now, before it was too cold. "What about my mom?" he said, crossing his arms, looking at the man. "Will you send her to Changes or not?"

Dr. Connelly exhaled. "He wants his mom in rehab, but not just any rehab—Changes."

"That might be a possibility," Cassie said. "If the mother would sign a letter saying that she's going there and designating you as temporary guardian, we could talk to Drossman about admitting her immediately. I'm sure he'd be happy to—"

"Thirty days? You have to be kidding."

"We could find other arrangements for them on Friday with social services. But the lengthy rehab makes the letter necessary and protects you from any number of possibilities. Assuming it's worded in such a way that it's clearly her choice to have you take care of her children, this limits her actions against you in the future, among other things."

"I wish I could think more about this after I get some sleep." He sighed. "Do we have to do it tonight?"

"The children are here now without parental permission. I think you have to either send them home or do it tonight, as quickly as possible. I'll help you, but first I'll have to call Gerald."

"No, I can't let you do that. Go. Be with your family. I can deal with it."

"At least let me make all the arrangements with Changes and work on a draft of the letter. And get a plane reservation for the mother, late tonight if possible, tomorrow morning otherwise. I can do all that from the car once you give me the go-ahead. That way, when she signs the letter, you just send her in a cab to the airport."

Danny was squinting at this woman, stunned at how serious she sounded. Like it was actually going to happen after so many years of hearing about Changes. His mom would be going there. His mom would be off drugs.

"Great," Dr. Connelly said. "That would be a big help."

"I'll also send a car over tomorrow morning with some toys and children's clothes. I have most of my kids' things; my mother insisted I save it all for Deana. She still believes my sister will decide to grow up and get married someday." Cassie shrugged. "I don't really mind. We have a very large basement."

"You don't have to bother with that."

"If you were in the process of adopting these children, I don't think you'd have them wearing these clothes and playing with nothing but cushions."

Isabelle had all the cushions off the big white chair and was jumping on them. Danny had noticed this earlier, but if the man wasn't going to object, he sure wasn't.

"But don't your kids want their toys?"

"My son is at Princeton and both my girls are in high school. I don't think so."

"Sorry. I forgot."

Cassie smiled. "You're not interested in children, Matthew. Everyone who works for you knows this. It's nothing to be sorry for."

Danny agreed with the last sentence. From his experience, most people weren't interested in children, and they weren't sorry about it, either. He wasn't sure why she was smiling; maybe because the boring conversation was about to be over.

"I'll need your mother's legal name," Cassie said to Danny. It was the first time she'd spoken to him, or even looked at him. "From her driver's license."

"Does she even have a driver's license?" Dr. Connelly said.

Danny nodded. It was from a few years ago, but he figured it would still work. He told Cassie his mom's name, and she punched the letters into a little computer-like thing that Dr. Connelly called her "crackberry."

A minute later she stood up, and Dr. Connelly walked her to the door. He whispered something to her and she gave him a quick hug. Danny was surprised by this, after the stiff way they'd been talking. Maybe they were friends, too, not just people who worked together.

Once Cassie was gone, the man was back to being grumpy. He complained that his head hurt and that he was tired about a million times before he said that Danny would have to go find his mother and bring her back here.

"Okay, Doctor Connelly. We'll do it right now."

"Not we. You. And don't call me Doctor Connelly." He was slumped on the cushionless chair. Isabelle was sitting at his feet, tugging on a loose thread in the rug. "Call me Matthew or Your Highness or even Fuckface. Anything but that."

"I can't go without my sister."

"You can and you will. I don't trust you, and I definitely don't trust your mother. What if she just scored a bag? She'll say rehab can wait, and then you won't come back, either, and I'll be fucked. Isabelle is my insurance that you will return, dragging your dope fiend mom with you." He smirked. "Think of it as déjà vu to the fabulous night we met."

"But who will watch her?"

"Who do you think? I'll force myself to stay awake until you get back. Better hurry, though. I'll have to call up the security guard to help me if you're gone too long."

Danny felt like he was going to cry, but he made himself sound angry. "I don't want to do this."

"Neither do I. I don't want to do any of this. I'd rather chew off my own leg than deal with the happy couple tomorrow, but those are the breaks. I have to do certain things, and so do you. It's part of being a man. Buck up and take it." Matthew laughed harshly. "I got that from my own father, and now I'm passing it on to you, my new son. Hope you appreciate it."

Actually, Danny did appreciate it. It chased away the crying feeling. It also made him feel older and even respected, to be talked to like he was becoming a man.

He went through the list of things to watch out for with Isabelle and Matthew listened, though he kept going "Yeah, yeah, yeah" after each thing. Then Danny took Isabelle into the bedroom and put a diaper on her, ignoring her complaints. He told his sister that he was running out for a minute to get Mommy, but he'd be right back.

"Back," she repeated, but her voice was quieter. He realized she'd missed her nap, which was good. Maybe she'd fall asleep and stay that way the whole time he was gone.

When they were back in the living room, the man asked him how far away his house was. "I don't know," Danny said. "Not that far."

Dr. Connelly, Matthew, reached into his pants and took out two twenty-dollar bills. "This should cover the cab both ways."

"Thanks," Danny said, because he was in too much of a hurry to explain that he didn't know how to take a cab. He knew a short-cut once he was over the bridge. He could walk there in less than a half hour, grab his mom, and be back before anything happened to his sister.

He was at the door when he thought to ask how he'd get back in. Matthew said he could just ask the guard to let him come up, the way Cassie had. "He'll see you leave. It shouldn't be a problem." He shook his head. "Obviously, he's not all that concerned with the security of my apartment."

"I don't think he'll let me in," Danny said. What he really meant was the guard wouldn't let his mom in, but he couldn't admit that without admitting he'd been inside the locked closet, and from there, he had a feeling that the man would get much, much grumpier.

"Live dangerously."

"Really. He won't let me in, I'm sure."

"All right, anything, if you'll just stop talking about this." Matthew disappeared into the bedroom and returned with something that looked like an ATM card. He explained how to use it outside the lobby and at his front door, too.

"Now, if you give my key to anyone else, I'll have to give your sister to someone else. Fair is fair."

"I won't."

"By anyone, I also mean your mother, or any of her friends."

"I promise."

"Fine, I'll accept your promise, despite how well you kept the last one. Any other requests, or are you finally leaving?"

"Take good care of Isabelle."

Matthew pointed at the door. "Go."

Danny did as he was told, even though leaving without his sister made his heart beat so hard he felt like it was trying to break through his chest. When he was out of the building he started running to the bridge, and he was still running as he headed over to Spring Garden. By the time he got to his house, he was holding his side and panting. Luckily, when he pounded on the door, some woman answered. She let him in even though she didn't know who he was.

As he walked around looking for his mom, he couldn't help noticing how ugly the house was—much worse than he remembered. Part of it was that the lights were on for a change, but the other part, he knew, was that he'd been spoiled by living in the man's place. He wondered how long it would take him to adjust again. The guy had mentioned getting rid of them on Friday, meaning he and Isabelle would have to come back here for a month, without their mom. It would be really hard, but at the end of the month, his mom would be off drugs. They could start their new life.

He found her on the third floor, alone in one of the bedrooms, lying on one of the dirty mattresses. She wasn't sick, but she wasn't normal, either. When she saw him, she blinked with recognition, but then she closed her eyes.

"Come on, Mom." He pulled on her arm. "We have to go to Isabelle."

"My baby?"

"Yeah, she's over in West Philly. We're going to get her, and then you're going to have a big surprise. You won't believe it."

She finally sat up. "Cobain? Where have you been?"

Cobain was Danny's real name. His mom had picked it because of some singer she'd liked in high school. The singer's first name was Kurt, which wasn't great, but it was a whole lot better than his last name.

"Danny," he said. "You have to call me Danny." He wiped his nose on his sleeve. "I'll tell you everything on the way there. Isabelle is waiting. We have to make sure she's okay."

His mom tried to stand up but she stumbled, and Danny had to grab her hands so she wouldn't fall. "Sweaty," she mumbled. He didn't bother to tell her that he'd run all the way there. Her hands seemed warm, too, and her face was very warm to his lips.

Of course he kissed his mom. He hadn't seen her for eight days.

She smiled, but her head fell forward, like it was too heavy for her neck. Then he knew what was wrong. She'd taken too much of the stuff in the needles. She'd be all right in a while, but it was going to be a struggle to get her to Isabelle.

Zeke, a guy who'd lived in the house forever, came in to see what was up. Danny had heard Zeke talking about Changes a thousand times, and he couldn't resist telling him that his mom was going there, tonight.

"Good news," Zeke said. He sounded genuinely happy for them. Danny wished he could send Zeke there, too. "Damn, Kim, you're lucky."

"Changes?" his mom said, blinking. "I thought we were going to get Isabelle."

"We are. Isabelle is with the man who's going to send you there. The one who's going to help us."

"Hold on a minute, champ," Zeke said. "Nobody does nothing in this world without a reason. What's this guy really want with Kim?"

Then Danny wanted to kick himself for bringing it up. "We have to go," he said to his mom. But Zeke kept saying it sounded suspicious, and then three other people from the house came up and said the same thing.

His mom was standing, leaning against him, but her voice was becoming stronger. "Cobain, did you give your sister to this man?"

"Don't call me that name! And no, the guy is just taking care of Isabelle until we get back."

"Oh, my god, we don't even know him. What if—"

"She'll be safe. He's a doctor."

"I hope he's not using that baby in some experiment," Salma

131

said. "I don't trust doctors. They act like they're your friend, when all they really want is your body parts."

"Ain't it the truth," another woman said. Danny didn't know her name. "I heard about a guy who went into rehab and came out without a kidney."

Danny was nervous, but he reminded himself that this couldn't be true. Even his mom said the people in the house loved to talk about the rest of the world plotting against them. Danny figured maybe they did it because they were afraid the rest of the world didn't really think about them at all.

"Mom, listen." Danny was looking at her, whispering. Two other people had come in to join the discussion, and he just wanted to get out of there. "Remember the guy we met on the bridge? That guy works for a big drug company. He's the one who wants to—"

"Drug companies are evil," Salma said. "They kill people with their bad drugs. All they care about is making money."

"True that," said some man with a big scar on his chin. "I got a friend who quit smack and the 'done with no help, nothing but his will, but now he's on Paxil and he can't get off that mother-fucker."

"That's how they do it," Angela said. She was the oldest person in the house, and she'd been an addict for years. "They make what helps you against the law so they can hook you on all their drugs that doesn't do shit except make you sick."

This went on for so long that Danny's mom slumped back on the mattress. Danny begged her to get up over and over. Finally, he said to the whole room of grown-ups, "Stop it! This is my mom's only chance. You're ruining it!"

"Listen, little man," Zeke said. He put his hand on Danny's shoulder, but Danny shook him off. "You gotta think about the way the world works. Changes is a whole lotta money. Why would some stranger pay for this unless he wanted something he couldn't get any other way? Whatever it is, I promise you, it's something real bad."

Danny didn't say anything, but he felt his throat close up like someone was choking him. He could imagine what Zeke would say if he heard the reason Dr. Connelly claimed he was helping them. To make some guests think he had a family? Yeah, right, and cops are all nice people, and Santa Claus will give you whatever you want if only you're really good. What if all the talk between Cassie and the man was like his train fare story—a put-on, meant to convince Danny they were considering Changes? What if Salma was right, and what they really needed were body parts for some drug company thing? He heard the guy say something about being run over by a bus. There were a couple of things like that he didn't understand. What if they all added up to something horrible, and his sister was up on the doctor's table, about to be cut open right now?

He grabbed his mom and pulled her from the bed. "We have to get Isabelle!"

"You want help?" Zeke said. Someone else said, "Yeah, bring along a can of whoop-ass for that doctor."

"No," Danny said, but only because Zeke was moving slowly, too, half dressed, and if he said yes to Zeke he might end up with half the house coming along. Getting them all to West Philly would take even longer.

He hurried his mom downstairs and outside. It was much colder now, which helped wake her up and kept her going all the way to the bridge, and then to the street where the man lived. On the way there, Danny told her about the letter and Changes and the woman, and she agreed with Zeke that there had to be something more to the story, something much darker and even sinister. Danny said maybe money didn't mean that much to this guy, but his mom reminded him that rich people were usually stingier than poor ones. He knew it was true, which was why he never begged from anyone who looked really rich unless he had no other choice. He felt like a stupid kid for forgetting how much he distrusted those people. He liked Dr. Connelly's apartment, but so what? He didn't know anything about the man himself except that he cursed a lot, like everybody in their house, but that didn't make him the same. There was no reason to trust him. He shouldn't have left Isabelle. He'd broken his vow to protect her.

When they got to the building, his mom thought to ask where they'd been when she came looking for them the week before. Danny told her they must have been out getting food. The fact that he had the key and knew how to use it helped make this believable.

The elevator couldn't go fast enough for him. He rushed down the hall and to the man's door and burst inside. He saw Dr. Connelly sitting at his computer, but he didn't see his sister.

He yelled, "Isabelle." His mom yelled her name, too.

"Keep it down." The man was typing so intently at his computer that he didn't look at them. "I need to finish this email. She can't hear you, anyway."

Danny was running around the apartment, searching for his sister. He didn't see her anywhere—not on the guest bed, not even in the bathroom. When he came back to the loft area, his mom was pounding on the guy's back with both her fists.

"Stop that!" Dr. Connelly stood up and struggled until he had her by the arms. He held her back, a few feet away from him. "What the hell is wrong with you?"

"What did you do to her?" Danny demanded.

"I didn't do anything. I was sitting here working and your crazy mother attacked me." He looked at her. "If I let you go, will you quit this?"

His mom's answer was to spit in Dr. Connelly's direction, but the spit didn't make it and drooled down her chin before landing on the rug.

"What did you do to Isabelle?" Danny couldn't help it; he was so scared his voice was shaking. "You said you would take care of her. You promised."

"I did not *promise*. I'm not a child."

His mom tried to kick the man, and Danny felt tears spring to his eyes.

"Wait, Christ, she's fine. She was listening to my iPod, watching some cartoon. She fell asleep that way and she's still in there. Go ahead, see for yourself."

Danny hadn't opened the man's bedroom door, but once he did, he saw it was true. Isabelle was lying flat on her back on the bed with the iPod still in her hand and the little plugs in her ears. The TV was on Cartoon Network. When he turned off the TV and took out the plugs, she woke up. And got mad.

He was so happy to see her that he didn't care when she pushed him away and climbed off the bed, still clutching the iPod in her fist. She toddled in the direction of the loft with the wires trailing behind her. When their mom saw her walking, she let out a little squeal of delight and breathed Isabelle's name. Matthew let go of her arms and she ran to her daughter and picked her up.

"No!" Isabelle wouldn't look at her and was pushing back, trying to get away. "No!"

"Belle, it's Mommy."

"Down!"

"Okay, baby. Okay, I'm putting you down."

When she did, Isabelle went straight to the leather couch, where Matthew was crumpled in the corner, holding his head in his hands. She climbed up and sat next to him, putting the iPod in his lap.

Matthew exhaled. "At least one person in this family is rational." He looked at Isabelle. "More Ramones?" She didn't answer, but after he put the plugs in her ears and started it up she patted his face, like he was her oldest friend.

After a few minutes, Danny said he was sorry for what happened. He said they were just worried about Isabelle, but Matthew snapped, "Save it. I don't care why."

"I guess you're not going to send my mom to Changes now."

"All I want is sleep. If she'll sign the letter Cassie faxed and leave and never come back, fine. Otherwise, you all need to get the hell out of here. I've had a very long week, my head is killing me, and I can't stand any more drama."

He closed his eyes and Isabelle closed hers, too, like she agreed.

Danny went over to his mom. He sat down on the floor next to her and took her hands in his. "Remember that story you used to tell me about your grandpa? When he took you fishing?"

His mom looked up. "I can't leave you and Isabelle with—"

"The boot became a pot for a flower. The sponge fit under the front step and stopped it from creaking. Even the—"

"We don't know this guy from Adam. He could be—"

" 'Trash is a good catch, too,' your grandpa always said."

"He didn't mean rich people," she said.

"But he told you any trash can be lucky."

Danny had forgotten about Matthew listening, but then he heard him say, "Perfect, just fucking perfect. Using a trash metaphor for someone who is saving your mom's ass has to be the irony of the year."

"You take your luck where you find it," Danny continued. He had to concentrate on his mom; he could make it up to the man later. "You've told me that a thousand times."

"I know, but this isn't right. I can feel it."

He argued with her for a while, but she wouldn't budge. Then Matthew said, "You have exactly one more minute to get her to agree. After that, the trash is rescinding his offer."

"I won't leave you and your sister here," his mom whispered. "I know something bad will happen. Let's go back to our house."

"Something bad has already happened." She wasn't a dragon, but still, he said it. He said it even though he knew it would break her heart. "You're the bad thing, Mom. You hurt Isabelle. She's better off with Doctor Connelly or anybody than with you."

His mom started crying, but when she recovered she signed the letter, as Danny knew she would. Matthew called Cassie; the last flight to Florida was at 9:52. When Matthew told Danny to walk his mom downstairs and talk to the security guard about getting a cab to the airport, Danny did that, too, even though he was scared. He gave his mom the forty dollars Matthew had given him earlier. Now she had eighty, since Matthew had given her forty, too—after getting mad that she didn't have any of his five thousand dollars. Danny didn't ask her what she did with all that money. He wasn't surprised it was gone.

When the cab drove up, she said, "You're so different, Cobain. I don't know what's happened to you."

"I'm ten and a half now," he said. He hadn't known what day it was until he saw the calendar at the security guard's desk. November 22, halfway to his birthday.

His mom always celebrated half birthdays. Nobody else thought they were important, but his mom did. "Oh, honey, I'm sorry I didn't remember. I would have tried to get you a little present." She paused and looked at him. "You're squinting. I know that means there's something you're wishing for."

"This is all I want," he said, pointing to the cab. He put his arms around her and hugged her. She was crying again, but he pulled away and forced a smile. "But when you come back, after you get a job and we get our own house, you can save up and get me an iPod."

CHAPTER NINE

A Moment of Weakness

Matthew slept until late in the afternoon the next day. He didn't feel great, but at least his headache was gone. When he came out of his bedroom to see what the kids were up to, he was relieved to find that Danny had handled everything, just as Matthew had ordered him to do last night. All the clothes that Cassie sent had been put away in the guest bedroom dresser. About half the toys were stacked against the wall by the bookcases; the other half were all over the floor, but that was probably unavoidable. Isabelle had to play with the damn things. Cassie had included toys for Danny, too, but Matthew suspected he hadn't touched them. He was too busy following his sister around, making sure she didn't fall off the little slide or swallow one of the hundreds of Barbie parts.

He had less than four hours before Ben and Amelia were set to arrive. He spent some time on what "his" kids should wear: he picked a pink jumper thing for Isabelle and jeans and a light gray cotton sweater for Danny. He went to the only grocery store that was open and bought a list of food they liked so they would stop consuming his gourmet dinners. While they were eating sandwiches, he worked with Danny to get their stories straight. He'd decided the easiest thing to do was to go with the truth, or a version of it, anyway. He'd let them in one cold night out of the kindness of his heart—but at the beginning of October, not a week ago. Their mother was a drug addict and their fathers were unknown. He was in the process of trying to adopt them, a lot of paperwork and hassle that his lawyers were dealing with.

Naturally, Ben would wonder why he hadn't mentioned these kids in the Caymans or at any time in the last two months—and his plan handled that, too. He was going to say he hadn't discussed them because he wasn't sure he could commit to this. He would even throw in a "guilty admission" that when he'd left them with a babysitter and gone to Grand Cayman, he was really hoping he wouldn't miss these kids. But it was too late; Isabelle and Danny had won him over, and now he just couldn't imagine his life without them. The last part certainly felt true. Since that night on the bridge, he'd had one problem after another and his normal life had disappeared. But it would be back tomorrow. All he had to do was get through this one night, and then Cassie would call social services. By Friday afternoon, he'd be answering messages and making his way through the hundreds of emails he'd ignored while he was out of the country. Today was a waste, but it was a holiday, after all. A stupid holiday, in his opinion, but they all were.

Danny had stayed up very late, stubbornly refusing to even try to fall asleep until he made sure his mom was safely in Miami. The intake clerk from Changes had been waiting at the airport. When she'd called to say the transition was successful, Matthew was dozing on the couch. He told Danny, and both of them finally went to bed. It had been a long, hellish day, but nothing compared to how bad tonight could be if he wasn't very careful.

The fake-family business wasn't the only thing he was concerned about. Ben had been to visit him numerous times over the last twelve years, but not since he'd been with Amelia. Matthew had assumed that in the unlikely event he ever had to have the happy couple over, he would have lots of time to prepare; specifically, that he would have time to unload all the furniture he still had from when he and Amelia had lived together.

She'd left all the furniture behind, claiming she didn't want anything that had been paid for with AD money, and what was he supposed to do? Amelia had excellent taste, and back then he'd thought thirty thousand dollars was a lot to spend on chairs and tables and lamps. He couldn't just give the stuff away, and he was hardly the garage-sale type. Over the years, he'd added state-of-the-art electronics and, with the help of a decorator, replaced the couch and furnished the guest bedroom. He'd invested in a few paintings. But he'd never gotten around to getting a houseful of new furniture. He was traveling all the time, and it was hardly a high priority. Why bother? Even the desk Amelia had picked out for him was still in great shape.

But now he had a decidedly weird problem. It bugged the shit out of him to think of her concluding that he'd kept it all as some kind of shrine to her (as if he could make a shrine to Amelia without voodoo dolls and severed heads), but he also knew that whatever happened, he could not afford to lose control the way he had on the morning-after in Aspen. He'd even shed a tear or two that morning, and the hard-hearted bitch had still called him "evil." She threw so many insults that Matthew couldn't help defending himself, which was a mistake, but hell, he couldn't just stand there and let her hand him his balls. When he shouted that he hated her, he knew he'd just blown the whole plan, but he didn't care. Even the best strategist has an occasional moment of weakness. Even the most seasoned manipulator can be pushed and prodded and egregiously insulted until he finally breaks down.

At 7:45 he was in his bathroom, touching up his shave, repeating "I hate that bitch" like a mantra. Had to get it all out of his system now, so no matter what she said he would remain calm as the Buddha. Isabelle was sitting on the bathroom rug, holding a bar of soap, watching him in the mirror. "Bitch!" she said.

"Exactly," he said.

His new daughter had become an unexpected ally. She followed him everywhere unless he shut the door to keep her out; she agreed with him on everything, from what kind of bread to use for the sandwiches to what color socks went best with her pink jumper; she'd even taken his side against her brother on the issue of Danny's ridiculous hair. Matthew wanted to trim it to something closer to normal, but Danny had vehemently objected, saying only that his mother had cut it that way. Isabelle said, "Icky," and pointed at Danny's head, but when the kid wasn't convinced, Matthew gave up. He certainly wasn't about to run after him with scissors.

When he heard the knock at the door, he was heading out of the bathroom. Isabelle held her arms out and said, "Up?" He couldn't have planned it better, answering the door holding this beautiful little girl in his arms. How very fatherly.

He let them in with a hearty welcome and the requisite introductions to the kids, though he immediately knew something was a little off between the lovebirds. Ben seemed his usual self, dropping his jacket on the chair, happily following Matthew into the kitchen when Matthew suggested a drink. Matthew recited the poignant story of his new children while he held Isabelle and fixed Ben's usual two shots of tequila over ice with a twist of orange. Danny lurked a few feet away, listening, as always; Amelia was somewhere in the vicinity of the kitchen, listening or staring at the furniture or getting ready to gun down the neighborhood—he really had no idea because he couldn't look for her and cut up the orange and pay attention to Ben while Isabelle was clutching him by the neck. At the end of the story, Ben clapped him on the back and said, "I really admire what you're doing," before changing the topic to the recent article in *Nature*.

Matthew hadn't had a chance to finish the article yet, but he knew the news of this genetic "breakthrough" had been reported in every newspaper across the world. He'd already gotten several emails about it; he was trying to answer one last night when the crazy mother started punching him. Short version: much of what scientists believed about genetics was apparently wrong. Mendel was wrong: children don't necessarily inherit two copies of each gene, one from each parent. The Human Genome Project was wrong: human beings aren't all 99.9 percent alike. CNV (copy number variation) is much bigger than previously thought; people can have up to ten copies of the same gene, or they might not have that gene at all. What this could mean for the future of drug development, Matthew wasn't sure, and he was glad Ben had brought it up. Ben could give him the deeper view, not to mention that it took the focus off the fake family.

"Are you sure you don't want something to drink, too?" Matthew said when he spotted Amelia in the shadow near the laundry room door. He was feeding a slice of orange to Isabelle, who still didn't want to get down. "I have juice and milk. Maybe decaf?"

She said no and Ben finished telling a long story about this guy he knew who was involved in the *Nature* study: a brilliant geneticist, worked in Cambridge at the Sanger Institute, a whiz at chess, made his own beer, and so on. He was just getting to the science part when his cell phone rang. He said he had to take the call and disappeared into the loft area.

A moment later he was back. "That was Richard," he said to Amelia. Then he turned to Matthew. "Richard Langer at HUP. He wants to talk to me about working on trypanosomiasis."

Trypanosomiasis, or African sleeping sickness. No wonder Ben was interested. It was another parasitic disease transmitted by an insect. HUP, Hospital of the University of Pennsylvania, was only a few blocks away. Matthew knew who Richard Langer was, though he'd never spoken to him, primarily because Langer was a do-gooder who'd never done any collaborating with Astor-Denning.

"From mosquitoes to tsetse flies," Matthew said. "Sounds like fun."

Ben laughed. "I didn't think Richard would be able to get away from his family this early, but I'll try to keep it short." He finished his tequila in one gulp before he walked over and put his arm around Amelia. "An hour at the most."

She said, "I still don't understand why this has to be done on Thanksgiving."

Matthew and his appendage Isabelle walked out of the room to give them privacy. The illusion of privacy, that is.

Ben whispered, "I already told you why. It doesn't have to be done today, but Richard won't be around this weekend, and I don't want to wait to talk to him. And I set up the meeting days ago, before you insisted on coming here. I still don't understand why we had to see Matt tonight, either. It's fine, though. You can stay and rest while Richard and I talk. He wants to discuss his lab. You know that wouldn't interest you anyway."

"I can't rest here."

"Why not? Matt will get you anything you want."

"I'm going with you."

"Okay, babe." Kissing noises. "It won't take long, I promise."

A minute later Ben and Amelia came out of the kitchen. Luckily, during that minute, Matthew and Isabelle had moved over to the couch, where they were innocently sitting together when Ben apologized that they had to take off so soon.

"No problem," Matthew said. He was used to this from Ben. Work came first, period, even on a holiday. Not to mention that he was struggling not to grin. Finally, something to be thankful for: the witch was leaving already!

Too bad his adorable new son promptly ruined it. Matthew was stunned when Danny went to the door, looked right at Amelia, and said, "I wish you didn't have to go."

"It is too bad," Matthew said, "but she has to. Maybe we'll see her some other—"

"I'll stay, then," Amelia said, still staring into Danny's eyes. Like she was reading the truth there? She turned to Ben. "You're right. It'll be better if I wait here for you."

As Danny retreated, he glanced in Matthew's direction and shrugged as if to say he didn't mean for this to happen. Maybe he was taking Matthew's request that he be polite too far? Whatever his reason, it was too late to do anything about it now. The happy couple was kissing good-bye. Ben left with a request that Matthew "look out for Amelia."

Matthew said, "Of course," but the instant Ben was gone, Amelia turned to Matthew and hissed, "You can cut the crap now."

She sat down on the white chair—her white chair, oddly enough. She'd always sat in that chair at their house, while he sat on one of the other chairs or the couch.

"I have no idea what you're talking about."

"You and your quote-unquote children."

His voice was all paternal protection—at least as paternal as he could make it. "You can say what you want about me, but please leave Danny and Isabelle out of it."

"I don't buy any of this."

"I'm sorry you feel that way." Have I mentioned how much I hate you? "I wish you could see that I've changed, too."

Isabelle was finally getting bored. She climbed off the couch and went to the Barbie pile. Danny knelt down with her.

"Could you make me a piece of toast?" Amelia said.

"Sure." Talk about a psycho. Bitching him out, then expecting him to wait on her. "What would you like on it?" Poison?

"Dry. Two pieces."

He brought back the toast without any butter or jam. "Here you go." Take that to your coven. "Want something to drink?"

She shook her head and started wolfing down the toast like she was starving. Apparently, Ben's cousin's Thanksgiving dinner hadn't done the trick. While she ate, she watched the kids playing like she was gathering evidence. Matthew turned up the Bach CD on his stereo, wishing he had an Ativan.

When she was finished with the toast, she put the plate on his (their) coffee table. "I want to talk to Danny now." She looked at Matthew and sneered. "Is that all right with you, Mr. Mom?"

"Of course. But it's not up to me. He's a child, not my slave."

When she smiled, Matthew suspected he'd just made some kind of mistake. Amelia walked over to them; Isabelle had a piece of rubber bread shoved in her mouth, probably imitating the toast, and Danny was building Legos because Matthew had ordered him to play, too, and not just watch his sister all night. She knelt down next to Danny, and the next thing Matthew knew the two of them were getting up, moving toward the hall.

"What are you doing?"

"You said I could talk to him."

"But why in the hall?"

145

"Not in the hall, in Danny's bedroom. He said he'd show it to me."

"Fine." He'd already told Danny what to say if the obviously adult-looking guest bedroom came up. No, it hadn't been furnished for them yet, but only because they weren't staying in this apartment much longer. They were planning to move to a house so he and Isabelle would have separate bedrooms and a yard to play in. Of course, before Ben could wonder why Matthew hadn't moved, the adoption would fall apart. The lawyers would uncover a long-lost aunt or uncle and Matthew would have to let his beloved children go. Poor Matthew, lonely again!

He waited a minute, but when they didn't return, he turned down the Bach and went over to Isabelle. "Go find Danny." She toddled off down the same hall and he followed behind her, ever the protective father. When they got to the guest bedroom, they both discovered the door was closed.

"Knock," he told his sidekick. She complied. The door swung open and Amelia was standing with her arms crossed.

"Sorry. Isabelle wants in, too. You know how kids are."

"She can come in, but I assume that doesn't mean you have to come with her?"

"You don't really have any experience watching a three-year-old. I think I should, just to make sure she's safe."

Amelia stood back, but he could tell she was fuming. Just as he was thinking Ha, ha, you scheming bitch, you can't outsmart me that easily, Isabelle decided to go back the other way, where all the toys were.

"Isabelle," he said. "I thought you wanted to find Danny?"

"No." With unusually clear diction. "You did!"

Amelia snorted and shut the door in his face. Naturally, he tried to listen in anyway, but the door was too thick. Damned high-quality materials.

He went back to Isabelle. She had the rubber bread clutched in her fist, and hanging out of her mouth, covered in slobber, was another rubber food, yellow with a darker yellow center, which he assumed was an aging fried egg.

"Go find Danny again."

"No."

No? "Come on. He's hiding. We have to find him."

"Don't want to."

He tried everything, but she wouldn't budge, and finally he said, "Some ally you turned out to be." Which made her laugh, god knows why, so he tried again, this time telling her to find Amelia. Back to no, no, and no again.

He waited as long as he could stand to, maybe fifteen minutes, before he went back to the guest room and opened the door. Danny was sitting on the chair; Amelia was on the bed. The kid didn't look as uncomfortable as Matthew had expected he would, given who he was stuck in there with.

"What do you want?" Amelia barked.

"You seem to have forgotten that this is my house." He sounded angry. Shit. He forced himself to smile his most innocent, would-never-dream-of-admitting-he-hated-her-interfering-guts smile. "I was just concerned about Danny. He must be getting hungry." He glanced at Danny as he said this, telegraphing to his new son that he'd better be hungry, now.

"I'm okay," Danny said. "I got pretty full from the peanut butter and jelly sandwiches."

"You fed them peanut butter and jelly on Thanksgiving?" Amelia said. "Very classy, Matthew." She shut the door after ordering him to stay out this time. "If you don't, I'll tell Ben you were rude to me."

He muttered a stream of curses before going back to check on Isabelle, who was fine but unfortunately still in full rebellion. Oh, well, he'd just have to trust Danny to keep his mouth shut. He'd already threatened the kid that if he screwed up tonight, Matthew would screw up and forget to buy his mom a ticket home from Florida. He'd thought of telling Danny that he wouldn't pay for Changes, either—though he wasn't paying, at least not directly; Jerome Drossman had been happy to help this "poor unfortunate woman" as a personal favor to Matthew, meaning he would expect even more ass-kissing and an even larger donation next year from AD—but he didn't do it because the ticket-home threat had already made the kid turn so pale (a paler shade of pale at least). At the time, Matthew had wondered why Danny seemed to just expect that Matthew would do something cruel to him eventually. Why the trash metaphor, for example? What had he ever done to this kid? It couldn't be only that Danny and his mother considered him "rich." It was an absurd assessment, anyway, given that they'd seen only this apartment, a place where even the poorest academics felt comfortable. True, the furniture included some antiques, but Danny's family couldn't know that since Matthew himself hadn't known it back when Amelia used to brag about her estate-sale finds. The same was true with the art he'd acquired; it took a trained appraiser to explain why one painting was worth fifty thousand dollars and another was worth five thousand. His electronics were more obviously impressive, but hell, everybody had expensive computers and stereos and televisions these days.

Now, as he watched Isabelle smash a Lego on the rubber bread, he realized that there was no reason whatsoever for Danny's attitude. Since the night on the bridge, Matthew had been unfailingly decent, if not outright kind. It was the kid's problem if he couldn't appreciate that. Too bad he wasn't more like his sister, who, despite her recent betrayals, had just flashed Matthew one of her best whole-face grins.

Cute as she was, after only a half hour of watching her play,

Matthew concluded that taking care of small children had to be one of the biggest unrecognized causes of mental illness. How did people do this all day? It was both excruciatingly boring and alarmingly stressful. Every other minute Isabelle was in some kind of danger: rocking too fast, causing the horse to tumble over; biting off a choke-sized piece of the yellowed egg (which he had to pry out of her mouth when she refused to spit it out); trying to lick the outlet (why, oh why, would she want to do something that dumb?). He'd just decided that he would rather choke himself to death on that disgusting egg than deal with another minute of this when Danny appeared, panting and pale, as though he'd narrowly escaped torture.

"Oh, thank god," he said. He looked around the corner. "Where's Amelia? Kill her by chance?"

"I didn't do it. She was throwing up, and it just happened."

Matthew stood up and ran toward the hall. "Amelia?" She didn't answer. "Amelia?" he repeated, coming into the guest room. "Where is she?" he yelled, but Danny was right behind him.

"In the bathroom. On the floor."

It was just as Danny said: Amelia was on the floor of the guest bathroom, unconscious. He knelt down and checked the ABCs: airway, breathing, circulation. He turned her face to the side and told Danny to get the pillows off the bed. After Matthew put the pillows under Amelia's feet, he said, "Tell me exactly what happened. Wait; go get Isabelle, and then tell me."

Danny was back, holding his sister, who was griping and kicking him. "She threw up a lot, maybe five times while we were in here. I don't know. She said it had been happening all day. I wanted to go get you, but she said you wouldn't care. She said you didn't—"

"When she passed out, was she standing or kneeling?"

"Kneeling. She didn't fall very far. The back of her head hit the rug."

"Good boy. That's what I wanted to know." He threw two washcloths in the sink and ran cool water. He wrung them out and folded them into squares; one he put on her forehead, and one on the back of her neck.

He estimated that all of this had taken less than a minute. Adding another half minute for Danny to get him, that left thirty seconds before she reached the two-minute danger point for being unconscious. If she didn't wake up in the next few seconds, he was calling 911.

He repeated her name three times and she opened her eyes. She was obviously confused because she tried to reach for his face. "Matthew?"

"It's all right. You fainted."

"Where am I?"

"At my house." He checked her pulse: it was still slow. Her skin was dry.

She struggled to sit up but her face grew paler than Danny's.

"Just relax for a minute," Matthew said. "Wait until the dizziness passes." He told Danny that he could take Isabelle back into the loft. After they left, he said, "I wish you'd told me you were sick."

"I'm not sick. It's just morning sickness, but today it's been morning, afternoon, and night."

"Have you been staying hydrated?"

"I'm trying, but I can't hold down any liquids. That's why I wanted toast."

"Forgive the personal question, but have you been peeing on a regular basis?"

"No, I don't think so. Not since this morning."

"Do you mind if I look in your mouth?"

Her saliva looked sticky. No question, she was dehydrated. "I think you need to go to the ER for IV fluids. You'll feel a lot better once they get a bag in you."

"I'm fine," she said, but when she still couldn't lift her head, she said, "I guess you're right." Then a sound that was like crying, but there were no tears. She was probably so dry she couldn't make them.

"It's not so bad." He moved the washcloth off her forehead and pushed back her red hair. She still wore it long, ever the serious schoolgirl, and it was a mess now.

"I don't want to go in an ambulance."

"Fine, we'll take my car."

"But how will I get to it? I can't even walk."

"I'll carry you, of course. Don't be dumb."

He knelt down and put one arm under her shoulders and the other under her knees. The worst part was getting to a standing position. He groaned a little and told her he must be out of shape. Didn't want her crying again, thinking she was getting fat.

"You're not out of shape," she said. "It's so strange the way you always look the same to me." She was babbling the way people do after a health scare; he remembered this from medical school. "Everyone else gets older, but you don't."

"I sold my soul for the fountain of youth. Got a nice black robe in the bargain." He was panting as he moved her out of the guest bedroom and into the hall. He called Danny, and the kid was there. "I have to take her to the hospital. Can you watch Isabelle?"

"You can't leave them alone," Amelia said. "They're too young."

Shit. "Danny, get Isabelle ready. Also, could you find my wallet and keys and cell phone? They should be on the table by my bed."

He adjusted Amelia's weight as they moved into the loft. It was still so difficult to carry her that he was breaking out in a sweat. "I don't suppose you can lift your arms?"

"I think I can."

"It would be much easier if you would put them around my neck."

She did it without saying anything. Danny and Isabelle were at the door. Matthew asked Danny to put the wallet in Matthew's pants pocket and the keys on the end of his finger, and to hold his sister and the cell phone. "As soon as we get to the car, I'll call Ben."

Ten back-wrenching, knee-destroying minutes later, he had the whole bunch settled in his Porsche: Amelia in the passenger seat, the kids in the back, with Isabelle strapped in with the neck belt pushed behind her, since he "forgot" her nonexistent booster seat. He decided to go to HUP because it was so close and Ben was already there, somewhere. Also, Matthew knew a few docs at that ER; he hoped one would be working today and could rush Amelia in.

He called Ben and got voice mail, which was irritating, but he left a message that he was taking Amelia for IV fluids and Ben should meet them in the ER. "We should be there in a few minutes," he said, and closed the phone.

Danny said, "How will he know what time a few minutes means?"

"Cell phones keep a record of every call, with the time it came in. Ben can add a few minutes to that time."

"Cool," Danny said.

"Cool," Isabelle repeated.

Amelia stayed quiet. He wondered if the trip downstairs had made her sick again. He hoped she didn't vomit in the car.

The hospital was a mob scene, as usual on a holiday. If the ER was any indication, the world was a much safer place when everyone was at work. One of the docs Matthew knew was doing a shift, and he brought out a wheelchair for Amelia. He said he would get her bagged and out of there as soon as possible. Before they took her away, she insisted on talking to Danny for a moment. When Matthew asked what she wanted, Danny said she just wanted to say good-bye.

After Matthew was settled down with the kids in the waiting room, he called Ben again. Still the voice mail. No point in leaving another message.

Everyone in the waiting area was staring at the loud TV in the corner. The show was some crap about TomKat's wedding. Matthew said to Danny, "Why are you watching this shit?" Some old lady told him not to curse around his children. He nodded and smiled and told her to mind her own damn business.

The doc who'd taken Amelia in asked Matthew if he could come in with her. "You can leave your kids," the doc said. "I'll ask one of the clerks to keep an eye on them." Matthew couldn't remember the guy's name at the moment, and he didn't have on his name tag. Probably on call and had hurried in without it.

"She keeps asking for you," the doc said as they walked past the triage station.

Really? "Fine," he said. "Whatever she wants."

The IV was in place, but the drip had barely started. She was lying in a bed, behind a wall of curtains, crying that pitiful tearless cry.

He sat down in the chair next to her and picked up her hand. Ever the nice guy. "What's wrong? The IV looks good. It doesn't hurt, does it?"

"Why isn't Ben here?"

She was looking into his eyes, but he shrugged. "His phone is off, remember? He probably turned it off when he walked in the building. It's hospital policy."

"If you had a pregnant girlfriend who you knew had been throwing up all day, would you turn off your phone?"

"No, but I'm amoral. Rules don't mean anything to me." He grinned. "You can hardly hold other people to my high standards."

Not to mention that Matthew knew the no-cell policy was bullshit. Medical staff used their cell phones all the time; as long as the phone was kept six feet away from the monitoring equipment, it didn't cause any problems. Ben would undoubtedly have come to the same conclusion if he'd spent a minute thinking about it, but Matthew wasn't surprised he hadn't. Pointless restrictions had never bothered Ben; plus, he was a little too busy with his curing-disease, saving-lives thing.

"If I were having your child," Amelia said, "you'd be here. You know it's true. You're here now. You wouldn't have left me sick on Thanksgiving."

Jesus, where did that come from? "All I know is that you're delusional. It's normal after fainting, especially as dehydrated as you are."

"Ben and I had a fight on the plane home from Paris. It was—"

"International flights are stressful. I'm sure he's already over it. He doesn't hold grudges."

"About you." Her voice was so weak he could barely hear her. "Ben said I had a vendetta against you based on nothing. He said I never even understood you."

Go, Ben. "If you're saying you want to call a truce, consider it called. But you might want to hold off a bit. I have a hunch you'll change your mind once you get some fluids."

She waited for a long time before she spoke again. Matthew watched the drip. Hoped the kids weren't going nuts and driving the other people crazy. Wished Ben would get the hell over here. Tried not to think about how much he hated being in hospitals. Refused to think about all the times he'd sat in a chair like this, holding his mother's hand while she was dying. Senior year in high school. His stupid decision to be a doctor came from that experience. Every decision he'd made for emotional reasons turned out to be stupid, which was why he didn't make decisions like that anymore (with the notable exception of the night he had taken E, and obviously that had been beyond stupid).

"I have to ask you something," she said. "About Palm Beach."

Uh-oh. This was going beyond delusional and becoming just weird. "Why don't we play What If instead?" He pointed to an old man parked in a wheelchair in the hall. "What if you could get out of here right now and feel better, but only if you agreed to cut that guy's ear hair?"

"Ben said I was wrong about what happened that night."

"Who cares? It was years ago. But that guy may not be able to hear if you don't trim down that forest of hair growing—"

"He said it really was the first time you'd done that, and when you told me women like her approached you everywhere, I was the one who jumped to the conclusion that you'd slept with them all."

Matthew was still staring at the old man's ears, but he casually let go of Amelia's hand. Sat back like he wasn't listening. Wished he could pull an Isabelle and cover his own ears and yell, "Don't want to!"

"Ben said you'd had enough of my always assuming the worst about you. So you let me believe that, knowing I was looking for a reason to leave you. But he said you never wanted me to go and you were heartbroken when I did."

Thank you very much, Benjamin. May I offer you my liver to dissect in your next argument with your girlfriend?

"What if you had to live in Antarctica? In an igloo. They still have igloos, right? Global warming hasn't melted them all yet. But in this igloo—"

"Is it true?"

"Wait, here's one I know you'll like. What if Bush calls you for advice and whatever you say, he'll do tomorrow. Only one thing, and it can't be resign. Would you tell him to bring home the soldiers from Iraq or change the Medicare prescription—"

"Please, Matthew, I really want to know."

He told her to forget about it, it was a long time ago, who cared anymore, and so on, but when she just kept pushing him he snapped, "Do you seriously think I'm going to have a heart-to-heart chat with you? After everything that's happened over the last twelve years?"

"I know, it sounds crazy. It's just that in the bathroom, and when you were carrying me to your car, you were so gentle. I felt really safe with you. And you're here now with me, and I really appreciate—"

Safe? Gentle? What the hell was next, shopping together for cute little shoes? And why was she pushing so hard about that night in Palm Beach anyway, when she was living with another man, pregnant with his kid? It was not only tasteless and tactless; it was absolutely infuriating.

He could feel his jaw muscle popping, but he did remember not to say that he hated her. Unfortunately, what he fired off was probably worse. "I'm sorry to break this to you, but I'm only here because of Ben. He's my friend. You're nothing to me anymore."

Thankfully, friend Ben arrived a moment or two later, before she could respond, before it could deteriorate even further. Filled with concern for Amelia. Apologizing for turning off the cell phone; thought it was policy. Eternally grateful to Matthew for taking such good care of his girlfriend for him.

"I'd better get going," Matthew said, standing. "Get the kids to bed."

"Thanks again, buddy," Ben said. "Sorry we didn't get to talk. Next time."

Matthew had already breathed a sigh of relief when Amelia delivered the deathblow: "When we're done here, can we spend the night at your place?" She smiled sweetly. "The doctor told me I'm not supposed to travel tonight, and all the hotels around here are full."

He strongly doubted that all the hotels were full, but he could hardly call her a liar. Was this her attempt to pay him back for what he'd said? Or was she determined to gather more evidence about Danny and Isabelle? Maybe she was actually trying to make his life a living hell? Probably all of the above.

"Matt doesn't really have room, babe. There must be a hotel somewhere in this city."

"But I can't ride all over looking for one. I'm exhausted. I just need to sleep, and Matthew's house is right around the corner."

Ben shot him a please-humor-her look. So what could he do? He said, "Of course you guys are welcome. It's not that crowded. We'll get by."

As he walked back to the waiting room, he decided to talk to doctor no-name and get some Ativan.

He was back in the Porsche with the kids, listening to an angry rap song, when it struck him that he might have made a terrible mistake getting Ben together with Amelia. Yes, he did it for Galvenar, but he also felt sorry for Ben. After Karen left, Ben was freaking out; he couldn't deal with the PR, and it was the first time he'd been without a girlfriend in ten years. Thanks to his sudden fame, he was being hit on right and left by hot young women, but he didn't want any of them. He wanted someone who liked him for himself (how Hallmark), someone his own age (no comment), someone who was moral and still believed in doing the right thing (wait, where have I heard that before?).

Which meant, Matthew realized now, that as recently as a year ago, he'd made another decision that was partly based on emotion, a decision that was at least poorly thought out and possibly as stupid as anything he'd ever done. Obviously, he deserved whatever hell it would bring him. When would he ever learn?

He turned the radio up. When the rapper said, "That's right, she's a ho," he said it, too, feeling pissed off all over again.

By the time they were back at his building, he'd decided that the next morning, he was going to call Ginny or Rachel or Christine or one of the others he was still speaking to. Then, after he got rid of Ben and Amelia and the kids and did some work, he could pick up the woman, have dinner, and bring her home with him. This stress was getting unbearable. He needed to get laid.

CHAPTER TEN

The City of Brotherly Love

Amelia had always hated being sick, but it was different with Danny there. He was such a gentle boy; he'd even followed her into the bathroom to hold her hair back while she knelt over the toilet. He told her he liked taking care of sick people and he knew how because his mother had been sick a lot. Amelia told him he was very kind. She also promised him, at the hospital, that she would come back to finish their talk as soon as they made her all better. The next morning, watching him with his sister, she was struck again by how unusual he was. She'd never met a child like this.

Ben and Matthew were sitting at the table, drinking their umpteenth cups of coffee, talking about genetics and trypanosomiasis and blah, blah, blah. Amelia was sitting on the floor with Danny and Isabelle—and refusing to see this as some kind of gender division of labor. She'd rather be with the kids than those two even if they weren't nerding out. She was still mad at Ben for yesterday, though she'd learned her lesson. She would never again tell him any of her suspicions about Matthew. The whole lousy day would never have happened if they hadn't had that argument when she'd insisted that Matthew was lying about starting a family. Now, of course, Ben was convinced he'd been right all along. He'd swallowed the ridiculous story about Danny and Isabelle without hesitating. Men could be so gullible.

Even men like Matthew, as it turned out. He'd really believed that she was pouring her heart out to him the night before; he even thought she meant it when she said how safe she felt with him—as if his despicable treachery in Paris hadn't just happened. Admittedly, when she asked Matthew to come into her room in the ER, she was feeling alone and a little scared. And yes, she was somewhat confused by how gentle he'd been with her back at his apartment. But when it struck her that he might be pitying her, the idea was so revolting that she immediately decided to use the chance to get him to admit that he'd lied to Ben about Palm Beach. Unfortunately, she discovered he hadn't lied to Ben; he'd lied to her. She'd suspected this when he'd refused to answer, and she knew it for sure when he got mad at her for pushing him. Matthew only got angry when he was losing control. He'd always been very transparent that way.

When she woke up in the morning, she was still thinking about how he'd let her cry and cry about his infidelities without saying a word. The excuse he'd given Ben for doing this was at least unethical and possibly self-deceptive. He claimed he wanted to give her a reason to leave him—as though sex with one woman wouldn't have been enough. As though she couldn't have come up with excellent reasons all on her own, without his help. The entire business was patronizing in the extreme. How could Ben see this as noble, for Matthew to act as if he knew what she wanted more than she herself did? To sacrifice the truth in service of a unilateral decision about their future?

Of course she didn't buy the brokenhearted part, not for a minute. If there were even a grain of truth to that, Matthew wouldn't have set her up with his best friend. Yes, he'd obviously done it for his damned drug, but Matthew was still a human being, she assumed, and a man, undoubtedly. No man would hand over a woman he'd ever really loved to his best friend. It was about as likely as Matthew truly caring about these children.

Amelia had one goal before she and Ben left for New York: to find out what Matthew was really doing with Danny and Isabelle. She had to know.

When she'd taken Danny into the bedroom the day before, she'd found it very suspicious that he called Matthew "Dr. Connelly." She asked him if Matthew had told him to use "doctor," but he said not at all. "He told me not to call him Doctor Connelly, but I keep messing up. My teachers said it's not polite to call a grown-up by their first name."

"What did he say to call him?"

"Dad," he said slowly. "But I can call him Matthew if I want."

"Do you like him?"

Danny nodded. "He's funny, even though he gripes a lot."

"What does he gripe about?"

"Being tired and having a headache. Those are the main things. But also that the jelly jar wouldn't open and the bread loaf got crushed and Isabelle's jumper was missing a snap. He gripes about all kinds of stuff. It's like the way he talks."

"Poor Matthew." Her voice was a little snotty.

"I don't think he wants people to feel sorry for him. He works all the time and he never gripes about Astor-Denning."

She was losing track of the topic—and beginning to feel nauseated. She told Danny she had to lie down. Then she said, "Tell me the truth: Is Matthew really adopting you?"

"Sure he is. If he can. He said his lawyers are working on it now."

"Do you want him to adopt you? I thought you had a mom."

"My mom's a drug addict. She can't really take care of us. She signed a paper to make Matthew our guardian."

Amelia had to throw up then, and every few minutes for the next hour. In between, the only thing she got out of Danny was that Matthew was good with Isabelle.

"Whenever Isabelle smiles at him, even if he's in the middle of griping about something, he always smiles back. And it's not in that phony grown-up way. It's like he can't help it, like he doesn't even know he's doing it."

"He probably doesn't," she said, before running back to the bathroom. From that point on, she stayed kneeling in front of the toilet. And Danny stayed with her, to help. No one had done that for her since she was a little girl.

Before she got dizzy, she told Danny that she wanted to help him in any way she could. He said he didn't need anything, but she could tell there was something he was thinking about. Now, while Matthew and Ben were busy with their endless science talk, she repeated the offer to Danny.

"Why do you want to help me?" Danny said, retying Isabelle's shoe. "What would I have to do?"

The little girl's shoes were too big and a little worn out. Could Matthew really be so cheap as to buy these kids used clothes?

"Nothing," she told Danny. "I believe in giving away my money and time to people who need it." Then she told him the story of sponsoring children when she was Danny's age. "My grandma taught me that everyone deserves a home and food and medical care. No one should ever go without these things."

He paused for a long time. Maybe he was waiting for Ben to laugh at another thing Matthew said, so they couldn't possibly overhear. "I might need a ticket from Florida to Philadelphia."

"If you do, let me know. I'll get it for you, no questions asked."

"Thanks," he said, and smiled. "I'm glad you're here."

"Sorry we took your bed."

"It was okay. We started out on the floor, but we ended up in Matthew's bed."

He was putting a dress on one of Isabelle's Barbies. What other boy would do that for his sister when a tub of Legos and a Game Boy were a few feet away?

"That must have been interesting," she said.

"When we woke up, Isabelle was upside down, with her foot against Matthew's nose. Plus, we were out of diapers and she peed in the bed."

"I'm sure he wasn't happy about that."

"He griped a lot, but he wasn't mad at Isabelle. He never gets mad at her."

"Does he get mad at you?"

"Sometimes. But he's teaching me stuff, like if he was my real father." Danny handed the doll to his sister, who handed him another one and a skirt.

Before she could ask what this meant, Ben called her over to the table. It was time to make their announcement. They'd discussed this last night, and Amelia had accepted it. She was dying to hear how Matthew would take the news.

"I've decided to work at HUP with Richard Langer," Ben said. He was smiling, holding Amelia's hand. "This means we'll be in

Philly for a while. We just have to find a place and get our things from Amelia's apartment in New York."

Matthew sputtered, "Wow. That's. Excellent."

"Tell him the other part," Amelia said.

"We were talking last night about this apartment," Ben said. "We both love it. And since you're moving anyway, we were wondering if you'd let us sublet it from you."

Actually, Amelia didn't "love" the apartment, and she really didn't love the idea of asking Matthew to give them a break on the sublet price, as Ben was planning to do. She thought it would be a conflict of interest, but she knew Ben would say the same thing he'd said about their trip to the Caymans—which Matthew had paid for, as it turned out, though Amelia certainly didn't know this until Ben told her during their fight. But Ben said there was no conflict of interest because it wasn't AD money, it was Matt's, and Matt was a friend.

"I don't know when we're moving," Matthew said. "We have to find a place."

"Don't you own several houses?" Amelia hoped he was surprised she knew about this. She'd gotten a copy of his tax return last year. She had her sources, too. "Why not move into one of them?"

He flashed her an indulgent smile. "They're all rented out. I can't just kick out my tenants. It wouldn't be fair, not to mention the pesky detail of the leases."

"Richard knows of a place in Wayne," Ben said. "He told me about it, but we want to be closer to the lab. Why not look at that house, Matt? It might be perfect for the kids and you since it's closer to Astor-Denning."

"The problem is I really can't move right away. Work is too intense right now. I think you guys should find another place, at least temporarily."

"Maybe you're right," Ben said. A moment later, he smiled. "At least we'll be in the neighborhood. We can drop by anytime and talk."

"Won't that be great?" Amelia said, though it sounded horrible. But she was watching Matthew, waiting for him to squirm his way out of this.

"It would be great," he said. "But . . ."

"But?" she said. "What is it, Matthew? Don't you want to live near your friends?"

He swallowed and looked at Ben. "Can I talk to you privately for a moment?"

Ben said, "Sure." He turned to Amelia. "Are you feeling up to watching Matt's kids for a few minutes while we take a walk?"

"I'm fine," she snapped. She was keeping down fluids and feeling much better. The ER doc had told her yesterday's episode had probably been triggered by exhaustion. She went back to sit by Danny, which was where she wanted to be anyway.

A few minutes after they left, Matthew's phone rang. She thought about whether what she was about to do was ethical, but not for long. She answered it and said, "Doctor Connelly's residence."

"This is Rachel. Is Matthew there?"

"He just ran out. I'm his housekeeper. He asked me to take a message from you."

Rachel, who sounded about twenty, said, "Tell him I would love to go out tonight. I'm glad he's back in town."

"Will do, though I don't know if he's found a babysitter."

The woman giggled. "A babysitter? What for?"

"How long has it been since you've seen him?"

"Last weekend," she said, sounding so defensive that Amelia knew she was lying. "What are you talking about?"

Amelia tried not to laugh. "Then you've met his children, obviously."

"Sorry, housekeeper chick, but you've confused him with some other person whose toilets you scrub. Just tell Matthew to call me, okay? And be sure to clean the bedroom."

She went to Danny, who was on the couch, helping Isabelle put in the earbuds for an iPod. "I was just wondering," Amelia said, "who takes care of you when Matthew isn't here? I know he works constantly, and he's always traveling."

"We have a babysitter."

Isabelle was singing along, but Amelia couldn't make out the words or the melody. Probably some children's tune.

"That's good. I assume it's a woman. Who is she?"

When he didn't answer, she asked him again. Finally she said, "You don't have a babysitter, do you, Danny?"

"We do, too." He looked so afraid her heart went out to him. "I just can't remember her name."

"It's all right," she said, looking into his bright blue eyes. "I'm a friend. I won't hurt you, no matter what you tell me. I promise."

When she put her arms around him, she thought he would pull away, but he didn't. Instead, he started crying, and soon he was crying so hard his chest shook. Even his sister felt bad and patted his foot. Amelia couldn't understand everything he said, but she got the basics. His mom was in rehab for a month. Matthew had paid for it (which Amelia found incredible), but he was only keeping them for a few more hours, until she and Ben left. Then they would be out on the street with nowhere to go but a crack house. Danny was scared of that place. All the people there were drug addicts.

She wondered if she could take care of these kids until their mother came back. She knew Ben might not like it; he was already stressed about joining Richard's lab, and worried about money. Amelia's trust fund was already gone for the year and committed for two years after, all to important charities. They were living off her job and Ben's salary from the foundation, which was about to end. Ben needed a good research position, and he was glad the one he'd accepted was in Philly, where the cost of living was cheaper than New York.

She asked Danny, "What if I kept you until your mom's out of rehab? Would you like that, or would you rather stay with Matthew?"

When Danny answered, "Matthew," Amelia tried not to be hurt. It was probably just that the poor kid was afraid to go somewhere new. "But he won't do it," Danny said. "I asked him already this morning. I thought since he likes Isabelle so much, he might say okay, but he said, 'Dream on.'"

The bastard, Amelia thought. Using these kids to fake out Ben and then throwing them out on the street.

"How about if I talk to him for you?"

"That might work." Danny sniffed hard. "I know he really likes you."

"What makes you say that?"

"He was really worried last night when you passed out. Also, he has a picture of you that looks really pretty. You have on a green and white dress. It's from a long time ago."

Her interview dress for the health policy think tank. The last time she spent real money on clothes. She was surprised, but then she remembered what a packrat Matthew was. He'd even kept all their old furniture rather than replacing it, which seemed insane given the money he made. "Does he have any pictures of my boy-friend, Ben?"

"Some. One with you in it, too. And Matthew. You're all stand-ing by a boat."

She remembered that day. The second summer they lived in Baltimore. An older woman had taken the picture for them, but the pose in front of a sailboat was Matthew's idea, so they'd look like rich preppies summering at the Cape rather than poor students who'd taken a bus to Rehoboth. Matthew made them all copies. She wasn't sure where hers was, but she knew Ben didn't have his anymore; he always threw away everything except journals and lab books and things he needed for research.

"Don't worry," Amelia said. "I'll talk to Matthew, and I promise he'll agree to keep you until your mom comes home."

Danny was squinting and Amelia thought to ask if he needed glasses. She said she could talk to Matthew about that, too. He said no, he didn't think so; then he hugged her. When Ben and Matthew returned, Isabelle ran over to Matthew but Danny stayed put, holding on to Amelia, trusting her to do the right thing for him.

She told the men that she needed to talk to Matthew privately now.

Ben said, "First, come into the bedroom for a minute. I have to tell you something."

"Fine," she said, but she winked at Danny, promising him that nothing Ben said would change this.

Ben shut the door behind them, but even so, he was whispering. "You can't talk to Matt, babe. He just confided in me that he realized last night he's still in love with you. It's not fair to him if we stay here any longer. We shouldn't move too close to him, either. We don't want to hurt him any more than we already have."

Amelia thought for a moment. This was an unexpected but very smart move on Matthew's part. It gained Ben's sympathy while blocking her out for good, making it impossible for her even to suggest dropping by to see him. He could dump the kids, knowing she couldn't come back in a few days to check up on things.

"I have to tell him something." She took Ben's hand. "Trust me, I'll be very sensitive to what you just told me. It won't take long. It's very important."

Ben looked at her. She wondered if he was a little jealous, or just worried about Matthew. Either way, she wasn't about to back down. Finally, he agreed, but he said, "I don't think Matt will do it. Haven't you noticed that he's been trying to stay away from you all morning? Even I noticed that, but I would never have suspected why."

"Give me a minute to talk to him. Go to the bathroom or something. I know I can get him to say yes if you're not standing right there."

Ben agreed. He was at his limit for emotional complexity, a fact that she was counting on.

She went into the loft. Matthew was holding Isabelle, and Danny was sitting on the couch, watching them. She whispered, "I know," in Matthew's ear. Then she smiled. "Can we take our own walk now?"

Ben was blinking with surprise, but he nodded when Matthew reminded him to watch Isabelle. Neither Amelia nor Matthew said anything on the elevator. When they were outside, walking against the wind, she told him she knew he was kicking the kids out today.

"Congratulations on your powers of investigation," he said. "Now tell me why I give a damn."

She was rattled, but she said, "I'll tell Ben."

"Go right ahead. I already told him it was all a ruse." Matthew looked at her. "Surprised you, didn't I?"

Stunned was more like it.

"All I had to do was admit that I was oh so jealous of him when he told me in Paris that you were pregnant." He smirked. "Poor lonely Matthew, making up a family because he can't have one with his only true love. Cue violins."

They were a block from Matthew's building. She looked up to his apartment, saw the wall of windows, thought about Danny. She'd promised to work this out for him.

"Are we finished here?" he said. "Because I have a life to get back to."

"Rachel, right? She called while you were out. She sounds like she's an imbecile, and all of twenty years old."

"Not that it's any of your business, but yes. First I plan to work for a while, then I'll have a pleasant dinner with Rachel, who's twenty-six and absolutely gorgeous, after which I'll take her back home and have sex with her for hours." He grinned. "Poor me, I have to do what I can to soothe the pain of my broken heart."

"You're such an evil bastard."

"So I've heard, many times." He clutched his chest. "I can't tell you how it hurts to have my one and only love assess me so harshly. But so long, farewell, hope your move goes smoothly and your kid is healthy and you stay the fuck away from me until we're all at least a hundred."

He turned around and started back to the apartment. Amelia was desperate to stop him, and then she remembered the one thing he did care about.

"Pain Matters," she said to his back. It worked; he stopped. She walked up to him. "The phony 'grassroots' group you created to sell Galvenar. Very clever, the way your PR firm hid everything behind wall after wall of true pain advocates. I'm going to make sure the whole intricate scheme is exposed in the *New York Times*. I've already put in a call to my contact there."

"I don't believe it. I know Ben told you that you can't say anything about Galvenar. He didn't mean the panel in Paris; he meant anywhere."

"I won't be. The *New York Times* will."

"You'll still hurt Ben by doing this."

"No, I don't think so. I considered that yesterday, before I left the *Times* a message while we were at Ben's cousin's house. Ben had nothing to do with the creation of Pain Matters. Even you can't think I'd believe something that ludicrous." She paused and looked at Matthew. "Whatever you have on Ben, it won't come out if this is exposed."

"Yes it will, because I'll release it. If you think I care about a friendship, even Ben's, more than—"

"Of course you don't. Nothing and no one is as important as your stupid company. But I also know that you'd be reluctant to release your secret when whatever you stand to gain from dropping Ben's name would be muted in the furor over Pain Matters. Then, too, if you use Ben now, what will you have left to use in the future?"

He cursed several times before he asked her what she wanted.

"Not that much. I just want you to keep the kids until their mother comes home from rehab. You can hire a nanny to help you take care of them."

"And at the end of that, you write the article anyway? No thanks. It's not worth it."

"No. I'll never talk about Pain Matters. I'll bury all my research about that, even though it took me two years." She inhaled. "I give you my word."

He believed her, she could tell. Since she hadn't lied to him before, he thought she was incapable of it, and even morally opposed to it. As if her morality were that simple. Even freshman philosophy students learn that lying is sometimes necessary, usually through the exercise of imagining the Nazis at the door, asking if you're harboring a Jew. In this case, Matthew was the Nazi and Danny was the Jewish child she had to protect. Any lie was not only allowable, but a moral good.

Too bad for Matthew that he'd never taken a philosophy course. He seemed thoroughly confused. "How can you agree to this? Doesn't it go against your own ethics?"

"Galvenar isn't a bad drug; it just doesn't belong on the essential medicine list. But I can let that go. Most ministries of health can't afford it anyway. And Danny deserves to be taken care of. He's a wonderful kid."

She saw the flash of relief in Matthew's eyes when she said Galvenar wasn't a bad drug. She wanted him to think the creation of Pain Matters was all she had, which was true at the moment, though it wouldn't stay that way for long. She'd just sent one of her staff to Jakarta, following Matthew's trail. She'd warned him that she would pull out all the stops to find out what hold he had on Ben. He should have believed her about that, too.

"Will you take care of them or not?" When he hesitated, she said, "I won't write the article about you, either."

"The one where you attempt to show that the guy who broke his back taking care of you last night is really an incompetent buffoon?"

"Yes."

More cursing, but finally he agreed.

"You know I won't break my word," she said. "But if you break yours, I will call the *Times* and say I remembered what I was going to tell them. And don't think I won't find out, because I am going to check on those kids every few days."

"Ben won't like that."

"Ben will be busy at the lab."

"So you're going to keep this from him, too? For some kid you just met? Amelia, you disappoint me. Being pregnant has warped your moral code."

"Don't flatter yourself. You never understood my moral code any more than you understood what I wanted in Palm Beach."

That shut him up. They walked back to the building, but Matthew walked on the street, refusing to even share the sidewalk with her. When they were waiting for the elevator, Amelia remembered to tell him that if he retaliated against Danny in any way for telling her the truth, the deal was off. "He didn't mean to. He really likes you. He said having you around was like having a real father."

Matthew pushed the elevator button again.

"Don't you have any sympathy for him?" she said. "You're really not that different. He doesn't have a father; you lost your father when you were twelve. He's very poor, but you were poor, too. His mother is sick, and so was yours."

"My mother had cancer. His is a drug addict who stole five thousand dollars from me. But I refuse to discuss this with you. You consider me capable of retaliating against a ten-year-old. I think that sums up the hopelessness of trying to get you to understand anything about me."

She was relieved, thinking what this meant for Danny. Matthew would be nice to him, just as she'd hoped. Even after she and Ben left and they were heading to the train station to go to New York, she was still thinking about Danny. Could you fall in love with a child at first sight? It had never happened to her before. Maybe it was being pregnant, something about hormones.

"I hope we have a boy," she told Ben.

"I don't care as long as it's healthy."

She hoped he wasn't making some reference to her age. She'd already agreed to do every prenatal test for older mothers. She decided he was just being sweet.

"Which one did you like better, Danny or Isabelle?"

"What a question. I liked them both. They're kids."

"Are you glad I talked Matthew into keeping them until their mother comes back?"

"I don't know. He was going to call social services and find them a good foster home. I wonder if that wouldn't be better for them, since Matt has to work all the time."

A foster home? That made more sense than kicking them out

on the street to live in a house with drug addicts. Danny must have misinterpreted something Matthew said.

"But for Matt's sake," Ben continued, "yes, I'm glad you talked him into it. I worry about him being alone right now. He told me he hasn't been sleeping, and he looks wiped out."

"He does?"

"Didn't you notice? I've never seen him look this bad. I felt even worse listening to him talk about last night with you. He's really a mess."

"Are you saying that a tiny little part of you didn't feel—I don't know—proud? Like you had something he wanted?"

Ben gave her a look like she'd just suggested murdering puppies. "Of course not. I love Matt. I just want him to be happy."

"Maybe you should give me back to him, then." She knew how childish that sounded, but she was annoyed by his passionate declaration of feeling for stupid Matthew.

"Even if I wanted to, which I don't, I couldn't. Matt cares about me, too, and he wouldn't want you, knowing it would hurt me."

This was way too much male bonding for her to handle. Luckily, they were at the train station. They were finally going home, but just to pack a few things. Tomorrow it was back to Philadelphia, to stay in a hotel the lab would pay for while they looked for a new place.

"At least we'll be in our own bed tonight," she said. They were walking inside 30th Street Station. Ben didn't say anything, but he squeezed her hand. He was already looking for the ticket booth. She knew he was tired, and no wonder, after everything he'd been through in the last week and the last year.

They were waiting on the platform when she thought of what Ben had said about how bad Matthew looked. Was it possible he was right? She'd noticed Matthew's cashmere sweater and expensive jeans; his stylishly cut, still thick brown hair; his teeth, so white she knew he had to be having them bleached at the dentist. Even when he was sitting right next to her at the hospital, she'd seen nothing but his unfairly long eyelashes and obscenely handsome face, the same disgustingly good-looking man he'd always been. Yet even Danny had mentioned that Matthew griped a lot about being tired. If it was really true that he looked wiped out, why hadn't she noticed this? Not that she would have cared if she had, but it was still so strange to think she could have missed it completely.

The train was only a few miles from Philly when Ben fell asleep with his face smashed against the window. Amelia pulled his head onto her shoulder and thought about the genetics study he and Matthew had talked about. She hoped it was true and the baby would get more of Ben's genes than hers. He was obviously much smarter than she was, and, she suspected, a much nicer person deep down.

CHAPTER ELEVEN

His Father's Son

After Ben and Amelia left, Matthew told Danny it was time to have a talk. Isabelle had gone down for her nap early, no doubt because she'd been awake most of the night, tugging on Matthew's earlobes, hitting him in the face, kicking him right in the middle of his sore back. He'd woken up exhausted and in agony and soaking wet, because, as his crap luck would have it, she'd picked that night of all nights to pee in the bed. He was extremely annoyed that Danny hadn't mentioned they needed diapers, but he'd gotten over that as the morning went plunging downhill.

Now he was sitting across from the kid at the table, plying him with potato chips and orange soda. He could tell Danny expected him to be angry, but he wasn't and he told him so. He also told Danny that he and Isabelle could stay until their mother came back. "But I do want to know how you did it. I think you owe me that."

To his credit, Danny didn't pretend not to know what Matthew meant. Was that a smile on his clever little face? Yes, it was, and no wonder. He'd run an elaborate con on an adult and gotten exactly what he wanted.

At first, he would admit only that he'd cried.

"What do you mean?" Matthew said. "A few tears or complete hysteria?"

"As hard as I could." Crunch, crunch. "I cried so hard it made my throat hurt."

"And how did you manage that?"

He shrugged. "I can cry when I need to. I do it all the time when I'm begging for money."

"An unusual skill. But how did you know it would work with Amelia?"

"She's the type I always pick to beg from." Crunch, crunch, crunch. A gulp from the soda. "I knew it as soon as I saw her."

"Meaning what? Bleeding-heart do-gooder?"

"She was wearing a jean skirt and kneesocks. Women who wear that kind of socks usually give me money."

"Interesting observation. I call that the liberal schoolgirl type, but your point works just as well." He stood up and got a napkin for Danny. "You're getting an orange mustache."

Danny wiped his lip and consumed another handful of potato chips.

"How did you know when to cry? Did you wait for the right opportunity?"

He nodded. "She asked who babysat us while you were at work. I pretended to be scared and said I couldn't remember her name."

177

"Rather than making up a name?"

"Yeah."

"What else?"

"Nothing much."

Matthew raised his eyebrows. "We both know that's not true."

He crunched for a while. "You promise you won't get mad?"

"Please stop asking me to promise. I'm not ten. But no, I won't get angry, even if you told her I fed you gruel instead of peanut butter and jelly." He smirked. "Which I'm guessing you didn't mention you insisted on eating yesterday, rather than turkey."

"When she was in the wheelchair last night, she said she was going home to New York. You know, as soon as she got out of the hospital." Crunch, crunch. "I said I wished she could stay with us a little longer. I said I really wanted to talk to her some more."

"Oh? Well, thank you again for giving me the opportunity to spend a fabulous night soaking in urine."

"I'm really sorry about that."

Matthew waved his hand. "What else?"

"I said I asked you to let us live here until my mom comes back."

"And what was my response to this imaginary question?"

Danny looked guilty. "You said, 'Dream on.'"

"Very pithy. Sounds like an expression I might use. Nice touch. What else?"

"I said you were kicking us out in the street with nowhere to live but a crack house."

"And you knew my assistant Cassie was going to call social services?"

Openmouthed crunch, crunch. "Yeah, but I don't want to go to foster care. They won't let me be with Isabelle."

Matthew thought for a minute. "Why did you claim you wanted to live with me rather than with Amelia?"

"I didn't say that. I just said you were like a real father and I liked you and you were nice to Isabelle." Danny took another drink. Matthew pointed at the kid's lip and he wiped off his mouth with the napkin. "She said she'd ask you if we could stay. I said it might work because you liked her."

"Surely you didn't expect her to believe that."

"No, I just said it because I knew she needed me to be young. Like innocent."

Matthew smiled. "I wish I could hire you. You're good."

"Really?"

"Amelia may wear kneesocks, but she thinks of herself as tough. Believe it or not, everyone in my office is afraid of her. But thanks to you, I know what she has on one of our products. You inadvertently did me a big favor."

More crunching, crunching, until Matthew finally removed the bowl. "I think you've had enough. Don't want to spoil your dinner."

Danny squinted. "So you're really going to let us stay with you?"

"What the hell, you've earned it. But Amelia will be coming by to check on you every few days. Can you keep up the innocent act?"

"Sure. It's easy."

"Do you think you can get close enough to her to be of use to me?"

"What would I have to do?"

"I'm not sure yet. But you must have noticed that Amelia is a pain in my ass."

"Yeah, I could tell that guy Ben wasn't the reason you were pretending to adopt us. I'll try to help you. I'll try really hard since you're not kicking us out."

"All right. We'll see how it goes. In the meantime, I have to do some work, and then tonight I'm going out for a while. I'll have to find a babysitter for you and your sister."

"We don't need a babysitter. I can take care of Isabelle."

"Perhaps, but that's not your decision anymore. For the next month, you'll do what I tell you to do." He shrugged. "This is what you wanted. No complaining now."

"Okay," the kid said sadly.

Matthew thought he was insane to be upset about having help with child care, but he said, "Come on, now, having a babysitter isn't the end of the world. You can con her if you want. Maybe she'll fall in love with you, too."

He blushed and Matthew could tell he did have feelings for Amelia. Which was so bizarre he didn't even bother wondering why. It was like the witch cast some kind of spell on every man in the room, even ten-year-old boys.

The rest of the day with the kiddies was challenging, but not terrible. He worked until Isabelle woke up; then she bothered him for several hours while he tried to work; then he fed them dinner, and by seven he was out the door, on his way to his date.

Rachel lived in Manayunk, which meant driving on the expressway, but the Black Friday, home-from-shopping-for-useless-crap crowd was jamming up every lane and he never got the Porsche out of second gear. Oh well, at least he had Talking Heads blasting out of the car's excellent sound system now that he was alone for the first time in days. It felt like his normal life, which was reassuring. This wasn't going to be so bad. As Pain in the Ass herself had pointed out, he could hire a nanny to take care of the kids. Cassie had already given him the names of several nanny services; she said if he was willing to pay top dollar, he should be able to hire someone right away. Moreover, he and Cassie had come up with a sensible plan to move the children and the nanny out to the suburbs, where they could live in blissful splendor with a yard and separate bedrooms until their mother returned. Despite what he'd told Amelia, one of his rental houses had been recently vacated; he could call the agent and ask her to take it off the market and arrange temporary furnishings. He enjoyed thinking of Amelia having to drive to the suburban paradise, given that she was afraid of traffic and hadn't had a car since she'd moved to New York. Of course he'd be dropping by the house, too, preferably not when Amelia was there, just to check up on things. The rest of the time he would be in his apartment, as always, where he could sleep or work or have a woman over, undisturbed. It was the best arrangement for him, but also for the kids since the excellent nanny would be much better at child care than he ever would be.

For tonight he'd had to accept an ordinary teenager, the not-too-bright-seeming Hannah, who Cassie had found through her daughter's school. As Cassie said, it was difficult to get a good babysitter on Friday night. Fifteen-year-old Hannah had years of experience, or so she said. She certainly charged enough—twelve dollars an hour, minimum of seventy-two dollars. Dinner with Rachel would be another four hundred; the restaurant was BYOB and he'd bought a bottle of her favorite wine. Almost five hundred dollars to get laid? Not a problem. He would have paid twice that if necessary.

Of course talking to the fascinating Rachel was another story. While they were at the restaurant, he found himself daydreaming while she told him the saga of her hair color change. From light brown to honey brown? He couldn't tell the difference. She had on a very tight, low-cut sweater; he did notice that, but she'd already told him to stop staring at her tits. So he was forced to look at her face and nod, while thinking about the Pain Matters problem. Obviously he couldn't just sit back and wait to find out if Amelia would expose this. She was like an unstable chemical now: she could do nothing, or she could react in an entirely unexpected way, or even blow up the building. What if she woke up tomorrow and realized that suppressing ethical research because you liked some kid was just a little bit problematic? Or what if the next time she saw Danny she didn't like him that much? What if she got mad at Matthew or even Ben and decided she'd feel better only if someone took her seriously, say, someone at the *New York Times*? The risk was unacceptable. He would have to step up and handle this proactively.

"Are you even listening?" Rachel said.

"Sorry," he said, taking her hand. Her nails were painted black, but this wasn't a change, either. Last time he saw her, he thought she'd done it for Halloween. He leaned closer and grinned. "To tell you the truth, I can't think about anything but getting you in bed."

She laughed happily. "I've missed you, too. You need to tell your boss that you can't travel for a month at a time. Your girlfriend doesn't like it."

He nodded and she went back to blabbing about something related to leather pants. Shopping for them? Hating them? Who cared? He went back to the problem at hand. The entire dinner was spent this way, with the sole exception of when she insisted he tell her what he'd done on his travels and he tried to explain one teeny, tiny thing—nothing proprietary, of course, just the reason the EU had held the conference. Her response? "If they want to help poor people, help them. Why talk about it?"

Why, indeed, when you can talk about hair color and leather pants?

She took forever eating and drinking and talking, but finally they were back in the car. When he insisted on going to her apartment, she whined that she liked his better. He told her he was sorry but his place was a mess. "You just had it cleaned," she said. "How is that possible?"

He had no idea what she was talking about, but he said, "The cleaner sucked."

"I can believe it. She had a real attitude, that one."

He was driving with one hand up her skirt. It was challenging just shifting gears and staying on the road. He mumbled in agreement.

Finding a parking spot in Rachel's neighborhood on a Friday night was close to impossible. When he'd picked her up, he'd driven around for ten minutes before he'd given up and asked her to meet him outside, but now a car was pulling out a few doors down. "My lucky night," he said. She lived on the second floor of an old row house with lots of stairs. She went first and talked about a creepy neighbor who was probably watching her ass right now from his peephole. Who wouldn't be? Matthew thought, but he said, "Want me to have a talk with this guy?"

Please have her say no, please have her say no, please have her say no.

"No, but you are such an alpha male." She turned around and smiled. "You'd do anything to protect me, wouldn't you?"

He nodded, though the only word he paid attention to was *protect*. He reached into his pocket until he felt the plastic condom package sticking out of his wallet. Protection remembered. Check.

Rachel's apartment was the real mess. Every piece of furniture was covered in clothes, as though she'd never heard of a laundry basket. Unless all of these were clean? Near the bed he saw several pairs of leather pants. No doubt he'd know why they were there if he'd been listening.

Near the bed, then on the bed, then her sweater and bra off. Kissing her to keep her from talking while he felt her large, soft breasts. No longer able to comprehend language when he put his mouth on those breasts. He pushed up her skirt, ready to go, but she said, "Wait, let me take it off. And you, get undressed. I know it's been a while, but we're not in that big of a hurry, are we?"

Hannah had to be home by one, which meant Matthew had to be back by twelve-thirty to put her in a cab. So he really needed to leave by twelve. It was 10:14, according to his watch. He needed time to satisfy Rachel (which could take a while, especially if she didn't shut up), and afterward, to hold her and make her feel appreciated as he fed her some bullshit reason he had to go home rather than spending the night. Didn't want to be a complete ass.

"Of course not," he said. He stripped as fast as he could without injuring himself. Jumped in bed. She was still arranging her skirt on the chair. "Rachel?" he said, playfully.

"Just a minute. This skirt wrinkles."

By all means, don't let the skirt get wrinkled. Ever heard of a hanger?

After an eternity, she got in bed, too. He turned her onto her side and lifted her hair to kiss the back of her neck, which every woman in the world seemed to think was the ultimate romantic gesture. He went through the rest of his foreplay arsenal and finally she was so turned on that she was quiet while he licked behind her knees and up her thighs. She pulled him on top of her, but he had to roll off to put on the condom. As he entered her, it felt unbelievably good, and he was instantly worried that he wouldn't be able to last. He did what he always did—searched for something bad to focus on, which he and Ben used to jokingly refer to as the "dead baby solution." It worked; he kept going until Rachel came the first time and then again, but unfortunately before he could get there himself his focus on Pain Matters led to Amelia, which led to Danny and Isabelle, which made his cell phone start ringing. At least, it sure as hell felt that way.

"Don't answer," Rachel whispered.

"I have to," he panted. "I think." Maybe it wasn't them. He managed to stay inside Rachel while he ripped his arm out of its socket reaching over the edge of the bed and into his pants for the phone. The caller ID showed his own number. He flipped open the phone. "What?"

"Doctor Connelly?" Hannah. "Um, we have a problem?"

Hannah ended every sentence with a question mark. He waited. Rachel was running her long nails over his back. Her nipples were still hard, demanding that he pay attention. Finally, he snapped, "Well?"

"Isabelle cut her foot? It's just a little cut, really, but—"

"Bandage."

"I can't find a bandage or Neosporin or anything?"

"Ask Danny. He'll think of something."

"That's the other problem? Danny ate too much pizza, and he's not feeling very well? He's already asleep?"

"Wake him up."

She laughed nervously. "I get it? It's a joke?"

"Make a square of Kleenex and tape it on her foot." Rachel was moving her hips. It was all he could do not to moan. "Bye."

"Are you sure you can't come home now? She's been crying pretty hard?"

"Give Isabelle the iPod."

"Doctor Connelly, I really think—"

He closed the phone and threw it over the side of the bed.

He kissed one of those beautiful nipples, but before he could kiss the other Rachel started pulling on his shoulders, telling him to get off. "Yeah," he breathed gratefully. No more foreplay; it was time. After a few thrusts, he was just about there, when her voice pierced through the pleasure.

"Get off me!"

Of course he did as she asked, but he let out a loud groan of protest.

She rolled away and pulled the sheet to her chin. "Who is Isabelle?"

"Oh, Christ, is that all?" He laughed and reached for the sheet. "Isabelle isn't another woman. She's three years old."

He pulled the sheet off, but then she jumped up. "So it's true! I thought there was no way you'd keep this from me."

He hadn't a clue what she was talking about, but he said, "I wouldn't," and tried to grab her arm.

"Don't treat me like I'm stupid." She put on a baggy shirt that she grabbed from the floor. No more nipples. At least she was still naked from the waist down. "Just because I'm a makeup artist and you're a hot shit doesn't mean I can't add two and two."

"I know that," he said, though why they were talking about addition he couldn't have said if his life depended on it. He stood up, too. Advanced. Managed to kiss her neck. Said, "Come on, Rachel," in his most seductive voice. Played with her hair. "Let's go back to bed."

"You don't love me, do you?"

"I do." He put his hands on her ass and squeezed. "I love your gorgeous—"

She wriggled away and stood with her arms crossed.

"Of course I love you." He advanced. "Now come on, I'm dying here. Let's—"

"How long have we been together?"

"Can't we talk about this after—"

"No."

A quick mental search revealed that he didn't know when he'd met her, though he remembered where. A party in Queen Village. They were outside, so it was warm. Probably August? Better to overestimate than underestimate. "Six months." He smiled. "Is that right?"

Obviously it wasn't, because she yelled, "A year and a half."

Oh shit, wrong summer. He tried, "I guess it only feels shorter because it's been so great."

"No, it's because you're always out of town. That's what you tell me." She glared. "You big liar."

He knew from long experience that once a woman used the *L* word, all hope was gone. He threw away the condom and put his clothes on without saying anything. He was so pissed he couldn't have spoken if he'd wanted to. If only he'd called someone other than Rachel. He knew she wasn't that smart (to put it mildly), but he had no idea she was so crazy that she would get furious at the mere mention of Isabelle's name. Obviously she still believed that a three-year-old was really some woman he was sleeping with. Maybe she was off her meds.

Right as he finished buttoning his shirt, the cell phone rang again.

"I'm leaving now," he told Hannah.

"That's good? Isabelle stopped bleeding but she's still crying? I think she needs you?"

He told her he'd be there as soon as he could and hung up.

"Isabelle cut her foot and she's crying. Because she's a *child*. I have to go."

"You big liar," she repeated. She lit a cigarette and blew smoke in his direction. "I should have listened to your housekeeper."

He'd never seen her smoke, or had he? If so, he couldn't remember. "All right, I give up. What in the hell are you talking about?"

"Your housekeeper told me you had kids, but I didn't believe it."

"My housekeeper?" he said, but then it hit him. Of course. Amelia had mentioned talking to Rachel, but she left out the strange pretense of being his housekeeper. Christ, what was wrong with that woman?

When his shoes were on and he was ready to go, he couldn't resist telling Rachel that he didn't have kids. "I'm just taking care of them while their mother is sick." He moved to the door. "But you're right, I don't love you. You don't love me, either, if that's any consolation."

"You lying prick." She threw a wad of clothing at him. "Screw you and screw that stupid song you made me listen to. It bites like a dog turd."

The song she was so brilliantly critiquing, Talking Heads' "Once in a Lifetime," was not only one of his favorites, but also one of the hundred most important American musical works of the twentieth century, according to some authority. CNN? NPR? An eminent music critic? He wasn't sure, but he'd read it on Wikipedia.

He smiled indulgently. "I believe the simile you're striving for is 'stinks like a dog turd.'"

"Whatever," she said, and gave him the finger.

When he got home, he found Isabelle face down, sobbing on the couch. Hannah was singing to her—a valiant effort, even if her voice was badly off-key.

"Isabelle," he said, leaning down to her. "What are you going on about?"

"Ma-ew," she said, and sat up, only to throw herself in his arms. More crying and some babbling, which he took to mean she was mad that he hadn't been there for the foot injury.

He patted her back. "You're becoming a pain in the ass, too; you know that, right?"

"I not," she stammered.

He laughed. "It's a good thing you're so cute. Otherwise, I'd have to throw you out the window."

Hannah looked horrified. Matthew told her it was a family joke. For some reason, that made Isabelle laugh.

"It cheered her up?" Hannah said. "I guess it's okay, then?"

He paid the seventy-two dollars plus cab fare. Sent Hannah home. Walked Isabelle around the apartment until she was completely calm and then told her she had to go to bed.

"You bed?"

"Absolutely not." Her face scrunched up again, but before she could let loose he reminded her that Danny was waiting for her in their bed. "You love Danny, and if you don't, you should. He treats you like a princess. Be nice to him or you'll grow up to be a bitch, too."

He had no idea whether she understood, but she didn't object when Matthew put her next to her brother. A few minutes later, he checked and she was snoring.

Another perfect night, but thankfully almost over.

When he sat down at his computer, he wrote Walter an email. "Something's come up that we need to talk about this weekend. Give me a call when you have a minute."

Walter would know it was an emergency because Matthew only bothered him on the weekend if a potential disaster was brewing. This certainly qualified. If Amelia could pretend to be his house-keeper, all bets were off. The woman was dangerous. They would have to release their own statement about Pain Matters as soon as possible. The only question was how to do it, and Matthew had already worked out a few possibilities during the evening with Ra-chel. At least it wasn't a total loss.

The next morning, Matthew sat down at his computer to dis-cover that Walter had already emailed him back. This was a little strange since the boss didn't like checking email on the weekend, and he usually did so as little as possible, once a day, late in the af-ternoon. But it was the message itself that was really disturbing: "I need to speak to you about something as well. How about coming over to the house today around two?"

Walter had never issued such a weekend summons. Naturally, it crossed Matthew's mind that he'd done something wrong, possibly even stepped in some very deep shit. He called Hannah and bribed her to come back, this time for a minimum of a hundred dollars. He also told Danny to stay alert and not eat too much. "I can't deal with any problems this afternoon," he said to Danny. "This is serious."

Walter lived about an hour outside of Philadelphia, in a relatively

189

undeveloped part of Chester County, mainly horse farms and old money. The drive took Matthew right past Astor-Denning and then about fifteen miles down tiny curving roads with names like Three Ponds Lane and Whitetail Run. Several AD execs lived out here, including the CEO, presumably because it was so convenient—unless it snowed; then getting out of here would be a bitch. Cassie lived in the other direction, nearer to civilized Paoli, and even she needed an SUV to get to work. Walter had a Jaguar and a Hummer, though how he got down these roads in that Hummer without knocking over mailboxes and running down little animals was a mystery. Harold Knolton, the CEO, had only been at the company since last spring, but the first time it snowed he'd probably charter a helicopter to take him to the roof and hire a band to congratulate him for making it in.

Matthew never complained publicly about the new CEO, though just driving by the man's forty-acre estate—on the way to Walter's more modest mansion—made him feel pissed off. Why the board had made Harold Knolton CEO instead of Walter Healy was something he would never understand. Knolton was an outsider whose only experience was in retail, while Walter had put twenty-eight years into AD, earning the respect and loyalty of nearly everyone in the company. During Knolton's very first week on the job he'd managed to alienate the entire workforce with his foolish comparison of AD and Microsoft, braying in his teleconference: "We must become the Windows of pharmaceuticals. Our goal is one hundred percent penetration of the market and the same reputation for safety and utility as the best Microsoft products." Ignoring the fact that even Windows didn't have 100 percent penetration (ever heard of Apple, asswipe?), the bigger problem was that pharmaceuticals are legally classified as "unavoidably unsafe products," meaning that, unlike software, you can't make them so they don't cause harm to *someone*. The key was always a careful risk/benefit analysis,

which Knolton claimed he fully understood from his vast experience launching . . . department stores. Thankfully, Matthew rarely
had to see the man or his house. He'd been to the estate only twice:
once in March, for the welcome party Knolton threw to welcome
himself, and once for the Fourth of July picnic and fireworks display. Both times, Walter had pushed Matthew forward and praised
him as the next big thing, and Knolton had shaken his hand before
walking off to someone more worthy.

He was about a mile from Walter's house when he suddenly
wondered if he was being fired. He'd heard of weekend firings at
other pharma companies, but surely AD wouldn't stoop that low.
And Knolton had just called him in Paris; why use effusive praise
as prep for a firing? Then, too, Matthew knew Walter wouldn't let
this happen unless the only choice was cutting Matthew loose or
facing jail time, and Matthew was positive (well, almost) that he
hadn't broken any laws. He consulted with the legal department on
every important decision. The last thing he wanted to do was get
the company in trouble with any government, not to mention his
personal opposition to going near a prison.

Walter lived in an old stone farmhouse, built in 1768 and on
the national register of historic places. (The plaque on the front
proclaimed as much.) The house was surrounded by hundreds of
trees, and Matthew heard the leaves crunching under his feet as he
walked up the long path from the parking area to the front door. He
could hear the brook in the back and smell the fire billowing out
of the chimney. It was an unusually warm day, almost 60 degrees,
but Walter loved to have a fire in his den or in one of his eight other
fireplaces.

"Son, you're right on time," Walter said in his great southern
drawl. Whenever they were alone, he always called Matthew "son."
He'd started this years ago, but the older Matthew got, the more he
appreciated it. Made him feel young.

Walter looked very tired, but that wasn't surprising. He'd come home from Paris a few days before Matthew had, but he'd probably had a houseful of kids and grandkids for Thanksgiving. His wife implied as much when she told Matthew they had lots of leftovers if he wanted anything.

He thanked her, but said he'd just eaten. He couldn't choke down a bite until he found out what the hell was going on. While he followed the boss through the long left wing of the house that led to the den, Walter congratulated him for the latest CESS results, joking that Matthew "must have paid them off again." The Confidential Employee Satisfaction Survey, or CESS, was called the "cesspool" by most of the employees, since filling it out was mandatory and it was way too long. One section was devoted to the employee's immediate boss and another to the leader of the employee's division, with statements like "My team leader supports and encourages my development"; "My team leader knows of my work"; "My opinion is valued by the team leader and sought out when appropriate." Every year for the last three years, Matthew had come in with the highest results in the company. This year's was his best score yet, and the director of human resources took him to lunch to pick his brain on how he kept his people so happy. The true answer, he didn't know. The BS answer, a reformulation of the same categories in the CESS. "I support their development in every way I can. I know all their names and what they're working on. I value their input." She took notes, which seemed so hilarious it made the wasted time for lunch almost worthwhile.

It struck Matthew that Knolton might have a different view of his CESS results, since the CEO was known for his boasts that "Being feared means I'm doing something right." True enough, if by "something" he meant being an incompetent asshole. Indeed, he was not only doing that right, he was doing it almost perfectly.

The den was Matthew's favorite of all the rooms in this great house. It wasn't as cavernous as Walter's office at AD, and it was much more personal. The shelves on the facing wall contained hundreds of books about the usual things—management, medicinal chemistry, the stock market, drug development—but also dozens of volumes on the boss's three passions: bird watching, poker, and American history. All over the room were photographs of Walter's children and grandchildren taken at holidays and birthday parties and summers at their vacation house in Maine. Even the mahogany bar seemed intimate, flanked as it was by a painting of Walter's wife, sitting in this den, smiling with the absolute confidence of a woman whose husband adores her. From what Matthew had seen, it was really true. They'd been married for almost forty years and Walter had never strayed; he said Cynthia was the love of his life, so why would he?

Walter fixed himself a scotch, but he knew Matthew didn't drink unless he was with a client, and then only a glass of wine, less if he could get away with it. "The only thing I don't like about you," he always joked. But not this time.

When they were seated in the wing chairs, Walter took a drink of the scotch and then announced that he'd decided to retire from AD. "Effective immediately. I wanted to tell you before they make it official."

"Knolton is forcing you out, isn't he? That dimwitted bast—"

Walter shook his head. "Harold had nothing to do with my decision. He asked me to stay for a transition period, but I told him I can't do it. For years I've been promising Cynthia a trip around the world." He smiled. "I've always told you, don't make promises. They have a way of coming back to bite you on the ass."

Matthew sat forward. The boss was obviously serious. "I'm glad for you if this is what you want. Selfishly, I'm worried about my division. Who is replacing you?"

"The board has been considering several internal people, but they've also been talking to outside candidates."

Walter was still talking about the board's process, but Matthew wasn't paying attention. Those jackasses. Outsiders like Knolton? Maybe the new boss would have substantial expertise selling toilet paper. He could explain how drugs should be 100 percent absorbent, as safe and effective as Charmin. And even if by some miracle the board picked someone inside the company, this was still bad news. No one else would be as good as Walter. He was fucked.

"They've authorized me to offer the position to you."

Matthew sat back. Wondered, did he just say you? As in me? As in, oh shit, now I'm really fucked?

"I'm not ready," he said, because it was absolutely true. Walter was one of only eight people on the corporate executive team, and his area, International Pharmaceuticals, covered everything from regulatory to IT, marketing to product development, ethical compliance to finance, medical alliances to clinical trial management, public relations to administration. A few others that Matthew couldn't remember at the moment. How could he be in charge of departments he couldn't remember? It was ridiculous.

"You are ready, son." Walter took a drink. "This is excellent news. If only you were a drinking man; this is a hell of a moment for a drink."

"All right, I'll have a scotch."

Walter gave him a curious look, but he stood up and poured him a drink. Matthew sipped it, afraid he'd wuss out and choke. It helped him calm down and listen as the boss started to tell his favorite story: the day Matthew interviewed for his first job at Astor-Denning. He felt about the story the way other people felt about watching home movies with their parents: a little fascinated, more than a little embarrassed, mainly just bored. The story always took forever because Walter was a southerner, and southerners have to tell you what kind of day it was (raining and "cold as a well-digger's tail"), what month (March), what Matthew was wearing (a blue suit that didn't fit him well and a clip-on tie), and what his clothes said about him ("so poor he couldn't rub two nickels together"). Several other colorful details that Matthew sat through, waiting for Walter to get to the real point of the story: what he was thinking throughout the process.

"I didn't want to interview you. HR insisted, because they were always impressed by anyone from Hopkins. But I was looking for a doctor to join my trials division and I knew you weren't my candidate. You sat across the table from me and said you'd done a residency in internal medicine. I had your college and med school transcripts. I thought either this kid has never been on an interview or he's just as dumb as a box of rocks."

"The latter," Matthew said, because it was undeniable. To think he could fake an entire residency. He'd never hire anybody who tried to pull something like that.

"So I told you the problem as I saw it. You'd done well in medical school, but you weren't a licensed physician. You needed to come back after you'd done a good internship and a residency, and then we'd talk." Walter paused. "You remember what you said to me?"

Of course he did. He'd answered the same question every time Walter told the story. "I can't stand hospitals."

Walter slapped his knee. "Another confession so stupid it boggled the mind. Applying for a job in clinical trials and admitting you don't like hospitals."

Matthew took a bigger drink. The scotch was warm going down his throat. No wonder the boss loved this stuff.

"So then I asked you, 'Son, what is it you think you can do at this company? What are you looking for?' And you said, 'I made a mistake going to medical school and now I have a lot of student loans to pay off. I was hoping I could make some money.'" Walter was laughing and coughing. "And I thought this kid is green as a gourd. How did he graduate from college, much less get through Hopkins? He has to be putting me on."

This was the most embarrassing part, which always made Matthew feel like Walter had to be talking about someone else. Yes, he'd been young and stupid, but green? *That* green?

"So finally I said, 'Tell me some skills you think you could bring to the job. Mind you, I'm only asking so I can tell HR the whole story and give them a good laugh, too.' But then you said, 'I'll work my ass off. I'll give the company my best effort not only when I'm having successes but also when I'm failing miserably. I'll be loyal to Astor-Denning and I'll be loyal to you—the most loyal person you'll ever hire. If you just give me this chance, I'll never let you down.'" Walter took a drink and waved his hand. "You also told me about working full-time in college, acing the MCATs, the clinical rotations in med school, the one patient you thought you might have killed, the couple of dozen or so you'd helped save. But the desperation is what got to me. I thought here is a kid who needs a goddamn job. And I can give it to him. All I have to do is find something he can do without screwing it up."

Matthew laughed. "And that wasn't much."

"You said you liked talking to scientists. I thought, I'll never turn this kid loose on our contacts. Instead, I gave you a job in marketing, at the bottom. Your first task was so impossible I knew you couldn't do any harm: to come up with a new strategy for one of our worst-performing drugs. It was our first SSRI and we'd given up on it after several studies came out saying it wasn't as effective as the others on the market. But you pored over all the numbers and discovered that our drug had one thing the others didn't. It had a lower sexual side effect profile for men. Not much lower, but statistically significant. You came into my office and said that from now on, we can promote this drug as the only antidepressant that doesn't depress your boner."

Matthew was certain he hadn't put it that crudely, but Walter, for all his soft-spoken manners, loved the word *boner*. He always ended the story this way. "The rest is history," he'd say, meaning everything Matthew had achieved up to this point. But heading up International Pharmaceuticals was such a reach that he couldn't imagine how he'd pull it off. He told Walter that, but the boss said he had complete faith in him. Walter also said that the board wanted Matthew to give his first press conference when they announced his own resignation, so Matthew had better start thinking about what he wanted his tenure as leader to be.

"Knolton is gung ho for this," Walter said. "You know he's not a hands-on man. His only loyalty is to the shareholders. Of course you'll have to work with him, but you can decide how you want to accomplish the board's goals. You'll have full autonomy."

Walter's wife came in to check on him. She said she wished he'd eat something. "Later, honey," he said, and kissed her. After she left, Walter told Matthew about the new salary, which was staggeringly high. More stock options and a huge bonus, of course. The choice to hire two or even three people to replace him, if he didn't think one person could do his current job. Walter also told him the downside, including some of the problems he'd be inheriting. The difficulties of working with the board, and the constant meetings. The significant changes to his lifestyle. He wouldn't be able to travel to the problems; he'd have to delegate. His alliances would have to be delegated, too. He'd have a public presence that he'd have to remain aware of at all times. He would represent AD at important functions all over the world. "You really should get married," Walter said. "It's time to settle down, and it's better for your image."

Matthew nodded through it all, but he didn't ask any questions. He'd already decided that he couldn't accept this promotion. He told Walter, "I'm sorry. I appreciate your confidence, but quite honestly, I wish you hadn't pushed them to choose me. I think McNeil is a much better fit."

It was true; Charles McNeil had been grooming himself for the top job in the usual way: by rotating areas every year. He'd started in product development, then moved to regulatory, then finance, and now IT. Matthew had stayed where he was because he thought his division had more impact.

Which, apparently, he'd been right about.

"I didn't push them, son. Hell, I didn't have to. The success of Galvenar made this inevitable. Tegabadol is our miracle molecule, and you're the man behind the miracle." Walter smiled. "They knew you could walk on water long before I told 'em so."

He reminded Matthew that if he passed on this opportunity, he'd be off the track for good. He'd be stuck where he was, and eventually he'd lose power. It was the way the game was played, and Matthew knew it as well as anyone.

Finally, Matthew relented. He said he would accept the job, but on one condition. "You have to stay on to advise me for at least a year. You can travel with your wife, but you need to be available by phone. I can't do this without you."

"Son, I wish I could, but I'm afraid that's not an option." He paused and Matthew finished off his scotch, already sensing that he didn't want to hear the rest. "The problem is, I have lung cancer. That's why I have to take my wife on this trip now. I don't have a year. I may not have three months."

Matthew was positive it couldn't be true. Walter was only sixty-three. He'd quit smoking years ago. He never coughed, at least no more than anybody with a cold did. "The doctors are obviously wrong. Have you gotten a second opinion yet? I know a great pulmonary specialist at—"

"I've done all the second and third opinions. I've known about this for almost a year. Tried radiation last summer, but it didn't shrink it. Chemo was a long shot, and I decided it wasn't worth the aggravation."

A year? A year???

"I wanted to tell you, but I knew it could put you in a difficult position. Before they brought in Harold, the board did offer me CEO but I turned them down. I knew I wouldn't be able to stay for long and you wouldn't be ready to step in for me. This way I can leave you in my job, and in a few years you can take Knolton's."

Matthew refused to let himself feel anything. He couldn't break down now; it wouldn't be fair to Walter. "You have to let me know what I can do to help you and your family. Anything at all."

"Take the job, run with it, and make me proud. That's all I ever wanted from you, and it's all I want now."

"I wish I knew how to thank you for everything you've done for me." His voice was breaking, but he swallowed hard. "Fifteen years. It's been a hell of a ride."

Walter cried then, but Matthew kept it together, though of course he got up and hugged his boss. Noticed how fragile Walter felt underneath his shirt and sweater. How old he seemed. Finally, he gave Matthew a shoulder slap and said, "Now, I've got to quit this, or Cynthia will worry."

They talked for another minute, but then his wife was back, insisting again that he eat something, soup perhaps, and rest for a while. Matthew knew it was time to leave them alone, though he didn't want to. He wanted to sit there until this stopped being true.

Before he left, Walter asked him what he'd wanted to discuss. The email he sent last night? What was the problem?

"I'll handle it," he said. "Go eat soup with your wife."

Walter's wife smiled and touched Matthew's arm. "Thank you for coming," she said, like he'd done something, when he hadn't done a goddamn thing.

Heading back through the horse farm country, with the sun setting behind him, he drove so fast that he could only concentrate on staying on the road. Once he was past Great Valley and onto the expressway, he darted in and out of traffic, slamming his hand on the steering wheel every time someone slowed down in front of him, getting up to ninety, then ninety-five, daring a cop to stop him. When he got into his apartment, he gave his wallet to Danny. "Pay Hannah and send her home."

"Ma-ew!" Isabelle said, running to him.

"I have to do something now," he said to Danny. "Can you keep handling everything?"

"Yeah," Danny said. "What—"

"Thank you," Matthew told him. And then he went into his room, shut the door, and got into bed. It was that or finish the tequila he kept for Ben, and probably every other bottle of liquor in the house. The scotch had reminded him of what he'd decided at a beer party in high school: he could become an alcoholic if he wasn't very careful.

Lying in the dark, he thought about the time he'd bragged to Ben that he was obviously brilliant since he'd known there was a gene for alcoholism long before *JAMA* said so on April 18, 1990. They were third-year med students, but Ben was already Ben. He said the research was wrong and gave an argument about dopamine receptors that was so convincing that even some of their professors started calling the research a hoax. At the time, Matthew wondered what Ben would think about all the other research he'd read on alcoholism: the countless studies that showed that sons of alcoholics, in particular, are more likely to become drunks because they have inherited everything from abnormal brain waves to deficiencies in coordination and perception, and even diminished intellectual capacity. But he never considered asking Ben to look over any of the articles and books he'd collected over the years. He used to be so afraid of finding out that it was true, that he could never escape his destiny as his father's son.

Walter had changed all that for him. So hell yes, Matthew was going to have his own private pity party right here, right now. He really didn't have a choice; this pain was so fucking bad. Walter himself always said that it was the hardest part of the job, accepting that all good things have to come to an end: the most profitable patent, the longest run in the market, the closest partnership. Whatever you think you can't stand to lose, the boss warned, that's your weakness, that's what will kick you in the ass. So prepare to lose it. Plan for the worst-case scenario. Be ready.

CHAPTER TWELVE

Fairly Odd Parent

At first Danny tried to convince himself that it didn't make any difference. He and Isabelle had been just fine before, with the house all to themselves. They didn't need Dr. Connelly for anything. The problem was that Isabelle didn't see it that way. Danny wore himself out trying to distract her, yet every time he looked away for a minute, she was back at Dr. Connelly's bedroom door, banging on it with her fists, yelling for him, crying for him, throwing herself on the ground and even kicking Danny when he tried to move her back into the loft.

His sister's weird attachment to a guy she barely knew might have bugged Danny if she wasn't so pitiful about it. She never once mentioned their mom, which was just as well, since there was nothing he could do if Isabelle was missing Mom. Unfortunately, there was nothing he could do about Isabelle's reaction to Matthew being unavailable, either. Even on Sunday afternoon, when Isabelle showed just how smart she really was by pushing the plastic slide to the door, climbing to the top, and turning the door handle without falling; even when she got in the bedroom—because, to Danny's surprise, the door wasn't locked—Matthew didn't move or speak or even look at her. His sister managed all this while Danny was in the bathroom, and he came out and discovered her up on Matthew's bed, kneeling next to Matthew's pillow, patting his face. No reaction, not even what Danny expected, which was "Get the hell out."

After that, Danny left Matthew's bedroom door open. He was afraid Isabelle would hurt herself if she kept using the slide to get in, and at least she could see that Danny wasn't keeping her from anything interesting. If Dr. Connelly wanted it shut, he could shut it on one of his trips to the bathroom. He didn't, so he obviously didn't care. Or didn't notice. Or whatever was going on, which Danny really couldn't figure out. He knew that some grown-ups spent days in bed, but those grown-ups were addicts, and Matthew wasn't on anything, Danny was almost sure. Something had happened to him, but what it was Danny didn't know, though he found himself thinking about it, not because he really cared but because it was so strange. On Saturday morning, Matthew had been his usual self: a little tired and grumpy, but smiling and laughing with Isabelle, even throwing her in the air and catching her as she squealed. While he made apple sausages for their breakfast, he ordered Danny around, as always, but he said "Use the Force, Luke" when Danny didn't know how to work the fancy toaster, which was like a joke of some kind from a movie Matthew liked called *Star Wars*. After they were finished eating, he sat down at his computer. When he stood up, he said he had to go see his boss later. For the next few hours he was quieter than usual, but still normal. He came whenever Isabelle called him. He told Danny to brush his teeth and take a shower. He said Hannah was a "lost cause," but he was going to call her again for the afternoon because he didn't have a choice.

When he got home, everything had changed. He stopped being Matthew and became the guy in the bed. He didn't move the rest of Saturday or all day Sunday; he didn't even react on Monday morning when Isabelle came in and discovered the remote control and hit all the buttons until the TV came on, blasting some news channel and scaring her to death. She cried and Danny came in to turn the TV down and find a better show for her to watch. She picked *Teletubbies*, which Matthew had called "Telerubbish" on Friday, but now he said nothing. Isabelle sat next to him and bounced and laughed and talked along with Tinky Winky, Dipsy, Laa-Laa, and Po—and Matthew rolled over. That was it.

Around ten-thirty, his cell phone started ringing, and then his regular phone started ringing, and after that one or the other was ringing constantly, every five minutes or so. Isabelle learned to ignore it somehow, but the ringing drove Danny crazy, and it worried him, too, as he wondered what would happen when Dr. Connelly didn't respond to all this. If anyone came here and saw the way he was just lying in bed, they'd know Matthew wasn't taking care of them and he and Isabelle would be back to where they were before, having to run away or be stuck in foster homes. And someone was going to come here looking for Matthew, Danny was sure of it. When they did, they'd discover his car parked in the garage downstairs, and they'd tell the guard he might be sick or dead or something bad, and the guard would let them in. This was the way the world worked: the people in their house could disappear and no one would notice, but someone like Dr. Connelly would be searched for until he was found. Even if the guy wanted to leave his life behind, he couldn't. His life would bust through the door and get them all.

All afternoon, as the phone kept ringing and ringing, Danny was hoping Amelia would show up first. She'd told Matthew she was going to check on them every few days, and this was the fourth day; why wasn't she here? She could protect them from whatever was about to happen. She could even take them home with her.

When he'd told Amelia he'd rather stay with Matthew, he was thinking how much Isabelle loved it here. But Amelia's house would be okay, too. Wherever they'd be safe.

By seven o'clock, when the phone was still ringing—not as often, but often enough that Danny felt like he would never stop hearing that stupid sound—he decided to call her. She'd given him her cell number before she left on Friday, and told him to call her anytime, day or night. He hoped Matthew wouldn't be mad, but he figured even mad Matthew was better than in-bed Matthew. He hadn't minded the griping, but he sure hated the silence. It was like living with a dead person.

Danny didn't tell Amelia anything except he had a problem, but she said she'd be right over. After he hung up, he decided to go in and tell Matthew what he'd done. He thought it was only fair, but he also had a feeling that if anything would get the guy up, this was it. On Thanksgiving, before Ben and Amelia came over, Matthew had spent more than an hour in the bathroom, blow-drying his hair and putting on cologne and shaving again, even though there was nothing to shave off that Danny could see. Now his face was so stubbly that Isabelle didn't want to touch it anymore. And he smelled, not bad like the people in their house, just a little sweaty, but even that was really noticeable for him since he was such a clean freak. He made them wash up before they ate and after they ate, and he constantly told Danny to blow his nose or wipe his face or change his shirt, even if it just had a tiny stain.

Matthew had been sleeping off and on, but he was awake now and he looked right at Danny when Danny said, "Amelia is coming," loud, like a warning. Matthew rolled over on his stomach and mashed his face into the pillow, but still he didn't say anything. Danny went back into the loft area to clean up some of the toys. He tried to get Isabelle to come with him to help, but she wouldn't budge from her half of Matthew's bed, where she'd arranged all the Barbies against the headboard and was talking to them. He wished he'd made her come with him because when Amelia knocked on the door about twenty minutes later, Matthew got up and shut his bedroom door. After Danny let Amelia in, he told her to wait while he got his sister, and that's when he discovered that Matthew had not just shut the door; he'd locked it.

"Danny?" Amelia said. She'd taken off her coat and she was right behind him, watching him shake the knob.

"Let Isabelle out," he shouted. "You can lock the door again. I promise, we won't come in."

"Matthew has your sister locked in his bedroom?"

"Yeah, but he didn't mean to. I think he was just trying to make sure you didn't see him."

"What?"

"I have to get Isabelle. She's safe in there, but she won't be when she gets bored with her dolls."

Amelia looked at him. "She won't be safe? With Matthew?"

"He's not really there. I mean, he's in there, but he's in bed. He hasn't moved since Saturday. He's not watching Isabelle. He didn't even say anything when she kicked him. Accidentally."

"Matthew!" Amelia knocked several times, much harder than Danny had. "Open this door right now!"

Danny whispered, "He won't do it if he thinks you're coming in."

Her voice stayed loud. "I have to come in. He might have had a heart attack. If he didn't go to work today, something is seriously wrong." She tried to turn the knob, shook it, pounded again. "Matthew, can you hear me?"

A heart attack? Danny hadn't thought of that.

"I'm going to call the police." Amelia was still yelling; she sounded really scared, which scared Danny. "Get them to break the door down and send the paramedics."

"No," Dr. Connelly shouted. "Leave me alone."

At least he said something for the first time in days. Danny felt better, but Amelia said, "It doesn't matter what he wants." She was quieter now, maybe so Matthew couldn't hear her. "We have to make sure he's all right, and we have to get your sister. I still think I have to call for help."

Danny didn't want the police to come if there was any way around it. "I can get the door open," he said. "I'll do it really fast." This lock wasn't a dead bolt; it was the regular push-in knob type. Danny had learned to unlock this kind of lock long before the kid taught him about the nail and the street-sweeper bristle. Some old man used to live in their house who was always shutting the bathroom door with the knob pushed in, so he could come back whenever he wanted and have the bathroom to himself. Danny watched this guy and discovered how easy it was to get in; all you needed was something hard that wouldn't bend, like a credit card.

He told Amelia, and she gave him her Visa. "I won't break it," he said, but she said she didn't care. While he was pushing the card against the latch, Amelia asked him to tell her what happened on Saturday. He told her he didn't know, that Matthew had gone to see his boss and come back like this. Before he could say anything else, the door opened.

Isabelle was fine, but Danny grabbed her and ignored her protests. Amelia came into the room, too, but she hesitated before she walked closer to the bed.

"Get out," Matthew said, but he didn't sound mad. He sounded like . . . nothing. It was creepy, like he'd turned into a zombie. Even Isabelle must have noticed because she stopped complaining and just whimpered.

Amelia came closer. "I just want to help you."

Danny took this opportunity to grab the iPod off the dresser where Isabelle had left it. He wanted to give his sister something to do because he had a hunch Amelia would tell them to go wait in the loft. And he was right; before Amelia sat down on the very edge of the crumply bed, she asked him to take his sister into another room. But she didn't say how far he had to go, so he stopped right outside so Isabelle could still see Matthew while Danny put the iPod earbuds in for her and started it up. His sister had a special playlist that Matthew had made of songs she liked, and Danny tried not to be jealous of the way the guy had basically given Isabelle the precious iPod. It was a good thing at the moment, because his sister sat and listened without moving while Amelia talked to Matthew. Danny sat down, too, and leaned against the wall around the corner, waiting for whatever was going to happen. He didn't care whether Amelia took them to her house or fixed Matthew and left them here, as long as nobody called the cops.

The phone wasn't ringing anymore, he just realized that. He wondered if Matthew had finally turned off his cell when he heard that Amelia was coming over. All day, that stupid cell phone had been ringing at least ten times more often than the other phone. Maybe Matthew was afraid she'd answer and say she was his house-keeper, like she'd done on Friday. Which was so strange Danny couldn't understand it, though listening to her had given him the idea to pretend he couldn't remember the name of a babysitter. It was part of his con, as Matthew called it, and it had worked, though now there was this new big problem. He would be glad when his mom was home.

He was a little bored just sitting there, but it was probably good that he could hear everything Matthew and Amelia were saying. He could never tell what it would help him to know.

"I can't leave until I'm sure you're all right. Maybe I should call Ben. He can at least check you out and make sure you haven't had—"

"It's not a heart attack." After a while, he said, "So you can leave."

She waited a minute, maybe more. "Danny told me you saw your boss on Saturday. And you didn't make it to work today." Another very long pause, and then she said in a completely different voice, "Did you get fired?"

She sounded lighter, happy even, and Danny was completely confused. He knew getting fired was bad. It was worse if you were poor, but it was still bad if you were rich, because then you would be poor unless you got another job before you ran out of money. And even if Dr. Connelly got another job right away, he would still be upset because he loved Astor-Denning. He'd never told Danny that, but he didn't have to; it was like the most obvious thing about the guy. Even when he talked about their commercial his face lit up. When Danny asked if he minded having to see his boss on a Saturday, he said, "No, I always work weekends. I really enjoy my work, as un-American as that sounds." He grinned. "Don't tell the Democrats or they'll have to hold hearings about that, too."

"Yes," Matthew said now. "I got fired."

His voice had changed. He wasn't a zombie, but he wasn't upset, either. He wasn't grumpy like usual or angry like he was when Danny's mom stole his wallet or happy like he was with Isabelle. It was so hard to tell what he was feeling that Danny wondered if he was trying to hide something. Maybe he was lying? It would make sense since he got an awful lot of phone calls for someone who didn't have a job. On the other hand, if he had gotten fired, that would explain why he'd been so weird since Saturday.

"I'm sorry if I can't see this as a bad thing," Amelia said. "You know what I think of that place."

"I do."

She acted like she hadn't heard him. "It's a corrupt company and you'll be better off without any of those people in your life."

"Any of them?" he said quietly. "Are you saying that the forty-one thousand plus people who work for AD around the world are all corrupt?"

"No, I'm sure some of them are fine. It's not the lower-level employees that I have a problem with at any of the Big Pharma companies. The executives are the ones who put profit above the public good. They're the ones I consider evil."

He didn't say anything.

"They have to be evil to do what they do. Don't you think so now that you're out of there and you can see it more clearly?"

He still didn't say anything.

"Well, it just happened. Give yourself some time to adjust. I really think you're going to see that this firing is the best thing that ever happened to you." She paused. "Why did they fire you, anyway? I thought you told me once that Walter Healy would always protect you. Did they get rid of him, too?" She snorted. "It's hard to imagine after what he pulled off in Paris."

"I don't think I told you that. If so, I wish I hadn't."

Right then, Danny knew that Matthew was really mad. His voice when he said "I wish I hadn't" was quiet but incredibly tense, like it was taking everything he had not to scream the words. No wonder he was mad. Amelia didn't understand how he felt about Astor-Denning at all. Even Danny could tell that Matthew didn't mean that question about the forty-one thousand people who worked there. And the way she said the word *evil* about some of the workers, which his mom had told him never to use about anybody, because only God knows who is truly evil. "You can call rich people bastards, but don't call them evil. It's bad karma."

Amelia was bringing a lot of bad karma on herself right now; Danny could feel it. He felt guilty, too, because he'd called her over here to help.

He decided to interrupt them. He stepped over his sister and went into the room. Amelia was sitting on the bed, and Matthew was sitting up now, too, which was good. But he'd moved over to the other corner, where Isabelle had her dolls, like he wanted to be as far away as possible from Amelia. She looked pretty with her pink cheeks and red hair curling down her back, jeans and a white sweater. Matthew still had on the tan pants and blue shirt from Saturday, and they were a wrinkled mess. His knees were pressed against his chest and one arm was resting on his knees, with his face pressed into that elbow. All Danny could see were his eyes, and even they were hard to see because his hair was all bent up from lying down so much, and the front part was hanging down on his forehead.

"I overheard a little," Danny said. "I'm really sorry you got fired." Then he looked at Amelia, hoping she'd take the hint and say something sympathetic, even if she didn't mean it.

"Thanks," Matthew said.

"I'm really sorry," Danny kept trying, "because I know how much you liked working at Astor-Denning. It must be sad not to be able to go there anymore."

Isabelle threw off the iPod and came in, too. She stood near Matthew and said his name, but much more softly than usual, like even she knew that he needed kindness. He picked her up and sat her next to him, but he was still looking at Danny. Finally, he said, "It is sad. You're right. I appreciate that."

Amelia stood up and said she had to go. Danny was desperate for Amelia to say one nice thing to Matthew so she could make up for the bad karma. He walked over to her. "Don't you think it's sad, too?"

"You're such a kind boy," she said, touching Danny's cheek.

"You are," Matthew said. Danny was very surprised. Matthew had never said anything like that to him. After another pause, Matthew said, "But even you can't change everything."

It was like somehow he knew what Danny was trying to do with Amelia. He knew, and he was saying it was hopeless. Which made Danny feel even worse. When Amelia was sick last week, Matthew had carried her to the car and been so nice. Why couldn't she see that he'd been sick for the last two days, even if it wasn't throwing-up-type sick?

Amelia said, "And some things you don't want to change. You're too young to understand, but sometimes it's better to be fired than stay somewhere that's evil."

She said it again! Danny was frantic. He had to get her to stop doing this. "My mom said it's wrong to use the word *evil*."

"Sometimes it is, but sometimes it's so obviously true that you have to say it."

He looked at her. "But you don't know all the people at Astor-Denning. Maybe they're okay." He thought about the equation. "They find cures for people, and that's a good thing."

"It's a lot more complicated than that. Believe me, they've done some very bad things." She patted Danny's hair. "But you shouldn't be thinking about any of this. You're a little boy. You have plenty of time to decide what's right and wrong when you grow up."

Matthew gave him a look and he suddenly remembered that he was supposed to be innocent. "Yeah," he said. "I don't really understand what you were talking about anyway."

Amelia hugged him. "I'm going to take off now. Ben is probably home from the lab."

"Thank you for coming over," Matthew said. "You've helped me more than you know."

"Glad I could do it," she said. Danny was relieved. Finally, one nice thing, but then she ruined it. "But I only came here to check on Danny and Isabelle."

"I assumed as much," Matthew said. And smiled.

If only Amelia had noticed that smile, she would have known how Matthew really felt about what she'd said. If only she'd listened to Danny when he tried to help her get rid of all that bad karma.

After she left, Matthew reached under the bed and pulled out his cell phone. He turned it on and punched some buttons. While he was listening, he said, "Two hundred and eighty-two messages. Christ, how is that possible?"

Danny said, "I don't know. It rang a lot, but not that many times."

"I had it off all day Sunday and the first few hours today." He shut the phone. "I don't know why I turned it on when I did. Must have been suffering from a bizarre impulse to punish myself."

Isabelle was pushing a Barbie into his hand. He took it. "Want me to rip her head off?" he said, looking at her.

"No!" she said, but she laughed.

Danny sat down on the floor. "Did you really get fired?"

Matthew shook his head. "I only told Amelia that because I couldn't trust her with what really happened." He paused. "But I will tell you. A good friend of mine is dying."

"That sucks," Danny said.

"It does." He looked at Danny. "I don't think I've heard you say *sucks* before. Fine by me, but don't do it around Amelia. She'll think I'm a bad influence, even recruiting you into my spooky cult of evil."

"I know you're not really evil." Even though his friend was dying, Matthew was tickling Isabelle's foot. No one who treated his sister this good could be that bad.

"Thank you. I consider myself a decent enough guy; not perfect, but hardly the reincarnation of Satan." He asked Isabelle if she was hungry and she said yes even though Danny had fed her dinner. "I'm starving," he said to her. "Let's go in the kitchen and see what's available."

Danny followed them to ask if Matthew was planning to do something to get back at Amelia.

"You are quick," Matthew said. He and Isabelle were looking in the refrigerator; his sister was pointing at her favorite cheese. "I wouldn't say I'm doing it to get back at her, but I admit, she won't be happy about it." He handed Isabelle a slice of cheese and glanced at Danny. "Since I know you have tender feelings for the Pain in the Ass, let me assure you that she brought this on herself when she tried to blackmail me."

He wasn't sure what *blackmail* meant, but he knew Amelia had brought it on herself. Still, he thought about sneaking the phone into the bathroom and calling her again, to warn her. In the end, he decided not to because though he liked Amelia, Matthew was here and she wasn't. It was as simple as that.

After Matthew and Isabelle had eaten cheese and two bananas and several cookies, he sat down at his computer, just like the last two days hadn't happened. "Banging out email," he said. He had the cell phone hooked up to headphones so he could listen to all the voice messages, too. Isabelle was watching cartoons. Danny was keeping an eye on her while trying to figure out the Game Boy.

"What do you think?" Matthew said, pushing down the headphones. "Should I call today my personal multidimensional agile enterprise summit?"

"I don't know what it means."

"Neither do I, but hopefully they'll think it's a cutting-edge leadership approach." He shook his head. "Knowing Knolton, he'll claim he invented the idea. He always says he knew the world was flat before Thomas Friedman."

"That's a really weird thing to say." Danny knew for sure that the world wasn't flat. He'd learned that in kindergarten.

"He's an asshole." Matthew shrugged. "But I'm going to have to learn to tolerate him. Until I can get rid of him, which won't be long. Want to bet I can get rid of him in a year?"

"No."

Matthew accused him of being scared to lose, but that wasn't why. Danny was thinking he wouldn't be here in a year, so he couldn't know if he won.

He figured out the Game Boy controls, but he kept dying because he couldn't get Mega Man to kill the first robot. It was frustrating and not very much fun. He wondered how the thief kid in their house could sit and play his Game Boy Advance for hours.

"I'm going to watch cartoons with Isabelle," he said.

Matthew didn't hear him; he had the headphones on again. Danny couldn't see a reason to repeat himself. He wasn't sure why he'd told Matthew where he was going in the first place.

He went to his sister and she sat in his lap while they watched *Fairly OddParents*. She watched the show, but he was busy thinking about everything that had happened. He'd been at Matthew's house almost two weeks now. Isabelle had changed completely, but he didn't feel that different. Maybe it was harder to change when you were older. He dreamed about his mom almost every night. He kept wondering how she was doing, wishing he could call her, wishing she would call them, though he knew she didn't have the number. After Matthew was back to normal for a few days, Danny was going to ask him if they were allowed to call Changes to check on his mom. He'd made a calendar, and he was marking off the days. Six down, twenty-four to go. For the next twenty-four days, if he kept being super nice to Matthew, maybe the guy would help his mom get an apartment and even a job. If only she could work at Astor-Denning—answering phones, filing, something. She had a lot of skills, or she used to have them, before her habit got so bad that she stopped working. She'd never liked any of the jobs she had back then, but maybe she'd like it if she could work there. Maybe she'd stay away from her drug addict friends and hang out with people like Matthew and Ben and Amelia, who were sort of weird, but so lucky. They all had nice clothes and great coats and thick gloves and money and credit cards and houses and food. Amelia could go to the hospital and get right in, rather than waiting on a bench moaning like so many other people in the ER. Matthew could spend a workday in bed and not be fired. Ben could even get a job on Thanksgiving, when hardly any jobs were open.

They had no idea how incredibly easy they had it. No wonder it was so tough to beg from normal people. They were so caught up in their own problems. He'd always thought they couldn't see him and his mom and Isabelle, but now he knew it was worse. They couldn't see themselves, either. They never got to sit back and think everything is fine now. Life is good.

At the moment, Danny was feeling pretty much like that. Isabelle was in his lap; he could smell her hair. It always smelled good now that she took a daily bath. He put his arms around her and she leaned against him, like the old days. She let him kiss her and she said, "Danny." Then she pointed at the little fairies on the show. And he said, "I see them."

"Poof!" Isabelle said, when the woman fairy used her wand to change a boy into an older kid who could drive a motorcycle.

He could hear Matthew typing away and talking on the phone now. He heard him say "Cassie." He heard him laugh.

"Life is good," he tried. If only his mom were there, it would be.

CHAPTER THIRTEEN

Heroes of the Twenty-first Century

Though Amelia had never heard of Danny's bad karma theory, she still knew something bad had happened to her that night. She worked so hard to keep it from meaning anything, but her life kept conspiring against her.

When Matthew was locked in his room and she thought he'd had a heart attack or a stroke, her fear was all too real, though she knew she'd feel this way about anybody: a neighbor, a friend, and, yes, someone from her past like Matthew. She didn't get worried about her own response until it struck her that he'd been fired, and then her anger was so sudden and intense it was like she'd been transported back to when they'd lived together. She took it personally, that he was finally doing the one thing she'd wanted all along; he was leaving that stupid company. Now, when it was years too late.

She was sitting on the bed with him. He looked dejected, but also vulnerable and strangely younger, like the guy in Baltimore who'd called her "little red-haired girl." She didn't decide to hurt him, but she had to distance herself from the sudden overwhelming sense that she didn't understand her own emotions. She couldn't show how she really felt about him being fired, so she chose a reaction that would make sense. She acted happy about it. She acted like it was a purely good thing, because, after all, it was. Her personal reaction was irrelevant. A smart man was leaving an evil corporation. That was obviously a reason to celebrate.

She knew Matthew was depressed about leaving AD, but unfortunately, his feelings didn't make her think he was a die-hard pharma sleazebag, still wishing he could spin lies to market his overpriced products to the unsuspecting public. His sadness made her feel sorry for him—and that infuriated her. Why should she feel bad for him? He had so much money now and the rest of his life to do exactly as he pleased. If he wanted to get married, he could; if he wanted children, he could have a dozen of them. Waiting all these years to leave that company hadn't hurt him in the slightest. And it hadn't hurt her, it couldn't have, unless she had some kind of unresolved feelings, which would mean she was losing her mind.

After she left, she thought she'd handled it as well as she could have under the circumstances. She didn't regret saying she'd come over only to check on Danny and Isabelle; why should she? It was just like Matthew saying he was only taking care of her for Ben. They were nothing to each other anymore, and that was the truth. Everything else was confusion, probably caused by the hormones that were making her breasts ache and her stomach churn and her mind an emotional wreck.

Since she and Ben had checked into the Philly hotel on Saturday, she'd been crying off and on for all kinds of reasons: because she missed her tiny staff, her friends, even her apartment in Brooklyn. Of course she'd been traveling for months with Ben, but this was different. The man she'd fallen in love with had been busy raising money to vaccinate children against malaria, but between the speeches and dealing with the media, he'd still had time to talk to her. Now he was back in the lab again, doing work he loved. He was happier than she'd ever seen him, which would have been great if he was ever home. On Sunday, he went in at six-thirty in the morning and came back after nine, when she was already asleep. He woke her up to tell her how well it was going. Richard was giving him everything he needed to get started. Monday, the day Danny called, she hadn't heard from Ben all day. She forced herself to wait up for him until ten-thirty, even though she had to splash water on her face to stay awake. (Her constant exhaustion was normal, according to her gynecologist, and caused by the surge in progesterone, according to Ben.) When he finally came home at a few minutes after eleven, she couldn't even rouse herself to tell him that Matthew had been fired. As the days went by and she didn't say anything about it, she might have worried what her silence meant, if she and Ben had ever had time to really talk.

For a full week it went on like this, but she told herself the first week had to be an exception. But then the next Monday, the day Ben had agreed to take off so they could spend it together, looking for a house, he left at six-thirty in the morning again. When she woke up she was confused, reaching for him across the king-size hotel bed, finding nothing, not even a note. At eleven-thirty she decided to take a break from her own work and take him lunch and find out what was going on. The hotel was on the Penn campus; she walked over to the deli and bought them sandwiches, spinach and turkey and provolone, which she knew he liked. She even went to a bakery to get butterscotch brownies, his favorite.

When she got to the lab she saw a group of twentysomethings at the benches, preparing vials and plates. Probably grad students or postdocs. She went down the hall and found Ben and Richard in a conference room. They were both talking animatedly, and Ben was standing at the chalkboard, writing furiously in an unreadable code of circles and arrows and letters, obviously trying to convince Richard of something. She waited a while, but when it looked like this wasn't going to end anytime soon, she stepped inside. "Ben?"

He turned around and smiled. "Babe, hey, what are you doing here?"

"I brought you lunch." She idiotically held up the deli bag. "I thought we could eat together."

"Oh. I can't stop for lunch yet. Do you mind waiting?"

Before she could answer, Richard told Ben, "Let's quit for a while." He laughed. "I can use the break to figure out where you're wrong."

"Fine," Ben said, and he laughed, too. He picked up his coffee and took Amelia's hand. "Want to eat in my new office?"

He took her around the corner. The office didn't have his nameplate yet, but someone had taped up a large index card reading "Benjamin Watkins, MD, PhD." It wasn't Ben's handwriting, but Ben had taped up one of his favorite sayings: "Experiments must be reproducible: they should fail the same way every time."

Inside, the office looked uninhabited. The phone wasn't hooked up yet. The walls were bare. Even the whiteboard had nothing on it. Ben's laptop was on the desk, still in its case, and the bookshelves contained nothing except one of Ben's notebooks and an unopened box of pens. The picture she'd given him of her was back at the hotel. He kept forgetting to take it with him.

"Good sandwich," he said. "Thanks." He was obviously hungry because he ate it and the brownie quickly. Unless he was trying to hurry back to Richard.

She asked him what had happened to their plan to look for a house. "I'm so sorry. I completely forgot." His voice was sincere. "How about this weekend? Will that work?"

She nodded, but she was still annoyed and she impulsively decided to go ahead and ask him the other, bigger question that had been haunting her since she found out she was pregnant. It was the wrong time to bring this up, but she wondered if there would ever be a right time in the foreseeable future.

She started off carefully, reasonably. "When I was in the hospital on Thanksgiving, I had a very large copay. The insurance I have for myself and my staff is really only for catastrophic illness. It won't even pay for my obstetrician."

He was sitting at his desk with his hands folded, but one or both of his feet were tapping against the floor. She could feel the vibrations. He said, "We'll have to get you a better insurance policy."

"The easiest way to do that is for us to get married. HUP is giving you great benefits."

"I see your point, but I don't think better insurance is a reason to get married."

She tried not to sound angry. "How about that I'm having your child?"

"I don't know if that's a good reason to get married, either. It may be, but I—"

"How about love?" She couldn't help it; she was both angry and really hurt. "That is, if you still love me."

"Why would you say that? You know I do. But I told you about my parents' divorce. It was a nightmare. I'm just trying to ensure we don't make a mistake."

Ben was thirteen when his parents divorced, and it was true, the divorce was horrible. His father, a biology professor, had gone on "sabbatical" to Las Vegas and developed a serious gambling problem; Ben had seen him only one time since, years ago, an uncomfortable reunion that Ben preferred not to talk about. His mom had to support three children on her salary as a middle-school librarian. They lost their house and moved into a tiny apartment. His two sisters hadn't even finished college because they didn't get scholarships and they couldn't manage working and going to school part-time. His older sister, Diane, worked at Home Depot. His younger sister, Melissa, was on disability because she'd hurt her back in a warehouse. Both of them had already been married—and both were divorced. Diane had two boys. Melissa was engaged to a new man Ben had never met. All of them still lived in the tiny college town in Kansas where Ben grew up. Amelia had never been there, though she assumed that would change now that they were in the States for a while. At the very least, when the baby was born.

"You can never be sure," Amelia said, because she believed this. "Love doesn't work that way."

"I can be surer than I am now. We haven't even lived together in one place for more than a few weeks. We have to give ourselves time to adjust to living and working together here in Philly. Find a place. Settle down. Get through this pregnancy and then decide."

She sat back and stared at him. "You want to wait until after our baby is born?"

"I don't know. Can you give me some time to think about this? I'm really focused on getting myself online here in the lab." He reached over and took her hand. His foot was tapping against the desk now; the thumping sound echoed in the empty room. "I know you believe in the work Richard and I are trying to do. Trypanosomiasis is a disease that afflicts only the world's poor. It deserves my full attention right now, don't you think?"

She said yes, but she wanted to say "What about me, Ben? Do I deserve any of your attention? I'm not an interesting problem, but I do need you, and waking me up to talk a little about your work and have sex isn't my idea of a relationship."

But she couldn't say any of that because Richard was standing in the doorway. "Can I borrow Ben back? I may have thought of something he hasn't considered." He laughed. "A miracle."

And off they went, leaving Amelia in the ugly, empty office to finish her sandwich and a brownie she didn't even like that much. While she was sitting there, she gave in and let herself think about Matthew. He'd always wanted her to come to lunch with him at Astor-Denning, but she never would. Maybe he'd felt like she did right now: rejected and alone.

Ever since that night at Matthew's, she'd been at war with herself, trying not to see any positive qualities in him. She'd spent days forcing herself to focus on the crimes of Astor-Denning, and Matthew's own crimes while he worked for them. She even made a list of AD's misdeeds, which included:

1) Not only creating patient advocacy groups like Pain Matters, but extensively funding existing patient groups to use them to persuade the general public that arguably rare diseases like adult ADD were actually widely undiagnosed and exclusively neurobiological in origin—that is, treatable only with drugs.

2) Enlisting the media in all their causes, including hiring celebrities to go on talk shows and talk about their high cholesterol or bone loss or whatever and how it was "cured" by one of AD's medicines. The public had no idea that these talk show appearances were really paid advertisements.

3) Downplaying clinical trial results that showed that any of their drugs didn't work. Using "thought leaders" to sign off on ghostwritten scientific articles that emphasized some trivial benefit of one of their drugs, while ignoring the fact that the drug wasn't much better than a sugar pill for the disease it supposedly treated.

And on and on. Amelia's list was eleven pages long—and this was without the dozens of additional crimes listed in the "contingencies and liabilities" section of AD's own annual report. Matthew loved to point out that it was normal for pharmaceutical companies to be sued constantly by consumers, and maybe it was true, but what about the federal and state civil and criminal investigations into everything from their marketing practices to kickbacks and antitrust? Naturally AD's annual report boasted that every action against them was "without merit" and would be "vigorously defended against," but somehow, every year, they still paid millions in government fines. But why should this stop them? Even the largest government fines levied against pharmaceutical companies weren't significant compared to the billions in profit. In this way Big Pharma was like the mafia: gladly paying off governments around the world so they could continue on their merry way, doing whatever they wanted.

And Matthew had not been some low-level "innocent" at Astor-Denning, no matter what he was implying with his question about their forty-one thousand employees. In retrospect, Palm Beach really had been the beginning of his rise to power, despite what he'd said at the time. Galvenar was now AD's biggest-selling drug, and Matthew had won several industry awards for launching it. That he'd somehow had time to run his "alliances" division, too, and even be involved with Galvenar's clinical trials (according to Ben) was just more proof that Matthew was an incredibly ambitious guy who really could have ended up being the head of that company someday. Meaning, or so Amelia had always thought, that she'd obviously been right to break up with him. If Big Pharma was like the mafia, then Matthew was like AD's Michael Corleone in *The Godfather*.

But what if Michael Corleone had left the business? Would Kay, his ex, have found herself feeling so incredibly confused? Could she have even found herself comparing the good man she lived with now to the corrupt guy she'd escaped, as Amelia did as she walked back to the hotel?

Admittedly, at that moment, it was hard not to compare Matthew's attitude about marriage to Ben's. They were the only two men she'd ever lived with, and Matthew had actually wanted to marry her. He'd even bought her a beautiful engagement ring before that Christmas party when he'd planned to ask her. He'd tried to give it to her a few weeks later, during dinner at their favorite seafood restaurant in Center City. He said, "You don't have to tell me yes right now. Wear it for a while and see if it persuades you." She was annoyed, thinking he was suggesting that the mere sight of an expensive ring on her finger could affect her judgment about something as important as marriage. Now, unfortunately, she could see another possibility. Maybe he'd been afraid she would say no.

Even when they were arguing constantly, Matthew would have married her if she'd gotten pregnant. She knew this because the subject had come up only a few weeks before Palm Beach. Her period was even later than usual, and he said if she really turned out to be pregnant this time they would get married right away so he could put her on his insurance. Ironically enough, she'd told Matthew she wasn't going to get married for such a flimsy reason.

"Insurance is a flimsy reason?" He was in the shower; she was sitting on the clothes hamper, straining to hear him. "Since when? You're always going on about the need for a national health-care system."

"I have my own money."

"Good for you, but if something goes wrong and the baby is premature, your entire trust fund could be wiped out trying to pay the hospital bills."

"It's a risk I'm willing to take rather than get married when we're not happy."

"And the baby?" He stepped out and grabbed a towel, which he threw around his waist. "I suppose you'll raise our baby without a father, too?"

"I could do that," she said, but her voice wavered. "If I had to."

"But you don't have to, and you know it." He walked over to the hamper. "Look, if you are pregnant, we'll just have to figure out how to be happy. We can do that for little Egor or Brunhilda, can't we?"

She didn't say anything, but she couldn't help smiling. He'd been joking about naming them Egor and Brunhilda forever.

A few days later, when her period started, she was alone and crying, knowing they wouldn't be forced to figure out how to be happy. No Egor or Brunhilda, just the two of them, fighting their way to the inevitable end.

Now, sitting in the hotel, staring at email she didn't have the energy to answer, it struck her how easily Matthew had said "our baby." Ben called the baby "it" or "the pregnancy." She told herself this didn't mean anything, but it was hard not to feel like it was somehow depressingly significant.

She did a long blog post about Big Pharma's newest ridiculous arguments against reforming the Medicare drug program, but her heart wasn't in it. What was she doing in this hotel in West Philadelphia when she'd loved living in New York? What if she'd made the worst mistake of her life? She wanted Ben's baby, but she wanted Ben, too. Maybe it wasn't enough that he was a good person if he never had time to be with her.

Around five, she tried calling him and telling him she wanted to go out for dinner. He said he'd be there by eight-thirty; she reminded him she was pregnant and couldn't wait that long to eat or she'd get nauseated. He mentioned that there was a good Italian restaurant downstairs, and she thanked him for his kind suggestion. He didn't hear the sarcasm and said, "See you soon, babe."

Unfortunately, he came home late again. She was already in bed and he joined her, saying he was worn out, too, but then he was so jittery and restless that it took him forever to fall asleep. When she finally drifted off, his light was still on and he was still leaning against the headboard, chewing his lip, scrawling page after page in his notebook. The next day, Tuesday, when he came in at nine-thirty, so exhausted he couldn't even tell her anything beyond how exhausted he was, she couldn't help asking if Richard was spending fifteen-hour days in the lab, too. When Ben said no, because his wife "didn't understand the mission," Amelia started crying. Ben was obviously surprised, but he held her and said he was so lucky to have found his soul mate. She was about to ask him if they could go downstairs to the restaurant and have dessert when she realized he was already asleep. She took off his Doc Martens and sat them under the chair where he'd thrown his coat, so he could find them in the morning; then she went downstairs and ordered a slice of strawberry cheesecake. But after one bite, her stomach felt queasy and she left the rest untouched.

On Wednesday she woke up extremely depressed, but she tried to make the best of it. She talked on the phone with her assistant Ethan. She emailed Sara for an update on the Galvenar situation in Jakarta. She walked to the campus bookstore and bought books about pregnancy. She worked on an article about an NIMH doctor who'd accepted hundreds of thousands of dollars from Pfizer in "consulting" fees. But by afternoon she was still profoundly lonely, and it took everything she had not to walk over to Matthew's apartment to check on Danny and Isabelle.

She had good reasons to be concerned about those children. What if Matthew had gone back into his depression and the kids were in trouble? What if he was thinking of breaking his deal with her, now that he no longer worked at AD? True, Danny probably would have called her, but what if all three of them just needed cheering up, like she herself did? Would it really be so bad to spend the afternoon at Matthew's place?

Yes, of course it would. If she couldn't control her mind, she absolutely would control her behavior. So she sat in the hotel, trying not to think about him—and failing, again, still. Around dinnertime, she blinked and saw him standing at the stove in Baltimore, holding out a spoon of soup, saying, "For you, I have included zee fresh mushrooms. Taste and tell chef if it pleaseth mademoiselle." She reminded herself that Matthew was the only person who had cooked for her since childhood, and even her dreams were about food these days. She knew her mind was telling her to eat more. If only she could. She was ravenously hungry and it seemed so unfair that almost everything—certainly everything good—made her sick.

But most of these memories had nothing to do with food, meaning there was no way to explain them away. She was taking a bath when she suddenly remembered him taking her to the oral surgeon's office when she had her wisdom teeth removed. She'd been scared of the anesthesia and Matthew said he'd try to talk them into letting him stay with her during the surgery. "Just in case the dentist is a serial killer," he said. She knew he was making fun of her, but still, he convinced the oral surgeon that he had to stay with his girlfriend, and the last thing she remembered as she was counting backward from a hundred was Matthew smiling at her, holding her hand.

She was trying to work on an editorial when she found herself thinking about the day they moved into their little rental house in the Philadelphia suburbs. Matthew had just carried her across the threshold when they discovered a woman from the rental agency waiting in the living room to take them on a walk-through and give them a copy of the signed lease. With a completely straight face Matthew told the agent, "We left her wheelchair in the car. I have to go get it." The poor woman stammered out something sympathetic and Matthew set Amelia down. "A miracle! This house has healed her!" Amelia hit him, but she was laughing so hard her sides hurt.

Could hormones really cause all this? Or was it possible that just being back in Philadelphia, his city, was driving her crazy? Why couldn't she control this? Even Thanksgiving night at his apartment was being completely reinterpreted in her mind—against her will. She kept seeing him holding Isabelle as he made Ben's drink, hearing him talk to Danny when they were leaving for the hospital, hearing him joking with both of the kids while he was strapping Isabelle in the backseat of his car. He made taking care of them look so easy. Even in the midst of his depression about being fired, when Isabelle said his name, he picked her up and sat her next to him on the bed. Somehow Matthew had already won over not only the little girl, but also Danny, who obviously felt bad that Matthew had lost his job. How odd that Matthew seemed to have some kind of natural ability with children. Ben, on the other hand, had almost zero interest in Danny or Isabelle. He'd barely spoken to them when she'd left for her walk with Matthew, and when she got back, Ben was sitting on the couch, reading some medical journal, and the kids were watching television. "Danny said they were fine," Ben told her. "There was nothing for me to do."

Wednesday night when he came home, late as always, but awake enough to talk, Amelia admitted that she was feeling desperate and half crazy. "I have to see you more often," she said. "It's been almost two weeks. I can't live like this."

He said he understood. "I'm taking the whole day off on Sunday." He was sitting in the chair next to the bed, but Amelia was watching his feet, which never stopped moving, tapping a hyperrhythm against the floor. "I promise, we can look for a house then, and do whatever else you want." He smiled. "I've missed you, too."

When she woke up on Thursday, she felt like she was in prison. The hotel room was pleasant enough, but she was sick of seeing the same beige/brown walls, the same floral bedspread, the same skinny desk and chairs, the same gold mirror, green-striped curtains, and green rug. She was sick of opening the minibar for juice, sick of the crackers and rice cakes she had to munch on constantly for nausea. Of course she could fight her way down a street crammed with students to find something else to eat, but she'd probably throw it up anyway, so what was the point? She needed to get out of there, but it was raining and cold and she couldn't think of anywhere worth going. She'd never liked shopping. She had no friends in this city. The tourist attractions like the Art Museum and the Franklin Institute were steeped in memories of Matthew, since he'd taken her to all those places the first year they lived here. Even thinking about the Art Museum made her think of the Chagall print they'd picked out in the museum store: *Birthday*. Their first framed painting. It was a perfect domestic scene: a small house with richly colored furnishings, a woman holding a bouquet of flowers and a man floating above her, leaning his head down to kiss her.

When she turned on the television in the middle of the day, she felt a little guilty for not working, but she had to have some distraction from the gloom that was threatening to overtake her. She planned to watch a movie, but first she flipped to CNBC to see how the pharma stocks were doing, and that's when she saw him. On the left side of the screen, Matthew, and standing next to him, one of the creepiest guys in the pharma universe, the AD CEO, Harold Knolton. The headline read: DR. MATTHEW CONNELLY APPOINTED EXECUTIVE VICE PRESIDENT OF INTERNATIONAL PHARMACEUTICALS, REPLACING TWENTY-EIGHT-YEAR ASTOR-DENNING VETERAN WALTER R. HEALY.

Amelia forced herself not to move or breathe as the reporter standing outside Astor-Denning corporate headquarters talked about the press conference that had just ended. In what the reporter called an "unusual move," Matthew had begun his speech by saying he would bring more "transparency and openness" to Astor-Denning's relationship with the public. They cut to a video clip of Matthew: "My first priority will be to communicate more effectively the kind of company Astor-Denning is. Despite what you may have heard about big pharmaceutical companies, we're not the enemy. We don't make firearms or alcohol or tobacco. Quite the opposite. Our scientists are innovators trying to find new means to treat gun wounds and alcoholism and pulmonary disease. We are passionate about our research and development; we are a science-centered company whose business is saving lives. As a socially responsible citizen of the global community, we are committed to the health of patients who rely on our medicines and to our company's mandate to operate with absolute integrity. All of our employees know we will not tolerate any deviation from our company's strict ethical guidelines."

Back to the reporter, who told the anchor what an effective speaker Dr. Connelly was: making several self-deprecating remarks, including one about his own resumé, that he'd finished medical school but never practiced medicine. The reporter also said that Dr. Connelly had "put his money where his mouth is" by being "open" about a recently discovered breach of ethics. The PR company that had launched their blockbuster drug, Galvenar, had apparently created the grassroots patient advocacy group Pain Matters. The PR firm claimed full responsibility, and Astor-Denning was investigating the situation. Another clip of Matthew: "But let me stress that because I hired this firm, I am ultimately responsible. I ask the several thousand legitimate pain patients who have joined Pain Matters to bear with me until I can uncover all the details of this troubling situation. I would also like to thank bioethicist Amelia Johannsen for bringing this important issue to my personal attention."

The reporter went on to the bigger news that Harold Knolton had announced that in the next few months, Astor-Denning would file NDAs (new drug applications) for two "first-in-class" medicines: one for schizophrenia and the other for diabetes. Of course the stock was already climbing and the reporter predicted that Astor-Denning would close the year as the big winner among the pharma giants. Blah, blah, blah about money and the market, but Amelia was already sitting at the hotel desk, desperately searching the web for a video of the entire speech, or at least a transcript. CNBC didn't have it; the newsroom page on AD's website didn't, either, though she did notice that Matthew's picture and bio were already up on the executive leadership page.

And to think she'd actually felt sorry for that lying bastard.

She googled herself, and it was even worse than she feared. Reuters had just reported on the press conference and, unfortunately, they mentioned that she had been credited with uncovering the problem with Pain Matters. Meaning it would be in a thousand newspapers by tomorrow. And everyone in the ethics community would think she was "consulting" for Astor-Denning. Why else would she tell an AD exec about it rather than the press? How could she even defend herself? What if the *Times* reporter revealed that she'd called him but then refused to share the story? God, it would look as though she'd taken a bribe or even accepted a job in that creepy company's "ethics" department.

She emailed her small staff to tell them to expect to hear from reporters. And to tell them to say that she had never taken any money from Astor-Denning and never would. Immediately she received an answer from Ethan, asking if she really had discussed their "two years of confidential research" on Pain Matters with an executive from Astor-Denning. She wrote saying yes, unfortunately, that was true, but she didn't explain. She also asked him not to share that fact with reporters.

Then she called Ben. When she asked if he was busy, he said yes, but thankfully he added, "Never too busy for you."

She started to tell him about Matthew's promotion, but he said he already knew about it. "He called me yesterday to talk about a speech he has to give. He's trying to get AD to pump an extra nine billion dollars into R and D. He wants to turn it into a science center and—"

She had to interrupt; she couldn't stand to hear him talking about this like it was a good thing. "Ben, he named me in the speech. He said I'd told him about an ethics violation at AD. It's already been picked up by one of the wire services."

"What ethics violation?"

"It doesn't matter. Don't you see? It looks like I'm working for them now."

"Hold on," Ben said to someone else. Amelia could hear talking in the background. Then he said, "Are you saying that he lied about you to the press?"

He sounded angry for her, and tears sprang to her eyes.

"Yes and no," she said, sniffing. "I mean, I did tell him about it, but of course he already knew. I just said I wouldn't make it public if he'd keep the kids. I was worried about Danny and Isabelle having to—"

"You tried to blackmail Matt?" He sounded very surprised, and she was suddenly nervous.

"I wouldn't call it that," she said slowly. "I just wanted those kids to be safe."

"But you were willing to suppress your research?"

"Not really. Just until their mother came home."

"I don't understand. Matt said their mother will be back before the end of the month. Why did you think he'd agree to this?"

She swallowed hard. "Because I told him I'd suppress it forever."

"You lied to him, too?"

His voice was pure disapproval and she felt like she'd been slapped. She wanted to defend herself, to scream that Matthew had obviously blackmailed them in Paris, but she knew this would only lead back to the argument they'd had on the plane, when Ben had insisted that Matthew had kept her off the panel not to protect his drug but to protect Ben's reputation and the work of the foundation. If she said that Matthew lied constantly, so what possible difference did it make if she lied to him, Ben wouldn't believe it. And even if he did, he would say that Matthew didn't have the same values as they did. Which was true.

"I thought I was doing the right thing." She paused and pushed her fingers over her eyes. "Ben, please, you have to back me up on this. If you don't, I'm not sure I can handle it."

He was silent for a little too long. By the time he said, "I will," she had already shut down her laptop. When he hung up, she got out her smaller suitcase. It took her only ten minutes to pack up a few essentials. She was in a cab on the way to the train station when her cell phone rang.

She was hoping it would be Ben, but she was still glad to hear from Danny. She was worried about those kids, knowing there was no way Matthew could take care of them now that he'd gotten this promotion and, of course, no reason for him to hold up his end of the bargain anymore. No one would care about her version of the Pain Matters story. They'd think it was like an AD press release, so why not use the real press release instead?

She'd just made up her mind that she'd postpone her trip if necessary to take in Danny and Isabelle until their mother was better when Danny surprised her and said he and his sister were fine. Matthew had moved them into a great house in the suburbs. They had a nice nanny named Mrs. Linnas. Everything was good.

"So you just called to say hello?" Amelia asked. She handed the fare and a tip to the cabdriver and got out at 30th Street Station.

"Yeah," the little boy said. "And to find out if you're okay."

"That's very sweet," she said, before she thought of something. "Did Matthew tell you to call me this afternoon?"

"Yeah," Danny said. "He said you might be upset."

"Well, I always like to talk to you," Amelia said evenly. "Would you mind giving Matthew a message for me? Tell him I appreciate his concern. Also, tell him Jakarta."

Danny repeated the word until he had the pronunciation right. Then he said, "What does it mean?"

"It's a place a long way from here. But Matthew will know why I said it."

Sara, her assistant, was flying home from Jakarta in the morning. Now that Amelia would be back in Brooklyn, she could meet Sara tomorrow night to discuss the odd fact that Sara had uncovered. It might be nothing, but it might be enough to scare Matthew into tipping his hand about whatever he had on Ben. On Saturday, Amelia planned to head over to a hospital on Long Island that had done an extensive Phase 3 study on Galvenar. She'd spoken to the principal investigator a few years ago and he'd done nothing but sing the drug's praises. But she'd gotten a tip that some of the nurses who'd managed the study didn't agree, and Ethan had managed to unearth a list of all the participating RNs. All she had to do was find one of the unhappy ones who would agree to talk to her, which shouldn't be too hard. Most people were desperate for someone to listen and take them seriously. Amelia knew that all too well.

Before she got on the train to New York, she picked up a newsmagazine because the cover blared: PREDICTING THE FUTURE OF THE 21ST CENTURY. The article was short on predictions, though it did have an advertising pullout that profiled ten people who they called "Heroes for the New Century." Number two on the list was Ben.

They called him "a man on fire" and said he routinely spent all day, every day, pitting his mind against the greatest challenges in medicine. They also noted that he always had a cup of coffee in his hand and that he drank at least a dozen cups a day to remain alert and stay focused.

All of the new-century heroes drank coffee, which wasn't surprising since a national coffee retailer had sponsored the pull-out. How Ben got in this advertisement, Amelia had no idea. She thought of his jumping feet and constant caffeine jitters, but she didn't laugh. Ben really was a hero; she never doubted it. He was working fifteen-hour days because he loved the lab, but also because he really cared about the diseases of the poor. Unfortunately, living with a hero had turned out to be a lot harder than she'd ever imagined.

Before she'd left the hotel, she'd written him a note. "Call me when you have time to see me. I have to leave and try to save my career."

She wasn't angry anymore, and the hurt was fading, too, but she was still glad she was doing this. She was tired of being confused. It was time to find out the truth.

CHAPTER FOURTEEN

Humpty Dumpty Is Not a Good Egg

I t was unseasonably warm in December, meaning only one thing (other than global warming): more golf. Matthew loved the game, but he quickly discovered that playing with his new boss, Harold Knolton, was like being kicked in the groin repeatedly while being expected to keep up his end of the dullest small talk on the planet. How (gasp) is (hey, that really hurts) your (not again!) wife? That's (turning pale) good (intense swearing burns hole in head) to (sniffing back unmanly tears at testicle eulogy) hear.

The first insult to Matthew's pride was Harold's unprecedented and stunningly lazy insistence on riding in a golf cart, meaning of course that Matthew had to ride with him, which was like riding on the short bus, complete with stares and snickers from all those with normal abilities, in this case everyone else on the course, including one man who was hobbling on a cast and another who looked about ninety. If that wasn't bad enough, Knolton refused to bet even the nominal twenty dollars that Matthew usually suggested when playing with his own employees, because, as Harold put it, betting, though a time-honored tradition in golf, really didn't belong in a "gentleman's game." He actually dared to call it that though he routinely and cavalierly violated the most sacred rule of that game: to play with absolute integrity. Golf was the only sport where players regularly called penalties on themselves. It really was a game of character and honesty (yes, even when played by people who had neither), and no one Matthew had ever golfed with—not the most corrupt doctor, not the slickest PR person, not the most fiercely competitive team from another pharma—had ever cheated, much less as shamelessly as the asshole Harold Knolton.

Matthew couldn't say anything when Harold lifted his ball out of the bushes and dropped it ten feet closer to the hole. He couldn't object when Harold consistently left out one or even two of his strokes when computing his score. He couldn't even complain when Harold claimed to have finished a par-five hole in two, which had to be physically impossible after dribbling the ball off the tee.

Walter had warned him that Harold cheated at golf and poker. "Ignore it," Walter said. "Don't contradict him, and don't win." While Matthew managed the first part, admittedly with great difficulty, the second part was as incomprehensible to him as Japanese and all the other languages he should have mastered by now. Simply put, he didn't know how to *not win*. He could lose, and he did on a regular basis, but only after he'd played, and playing was defined as doing his best—that is, trying to win.

Knolton should have won anyway with all his cheating, but somehow Matthew came in with an almost perfect game (crushed testicle rebellion?). He was a gracious winner and Knolton, amazingly, seemed to be a gracious loser. As they went into the club bar, Harold was still keeping up his mind-numbing small talk about his family and his horses and his yacht, but Matthew was relieved, knowing it was almost over. Then, all of a sudden, Knolton changed direction and brought up Matthew's least favorite topic, the RIF or "reduction in force."

It was considered bad form to talk about work at the club, but sometimes it was necessary; however, this was decidedly not one of those times. In the last week, Matthew had already spent a million stressful hours in conference calls with the executive team discussing the consultants' recommendations to reduce the size of the U.S. workforce. Most of the team agreed that substantial layoffs could be a disaster for the company's productivity, not to mention employee morale. Especially if they closed one of the research sites, which Knolton, ever the dimwit, was arguing for, but which Matthew and Paul Chan, the head of R&D, were vehemently against. Yes, it would increase profit, but at the risk of drying up the pipeline. The problem was Knolton had no interest in thinking about whether the cuts were appropriate; he was only looking to show the board that he wasn't afraid to make the "hard choices" (e.g., laying off people he had never met) and that he was "thinking outside of the box" (hint: if you're still using that phrase, you aren't).

But now, sitting at the club, Knolton said he'd spoken with the board, and the R&D sites were safe. Still, they would be going forward with the RIF, and Matthew would need to let go of 187 people from U.S. corporate.

Matthew wondered how they'd pulled that number out of their asses, but it was a lot better than the bloodbath Knolton had been threatening all week. He'd been forced to lay off people before;

it was never fun, but it didn't have to be a disaster. There were always employees who were screwing up and on their (carefully documented) way out the door. And Matthew had barely begun his analysis of all the departments that reported to him now: surely he could find 187 screwups somewhere. This was doable, if unpleasant. Walter had said Matthew would have to compromise with Knolton, and compromise he would. No choice—for now.

Speaking of bloat, Matthew had finally realized who Harold looked like, at least when the man was sitting down: Humpty Dumpty. The same wide, bald head, the same nonexistent waist, the same skinny arms, the same general egg shape. The big difference was that Humpty Harold was smiling a malicious smile. Uh-oh.

"One thing to be aware of," Knolton said. His drink was already empty, but he was still holding the glass, turning it around in his hand. "The board wants the RIF completed before the end of the year."

It was Saturday, December 9. Meaning only two weeks until nearly everyone would disappear until January, using vacation time to bridge the gap between Christmas and New Year's or working at home, which for anyone with a family was virtually the same thing. Meaning Knolton was not only a shit, he was a veritable Scrooge. Laying off people right before the holiday? Merry Christmas and hit the road? Not that Matthew gave a damn about Christmas or Hanukkah or Kwanzaa, but he knew his employees did. Their productivity always took a nosedive after Thanksgiving, when all but senior people began spending half the day online, designing silly candy cane ecards, downloading pie recipes, bidding on crap from eBay. It was hardly an ideal situation, but Matthew accepted it because he knew those same people worked so hard the rest of the year. They didn't deserve this. Even the screwups didn't deserve this. It was coldhearted and wrong and—dare he say it? Why the hell not?—*immoral*.

Knolton's voice was chillingly congenial as he delivered the final, lethal kick in the balls. The consultants would be choosing the 187 people through some formula of productivity and industry standards. Matthew would have no say, though of course he was welcome to discuss it with the consultants, but their decision would have to be final.

Matthew was already imagining Humpty Harold in pieces at his feet when the bastard added that it was really for Matthew's own good since he had enough to do getting up to speed in the new position.

"I appreciate the help," he said, but he was thinking that if Humpty Harold didn't fall off that wall very soon, he'd have to shove him. This cheater would not win.

On Monday morning, Matthew discovered that Knolton had done the same thing to everyone else on the executive team, including Paul Chan, who was told his RIF list would include 342 people from various research sites, but nothing about who those people would be or why a Manhattan consulting firm was making the decision about what *scientists* AD could afford to lose. Supposedly the consultants were bringing a crucial objectivity to the process (ignorance is objective?), while also ensuring that the employees kept their trust in leadership (yes, trust in us, because we are powerless to save you).

While Matthew and Chan and the other execs waited for their RIF lists, they were busy dealing with the morale crisis that followed Knolton's webcast interview with the employees on Tuesday to discuss the reorganization plan. When someone asked about site closures and layoffs, Harold said, "All options are on the table." Then he said announcements would be made within the next few days, meaning of course that all work ground to a halt as everyone gossiped about whether they would have a job by the end of the week and joked bitterly that the annual holiday party on Saturday could be their funeral. By Friday, Matthew was spending hours assuring his own VPs that they had to stay calm. Yes, the consultants were making a list and checking it twice like some kind of surreal Santa Claus, but their decisions would surely be based on performance reviews. Why the list had been delayed was anyone's guess, but in the meantime, they were to exude confidence and encourage everyone to attend the party the following night.

The holiday party was the biggest AD event of the year, and it took almost all year to plan it. Cassie had been stuck on some committee and she'd told Matthew some of the crap HR and Legal had to worry about. Employees drinking too much and suing AD if they were in a car accident (solution: strictly cash bar, and dozens of emails to remind everyone about "responsible alcohol consumption"). Employees feeling that their holiday traditions weren't represented and suing AD for discrimination (solution: represent no traditions; stick with snowflakes). Employees groping one another and suing AD for tolerating sexual harassment (solution: a thousand more emails about sexual harassment, and another all-day training seminar for anyone who still felt he or she wasn't "sufficiently informed"—the brain dead, perhaps? Someone from Mars?).

The party was held at the biggest and swankiest ballroom in Center City. Dinner was served buffet-style to accommodate the two thousand plus people from corporate headquarters and Chan's Princeton site, and their spouses or dates. Despite the alcohol consumption emails, nearly everyone was drinking nonstop, no doubt thinking they might as well eat, drink, and be merry, for tomorrow (well, Monday), they might be axed.

Matthew and Knolton were both slated to give rally-the-troops speeches. Matthew was in no mood to deliver a pep talk, but he tried to inspire the room by frequently quoting from a man they all respected: Walter Healy. He concluded by saying that Walter had taught him that loyalty and hard work would never go unnoticed at Astor-Denning. "Those of you who already know me can attest that I love this company, and I believe our people are what make us great." He looked around the room and saw so many of those people: Chris Hawkins, a smart guy who was now leading up alliances; Paul Chan and Beth Dwyer, whose team had discovered AD's about-to-be-launched diabetes drug; Darryl Goodwin, a staff neurologist who'd managed the new schizophrenia drug trials; Martha from the Galvenar marketing team, hugely pregnant, standing in a line with Karen and Srini and Johanna and Link and all the other people who'd busted their asses for Matthew and his miracle drug. He smiled. "This year, we had the largest profit in the company's history, thanks to you. Your talent is our most important resource. You've earned this party. Now let's celebrate."

He got a loud ovation complete with whistles and cheers, unlike Harold, whose speech had been met with tepid applause. Too bad it wasn't a popularity contest. Old Humpty could be thrown from the stage and Matthew could be hoisted on the shoulders of his people and carried to the throne.

He had to indulge the occasional fantasy, especially at this moment, with the hit list in his pocket. Harold had given it to him right before his speech, probably thinking Matthew would scan it and choke. Sorry, Humpty, maybe that shit works in retail, but you don't get ahead in pharma by acting on impulse. We deal in numbers and reproducibility. We're a science company, even if you don't understand what that means. I'm not looking at that list until I'm damn well ready.

Meaning a few minutes later, standing in a bathroom stall.

Most of the names on the list were unfamiliar to Matthew: several dozen from finance, an entire "redundant" department in technical writing, two graphic designers, an entire department of programmers whose jobs were being outsourced to India. The only people from his former division were one alliance guy and two people from marketing, all with performance problems. Probably nothing he could fight, with one very significant exception. He stared at her name, knowing it had to be a mistake, but worried because her assistant, Geoff, was on the list, too. Cassie?! His own assistant was part of the RIF? It would have been impossible when he was a mere division VP, but now it was unthinkable.

He left the bathroom determined to track down Harold. If it wasn't a mistake, it would have to become one. Harold was dancing with his wife so Matthew waited, making small talk with whatever employee stepped forward to introduce himself or herself and do a little understandable brown-nosing. Matthew remembered being on the other side, and it was easy to be gracious. "I'll remember you," he said, because it was true. He had a great memory for the names and faces of his employees. Unfortunately, some of these names were already familiar to him from the list. In those cases, he also wished them a happy holiday, knowing they'd need all the wishes they could get.

Finally, Harold escorted his wife back to the exec table and Matthew asked if he could have a word with him. From the way the asshole smiled, Matthew suspected he already knew that Matthew would be pissed. But after he told Humpty about the problem, Harold said it was, in fact, a mistake. Of course Matthew's assistant wouldn't be laid off. The consultants must have gotten confused in their bid to eliminate redundancy. The names on the list shouldn't have been Cassie and her assistant; it should have been Phyllis Francis and hers.

Matthew was speechless. Phyllis Francis had worked for AD for almost fifty years. She was seventy-one, but she wasn't considering retirement, due to some kind of personal situation that made it essential for her to keep working forever (grandchildren she had to support? A daughter with some handicap?). Everyone at corporate knew and loved her. She was also famous for her great basket of teas: one for stress, another to boost your immune system, yet another if you felt depressed, and so on. Actually, Phyllis had been the first person to help Matthew when he started at Astor-Denning. He'd been told to fill out his W-4 and other forms, but he stupidly hadn't brought anything to write with. Phyllis Francis had given him a pen and told him how to get from Walter's office to HR.

How the hell could they lay off Phyllis? She'd given her life to this company—and specifically to Walter Healy. She'd been Walter's Cassie, and Matthew had inherited her with his new job. He now had two assistants, and though he found plenty of work for them both, the redundancy police must have decided one had to go.

He imagined how Walter would feel if he discovered that Phyllis had been laid off a week before Christmas. He and his wife still hadn't left for their trip around the world; he'd been in the hospital twice with breathing problems. The sad truth was he'd probably waited too long, and now he wasn't strong enough to travel. He'd waited because of the EU conference, knowing how important it was for AD. After everything Walter had given to the company, it was horrifying to think of his assistant being treated like this. Matthew could not and would not let this happen.

He knew the holiday party was not the place to have this argument, though every cell of him wanted to punch Harold Knolton. Instead, he made his way through the throng of dancing couples and headed toward the door. He had to get some air.

Before he made it, though, he spotted a traitor. There she was, dressed in a long blue gown and high heels, looking for all the world like any other woman standing in the buffet line. At least he knew how she got in; the holiday party wasn't a proprietary event, and security was only supposed to handle any trouble, meaning escorting drunks to the coffee station. How could they know that Amelia was trouble incarnate?

He walked over and grabbed her arm. "Crashing my party?" he said in her ear. "Are you really this desperate for a social life?"

"No, I'm working."

"Not here, you're not. If you don't leave this instant, I'll have security throw you out."

"Fine, I'll go." She looked up at him. "After you answer a few questions."

"Follow me." He dropped her arm, but she followed him to the exit. Once they were outside, they walked down the steps to the sidewalk to get away from the crowd of smokers huddling by the door.

Immediately, she said, "Tell me what happened in Jakarta."

They were standing under the yellow streetlight. He could see goose bumps on her bare arms. "Where's your coat?"

"I didn't bring it," she said, shivering. "Don't change the subject."

"Oh hell." He took off his jacket and gave it to her. She said she didn't want it, but finally she put it over her shoulders. He looked down Chestnut Street for a cab. His only goal was to put her in a cab and send her home to Ben.

"Look, Danny gave me your mysterious message, but I can't imagine why you think this is worth talking about. It's nothing more than—"

"You kept out anyone with hepatitis. From the postmarket trial."

He nodded. "It's standard procedure. We don't want to—"

"It causes liver damage, doesn't it? That's what you're trying to hide about Galvenar."

She looked so proud of herself. Too bad her theory was so ridiculous; he wondered if she was losing her touch. "You're way off.

Sorry, but I have real problems tonight and I'm just not up to your usual—"

"I spoke to the nurses in Long Island. They told me that some patients had to quit the trial when they developed jaundice."

"I'm aware of that. Independent statisticians determined that our drug didn't cause it. You can check the data yourself."

"Did you keep this information from the FDA?"

"Of course not." He stepped into the street, hoping to hail a cab down the block. "The FDA hearing is a public record. Look it up."

"I have. I did. But nine out of twelve people who recommended Galvenar at that hearing had ties to AD. The FDA was acting as an arm of your company."

"That's not true, either, but even if it was, so what?" He turned around and looked at her. "Would you like me to personally reform the FDA? How about the Justice Department and Congress while I'm at it? Maybe I should go after the media; it needs to be reformed, too, don't you think? Of course *every* corporation would have to be changed; that goes without saying. Every person in America, too, since we're all part of the problem, right?" He forced a laugh. "If only I were that powerful, Amelia. Sorry, not even close. I can't give you a cure for modern life."

A car was honking across the street. The smokers were laughing. He needed to get back to the party and meet and greet. After a minute he said, "Ben was really upset when you left him. I'm glad you two worked it out." She looked strangely sad, so he added, "He said you already found a house? That was quick."

"The movers delivered our things today. Ben is unpacking boxes right now."

Matthew smiled. "See, he does know how to do things other than fight disease." Finally, an empty cab. He hailed it and it stopped. "As enjoyable as this is, it's time for you to go. And I'll need my jacket back."

She took it off and handed it to him. Right before she got in, she said, "You really hurt me with that speech, Matthew."

He didn't say anything, but he felt a little bad. She looked worn out; Ben had told him that her pregnancy wasn't going well, but he didn't elaborate. Matthew hoped it wasn't serious.

As the cab drove away, he wondered why she'd come here rather than calling. Something wasn't right, but he was too distracted to dwell on it. Humpty was the immediate problem, and his consultants, who Matthew thought of as Thing One and Thing Two—thanks to Isabelle, who loved *Cat in the Hat*.

Since Matthew had moved the kids to the suburbs, Danny had become aloof and quiet, but Isabelle was still happy to see him even if he didn't visit often or stay very long. He couldn't fathom what Danny's problem was, though admittedly he hadn't spent much time thinking about it. He'd already given them his Malvern house and a nanny who charged an outrageous sum to work around the clock. Where was the gratitude?

Unfortunately, back at the party, Matthew found more gratitude than he could handle. Dozens of employees wanted to thank him for what he'd said in his speech. Even the people on the RIF list were grateful, which made him more pissed at Knolton and the board. The company really was having a great year; the profit margin had never been higher. Why did the shareholders need this reorganization? Why risk morale when the pipeline was paying off and Galvenar was making them all rich? Were they really such greedy bastards that they'd insist on firing Jessica, a single mom and technical writer making fifty thousand a year? A fifteen-minute meeting between Knolton and the consultants cost the company more than that. Why was this happening—and why couldn't he understand it? Was it possible that he was losing his focus, even becoming soft on profit? He loved money as much as the next guy, but Jessica was standing in front of him. On Monday she would be called into HR to receive "options counseling," the euphemism they were using for being laid off. Even "layoff" was a euphemism, since no one was ever called back to work. They weren't being counseled or temporarily sent home; they were being fired.

He dreaded Monday, and it was just as bad as he feared. It was December 18, only a week from Christmas, and everyone sat around waiting for the call from HR, crying when they got it, coming back to find security waiting for them at their desks. They were all escorted out of the building like budding Unabombers, transformed from employees to threats in little more than an hour.

Thankfully, Phyllis Francis did not get the call; she'd been removed from the list pending Matthew's meeting with Knolton and the consultants. Meaning if he didn't win, she'd be fired later in the week—even closer to Christmas. Meaning if he didn't win, he would have to go over Knolton's head and talk to the board chairman, Stephen Mezalski. Mezalski had been CEO for three years before he retired and they brought in Knolton. He knew Phyllis, and he knew Walter. Surely he would see how wrong this was; maybe he would even agree that Humpty was a psycho who had to be stopped.

Matthew was so focused on the RIF that it was almost noon before he read Amelia's latest newspaper article: "Big Pharma Blues." Cassie was home taking care of a sick daughter, but Phyllis had left it on his desk first thing in the morning, and he'd given it a quick glance and gotten the impression it was about pharmas having trouble with pipeline failures and dropping stock prices—in other words, not AD. The first few paragraphs were about this, but then Amelia discussed recent layoffs at Bayer and Pfizer, and finally the reorganization at Astor-Denning.

First she claimed that the mood at the holiday party was "somber" and "bitter." That spying bitch. She also said an anonymous source had revealed that AD was laying off nine hundred people. That was about right, but where in the hell had she gotten that information? The number had not been made public yet; in fact, all RIF employees were being forced to sign nondisclosure agreements as a condition of getting their severance pay.

At 2:32, Matthew got an email saying his meeting with Knolton and his axmen had been canceled. He immediately picked up the phone to call Harold, but then he noticed Phyllis standing in the doorway of his office, too polite to enter without an invitation, even though she was crying. She looked every bit the grandmother—white hair in a bun, a navy shirtdress that had to be from the eighties, papery skin and gnarled hands clutched together like she was praying—but what struck Matthew was that she was exactly thirty-one years older than he was. The age his mother would have been had she lived.

He knew HR had called. He told her it was a mistake and not to worry; he would fix it, but in the meantime, don't go to the HR "counseling." He didn't mention that security might come looking for her, but he did ask her to stay in his office and keep the door closed. She thanked him profusely and gave him a grandmotherly hug. She was still sniffing back tears, but she sounded confident. "I knew you wouldn't let this happen."

As he stomped in the direction of Knolton's office, he decided he would threaten to quit if necessary. Of course he wouldn't have to go through with it, but it would still cost him political capital. Oh well, he could afford to put himself on the line every now and again. He was the man behind Galvenar, after all. Mezalski and the board knew what he was worth, even if Humpty didn't.

Knolton was just coming back from lunch, and Matthew ran into him in the long hall that led to the CEO suite. Instantly, Matthew knew something was wrong because Knolton refused to discuss it, saying only, "The Phyllis Francis decision is final." When Matthew hinted that this was a make-or-break issue for him, Knolton said ominously, "I wouldn't push this if I were you."

"Thanks for the advice," Matthew snapped, turning back to his office.

Phyllis was sitting in one of the leather chairs by his window, working on her laptop. He asked her to wait outside but said she should buzz him if anyone from HR or security showed up. Then he picked up the phone to call Mezalski, but Mezalski's assistant put him on hold for a full minute before claiming the man was out for the day. Meaning Mezalski had refused to take his call. Meaning something was very, very wrong.

He took an Ativan and sat still, thinking, before he remembered to check on Phyllis. She wasn't at her desk. He hoped she was in the bathroom, but after ten minutes, he knew HR had abducted her. When she returned, a security guard was with her. Matthew tried to stop it, but Phyllis told him it was too late. She'd signed the form. She just wanted to clean out her desk and go without making a scene.

She put her family photos in a box, but she left the basket of teas. "Hopefully someone else will replenish it," she said, forcing a smile. Before she left, she told Matthew she'd be okay. "You know what Walter always said: 'That which does not kill you makes you stronger.'"

Matthew nodded, though he'd never really believed it. What if your leg got cut off? Would you be stronger then? How about both your arms?

He was so disgusted that he was thinking about going home, even though it was only four-thirty. He'd never left that early unless he had a plane to catch or a client meeting. He had a shitload of work to do, including more damage control on Pain Matters, but he could do it at home, away from this stupidity. He needed to get in his car and drive until he understood what the hell was going on.

When his phone lit up, he instinctively waited several flashes before he remembered that neither Cassie nor Phyllis was there to answer. It was Mezalski, thank god. All Matthew had to do was tell him what happened, and Phyllis's form could be ripped up and she could come back the next day.

But before Matthew could say anything, Mezalski said he was calling to inform Matthew that he was being investigated. Naturally, his first thought was the Department of Justice, but then a stunning array of possibilities passed through his mind, from the Japanese Ministry of Health, Labour, and Welfare to some state's attorney's office, or even congressional hearings. But the truth turned out to be worse than any of these. He was being investigated by Astor-Denning. His own company was accusing him of leaking proprietary information to the press.

The proprietary information was the number of employees being laid off; the press, of course, was Amelia. Only the board and the executive committee had been told that 908 people were being laid off. And, as Mezalski explained, Matthew was obviously in touch with Amelia Johannsen, as evidenced by his mentioning her in his speech. Moreover, he'd been seen stepping outside with her at the party, talking to her for several minutes. In fact, he'd been photographed by security, standing next to her, with his jacket on her shoulders.

Photographed? Spied on? Was this his company or the CIA?

"I didn't tell her anything about the RIF," Matthew said, not even trying to keep the anger out of his voice. "I'm being set up."

Mezalski asked if he had any proof. The truth was no. If he called Amelia, she would say she couldn't reveal her source, and most likely she didn't even know that her anonymous tip came from Knolton. She'd been used. But it pissed him off that he would need proof. Weren't the last fifteen years busting his ass for AD proof enough?

"I'm happy to discuss it with the board," he said. "But I must admit, I'm disappointed that this is on the table, given my contributions to this company."

"We're disappointed as well," Mezalski said, but his tone was unreadable. Matthew couldn't tell if they were disappointed in him or in what they were doing to him.

He thought how strange it was, hearing this in his gigantic new office, surrounded by opulence and elegance. And all of it—the gray suede couch, the black leather chairs designed by Mies van der Rohe, the floating bookshelves, the dark gray tweed carpet, the silver lamp, the glass desk—a testament to his important role in the company. Of course he still thought of it as Walter's office half the time, and especially when he looked at the photographs Walter had chosen from AD's art collection: three Dorothea Lange shots of Americans during the Great Depression.

He was at the pinnacle of his success, and he would have gladly worked at AD forever. Weird or not, he'd always rather liked the idea of being eightysomething and working on a PowerPoint presentation and just flopping over dead at his keyboard. Like the good soldier dying with his boots on.

But he really had believed that AD was a team. A team to make money for the shareholders, absolutely, but a team that also rewarded those people who dedicated their lives to finding and selling the drugs that made the money. And, as embarrassingly naïve as it sounded to him now, he'd really believed that loyalty and hard work still mattered here. Walter had always emphasized this, and Matthew had believed him.

"I need to have Phyllis Francis reinstated," he finally said. "I think the company owes me that."

Mezalski didn't say anything.

"After HR reinstates her, I'll be happy to comply with whatever the board wants."

"You're hardly in a position to make demands." Mezalski took a breath and lowered his voice. "If you want my advice, I'd suggest you cooperate fully with Knolton. If you do, I think you'll find this will all go away."

He thanked Mezalski for being candid and hung up. Then, without hesitating, he ransacked his own office, stuffing the most important files in his briefcase, along with his laptop, then filling a box with other files and papers and the old Rolodex he hadn't used since he'd started keeping his contacts on his computer. He made it to his car without security stopping him. Unfortunately, the five o'clock rush to get home had already begun and he sat in traffic forever trying to get on Route 202.

Which gave him plenty of time to think, though it was obvious what Mezalski was saying. This was all a strategy on Knolton's part. The man wanted to be feared, and Matthew hadn't feared him, so he set Matthew up. The goal wasn't to get Matthew fired, but to change him into someone who would play the game Knolton's way. The "investigation" would be inconclusive, but Matthew would be diminished in the eyes of the board. That was the point, and probably the way the asshole always won.

By the time Matthew reached the Schuylkill Expressway, he found himself thinking about something he rarely considered—how he felt. Of course he knew it was possible that he'd been promoted past the level of his competence, a textbook case of the Peter Principle, but oddly, he didn't care about that. He wondered if the company had really changed or whether he had, and if so, why? Was he having a (gulp) midlife crisis? If he lost his faith in AD, what would he believe in? What did he really care about?

An hour later, back at his apartment, he was still in this bizarre reflective mood, though he was positive of one thing. Phyllis Francis was going to get her job back. The game wasn't over yet, not by a long shot. If he'd underestimated Knolton, old Humpty had also underestimated him.

CHAPTER FIFTEEN

A Pink Tulip in December

Danny knew how to spend his days walking around the city, hustling for money, scrounging for food, running from older kids and men and cops; he knew how to pick a lock and sneak into hotel bathrooms; he knew where the good dumpsters were and what alleys were dangerous. For the last two and a half years, he'd been always in motion, always scheming, always busy, until that December, when Matthew moved them to the suburbs. Suddenly he and Isabelle had food and beds and no fear of anyone coming to take it all away. Danny had time on his hands, which he wasn't used to at all—and he found out he hated it. Maybe it would have been okay if he hadn't been waiting for his mom, but waiting was the worst. Waiting meant thinking and worrying about the future. Waiting made his eyes go squinty with hope that, this time, his mom really would get off drugs for good.

The first time she called from Changes, she sounded shaky and tired and a little nervous, but there was something else in her voice, something he couldn't put his finger on. His mom had made it through prescreen and detox and now she was in the rehabilitation phase, though she didn't say what it was like. She really didn't say much at all, but she wanted to know how he and Isabelle were doing. He said they were fine. They'd just moved into the suburban house and he told his mom about it, though he left out the bad parts because he didn't want her to worry.

At first he'd felt like the luckiest kid on the planet. Matthew said the house had everything they needed, including furniture he'd rented and a good yard and a swing set left behind by the last family. As the nanny was driving them there, he couldn't wait to see this amazing thing: their very own yard. The nanny's name was Mrs. Linnas and she was really old, maybe fifty or even sixty. Matthew called her Theresa, but she'd already told Danny and Isabelle to call her Mrs. Linnas. Danny didn't mind, but Isabelle couldn't say Mrs., and she couldn't remember to say both syllables of the woman's last name. "Lin" didn't bother the nanny, but "ass" did, and Danny kept correcting his sister. Matthew thought it was funny, which didn't help, but he wasn't with them anymore. He'd gone back to work.

They were driving down a street called Lancaster Avenue when Danny noticed the name of the town. He asked Mrs. Linnas if this was where the house was and she said no, but still, he couldn't believe this place was right there, in front of his eyes. Ardmore, the town where he always said he lived in the train fare story. He took it as a sign that everything would work out.

The house was even better than he'd expected. He had a room of his own, with bunk beds, like at the homeless shelter, but these were wood instead of metal. At one end of the bed was a desk, and on the opposite wall was a dresser for his clothes. He even had his very own closet. Isabelle had a room, too, with a little pink and white bed, just her size, and a toy box for all the toys they'd brought in boxes from Matthew's apartment. Between the two rooms was a bathroom with a big white tub with claw feet, just for them. Mrs. Linnas was staying down the hall, and there was another bedroom downstairs, in a hall off the kitchen, where Matthew could stay if he wanted to, but Danny didn't expect that to ever happen. He knew the guy was sending them here so he wouldn't have to deal with them, and Danny didn't really care, though he knew his sister would have cared a lot if she'd understood what had happened. Luckily, she was too excited by all the things to see in this great new place.

Of course the first thing she wanted to do was go outside and swing. She always loved the swings at the park, but this was so much better because she didn't have to wait her turn. Danny pushed her until his arms hurt, and even then she yelled at him for stopping. But they had to quit because Mrs. Linnas said dinner was ready.

She made them wash their hands before sitting down at the table, but that was okay. The only thing that bothered Danny was the way Mrs. Linnas picked up Isabelle: with no tender feelings he could see, almost like she wished she didn't have to touch his sister. She didn't talk to Isabelle much except to tell her to eat the meat loaf. Danny wondered if she just didn't like little kids much, but as long as she wasn't mean, he wasn't going to complain. Matthew had warned that he had to cooperate with Mrs. Linnas. "I know you're not used to being treated like a child, but you need to get used to it. No doubt it will be difficult, but remember, every man has to do things he doesn't like."

Danny promised he would. He wanted to be a man. He also

wanted to stay on Matthew's good side, so Matthew might help his mom when she came back from Changes.

But on Monday, when Matthew came to check on them, Danny felt like he had to say something about the nanny. Mrs. Linnas had ignored all of Isabelle's attempts to make friends, even turning away from his sister's goofy smiles and jokes. The nanny didn't really play with his sister or even talk when she took Isabelle to the bathroom.

It was after dinner, around seven-thirty; Danny was following Isabelle up the stairs and down the stairs, over and over, knowing she needed to practice handling stairs no matter how boring it was for him. Mrs. Linnas was sitting in the living room, watching some woman show on the big television, ignoring the Rent-a-House sticker along the bottom of the TV. All of the furniture had these stickers, and Mrs. Linnas said they probably shouldn't remove them, but Danny peeled them off his sister's bedroom stuff anyway. Isabelle loved her room so much, and it made Danny feel bad to be constantly reminded that everything his sister had now was so temporary.

When Matthew came in, Mrs. Linnas quickly turned off the TV, but Danny knew Dr. Connelly saw it first. He also saw Isabelle slowly toddling down the stairs, holding the rail, with Danny walking backward in front of her in case she fell.

"Ma-ew!" his sister yelled, and luckily Matthew came over and scooped her up, because otherwise she might have plunged down the last five stairs too fast for Danny to catch her.

"Is-elle," he said, holding her away from him so he could look at her face. "When are you going to learn the middle of the name is important, too?"

"I glad."

"I'm glad to see you, too, though I can't stay long. I'm working on the most important speech of my career, but don't let that concern you."

Isabelle laughed. Danny wondered why Matthew had come if he was so busy.

Mrs. Linnas said, "Everything is going very well, Doctor Connelly. We're all moved in. We've stocked up on supplies at the store."

"Good to hear. Now I need to talk to the kiddies. Could you give us a minute?"

They went upstairs to Isabelle's room and she jumped on her bed happily and woke up her "napping" stuffed elephant.

"This bed is made of plastic," he said, frowning. "The living room looks like it was furnished by a blind man. That brown sectional is stunningly ugly. You wouldn't believe how much Rent-a-Crap charged for all this."

"We don't mind the furniture," Danny said. "But I'm not sure about Mrs. Linnas."

Matthew sat down by Isabelle and glanced at him. "Remember what I told you."

"I know. But I really think my sister and me would be better off here alone. You wouldn't have to pay anybody then."

"Tempting, but not an option. It's illegal to leave a ten-year-old with a three-year-old. I already checked."

Danny paused. "She's not very nice to Isabelle. I don't think she likes her."

"I find that hard to believe."

Isabelle was holding up her elephant and grinning at Matthew. Matthew smiled back and asked Danny what Mrs. Linnas had done or not done to his sister. Danny tried telling him what he'd seen, but it wasn't very convincing and he knew it. Isabelle did seem happy. Matthew said the nanny agency had told Cassie that Mrs. Linnas was their best. Maybe Matthew was right when he said that Danny would have trouble with anyone who took care of his precious sister.

After a few minutes of listening to Isabelle tell him about the pretend game she was playing, Matthew said to Danny, "Have you spoken to Amelia recently?"

"No. I haven't called her, and I don't think she has the number here."

"I want you to call her on Thursday afternoon." Matthew paused. "Just check in and see if she sounds all right. Not too depressed, not too insane."

"Okay." He waited a minute. "Have you heard from Changes?"

"Cassie spoke to them today. Apparently your mother is doing fine. She's cooperating fully with the rehab process." Matthew stood up. "Let me know what Amelia says. Now I have to go. I have four people sitting in a conference room, waiting for me to come back and get their input on the speech."

Isabelle called him over and kissed him. "Bye, bye," she said.

Danny didn't hear from his mom the next week. It bothered him, but he had something else to talk to Matthew about when he came by again, on Saturday, late in the afternoon. Mrs. Linnas was cooking a roast; Danny was reading and Isabelle was watching a cartoon—or at least she had been until Mrs. Linnas changed the channel without saying anything, like Isabelle wasn't even a person. Isabelle was just starting to cry when Matthew arrived. Of course seeing him made her forget what had happened, but Danny still told Matthew what Mrs. Linnas had done.

"Oh, the inhumanity," Matthew said. He was grumpier than Danny had ever seen him; he kept cursing this nursery rhyme character, Humpty Dumpty, which was so weird that Danny didn't even try to figure it out. After Matthew read two Dr. Seuss books to Isabelle and watched her play for almost an hour, he said he was going into the office "forever."

"You can still call me if you have a dire emergency, but otherwise, I hope you'll handle it." He was talking to Danny, not Mrs. Linnas, who was back in the kitchen. "Hint: an adult changing the channel is not an emergency."

Danny nodded. It was December 9; his mom would be home in only two weeks. Of course he could do this. He had a nice room and good food. He'd even met another boy in the neighborhood, Jeff, though Jeff was gone most of the day, in school. Matthew had mentioned Danny going to school, too, but it turned out to be a lot of paperwork and not worth it for a few weeks. It was a good thing, because he wouldn't have gone anyway. He wouldn't go to Jeff's house, either; though Jeff kept asking Danny to come over or ride bikes, Danny always said no. He didn't have a bike and he wouldn't have known how to ride one if he did. And he couldn't leave Isabelle alone with Mrs. Linnas—that was the main thing. Mrs. Linnas still didn't like his sister and Danny had a feeling he knew why. Isabelle had brown skin. He'd heard some people call his sister ugly names like wetback, and sometimes they told her to go back to Mexico. Danny yelled at these people, but he didn't know what to do about Mrs. Linnas since she wasn't saying anything mean. Nothing happened that Danny could put his finger on until Wednesday, December 13—obviously an unlucky day—at lunch.

Mrs. Linnas had cooked macaroni and cheese, which he liked. Isabelle had never had it, but it turned out she hated it. She took one bite and spit it back on the plate. Mrs. Linnas said, "Now, Isabelle, you have to eat so you can get big."

"Don't wike!"

"This is your lunch, you have to eat it."

"No."

"We'll see about that." Mrs. Linnas sat down and picked up a magazine.

Danny didn't feel like eating any more, either, but he did, every bite. Then, while Mrs. Linnas was flipping through the magazine, he tried to sneak a bite from Isabelle's bowl. Unfortunately, the nanny saw him and said, "Don't do that again, Daniel. That is your sister's food, and she has to eat it. You're excused to go play."

Isabelle would have jumped down, too, but the house had a high chair. She was belted in, trapped. And she started to wail.

"Let me make her something else," Danny said. "She likes almost everything."

"You're excused. Please leave the kitchen. Don't worry about Isabelle. She and I will work this out."

He left, but he lurked in the living room so he could hear what Mrs. Linnas did next. Nothing. She left Isabelle wailing and throwing macaroni and cheese. She didn't move or stop reading. When Isabelle hit her in the face with a piece of macaroni, she stood up and wiped her face with a paper towel. She said, "None of that," and slapped Isabelle's hands. The slap wasn't hard, but Isabelle started crying a lot harder, like she was afraid.

This went on for at least an hour. Danny tried to come in and help over and over, but finally Mrs. Linnas told him to go to his room. Poor Isabelle was holding her arms up, calling him, "Danny!" The crying was breaking his heart, but he didn't know what he should do. What if he picked up his sister anyway and Mrs. Linnas got even meaner? They couldn't run away out in the suburbs. He'd noticed police cars everywhere on Lancaster Avenue. One of those cops would pick them up for sure.

It felt like an emergency, but he wasn't sure if Matthew would agree, so he decided to call Amelia. She'd said she'd help him and he needed help, bad. He had to save Isabelle, who was crying so hard he was afraid she would throw up.

Amelia answered right away. He told her what was happening and their address and she said she'd be over as soon as she could get there. "Don't worry," she said. "I'll deal with that nanny."

It was another fifty-five minutes before she made it. Danny wanted to cooperate, like Matthew had told him to do, but Isabelle was crying and calling for him and finally he just couldn't take it anymore. He went back downstairs to get his sister out of the high chair, but Mrs. Linnas was standing right there, making it impossible for him to get Isabelle unless he physically moved the nanny out of the way. He felt like shoving Mrs. Linnas, hard, but his mom had told him never to do that because pushing or hitting a grown-up could land you in jail for a long time. Mrs. Linnas ordered him to return to his room, but he ignored her and talked to Isabelle, telling her it was all right, just hang on and he'd get her out of this. Mrs. Linnas got louder and louder; she even threatened to spank him if he didn't leave the kitchen immediately, but he told her he wasn't going anywhere without his sister. She was still yelling at him when Amelia finally knocked on the door.

Danny ran to the living room, let her in, and put his arms around her waist. "I'm so glad you're here." Mrs. Linnas started to introduce herself, but Amelia ignored her. She followed the sound of Isabelle's cries to the kitchen; then she walked over and removed Isabelle from the high chair. When Isabelle reached out for Danny, Amelia handed his sister to him. And then she told Mrs. Linnas she was fired. Just like that.

"I don't know who you are, but only Doctor Connelly can fire me. He hired me, not you."

"Fine, let's call him and see what he says, shall we?"

Danny was still comforting Isabelle, but he turned to Amelia. "He said not to call unless it was a real emergency. He has some kind of problem at work and—"

"He'll live." She took out her phone and dialed the number. When Matthew answered, she told him what was going on. He said it was fine to fire her. That's what Amelia told Mrs. Linnas, anyway, though from the length of time they were on the phone, Danny had a feeling Amelia was making it up and Matthew hadn't answered at all.

"Mrs. Linnas, I'm a friend of Doctor Connelly's. He told me if you don't want to be arrested for child abuse, you'd better go."

"I've never been treated like this."

"Neither has Isabelle," Danny said. His sister's whole body was still shaking, though she'd quieted down. "No drug addict ever treated her as mean as you."

Mrs. Linnas stomped up to her room. A few minutes later, she was back with her things. "You may want to remind Doctor Connelly that his fee for this week is not refundable."

Amelia shrugged. After Mrs. Linnas left, she said, "Where did Matthew find that witch?"

"A nanny agency," Danny said. "But he didn't find her, his assistant did."

"When will he call to check in?" Amelia said.

"I don't know," Danny admitted. "Do you have to go right now?"

"Of course not," she said. "I can stay as long as you need me."

Isabelle must have understood this because she reached out her arms for Amelia. "Well, hello there," Amelia said, smiling. "I wondered if I'd ever get to hold you."

Isabelle pointed upstairs.

"She wants to show you her bedroom," Danny said.

"I'd love to see it," Amelia said.

It was a little after six. Amelia played with Isabelle for a long time, then they cleaned up the kitchen and had a great cheese pizza that was delivered from a local restaurant Amelia found in the yellow pages. Now she was lying down because she felt a little sick. Danny was trying not to worry about Amelia being sick so much, but it was hard because he really liked her.

While Amelia was resting, Matthew called, sounding even grumpier than he had on Saturday. "The nanny agency has called my assistant repeatedly to ask why I fired Mrs. Linnas and threatened her with child abuse charges. They're hinting at a lawsuit, though of course they have no grounds. Still, any publicity is bad publicity right now. So, would you mind telling me why I did this?"

Danny told him the whole story and Matthew cursed, but he said Danny had done the right thing. He also said Cassie had already performed a miracle and found them a new nanny who could be there later tonight. "But in the meantime, we have a new problem. I was planning to come over and be with you two until she gets there, but I've just gotten an email inviting me to dinner with some investors and Humpty Dumpty. I'm dreading it, but such is life. I'll have to bother Cassie again and see what she can arrange."

Danny was reluctant to admit that he'd called Amelia, and that she was downstairs right now. He didn't want to deal with Matthew getting mad. But when he told him, Matthew sounded relieved. "Fine, if she can stay until the new nanny gets there. But if she can't, before she leaves, you'll have to call Cassie." He made Danny write down Cassie's home number. "Repeat after me. I will not stay here alone with my sister. It is illegal. If Amelia has to leave, I will call this number. I will not screw over my benefactor."

Danny repeated each sentence, though he wasn't sure what *benefactor* meant.

When Amelia came upstairs a few minutes later, Danny told her that a new nanny was coming. She seemed a little depressed, like maybe she wanted to take care of them instead of the nanny, but she said at least she could be with them until the nanny got there. She called Ben, but whatever he said upset her and she sat on Isabelle's bed and cried. Both Danny and Isabelle tried to comfort her, and finally she blew her nose on a Kleenex Danny brought from the bathroom and said, "What about taking a walk around the block? It's dark, but it's not that cold. Isabelle, can I push you and your elephant in your stroller?"

Isabelle nodded and broke into a grin. Danny felt a lump in his chest but he followed them and got his sister's coat on and grabbed his own jacket. Before they opened the door, he told Amelia that she was pretty.

"Thank you." She kissed him on the top of the head. "I really needed to hear that."

He knew she did, but he also thought it was true. She was so pretty that he wished it wasn't dark outside, so he could look at her. He liked to look at her; it made him feel safe. Her face was kind, like his mom's, and honest, like his mom used to be, before her habit. Even when the new nanny came at ten-thirty and she was really young and really nice, Danny still wished Amelia would stay, too. But he knew Matthew wouldn't like it.

Before she left, she asked Danny if Matthew had mentioned the holiday party at Astor-Denning. Danny said no, and then Amelia said, "I got the strangest phone call inviting me to the party and hinting that something newsworthy was going on at AD. The person never identified himself, but it certainly didn't sound like Matthew."

"Doctor Connelly is busy with this person he calls Humpty Dumpty." Danny shrugged. "Could anybody really have that name?"

Amelia laughed. "It's probably code for one of their scams. I don't know what's going on over there anymore." She rolled her eyes. "Since the evil jerk won't take my phone calls."

Danny hesitated, but finally he said it. "He's really not evil."

"I have to stop using that word, I know." Amelia smiled and touched his arm. "Your mom is right."

"Yeah, 'cause it brings bad karma."

"Well, I certainly don't need any more of that." She laughed, but it was a sad kind of laugh. Danny felt the lump again as he watched her go.

At least the new nanny, Rosalie, was nice to Isabelle. And a few days later, Sunday, December 17, his mom called. Again, she said she just wanted to know how they were doing. He told her about the kid Jeff with the bike and Isabelle walking and talking constantly and about Amelia, too, and how nice she'd been when the nanny had to be fired. He skimmed over what was wrong with Mrs. Linnas and focused on how great Rosalie was and how she sounded funny because she was from Ireland. His mom didn't seem to care about Rosalie, but she asked a lot of questions about Amelia.

"Is she Doctor Connelly's wife?"

"No, they're like friends. Sort of."

"But she helps him watch out for you and Belle?"

"Yeah, I guess. If anything goes wrong, I can call her and she'll come fix it."

"Is she a doctor, too?"

"No, she's a writer. I think. She said she writes about ethics, which is like how to be a good person."

"Wow," his mom said. "Do you think she's trying to be a good person by being nice to you kids?"

"Kind of." He told his mom what Amelia had told him about her grandma and sponsoring orphans from poor countries when Amelia was a little girl. "But she likes us, too."

"Do you like her?"

"Yeah." He felt himself blushing, and he changed the topic to the calendar he'd made to count down the days until his mom was home, with the biggest square coming in only six more days, December 23, which he colored in red and green. He also said he missed her, which was so true it was painful. Every night before he went to sleep, he thought about the way his mother used to be, back in the apartment, when he was in first grade. She made popcorn and they sat at their tiny kitchen table and played Uno and Go Fish. She told him stories about the town she grew up in: the lake and fishing with her grandpa, her grandma teaching her to use a sewing machine and the time she tried to make a blue skirt with a bright pink tulip on the pocket. But the pattern was cut wrong and the skirt was a square, with no waist. It kept slipping down to her hips, but she wore it anyway because fabric wasn't cheap and because she'd made it all by herself.

In all the stories, his mom was such a normal kid, but later Danny discovered the other side. Whenever she tried to quit using drugs, she talked about the bad part, and cried about it, too. Her own mom had disappeared when she was nine and her father drank and beat her. This was why all her happy memories involved her grandparents. This was why she ran away when she was seventeen, after her grandpa died and her grandma was put in a nursing home.

"The calendar sounds sweet," his mom said now. Her voice was flat, though, and Danny wondered if it made her feel bad.

He said, "You'll be here for Christmas."

His mom had always loved Christmas. Even when they lived in the car, she insisted on dragging back a scraggly tree and decorating it with strips of tin foil. At night, the lights of the city made the foil reflect red and green and yellow and blue, like real ornaments.

"Do you know what Belle wants from Santa?"

"Don't worry about it." He knew his mom didn't have any money, and he didn't want her scrounging on Christmas Eve.

"I guess Amelia and Doctor Connelly will get her everything she wants anyway."

"Yeah, sure," he said, though he doubted Matthew would even think of it now that he'd gone to work forever. Amelia might, but Rosalie was the best bet. She'd already said she was going to use some of the household allowance to get decorations. She'd also told them both to think about what they wanted.

"I have to go," his mom said. "We have meetings every hour."

She still sounded weird. Sad, but something else, too. What was it? He tried asking her, "Don't you like the meetings?"

"I don't know, Cobain. They make us talk about our feelings about what's happened. I guess I have a lot to figure out."

He didn't know what to say to this. After she hung up, Rosalie asked if he and Isabelle wanted to go bumper bowling. "It's a load of fun," she said, picking up his sister, who was nodding and smiling. He said yes and tried not to worry about his mom. Rehab was hard; he knew that from listening to all the people in the house. You had to change yourself, they said, not just stop using drugs.

He wondered if his mom could really change.

But as the day she was coming home grew closer, Danny held on to the hope that his mother would be back to the way she used to be, maybe even better. Cassie called to say the plane ticket was arranged, but her voice was so businesslike that Danny got nervous and forgot to ask what time. He hadn't seen or spoken to Matthew since the day Mrs. Linnas was fired, but it was okay. Rosalie kept them busy decorating the house for Christmas and taking them to the huge King of Prussia Mall so Isabelle could sit on Santa's lap. She also gave them each five dollars to buy presents for their mom. They put the money together and got a pretty brush and comb set.

On December 23, Danny woke up with the sun, too anxious to go back to sleep. Rosalie made Danny and Isabelle a special breakfast: waffles with chocolate chips and whipped cream, "in honor of our last day." The rest of the morning he was distracted, thinking about ways he could help his mom stay off drugs. First, she needed a good job and an apartment far from the city, away from her friends. There were lots of apartments on Lancaster Avenue; they could live out here if they had a car. Or maybe they could find an apartment right by the train station. The job came first, and he'd been cutting out ads from the paper, just in case Matthew couldn't or wouldn't help his mom get a job at Astor-Denning. He hoped his mom had gained some weight. It might be hard to get a job if she still looked as sick as she did when she left.

That afternoon, Amelia called to find out if he and Isabelle had gotten their presents. Danny said yes, Rosalie had put them under the tree. "Oh, good," Amelia said. "At least you'll have something to open on Christmas."

"We each have two presents. One from you and one from Rosalie."

"I knew Matthew wouldn't get you anything. Don't feel too bad about it. He's always been a complete Scrooge about Christmas. When I knew him, he used to spend the day watching stupid music documentaries. And I mean the entire day, from morning to midnight."

Danny wasn't sure what a documentary was, but he laughed because Amelia was laughing and because he knew Matthew could be really weird.

After a moment she said, "I better go. Hope you have a great Christmas with your mom."

"Thanks," he said.

"I'll miss you," she said, and it sounded like she was trying not to cry. "I hope I can see you and Isabelle again someday."

Danny said he hoped so, too. When they hung up, he wondered if their mom would like Amelia. He didn't think so, though he wasn't sure why.

By five o'clock, he was getting really anxious. Cassie had said his mom would take a cab from the airport, but what if his mom lost the address? What if she was too nervous to figure out how to get a cab? Of course she could call from a pay phone, unless she lost the number, too.

By eight-thirty Danny was desperate enough to call Cassie to find out what time the flight got in. When she didn't answer, he figured she was out of town; too bad he didn't have her cell phone number. Of course everybody went to see their family for Christmas if they had a family to go to. Even some of the addicts in their house went home for the holidays, and those who didn't talked about their families: sometimes missing them, usually griping that their family had cut them off.

Danny knew he couldn't call Matthew under any circumstances. Matthew had already told Rosalie that he was too busy to come over and she would have to deal with the arrival of Danny's mom. He'd also sent Rosalie a text message on her cell phone to show Danny, which said that Matthew had decided that Danny's mom could stay with them in the rental house until Christmas was over. Matthew even said he would consider helping Danny's mom get a job, as long as they "handled" everything until after the holiday—and didn't bother him in the meantime. He also added a P.S.: "Don't let your mother steal anything from Rent-a-Crap."

At nine, Rosalie gave Isabelle her bath and put her in bed. Then, around eleven, Rosalie herself said she was going to bed. "Tell your ma I'm sorry I couldn't wait up." Her voice sounded sure that his mom would be there soon. As she'd been saying all evening, lots of planes come in after midnight. And planes get delayed, too. There was obviously some explanation.

Danny sat on the couch, looking at the tiny lights blinking on the Christmas tree, willing that his mom would knock on the door in the next minute. The next five minutes at least. Every time he heard a noise down the street he ran to the window, looking for a yellow cab; every time, his disappointment was worse. At midnight he decided to turn on the TV to the news channel, just to make sure no planes had crashed. He muted the TV as quickly as he could, but not before the noise had woken up Isabelle.

She came down the stairs, slowly, quietly, with the biggest grin on her face, but when she saw it was only Danny, she started to cry.

He picked her up and carried her back to her room. When she was still crying, he lay down next to her and held her hand. He knew Isabelle was crying because she'd gotten confused about the date and thought Santa was coming tonight, not their mom, but still, he felt so sorry for his sister at that moment. The bed wasn't really hers; the house wasn't really hers; even the pajamas she was wearing weren't really hers. She deserved a place she could stay for more than a month. She deserved to belong somewhere.

He closed his eyes, just for a minute, and then he was asleep and already dreaming that his mom was standing in the room, wearing the square skirt with the pink tulip. When he asked her where she found it, she said, "Trash is lucky." She was smiling, but still, he knew she wasn't happy. Before he could ask her why, she'd slipped away.

CHAPTER SIXTEEN

Changing the Game

Ah, Christmas Eve morning in Philadelphia: sheets of rain and thick fog and way too many people on the road who didn't know how to drive in bad weather. And why was Matthew out driving on this day, the first day in weeks, when his only plan was to sleep in and exercise and do as little about the Humpty problem as his nerves would allow? Because "his" kiddies were having a crisis—or, to put it more precisely, the kiddies who were *never* his responsibility and certainly *not* his responsibility now that their mother had finished rehab were having a crisis. Their nanny had called repeatedly, starting at seven-thirty in the morning and continuing nonstop until he gave up and answered. At least it was a real crisis. Their thieving mother had not returned.

A quick call to Changes revealed that the mother had been released yesterday morning and left for the airport around noon. According to Drossman's assistant, she had to be in Philadelphia somewhere. Matthew suspected she'd gotten off the plane and gone straight to her drug dealer, but the assistant said this was very unlikely because Kim, Danny's mom, had worked so hard to finish the program.

It sounded like rehab promotional BS to him, but all he cared about was finding the mother, wherever she was, and handing over her kids. Today. Several of Rosalie's messages had included the depressing fact that this was the last day she could take care of Danny and Isabelle. Stupid Christmas Eve meant the nanny agency would be closed and social services would be, too. Even Cassie was out of town. If the mother couldn't be found, he'd be stuck with the kids on Christmas—and that was out of the question.

Amelia used to call him Scrooge; more recent girlfriends called him the Grinch or just a selfish jerk, but it didn't make any difference: he refused to interact with anyone on December 25. Since he was eighteen years old, he'd always spent Christmas the same way: watching rock documentaries. Just last night he'd gotten out his DVD collection, which included classics like *The Last Waltz, Imagine, Sex Pistols: The Filth and the Fury*, and, of course, *This Is Spinal Tap*. He'd also rented a half dozen crappier ones, most courtesy of VH1's *Behind the Music*. He probably wouldn't need all of this to get through the day, but what if one of the discs was scratched? Best to be on the safe side.

When he arrived at the Malvern house, he expected Danny to act like his mother's no-show was somehow Matthew's fault (wasn't everything?), but he was still surprised when Danny didn't move or speak when he came through the door. The kid was slumped on the corner of the monstrously ugly brown couch, staring at the Christmas tree. Isabelle was face down on the floor, kicking and crying, with the Irish nanny kneeling next to her, stroking her hair.

He put down his umbrella. "Oh Christ, it's not that bad." Nobody but Rosalie acknowledged his arrival. He walked over to Danny. "Look, we're going to find your mother." He swallowed, thinking about driving his Porsche through a bad neighborhood, but it couldn't be helped. "We can leave right now if you want."

"Really?" Danny said.

"Yes, of course. I know you need her back." Not to mention that he needed to get back to the nineteen hours of music documentaries stacked on top of his DVD player.

Danny smiled and ran up the stairs. Seconds later, he was back with his shoes crammed on his feet and his coat in his hands. Unfortunately, Isabelle wasn't ready to go.

"Ma-ew," she'd cried when she finally looked up. But she walked in the other direction, toward the tree.

"We have to hurry," he said. "We're going on a trip."

"Wait!" She leaned down and picked something up. When she turned around and started toward him, he realized it was an iPod.

"Now where did you get that?"

She handed it to him, still crying. "Broke."

He knelt down. "So this is what's upsetting you? You broke it?"

"No!"

Rosalie said, "It came without any music on it. I told Isabelle that was normal, but I don't think she understands."

"It's not broken," Matthew said, picking up the sobbing little girl. Wishing he'd remembered to give her his iPod before he moved them here. No doubt Amelia had bought this new one for Isabelle, convinced that Matthew was a selfish ass for refusing to share with a three-year-old. The truth was he'd simply been too busy to think about it.

He tried to explain about downloading music, but the only thing

Isabelle responded to was his promise to pick up his iPod on their way to look for her mom. "It will have all the music you like, all right?" She smiled and planted a wet kiss on his cheek.

When he put her down, she handed the iPod to Danny. "I sorry," she said.

"The iPod's mine," Danny said. "Isabelle got that." He pointed at a large stuffed bunny with floppy pink ears.

"Wrong holiday. Amelia must be slipping."

"We didn't open Amelia's presents." Danny pointed under the tree, where Matthew could see two gifts with Amelia's trademark perfectly tied bow. "The bunny and the iPod came in the mail this morning. From my mom." The kid blinked at Matthew. "That's how I know where she is."

"I don't follow." How could their mother afford an iPod? Why would she send presents rather than bring them here?

"She gave me her new address. In the letter."

After a few minutes of frustrating discussion, Matthew realized that Danny thought Rosalie had told Matthew about this letter in one of her phone messages, and Rosalie thought that Danny had left his own message for Matthew about it. Isabelle was saying "wetter" over and over, like even she knew what the thing said.

"Let me see it." When Danny hesitated, Matthew said, "You're trying my patience."

The boy reached in his pocket and handed Matthew a crumpled-up piece of paper. Matthew read it quickly, but the meaning was all too clear. Danny's mother was still in Florida. She'd moved in with a "friend" she met in rehab, to get healthy and stay clean. She claimed she would always be *there* for Danny and his sister, but she obviously had no intention of coming back *here* for them. And her reason? "I know Dr. Connelly will take better care of you and Belle than I ever could. Trust me, baby, this is for the best."

He was so surprised he was sputtering. "She can't be serious."

Danny smiled. "I knew you wouldn't let this happen."

"You're damn right, I won't. I'm going to have her arrested." But even as he said it, he wondered if abandoning children was illegal. Fathers did it all the time. Even mothers could do it if they gave their children to social services. It wasn't illegal to desert your kids if they were safe, as opposed to, say, in a dumpster.

He remembered Danny's mother's misgivings about leaving her kids with him—the infamous "trash" discussion—and he wondered why she'd done such a complete turnaround. Danny was begging him not to put his mom in jail when Matthew interrupted. "Why does she think this is such a great environment for you?" When the kid didn't answer, Matthew knew that Danny himself had told her this, probably many times. Maybe he was trying to reassure her, or maybe he really believed it. At least it was obvious that Danny hadn't wanted this outcome.

He thought about calling Drossman's assistant, but what could she do? What could anyone do about the run of shit luck he was having? His boss was dying; his job was screwed; he was having a hell of a time forgetting about a disturbing encounter he'd had with a strange woman earlier in the week; and to top it off, he still hadn't gotten Phyllis Francis rehired. But dammit, he was watching his DVDs tomorrow. It was an exceedingly simple desire, and he would see it realized. No matter what it took.

Unfortunately, Danny's mom hadn't provided a phone number, but even if he could do a reverse lookup from the address, calling now could give her a chance to escape before he could return the kids. There was no choice. He told Rosalie to get Isabelle ready. Then he told Danny to pack a bag of things for him and his sister. "Take anything you really care about. The iPod. Whatever toys Isabelle loves. A few outfits."

"We don't have a bag."

"Improvise," he said, looking out the window.

He thanked Rosalie for her work and told her to lock up when she left. They were walking out the door, Danny holding a cardboard box, Matthew holding Isabelle, when Danny thought to grab the presents from under the tree. Two from Amelia; two from Rosalie; and one for the last person on earth who deserved a gift: their thieving, irresponsible mother.

Ah, Christmas Eve afternoon on a crowded airplane to Miami. First class sold out, business class nonexistent. Coach completely full, except for the miserable last row, where Matthew had to sit with his knees against his chest as soon as the people in the row in front of them put their seats back. The seats in the last row, he discovered, didn't go back. Moreover, even the aisle seat didn't afford any leg movement because the last row was right in front of the restroom, where a steady stream of travelers stood in line. They were unusually patient and friendly with one another, no doubt filled with Christmas cheer, but Matthew still detested them because whenever the restroom door opened he was hit with yet another blast of putrid air. He felt like he was in hell and he told Isabelle so, repeatedly, when she complained that she wanted "out." "Of course you do," he explained. "But there is no way out in hell."

Even the pretty stewardess who kept smiling at him didn't make him feel better. True, the sight of her great legs gave him a momentary physical reminder that he could still have sex, but that only depressed him more because he knew he couldn't actually have sex until he managed to stop thinking about what had happened on Monday night, when he'd picked up a crazy woman in a hotel bar.

He'd been desperate to distract himself from the horrible day he'd had with the layoffs and losing Phyllis and discovering his own company could turn against him. He wasn't up to wining and dining a woman he already knew and, admittedly, he was afraid

278

of a repeat of the Rachel disaster. So he went to a hotel in Center City, hoping to find someone who wanted what he wanted: a little harmless fun, nothing more. Two club sodas later, she appeared. Hot body, tight dress, black hair, brown eyes. A guest at the hotel, meaning he wouldn't have to get a room. He never found out her name, and she didn't want to know his, either. She was fascinated by the What If questions he used to flirt with her—already odd, as he hadn't used that technique in years—but before long, she managed to twist the game around, insisting on playing her own version instead. "What if we weren't strangers?" she said. "What if we were in love?"

It crossed his mind to run, but then she was kissing him and whispering, "I love you, Harry." She said Harry was her boyfriend or her husband; he couldn't remember. At first he'd said, "I love you, Margarita," since she was drinking margaritas, but that hadn't satisfied her. None of the names he tried satisfied her because she claimed he wasn't convincing. They were in a relatively dark corner. Her hand was moving up and down his crotch. He said they should go up to her room, but she said no. "You have to use the name of a woman you really love," she said. "That's the game. Take it or leave it."

He told her that he didn't love anyone. She called him a liar, but his eyes were closed and he was a little distracted by her amazingly dexterous fingers. When he felt like he couldn't stand it anymore, he finally said, "I love you, Amelia."

She grabbed his hand and took him to the elevator, and he didn't hesitate, convinced that all of it had been some kind of weird foreplay and was now, thankfully, over. But it was just beginning. He was up in her room for over two hours; she insisted on being in control; she didn't even want him to kiss her or reach for her or move from lying on his back. He went along because everything she was doing to him was so freaking incredible, but he still found it disturbing that every fifteen minutes or so she punctuated the pleasure by saying "I love you, Harry," and demanding his reply: "I love you, Amelia." It was hardly the kinkiest thing he'd ever heard of (or done), but nevertheless, it did feel creepy to keep saying Amelia's name while staring into the eyes of this stranger. And even in the throes of passion, he couldn't entirely ignore the sense that this woman wasn't just turned on, she was angry, as if she was determined to punish him (Harry?) for some unforgivable crime.

When it was over, she pointed to the door and rolled onto her stomach. No good-bye, good luck, thanks for this, or even fuck off. He dressed as quickly as possible, feeling embarrassed and even cheap, like he'd do anything to get laid. He took a cab back to his apartment and told himself he would forget about this by morning, but it hadn't happened. If anything, as the days went by he found himself struggling not to conclude that his years of meaningless sex were over, destroyed in a single night by this nameless woman for reasons he would never understand.

Isabelle was crawling all over him but he was lost in thought, wondering what had happened to his reasonably content, if oblivious, life. Even What If had been changed into something he no longer understood and definitely wanted to avoid. The game used to be all about possibilities; it was innocent; it was fun; it was like Matthew himself, eternally optimistic. But now no amount of Ativan (well, no *PDR*-approved amount) could stop his brain from assaulting him with What If questions about all the bad choices he'd made: from lying to Ben in Paris to naming Amelia in his speech, which had not only hurt her and Ben, but had handed Knolton the ammunition to ruin him.

He might have been able to trace all this back to the night he'd become entangled with the bummed-out boy sitting in the window seat and the little girl kneeing Matthew's stomach while she bashed him over the head with the airline magazine—except, unfortunately, he was no longer sure about the past, either. Why had he agreed to the creation of Pain Matters, to give only one example? What if marketing Galvenar wasn't as important as he'd always thought? Money still mattered, of course—please, he was sitting in coach for the first time in over a decade, and it was even worse than he remembered—but money couldn't excuse every decision he'd made.

And the questions that really scared the shit out of him: What if none of it had ever been important? What if Walter had even been wrong to give the last good part of his life to AD rather than to his wife? Christ, what if the nameless woman really was a punishment for Matthew having put his career above his relationship with Amel—?

Wait a minute. Was that the pilot announcing that they were about to land? Excellent! He would soon be free of the kiddies. Perhaps he could fly home first class. He would go to his apartment and watch the rockumentaries. His life would be back on track. Reflection was hell, but he was getting out of hell now, thank god.

"Ma-ew?" Isabelle said, patting his face with her small, soft hand.

"You have to sit down," he said. "Danny, strap her in."

The boy came out of his own daydream and did as he was told. An hour later they were in a cab, headed to the address in the letter.

Matthew had never been the type to pray, but he sent a message to the gods of fate to cut him a much-needed break and have the mother be at this address. Stupidly, that was all he thought to ask for. Oh well. He was getting used to regret.

Christmas Eve, 5:21, carrying a sleeping three-year-old up the stairs of a rundown apartment complex while yelling to her brother to

"Wait for us." Apartment 6D was, as expected, on the sixth floor. The dirty elevator was out of order, of course.

After he panted up the last flight of stairs, he saw that Danny had, in fact, not waited, and was already inside 6D. The woman talking to him in the living room was fortysomething, educated, lucid, surprisingly normal-looking for a former drug addict—and not his mother. She introduced herself as Susannah. He introduced himself as Matthew, fearing that Dr. Connelly might connote a maturity to raise children, not to mention an unlimited supply of cash.

Assessing the situation, Matthew realized that Susannah had elected herself protector of Kim. What else could explain her refusal to let the child see his own mother because, supposedly, Kim was sleeping? Danny was upset, but Matthew was furious. As he told this Susannah, they'd come all the way from Philadelphia, and Danny would not only see his mother, he would live with her. As would Isabelle. "Sorry, but I only came to deliver them. I have to get back home to be with my own family for Christmas."

Not true, but close enough. He'd watched those rockumentaries so many times that John Lennon, The Clash, and the rest of the musicians might as well be his family. He knew them better than most people knew their visit-only-on-the-holiday relatives.

"Can I have a word with you first?" Susannah said. "It's important."

No good could come of a private chat, he was sure; still, he couldn't just leave the kids without knowing what she was going to say. What if Kim wasn't even there? It was a small apartment, only one bedroom judging by the number of doors. If Danny's mother was in that bedroom, he hoped she really was asleep. Otherwise, she was a heartless bitch, knowing her kids were in the apartment and refusing to see them.

He was right; there was only one bedroom. After he handed

Isabelle off to Danny, Susannah took him into the tiny bathroom. She sat down on the toilet seat. He sat on the edge of the tub and tried not to cough as she blew smoke in his face.

"Kim is sick," she whispered.

Oh Christ. Using again already. He shook his head, but before he could respond Susannah said, "You're a doctor, so you'll understand why the med staff at Changes said it was a miracle she was still walking around." Susannah took a deep drag. "She's been HIV positive for years, but now she has full-blown AIDS. T-cell count in the eighties, virus in the millions."

He shouldn't have been surprised, given how terrible Danny's mother looked when she left for Changes, but he was surprised—or, more precisely, stunned. Of course Danny hadn't been told about his mother's condition, but why hadn't Jerome Drossman called Matthew about this? Patient confidentiality? Drossman had never been a stickler for following rules; why start now?

Kim's case was undoubtedly serious, with a double-digit CD4—cluster of differentiation 4, or what Susannah called T-cell, count—and skyrocketing viral load; yet the right combination of drugs could conceivably turn it around. He told Susannah this. "I don't know what she's tried, but there are several new drugs for AIDS. My own company has—"

"She started treatment in rehab." Susannah stood up very slowly, as though her legs were unsteady or injured, Matthew couldn't tell, and pulled on the mirror above the sink to reveal a small medicine cabinet filled with prescriptions for Danny's mother. Matthew recognized AD's latest and best antiretroviral. The staff at Changes clearly knew what they were doing.

When Susannah sat back down she said, "The AIDS is only part of the problem. After Kim got clean, she was having bad headaches. They did tests and finally, last week, they told her she has AIDS-related CNS lymphoma." Susannah's eyes filled with tears. "She knows she's going to die, but she still finished the program. She told me it was important to her son. She's such a strong woman."

CNS lymphoma: cancer of the brain. Matthew knew that as a complication of severe AIDS, it was very aggressive and usually fatal in months. But still, it was impossible to predict how long Danny's mother had left. He told Susannah that the right drugs and radiation could even bring on a remission. It was unlikely, but worth a shot.

Susannah already knew all this. She said the staff at Changes had explained it to Kim. "They gave her the forms to follow up at the clinic here. She's going to do it. She wants to fight this."

"Then why doesn't she want her kids with her?"

"Because she can't support them." Susannah paused and put out her cigarette in a planter of dirt on the windowsill. She looked at him. "You obviously can."

"She could get public assistance. Hell, I could give her some money if that's—"

"And what happens to them when she dies? I have multiple sclerosis. There are days when I can't even walk." Susannah glanced at the door. "Should I send them out to stand on the street and hope another rich guy with a good heart comes along to save them?"

"But I don't want to save them." He knew how bad that sounded, but shit, wasn't this an insane request? "Look, I work constantly. I don't have a good heart. This is all a bizarre mistake."

"Kim says you're a gift from God, to make up for everything that went wrong in her life. She calls you her kids' guardian angel."

No one had ever thought of him in this way, for the obvious reason that it was utterly ridiculous. He told Susannah as much, and when she didn't believe him, he brought up the one thing he thought would convince her. He said that he worked for a multinational pharmaceutical company. "I'm sure you have a problem with that." He exhaled. "Everyone in America seems to."

"I don't trust drug companies, if that's what you mean." She lowered her eyes. "Mainly because I was in rehab to get off a prescription medicine my doctor gave me for pain. You've probably heard of it. It's one of those new drugs, constantly advertised on TV. In the ads, the people are always outside, hiking and jogging and riding bikes. They call it the 'miracle drug.'"

Uh-oh. Just when he thought this day couldn't get any worse.

"The doctor promised me it wasn't addictive, but I guess my body didn't listen. I kept trying to quit. I ended up losing my marriage." She hugged herself and rocked back and forth, still looking down, staring at her knees. "The rehab guy said he's only seen a few dozen cases like mine, but he's sure there will be more once . . ."

He couldn't bring himself to listen to another word. It was obvious she was talking about Galvenar, but he didn't want to accept that his beloved baby had hurt this woman. Despite a *slight* chemical similarity between Galvenar and other narcotics (like codeine and morphine and, yes, okay, heroin), the FDA had concluded that Galvenar had such a low addiction potential that it didn't even need to be a controlled substance. Of course the FDA wasn't perfect, but they weren't always wrong, either. The clinical trials had shown that Galvenar was a good drug, and AD had the (ghostwritten) science articles to prove it. There was no hidden data, no spooky cover-up.

And yet Matthew could hardly pretend that this was news to him, though god, did he want to. He'd been in dozens of meetings about the Galvenar postmarket *problem*, but it was always discussed in terms of numbers and cases, not real people like Susannah. And yes, it might have been his idea to pump donations into rehab clinics like Changes to ensure that Galvenar was kept off the list of treated addictions in those clinics' press materials, but he'd convinced himself he was just doing his job and protecting the company. After all, wasn't it the prescribing doctor's responsibility to read the

Galvenar label that specifically warned to use with caution in people with a history of addiction? Obviously Susannah qualified; she was smoking another cigarette right now. And each and every day, AD received *real* letters from chronic-pain patients saying Galvenar had given them back their lives. The risk/benefit analysis was conclusive: the drug helped a lot more people than it harmed. It was just bad luck that the woman in front of him had been in the latter category. No one to blame. Certainly not his fault, right? Right?

Shit.

At least Susannah no longer insisted that he had a good heart after he told her he'd been in charge of marketing Galvenar.

"I hope the money you made was worth it." Her voice was bitter. She blew smoke in his face. "Go on back to your job."

If only he could blink and find himself back at work. Even the disaster with Humpty was better than this mess.

Susannah reached over and opened the door so quickly that Matthew saw Danny moving away. He'd been listening to everything, as always. Damn.

Isabelle was still asleep on the couch, but Danny was already out the door and running down the stairs. Matthew followed the sound of the boy's crying. He finally caught up with him behind the building, standing in the patchy grass, pathetically hugging a ratty palm tree.

"Go away!" Danny yelled. "Don't touch me!"

Matthew was bent over, trying to catch his breath. "I don't plan to."

The boy cried for a while, mumbling largely indecipherable things, though Matthew did hear something to the effect that it was all Matthew's fault for sending his mom to Changes. No surprise there. The sun was lying on the horizon, a pink and orange ball, when Danny's cries turned to agonized sobs as he shifted the blame onto himself.

"That is not true," Matthew said. No response. He repeated it. Still no response, and finally he grabbed the kid by the shoulders and pried him loose from the tree. "It's not your fault your mother has AIDS. That's absurd."

Naturally, Danny took out his frustration on Matthew, hitting him in the chest and arms multiple times. All the while he was stammering out his blame theory, starting with the first night in Matthew's apartment, when he'd told his mom he wouldn't go with her after she stole the money, moving to when he'd convinced her to go to Changes by claiming that Isabelle would be better off with "stupid Doctor Connelly" (hello?), and ending with the saddest shit in the world: that he'd thought of her as a "dragon" and he'd been mad at her since Isabelle was born.

"You think being angry with someone can make them sick? I can prove you're wrong."

The boy wiped snot on his shirt. "How?"

"You're mad at me right now. I'm fine."

"I hate you."

He shrugged. "More proof."

"You're mean!" Another thump on the chest from the kid's skinny arm, more tears. "I thought you liked Isabelle, but you don't even care."

Actually, this was untrue—surprisingly so. Even while Susannah was talking, he'd been obsessing about the little girl's health. Surely she'd been tested for HIV, but what about HCV (hepatitis)? Given her mother's history, Isabelle needed to see a specialist, and Matthew knew a great one at Children's Hospital of Philadelphia. Except Isabelle wouldn't be in Philadelphia anymore. He kept forgetting that part.

"I do like your sister. My decision has nothing—"

"Why don't you like me?" He was spitting out the words. "Why didn't you ever like me at all?" Here the boy broke down again and gasped out something about the iPod playlist. What? He'd wanted one, too, but Matthew hadn't noticed? More crying, then another airless stammer about how hard he'd tried to make everything okay. But nothing ever worked out. He was so scared. His mommy was dying.

Matthew was having chest pains. From the humidity and the heat? From running around after a ten-year-old? It occurred to him that if he *was* having a heart attack, he could drop dead behind this ugly beige apartment building in Miami and never have to think about how this kid felt right now, confronting this unimaginable loss. Or what would be an unimaginable loss unless, like Matthew himself, you had experience with it. Failing to save an addict parent—check. Losing your mother—check. Finding yourself alone with the worst shit life has to offer—check and check and check again.

He felt his chest muscles constricting. Heart attack or sympathy: either way, damn, this really hurt.

He stood there for another minute, cursing the pain, until finally, against all his better judgment, against reason, against his own nature, he reached out and collected Danny in his arms. The boy struggled for a minute, but then he collapsed and let Matthew hold him up. Danny's tears and snot were staining Matthew's suede jacket, but what the hell. At least his chest wasn't getting worse; he wasn't going to die of this. And neither would Danny. He would be changed in ways he might never understand, but he would keep going. Such was life. No other choice but to go on.

After several minutes, when Danny had finally calmed down, Matthew said, "Are you ready to go back upstairs? Your mom may be awake now. Maybe she'll feel well enough that you can spend Christmas with her."

It was too dark to see Danny's face, but Matthew heard the jumpiness in the little boy's voice. "Where will you be?"

Ah, Christmas Eve, standing outside a slum, sweating in a jacket that he should have taken off before he left the Miami airport, confronting the million-dollar question. What would he do with these kids?

He looked in the direction of the ratty-ass palm tree. He didn't want to be involved—this wasn't his responsibility, it had nothing to do with him—and yet the unfortunate truth was that he did care about Danny and Isabelle. There was no way to deny it, and he was too tired to even try. The happiness of two homeless kids was now more important to him than watching John Lennon and U2. He was screwed.

"Waiting for you," he said to Danny, and sighed. "Where else?"

CHAPTER SEVENTEEN

A Spot on the Heart

From the outside, Amelia and Ben's Christmas looked absolutely fine. They woke up early at their great new house near the Art Museum that had everything they needed, even a lovely yellow nursery with a wallpaper border of dancing teddy bears. They took a morning train to Connecticut, where they spent the day celebrating with her family in Greenwich. Amelia got along well enough with her stockbroker brother, and enjoyed seeing his wife and their two preteen daughters. Her nausea had finally become "only" morning sickness, not morning, noon, and night, and she was able to enjoy the delicious dinner her mother made: she-crab soup, glazed ham, potatoes lyonnaise, string beans with slivered roasted almonds, pecan pie, and apple tartin. Ben was friendly enough, and he avoided any mention of his work, as Amelia had asked him to, knowing that it confused her family (and that her mother thought it was not only dull, but a little bit egocentric). By nine o'clock that night they were back home, settled in their cozy living room, reading together. All in all, a good day with very little stress—except inside Amelia's mind, where she was being tortured by fear and uncertainty.

A few days earlier she'd taken a prenatal blood test. It was quick and painless and utterly routine, and she hadn't really worried about it until Friday, when her OB had called with the results. The numbers were confusing, but the one thing Amelia did understand was the conclusion. Her baby was now considered "high risk" for Down syndrome.

Of course she sobbed and called Ben and sobbed some more, but when she calmed down enough to think, she did what any good researcher would do: she spent the whole day in front of her computer, downloading articles, reading pregnancy blogs, searching for what this really meant. When Ben came home, she told him there was nothing to be afraid of. "False positives happen all the time with this test." She handed him an article that she'd highlighted. "See, it says ninety-nine percent of the time the babies are absolutely fine."

He sat down on the couch and quickly scanned the article. "It doesn't say anything about maternal age." He looked up and took her hand. "That's the issue here, babe."

She pulled her hand away. "I don't understand why you always talk like I'm so old. It's not true, and it's insulting."

Almost from the day she'd told Ben she was pregnant he had been pointing out something or other that was "a serious concern at her age." Every time he said it, she felt awful. He'd even given her the statistics for miscarriage and she'd been shocked to discover that she had a 33 percent chance of losing the baby in the first trimester.

There was nothing she could do about that, but she did decide to wait until the twelfth week before telling anyone she was pregnant. Only Matthew knew, and she still didn't understand why Ben had told him.

"I'm sorry," Ben said. "I don't think you're old, but from a medical point of view, you're considered an elderly *prima gravida*."

Amelia knew *prima gravida* was a first-time pregnant woman, but elderly? "Great," she said. "Thanks for sharing." She knew how snotty she sounded, but this test had made her feel like her body was not only old but defective, like it couldn't even protect her baby. "I don't care what doctors call it. I know a lot of women my age who had babies and everything was fine."

"That doesn't tell us anything about the risk. People you know can't be considered a representative sample. The plural of anecdote is not data." He sat up straighter and started thumping his foot against the couch leg. "Before the test, the risk was already high based only on your age. Recent research suggests that the father's age also increases the risk. Taking into account the figures you gave me for the serum test, the free beta-hCG and PAPP-A, and also—"

"Just tell me what they mean by 'high risk.' In English."

"The estimated chance is one in twenty-three."

She swallowed. "That's not so bad. Twenty-two babies will be healthy for every one who has Down syndrome. I'll just have to believe that mine is one of the healthy ones."

"And we'll know soon enough from the CVS. Nothing to worry about yet."

CVS was chorionic villus sampling. Amelia had agreed to have the test because Ben had told her, weeks ago, that it was "essential." It was scheduled for the day after Christmas, but she still wasn't sure she could go through with it. Originally she'd been happy about this blood screen, thinking that when it turned out to be normal Ben might agree that she could skip the test. It was such an invasive procedure; the doctor actually stuck a needle into the placenta. She'd even read about so-called limb-reduction defects—the baby losing a finger or toe. Ben said that was very rare, especially if the doctor was experienced, and her OB was sending her to one of the best specialists in the country. The risk of miscarriage was also overstated, according to Ben, but she didn't see how she could take that lightly if he was right that her chance for a miscarriage was already high.

"I've been thinking about the CVS," she said. "I know we want our baby to be healthy, but we could do an ultrasound first. Then, if—"

He shook his head. "An ultrasound can only show markers for Down. It's not definitive."

Amelia had read about these markers on the web. They were things like a missing bone in the nose or unusually thick skin at the back of the neck. Lots of others, including the one that had made her cry when she read about it: a bright spot on the heart. It sounded like something beautiful; maybe that's why it seemed so sad, thinking of the babies who had those bright spots on their tiny hearts.

"At this point," Ben said, "the only way to be absolutely sure is to do the CVS now or an amnio at sixteen weeks." He paused. "I'm sure you don't want to wait to find out if the fetus is healthy."

"No," she said, though the truth was more complicated. She felt like she couldn't wait five minutes to hear that her baby was all right, but she might never be ready to hear the other answer, that it wasn't.

When she woke up the next morning she told Ben she'd had a dream about the two of them in the park with a toddler. "And it was a beautiful spring day. Maybe it's a sign that everything will work out."

Ben didn't like listening to dreams, but he would if she kept it

293

short. This time, she wished she hadn't bothered because his response was so deflating. "It's a sign that you're thinking positively. That's good, even if it can't influence the outcome."

"How do you know it can't be a real sign?"

He looked confused. "Are you serious?"

Was she? She was hardly a mystical person, and yet being pregnant made her feel that she was connected to something bigger than herself. A universal life force? A benevolent being? God?

When she didn't answer, he said, "I'm glad you're keeping your spirits up. I'll be home around seven. We can have dinner together."

He'd promised to work fewer hours; it was part of their agreement when he asked her to come back from New York. So far he was keeping his promise, though their time together was still strained. Sometimes she thought he was a different person now that he worked at the lab. Or she was different from being pregnant. Or (her secret fear) that she'd never known him that well to begin with. But at least he was trying. He'd even stopped calling the baby a fetus—though she noticed that he'd reverted again last night, but maybe that was understandable. Maybe he was trying to keep himself from being heartbroken if the worst happened.

Since it was two days before Christmas, she had no choice; she had to finish her shopping. She went to the gigantic mall in the suburbs, which was mobbed of course. By the time she got home it was after seven. Ben was having a glass of wine and talking on the phone to Natalie, an old friend of his from Boston. They'd never been romantically involved, and Amelia wasn't jealous; she actually thought it was a good sign. He used to talk to Natalie a lot when he was traveling for the foundation, but he was always too busy since they'd been in Philadelphia. Maybe he was starting to relax into the work at the lab.

On her way home from the mall she'd picked up a broiled

chicken and pasta from Trader Joe's, but she didn't want to start eating without him. She put the food in the refrigerator and threw together a half-sandwich of ham and Swiss, just to tide her over. Her OB had said she could eat whenever she was hungry, and since she was always hungry, this was great news.

Amelia was sucking mustard off her fingertip when she heard Ben say, "She's not Catholic. I think she said her parents were Unitarians. She doesn't even believe in God, as far as I know."

Normally she made a point of leaving the room whenever Ben was talking to anyone, to give him his privacy. But this was different. He was talking about her.

"I've decided I do believe in something," Amelia said loudly. "I think of it as Universal Benevolence."

He nodded in her direction. Good; he knew she was listening. Now she could eavesdrop as much as she liked.

"I think you're right," Ben said to Natalie. "We have to discuss what I want, too."

Amelia took her sandwich and sat down at the kitchen table— her beautiful blue tile table, which she'd found in Mexico; it was so comforting to have her own things after far too long living in hotels. Ben was in the den, which was connected to the kitchen. He was on the floor, leaning against her walnut file cabinet. "I've never told her how I felt about that," he said. "Don't you think it's too late now?"

"No," Amelia said. "It's never too late." Then, for some reason, she giggled. The sandwich tasted so good, and she knew she wouldn't throw up. Maybe that was all it took for her to be happy, as long as she didn't think about that test.

"Hey, babe," Ben said, turning around. "I didn't know you were back."

He sounded sincere—and embarrassed. He was even blushing.

She finished the sandwich, but her happiness evaporated. She went into the bedroom and took off her tight jeans and put on her sweatpants. When Ben got off the phone, she was lying on the bed, curled up in a ball, thinking.

A half hour later they were sitting in the kitchen, eating chicken and pasta, when he said, "I need to ask you something."

"So I gathered," Amelia said coolly.

"Are you pro-choice?"

"Of course." She stared at him. "Why?"

He didn't say anything.

She put down her fork. "Do you want to ask if I'm a Democrat, too?"

"No," he said. He swallowed a bite of his chicken. "I'm sorry I brought it up."

"Brought what up?"

"Nothing." He was staring at his plate.

She waited for several minutes, finishing her pasta. Finally, she said, "Do you want to talk about what we should do if our baby has Down syndrome? Is that what you're hinting at?"

Ben exhaled. "I don't want to hurt your feelings, but yes. I do want to talk about what we'll do if the fetus has an abnormality." He grew quiet, but his foot was banging a nervous rhythm on the table leg. "I don't think I can handle that."

She paused. "Me either."

"That's great," he said. "Now you can see why I'm glad you're doing the CVS test after Christmas."

"Because if it does have Down syndrome, you want me to get an abortion?"

"Yes." His voice was grateful. "That's what I want. And I'm so relieved to hear that you feel the same way."

She nodded, but it hit her what this would mean. She would not have her baby anymore. She would probably never be a mother.

The next day, Christmas Eve, Ben biked to the lab in the morning to do a little work, but Amelia couldn't concentrate. She kept thinking about those babies with the bright spots on their hearts. Some of them would go on to be diagnosed as perfectly normal, usually through amniocentesis, but those that weren't would probably be aborted. The abortion rate for babies with Down syndrome was something like 90 percent—assuming their parents used the available genetic tests. It was obviously a bioethics issue, and Amelia wondered why she'd never really thought about it before. She read message boards and blogs where parents of Down kids called this a clear case of eugenics. Their passionate voices speaking out for their children's rights moved her. The pictures of the children—so beautiful in a wispy, otherworldly way—haunted and confused her.

When Ben got home she was determined not to discuss this, afraid she'd spoil the evening. She'd bought a red silk blouse to wear for their first Christmas Eve together, and she was hurt when he didn't say a word about the blouse or how she looked in it. She was finally gaining weight; maybe she was ugly to him now? They hadn't had sex once since they'd moved into this house. Was *she* defective to him, too?

Of course she didn't bring up the test on Christmas Day, either, at least not while they were in Connecticut. But that night, when she and Ben were back home, sitting in their new living room, she asked him to tell her everything that could go wrong with a Down syndrome child. He had a long list: from heart problems to epilepsy, from sleep apnea to blood disorders. He must have thought he was helping her remember that she was making the right decision about having the CVS.

She was sitting on her favorite green chair with the overstuffed cushions: wide enough for two, snuggly enough for one with a blanket and a book. She thought for a moment, then she asked Ben if he'd ever considered that Down syndrome could someday be accepted as a variation in nature. "I remember the day after

Thanksgiving, when you and Matthew were talking about the CNV breakthrough. You told Matthew that copy number variation would change the way we look at normal. You said it could change genetic testing, too."

"I was talking about Uniparental Disomy. When a child gets two copies of a chromosome from one parent and none from the other. We don't know the full effects of this yet, but we do know Trisomy 21. The condition has been in the literature since 1866, when John Langdon Down identified it."

"Are you sure there's nothing we can learn from people with Down syndrome?"

"I wouldn't say that." He looked at her. "I think we may be able to cure it someday."

"I mean the people themselves. The ones who are living with the disorder."

"I'm sure they have something to teach us about patience and kindness. They can help our compassion evolve."

"But they don't deserve to live, you're sure about that?"

"Of course not." He finally put his journal down. "How can you even think I'd believe something so inhumane? I only want the abortion because I know I can't take care of a child with significant health problems."

She curled up tighter into her chair. "But what if I can't bring myself to do it?"

"What do you mean?" His voice was cracking the way it did when he was really upset. He turned around and looked at her. "I thought we already settled this."

"I want to see it the way you do . . . but I—"

He shook his head. "It's your choice. I know that. I won't abandon you whatever you decide."

Amelia knew why he used the word *abandon*—because he always said his own father abandoned the family after the divorce. But still, it seemed odd the way he said this, though she forced herself not to be nervous and just listen to him.

"I feel so overwhelmed." His voice was miserable. He was running his hand through his hair. "I don't understand how we ended up here."

"It's nothing we did," she said gently. "You told me that the risk for Down syndrome is statistical, no one's fault, nothing that could be done to—"

"No, I mean I don't understand how we got into a position where we have to worry about this." He stood up and walked over to the bookshelves. He was silent for a minute. "Everyone who knows me knows I never wanted children. But apparently, you didn't know that. I can't fathom why we never had that conversation."

"Well, it's too late to have it now." She hoped she didn't sound as hysterical as she felt. "Obviously."

"I'm not blaming you. I know I shouldn't have assumed you were using birth control." He sighed and looked at his hands. "Ever since Matt told me that you always wanted to be a mother, I've been trying to adjust, but the last few days have—"

"Matthew told you that?" It was the least important of everything Ben was saying here, and so the easiest to focus on. "When?"

"In Paris, when I told him you were pregnant. He knew how I felt about having children, but he said I would have to change. He said he understood how hard it was because he was going to have to change himself, too, now that he was starting a family. At the time, I felt like he really did understand, though of course later he admitted he'd made it up. I was surprised, but I shouldn't have been. Matt has never been above lying if he thinks the ends justify the means."

"I thought he lied because he was jealous."

"Where did you get that idea?"

She flashed to the day after Thanksgiving, standing out on the sidewalk with Matthew, but she said, "You told me yourself that he was still in love with me. Supposedly."

"He is. That's why he was desperate to convince me to change, even if he had to lie to do it. He wants you to be happy. In the last month, he's told me a dozen times that I have to step up to my responsibility now that you're pregnant and marry you. 'She loves you,' Matt keeps saying. 'She's having your kid. You're a lucky guy, and you're acting like a jackass.'"

Amelia was speechless. Matthew had told that lie about starting a family for her sake?

Ben was still talking. "I want you to be happy, too, but I'm not sure I can change how I feel." He closed his eyes for a second. "Even if the CVS shows no genetic abnormalities, what if the child is born with another illness, one we don't have a test for yet? What if it develops autism? What if it's in an accident and ends up paralyzed? What if it gets leukemia?"

"I think every parent worries about these things. But you tell yourself that if something terrible happens, you'll—"

"What? Dedicate my life to taking care of it? Give up everything else—my lab, my commitment to the world's poor—for one child?"

"You could still work."

"But the child would have to come first, and the work would suffer. My life's work." He went back to his chair and sat, thumping his feet, messing with his hair.

"What choice do we have?"

"It's not really 'we,' Amelia. If you didn't want to be a mother, you'd have a choice. But if I don't want to be a father, I don't."

She didn't know what to say to that. After a few minutes, she stood up and went into the bedroom. She felt like such a fool, moving to this lovely house, unpacking all her things, spending so much time daydreaming in the nursery. Dreaming of a family with him.

The next morning she couldn't bring herself to have the CVS test and risk a miscarriage. She was watching an Adam Sandler movie when Ben came home. It was dark outside, and windy. The branches of a tree were slapping against the back bedroom window.

When she told him that she didn't have the test, he sighed but he didn't say anything. "I don't think our baby has Down syndrome," she said. "I have a feeling that everything is going to be fine."

"But you can't know that."

"No, I can't. And it's not the only issue anymore, is it?"

He looked in the direction of the window, and so did she. It faced their little yard. Amelia wanted to plant flowers there. Ben thought it would be a great place to put a barbecue grill. She'd imagined standing at that window, watching Ben and their son or daughter playing catch. It was a silly daydream, since Ben had never liked sports. He rode his bike to work only because he believed exercising was important for mental clarity, and he was opposed to driving unless he had to because it was bad for the environment.

"You do have a choice," she finally said. "You can leave me." She paused. "When the child is born, you can see him or her whenever you want, as much as you want, or not at all. That's your choice, too. But you can't stay and not be happy about this pregnancy. I don't want to live with you like that. That's my choice."

He walked out of the room and Amelia forced herself to concentrate on the movie. She'd seen it several times, but each time she was struck again by how good it was. Yes, it fit the classic romantic-comedy formula that "love conquers all," but the *all* in this case wasn't a misunderstanding or a nutty relative; it was a brain injury. Even more impressive, the brain injury was permanent. Adam Sandler and Drew Barrymore had to figure out how to live together in a world that was inherently unpredictable. Nothing was guaranteed in life, and Amelia was trying to make her peace with that, but it was so hard.

The next day Ben loaded up his few possessions in his backpack and left to stay at the campus hotel, "for a while." Of course he agreed to pay for the rental on the house and whatever she needed. Amelia didn't plan to stay in Philadelphia, but she felt like she had to be in this house, surrounded by her things, until she decided what to do next. She'd lost everything but her possessions: Ben, of course, though more truthfully, she'd never had him; her career and even her assistant Ethan, who'd quit a few days after Matthew's speech. She wasn't even sure how she would support herself and the baby. The trust fund wouldn't come close to paying the bills if her child really had a major health problem. Even her mother didn't have that kind of money, now that she was living on Amelia's father's life insurance.

Before Ben left, he sat down next to Amelia and cried. He said he felt terrible that he couldn't be what she needed or wanted.

She refused to cry again. "You couldn't help it. I wanted a child, you didn't."

"I tried to, for you."

"But you don't really want a family."

"I don't look at family in the usual way." He dropped his head in his hands. "I honestly thought you didn't, either."

She knew what he was referring to. Last spring, before he started calling her his soul mate, they'd had a long conversation about poverty and the developing world. Both of them had agreed that it was terrible that Americans lived in luxury while millions of people died of starvation and disease, that most Americans seemed to care only about their own families. "I think all the world's children deserve to be taken care of," Amelia had said. "They're all part of my family."

Now she said, "I guess I'm not as good as I thought."

She meant it. From an ethical perspective, how could one child matter more than thousands? And yet it was undeniable: her own baby now mattered to her more than every starving child in Africa. Having Ben commit to taking care of that baby—in sickness and in health and all the normal things in between, from the baby's first step to playing catch and going to the beach—obviously mattered more than how quickly he found a cure for trypanosomiasis, a disease that, every day, including this one, would kill at least two hundred real live human beings and sicken thousands.

Two hundred human beings with families who would mourn them.

Two hundred human beings, every day, that Ben might save—as long as he didn't get distracted. As long as he didn't give his heart away to Amelia and her one child.

Some magazine had just named Ben number one on a list of "The World's Most Ethical People," and maybe he deserved it. Maybe this was what a truly ethical person looked like.

All her life she'd been trying to figure out what good was. She still didn't know, but she was surprised to realize that she didn't care if she was doing the morally right thing this time. She felt oddly relieved.

The rest of the day she spent in a strange daydream, thinking about her past. She even went into the attic, where she had a box of things from her childhood, including pictures and letters from her sponsored children. She sat cross-legged on the dusty attic floor, looking at Esteysi and Pablo and Astrid and all the others. She'd been a child herself, the same age as each of these kids. Why had she felt like she could save them? Why was she always trying so hard?

And the questions before her now: Who would she be if she stopped? Would she ever believe she was good enough—just as she was? Could she even believe she deserved to have all the ordinary things other people had: a family, laughter, happiness?

CHAPTER EIGHTEEN

The Answer Is Four

It was December 31 and Matthew had already accepted the sad fact that, for the first time in his adult life, he wouldn't be out partying on New Year's Eve. He could have hired a babysitter for the kids, but he'd kept putting it off, hoping Danny would snap out of the depression he'd been in since they left Miami. If anything, the kid's mother being so much nicer now that she was off drugs had broken Danny's heart all over again. Maybe it had been a mistake to let the kids spend Christmas there. It had certainly sucked from Matthew's point of view, but apparently something sucking for him didn't prove it was good for the kiddies. Meaning martyrdom was not necessary to be an effective guardian. Thank god, as being a martyr was not one of his strengths.

Cooking was, though, so tonight, Chef Matthew was coming out of retirement, in the hope of distracting Danny, but also because it seemed like he should do something to celebrate his successful coup against Knolton this morning, though in truth it didn't feel like much of a victory. He and the kids went shopping and picked up all the ingredients for Matthew's mother's delicious spaghetti: sausage, zucchini, mushrooms, tomatoes, fresh garlic and basil, and baby mozzarella cheese. They also got two loaves of bread from Metropolitan, and a variety of teeth-rotting cookies and dough-nuts that Isabelle wanted and Danny said would be "okay." He said "okay" about everything, including the movie Matthew rented for them to watch after dinner, *Star Wars,* and even the music Matthew had been downloading for him all week. It was a tad irritating, but understandable. The poor kid hadn't smiled once since Kim had kissed him good-bye.

Matthew had promised to work out a way that Danny could see his mother again, soon, somehow. He wasn't trying to be vague; he just didn't know if a hospice in Philly would take Kim or if she even wanted to leave her life in Miami with Susannah. Of course the other alternative was for Danny to fly back to Florida, but the tim-ing would depend on Kim's condition. If she made progress with the meds and radiation, they'd have options, but if not . . . Matthew couldn't think about it yet, but he would deal with it when the time came. Somehow.

While Matthew was frying the sausage, he told Danny some interesting facts about Philadelphia, including that the city had the largest urban park in the country. He suggested going to Fair-mount Park the next morning, if it was warm enough and not raining. Or they could watch the parade. Or rent more movies. They had to think of something cool for the first day of the new year, right?

Danny was sitting on the opposite counter, morosely looking

at nothing. Isabelle was lying down in the middle of the kitchen floor, pretending to read one of her Dr. Seuss books. In the last few days, Matthew had read so many of the good doctor's books that the rhymes were all blurring together. He'd be glad when Isabelle really could read. Hopefully they taught that in preschool, along with tying shoes and starting up the iPod.

Finding a preschool for Isabelle was one of numerous things on his kiddie to-do list. He was waiting for Cassie to come back from her holiday—and hoping by then he'd have a better sense of how to handle all this. So far, he knew that Danny and Isabelle liked their iPods; they liked his television; and they had low expectations of him. Isabelle even seemed to prefer being at his apartment instead of the house in the suburbs, which was a good sign, given how god-awful that rental furniture was. A promising beginning.

He'd brought them back to the apartment because he was determined to solve the Humpty problem before the end of the year and he knew he could work better there than in the Malvern house. Each night when the kiddies went to bed, he took out the box he'd stolen from his office and pored over the files Walter had left behind, still searching for something he could use against Humpty. Finally, last night around two A.M., he'd found it. The details were very complicated and specific to pharma (thus, outside of the Dumpty's expertise), but the upshot was that Harold had made an under-the-table deal with a generic manufacturer that, in the wrong hands—say, at the Department of Justice—*could* be interpreted as a violation of antitrust laws.

Now that Matthew was in possession of this interesting fact, he had to decide what to do with it. There were several ways to play this, but in the morning he went with his hunch and called Stephen Mezalski at home. When Mezalski said that Matthew's information was "extremely disturbing," it was obvious his hunch had been right. Mezalski had been *hoping* Matthew would find some dirt on

Knolton. Of course. This was why he'd told Matthew to cooperate fully with Knolton in the investigation: to make it obvious that Knolton had set him up—and give Matthew the incentive to bring that bastard down.

Though Matthew was (always) glad to win, he was very disappointed in Mezalski. The man had refused to lift a finger to stop that psycho from screwing with him and the company. Still, ding-dong, the wicked egg would soon be dead, and Mezalski had already agreed that of course Phyllis Francis would be reinstated immediately. He also hinted that Matthew could have whatever else he wanted, but Matthew didn't know what he wanted anymore, nor was he in any mood to think about it. He had other, more pressing concerns.

When Danny didn't respond to Matthew's Philadelphia talk, Matthew went on to other topics as he added the rest of the ingredients to the spaghetti sauce. He was in the middle of an amusing rant about Humpty's personal-hygiene habits (that bald head couldn't shine like that without some kind of polish) when Danny said, "Why do you hate Amelia?"

"I don't hate her." Where did that come from? He looked at Danny. "If I hated her, why would I have invited her to come to dinner tonight?"

Danny rolled his eyes like he knew that Matthew had only asked the happy couple over in the hope that he could talk to Ben while Amelia provided a much-needed break from child care. He'd left Ben several messages and even emailed Amelia about it yesterday—after deciding that Ben's cell must be dead since he hadn't answered for a week—but no response. Maybe they were out of town? Oh well. He could handle the kiddies alone. He'd been doing it for a week now and, yes, it was boring at times, but it wasn't that bad. If only Danny's mood would improve, they could even have a decent night.

At least the kid was interested in something, so Matthew continued. "The problem with Amelia is actually quite complicated." Time to ratchet it up with an allusion to tonight's featured film. "You see, long ago in a galaxy far, far away, she was my girlfriend." He stirred the sauce and tasted it. Perfect. "Back when I was young and stupid. Much stupider than you are now, I should add." Oops, that didn't come out right. "What I'm saying is that you are already more mature than I was at the time when I fell for Amelia."

Danny thought for a minute. "Is that why you kept all the pictures of her?"

Matthew said yes before he realized what this meant. How could Danny have seen those? The pictures were in his personal vault closet. Most of the closet was full of useless personal memorabilia, but there was another box that contained very important documents about Ben and Galvenar.

Before he could interrogate Danny, someone was at the door. The happy couple? This would be great; he had more than enough food. His New Year's Eve was looking up.

But wait; it wasn't Ben, only Amelia. Where was his buddy?

No choice but to show her highness into his apartment. She looked much better than she had the last time he saw her, at the Christmas party. Her face was filling out, and her corduroy pants actually looked tight. She'd need maternity things soon. How weird to think about what was going to happen to her over the next six months. She would get huge, but also wobbly and awkward and strangely fragile. He'd seen it happen to women at work. He'd often wondered if it was hard to concentrate on email and memos and presentations with your body morphing itself to accommodate another being.

"Danny!" Amelia said, kneeling down to hug him. When Isabelle came in, Amelia put her arms around her, too.

Matthew's email to Amelia had included a quick version of

the Florida disaster and their mom's health. Perhaps this was why she'd come over—to see them. Who knows, maybe she could cheer Danny up.

"I'm really amazed." She looked up at Matthew. Amazed by him? He'd done something she approved of, finally? "Let me know if you need a babysitter. I'm happy to help."

"I will, thanks." She sounded positively congenial, so he threw in, "I can use all the help I can get."

"What else can I do?"

"I'm not sure yet." He laughed. "Unless of course you'd like to help me raise them, in which case, feel free."

She hugged the kids harder and Matthew realized she was crying. Why the hell would that upset her? "I was only joking," he tried. More crying. "Or not?" Same.

She let the kids go when Isabelle started squirming to be free. But she was still crying, so he said, "Jesus, what is it?"

He stuck out his hand and she let him help her up. She sat down in the white chair and he sat on the couch, with Isabelle standing next to him, trying to comb his hair. What Amelia told him was unexpected and yet sadly predictable. Apparently, the week before, Ben had bolted from the whole father thing. No wonder he wasn't taking Matthew's calls. Dammit, another problem.

"Where is he staying?" Matthew said.

"At the campus hotel," she said, sniffing. "He's been there for almost a week."

She turned her attention to Danny and Isabelle; he went back to setting the table. The meal with the kids was fine, if stressful. Isabelle wanted apple juice, which he'd forgotten to buy at the store. Danny kept looking at Amelia as though he was trying to telegraph some message to her, or maybe he was just glad to see her; Matthew couldn't tell. Isabelle finally got over the juice crisis and went back to being her happy self, though her reaction to the spaghetti was to eat all the zucchini and play with the rest, wrapping the noodles around her fingers before letting them slide onto the floor. Each time, Matthew wiped off the rubber sheet he'd put under her chair and asked her not to do that. Her response, predictably, was to laugh. Amelia thought it was funny, too, and Danny was paying attention, at least, though he still didn't smile.

Amelia ate two enormous helpings and thanked him for the delicious meal. Danny asked if he could take Isabelle into the loft, where Matthew had moved the TV. Matthew said fine and Amelia helped him put the dishes in the dishwasher. When they were finished, as he was wrapping up the bread, she started crying again and sobbed out another twist to the story. Her baby might have Down syndrome, or at least Ben thought so. The OB said it was very unlikely. They'd done an ultrasound a few days ago and none of the markers were there, but just the idea that the kid could be screwed up was unacceptable to Ben.

Matthew said, "He doesn't like uncertainty outside of the lab. He'll come around, but in the meantime, you have to remember that he's not just a man, he's superman. He can't be held to the ordinary standards of mere mortals like—"

"But I want an ordinary life," she said, sniffing. "I want someone who is happy that I'm pregnant. I want someone who doesn't constantly tell me I'm too old to have a healthy baby."

Matthew could imagine Ben telling Amelia that; the guy had never pulled punches with his girlfriends. He once told Karen that her sagging breasts were normal for her age. After she threw a jar of pickles at him (and missed), he called Matthew, mystified as to what he'd done to upset her. "It was the truth," Ben said, as though that meant it couldn't be upsetting. Matthew had explained for the millionth time that truth was not the standard by which to judge what to say to a woman, or almost anyone for that matter.

But Amelia was different since she was such a stickler for the truth. Unless she'd changed. An ordinary life? That didn't sound like her.

"It will work out," he said. "Ben does love you, I know that. He—"

"No," she stammered. "It's over between us." And then, horrifyingly, she reached out and put her arms around him. He waited a minute and finally put his arms around her, too, but stiffly. At which point she dropped her head against his chest. Snuggling there? What?

"I think I should talk to Ben," he said, pushing her back as gently as his panic would allow. "Find out when he's coming home. Can you watch the kiddlings until I return?" he said, nodding in the direction of the loft. She said yes, and walked in that direction. He tried not to run to the door, but he did hurry once he got to the parking garage. He got in the Porsche and drove as fast as was safe, straight to Ben's hotel.

He had to fix this, and pronto: for Ben's sake and for Amelia's, too. Admittedly, he was also concerned about protecting himself from getting royally screwed over. The last time she'd put her arms around him was in Aspen, and the end result there had not been pretty. At least she was full of surprises, if most of them were of the cut-your-heart-out-and-eat-it variety.

Ben was in his room, already drinking, celebrating New Year's Eve alone, and obviously, annoyingly, feeling sorry for himself. They walked to a campus bar to have this talk. Matthew drank three Diet Cokes before Ben said he was "calm" enough to talk about Amelia. He'd already had several double shots of tequila, but he seemed to be serious when he claimed he'd realized something "important." He even lifted his finger and pointed it at Matthew, for emphasis. "Amelia belongs with you, not me."

"And just when did you arrive at this fascinating realization?"

Matthew leaned back and stared at Ben. "Ah, let me guess. Right after you walked out on your pregnant girlfriend?"

"Yes," Ben admitted, looking wounded. "That doesn't mean it's not true."

"Oh please. It's a justification, and an exceedingly lame one at that."

"I can't do it. I'm sorry, Matt. I did try, but I don't—"

"You'll just have to try harder, then," he said, and launched into yet another rant about Ben's responsibilities in this situation. Ben seemed to be listening, but he was also continuing to drink nonstop and, unfortunately, by the time the little speech was finished, he was so plastered he actually thought something in all this was funny.

Matthew frowned. "I fail to see the humor here."

"I was just thinking that I would choose you to be my kid's father over any man alive. That's how much faith I have in you, buddy."

"How flattering." Matthew's voice was clearly sarcastic, but Ben was smiling like he'd just offered Matthew a little present. "Do you hear how ridiculous you sound? The father has already been chosen. Tag, you're it."

"But you know I can't be a father. How can I, when I can barely take care of myself?" A little drunken sigh of self-pity. "I'll just screw the kid up the way my dad screwed me up."

Ben was still talking about his father, but Matthew wasn't listening. He'd heard all of this before, dozens of times.

"What about Amelia?" he finally said. He was trying not to yell, but he was getting really angry. "Are you telling me that you don't love Amelia?"

"I should never have started going out with her. She was too much for me from our first date."

"You certainly didn't think so at the time." Matthew could feel a headache coming on. The bar was too noisy, already packed with people celebrating. He rubbed his temples. "Tell me why Amelia was 'too much' for you on the first date. Enlighten me about this, because I can't imagine why you continued to see her if you felt that way."

"Okay." Ben leaned forward as if he were about to share his deepest secret. "You know how I am, Matt. I like to think."

He broke off in drunken laughter, which even Matthew couldn't entirely resist. Talk about an understatement; Ben's idea of down-time was daydreaming about chemical databases.

"When I'm with Amelia, it's hard to think because she always wants to talk. She thinks we should talk about everything. She's so intense, it makes me nervous. Even in bed, she's so passionate she intimidates me, though she does give the best blow jo—"

"Christ, have some respect." Matthew was instantly pissed off again. "You're talking about the mother of your child, and our oldest friend."

"And I will always care about her." Oh no; he was gulping, meaning it was time for the serious drunken tears. "Even on the day you marry her." He grabbed Matthew's hand. "You've always been like my big brother. I want to know my big brother is taking care of my wife and child."

Matthew smirked. "I believe she's my wife in your insane scenario."

"Right," Ben said, sitting up straighter. "While I'm working on trypanosomiasis, you'll be here with Amelia and your son or daughter. That's the way I'm going to think of the child. It's yours now." He waited for a moment, then unaccountably laughed. "If you want, I'll even sign papers saying I give up my rights like I did with tegaba—"

"Have you lost your mind?" Matthew jerked his hand away. "I know you're drunk, but can you honestly think it's funny to compare your kid to some fucking molecule?"

Had he really just called his beloved Galvenar *some fucking mole-*

cule? Yes, strangely enough, he had. But he didn't have time to think about what this meant before Ben dropped another bombshell.

"I know it's not the same," Ben said, sniffing, clearly insulted. "I was just trying to lighten the situation. This is very hard for me. All I meant is that I'm giving it to you forever, not just while I'm in Africa."

"Africa? You're leaving, too?"

"Richard and I both think someone needs to be there. I'm going on Sunday. I won't be gone long, probably less than a year. It's an incredible opportunity to—"

Matthew ignored Ben babbling on about the point of this trip. Finally, when he couldn't think of anything to talk Ben out of this, he snapped, "You're being a complete shit. You should have had a vasectomy years ago, when you first mentioned it."

Ben smiled. "Bro, you know me so well."

And that was the end of that. Matthew pulled Ben to his feet and lugged him out of the bar. When they were on the street, heading back to the hotel, Ben told Matthew that he loved him. As usual. So, what the hell, Matthew said, "Same, asshole," but he couldn't resist throwing in that if Ben wasn't so brilliant, he'd be fucking useless. "I know, buddy," Ben said. He was still smiling. "I know."

Matthew was driving in circles around the city, cursing the traffic and thinking about the million things he'd had to do for Benjamin over the last twenty-two years. Helping him move into not one but three apartments. Taking over his checking account and hiring someone to pay all his bills and handle his insurance and even remind him to renew his driver's license. Flying to Boston or London or wherever Ben was to help him with a woman problem or a money problem or just a typical Ben moment of freaking out about life in the real world. And, of course, the big thing, when they were both twenty-seven. Thirteen years ago.

Ben had just moved to Boston when, out of nowhere, his loser dad showed up. Ben hadn't even seen his father since Ben was in middle school, but somehow the deadbeat tracked him down. He told Ben some vague shit about a gambling problem and being afraid of what would happen if he didn't get hold of a hundred grand by the end of the summer. Matthew was living with Amelia then, working at AD, but at the bottom, before his first promotion. He had less than two thousand dollars in the bank. He told Ben to let his dad rot, but of course Ben wouldn't consider that. He loved his father and, probably more important, he'd never felt like his dad loved him.

For months, Matthew spent every waking hour trying to solve this impossible problem. It was Ben's idea to try to sell what he always called "the accident"—a molecule he'd discovered during his PhD program, purely by chance, while he was working on something he considered much more important. In the past, Ben had insisted the accident was worthless chem-trash, but now he wanted Matthew to convince somebody it wasn't. Couldn't Matthew get AD to invest in it, on the off chance it could become a new drug?

No, of course not. It didn't work that way, though Matthew did go to a friend in R&D and beg him to take a look at it. The friend was encouraging about the molecule's potential, but he said what Matthew already knew: the company couldn't buy anything without making sure it was eligible to be patented, and that process took a very long time. Matthew also approached several biotech start-ups, and when that didn't work, he went to Wall Street to pitch the molecule to venture capitalists. He was so over his head (still a little *green*, as his boss had called him), and by the middle of August Ben was panicking. Ben's dad was spending his days in Ben's apartment, peeking out of the blinds, refusing to answer the phone or even turn on the television. Matthew suspected Ben's father was making the whole thing up, but Ben insisted his dad was in real danger of being hurt or even killed. They had to get the hundred grand, somehow.

Finally, Matthew decided to get it the old-fashioned way: by opening fourteen credit card accounts and maxing out their cash advances. But he didn't want Ben to feel bad about him taking on more debt—since Ben's father, no surprise, had disappeared as soon as he'd gotten his hands on the cash—so he told Ben that surely AD would buy the accident molecule eventually. He had Ben sign papers, turning over all rights to the formula to Matthew. In the meantime, Matthew's friend in R&D and the friend's supervisor had been running tests on Ben's accident and, amazingly, the molecule continued to look promising. After a lot of legal wrangling, AD did end up buying it, for $250,000. Matthew's good deed had been rewarded. He not only paid off the credit cards, but also his student loans, since Ben didn't want any of the profits.

Ben also didn't want his name associated with the molecule in any way because he'd violated a legal agreement to share any discoveries he made with the university. It was the only unethical thing he'd ever done (except for all the other things he didn't think of as unethical because they didn't matter to him). Over the years, he became obsessed with what would happen to his reputation if it ever came out. Matthew told him countless times that he was being silly, but after the molecule became a blockbuster, it struck him that he just might be able to use Ben's fear to protect his billion-dollar baby. He hooked up Ben and Amelia, knowing that if Amelia threatened to release anything bad about Galvenar, Matthew could play off Ben's paranoia that *everything* about Galvenar was in danger of being exposed. And Ben would shut her up; that was the idea. Simple but effective, or so he thought.

As warped as it sounded to him now, at the time he really didn't think he was doing anything wrong. Ben and Amelia were both so irritatingly moralistic and self-righteous; why wouldn't they be ecstatic to find each other? It was almost a good deed to play matchmaker for them because they had so much in common. When he met up with them in the Caymans to make sure their relationship was still on track—and to reassure Ben that Galvenar was doing fine in the postmarket, no reason to worry despite the jackass TV journalist's scare tactics—they seemed quite happy together. Where was the harm?

But somehow he'd let himself forget about one very important difference between them: Amelia's fierce desire to be a mother and Ben's equally fierce desire to avoid being a father. So once again he was back in reflection hell, but this time with a new twist. He had to go back to his apartment and face Amelia with no hope of giving her back Ben. She'd moved to Philadelphia to be with the guy, and now the screwup wouldn't even be in the country when she delivered their baby. Matthew wasn't sure he could forgive Ben for this outrageous selfishness, but at the moment he had to focus on Amelia. He felt so damned sorry for her, pregnant and alone.

He came home to find that she'd put the kids to bed and was resting on his couch. She had the lights dimmed, but he could see her schoolgirl long hair hanging halfway to the floor.

Naturally, he told her that Ben absolutely loved her, no question whatsoever about that. But, sadly, he was too irresponsible to be a father. Then he started sharing a few details with her, including the fact that Matthew had paid the security deposit on their new house. Matthew had had one of his minions (not Cassie; this was beneath her) turn on all their utilities. Everything was in Ben's name, yes, but Ben hadn't done any of it—though he'd promised to handle the move when he talked Amelia into coming back from New York.

At first she was stunned, but as he warmed up and moved to the litany of strange things Ben had done in the past, she relaxed. Eventually, he got her laughing with the story of the time Ben left one of his notebooks on a plane to London and then insisted on flying to the city where the plane was headed next, Madrid, rather than waiting for the airline to return it to him. Unfortunately, by the time he got to Madrid, two hours after the other plane had landed, the notebook was already on route back to London. He had no money and it was the middle of the night. He had to wait in the airport, on the floor, and since he didn't have the damned notebook, he took notes on his arms. Airport security thought the notes were suspicious and made him wash his arms before he could go back to London. He insisted on being given paper first, so he could transcribe them, but when he mentioned the word *anthrax* to someone—god knows why; Ben said he was just trying to be friendly and let them know he understood why they were being careful—airport security took him into custody, where he stayed for hours, being questioned, until Matthew rescued him. Matthew was in Berlin at the time and he flew to Madrid, with a Spanish translator, to explain Ben's ways to the security police. And to give Ben some fresh paper, of course. And to buy him a meal, because he hadn't eaten since the notebook was lost and he was so dizzy he couldn't stand up.

"You really don't want this guy taking care of your baby," Matthew said. Amelia was sitting at one end of the couch. He was sitting next to her: friend close, nothing more. "His genes are valuable, though. If he wins the Nobel, women all over the world will want to buy what you got for free."

He said this in the same jocular tone as the rest, but Amelia fell silent and he realized that he shouldn't have mentioned anything about genetics. He reminded her that the ultrasound had been normal, and when she didn't respond, he told her that the media push for all women to have tests for Down syndrome had to have been funded by some med-device company. "They just want to scare the shit out of mothers and make them pay for more expensive tests. Hell, you know how it works. You can't take any of this too seriously."

She looked at him. "Do you really think my baby will be all right?"

"No, I think the baby will be very strange, but that can't be helped, given his parents." She laughed. Good. "Seriously, I think your baby will be just fine. I can already imagine her throwing a baseball and hitting me in the head."

At which point, before he could comprehend what was happening, she leaned over and kissed him. A real kiss, too, not a friend-to-friend peck on the cheek.

He pulled back. "Um, I'm not sure w—"

She interrupted to kiss him again. Uh-oh. "Amelia, I'm the enemy?" He forced a laugh. "The speech, remember?"

"I've decided that was unimportant," she said, into his neck. "Good is meaningless in the modern world. I was wrong."

All she was doing was breathing on his neck, but Ben was right—it seemed intensely passionate, though hardly intimidating. Of course then his mind flashed to the other thing Ben had mentioned, which turned him on, remembering that unusual skill of Amelia's, but then turned him off, thinking about her performing it on his best friend.

She'd moved to kissing his ear, and he said, "Wait." He was losing it already. This was just not right on a million levels. He moved to the other end of the couch. "I'm sorry, but I can't do this."

Can't do this? Had his balls been cut off? Yes, actually, in Aspen. And he had absolutely no intention of repeating that disaster, no matter how horny he was. No matter how much he wanted to just—

"First of all," he said, "good is not meaningless, and you know that, or you will if you get past Ben's recent bad behavior. Second,

319

I think you're afraid of being alone right now, and I don't blame you. You've had a lot of bad luck recently. But third, you don't want to do something you'll regret in the morning to get your mind off your problems. Believe me, I've tried that, and it doesn't work."

"You're probably right," she said, but he heard her voice catch. Was she going to cry again? Yes, unfortunately, she was. Her reason, when he finally got it out of her, was laughable, but he didn't dare laugh. She claimed she was obviously too old for him now. Old and not pretty enough. Not sexy like that woman Rachel.

"That is not true." What choice did he have but to confess? "You have always been beautiful to me." He raised his eyebrows in what he hoped was a playful gesture, certainly not embarrassed. "Just my bad luck."

"Then why did you sleep with her?" She looked at him; her big green eyes were glistening with tears. "I don't mean Rachel; I mean . . ."

Oh shit, not Palm Beach again. The truth was he didn't even know anymore why he'd slept with that woman, but he still considered it one of the stupidest decisions he'd ever made, and he admitted as much. "And I've made a lot of stupid decisions in my life, so that should tell you something."

"Me, too," she said. He was expecting her to say any number of things: blackmailing him, getting together with Ben, even the choice of her career. But instead she said, in a voice as earnest as if she were confessing a real crime, "I should have gone to lunch with you at Astor-Denning."

Then he did laugh, because it just seemed so damned funny. The whole situation. Amelia smiled, too, and said, "God, we've made a real mess of this, haven't we?"

Before he could answer a resounding yes, Danny appeared, rubbing his eyes, but he was clearly relieved when he saw that Amelia was still there. He went to her to whisper his request that he be allowed to watch something because he couldn't sleep. Specifically, he wanted to watch the movie that Matthew had rented for them.

What the hell; Danny never asked for anything, and it *was* New Year's Eve. But Matthew didn't like the idea of the depressed kid watching the movie alone, so he asked Amelia if she wanted to watch it, too. She said yes so enthusiastically that he knew she still didn't want to leave them. Or was it him she didn't want to leave? Or was it just that she didn't want to go home? Christ, this was so beyond his ability to parse out the meaning that he didn't even know where to start. What if she was still here when the movie ended? What if she wanted to sleep here tonight? What if she stayed around tomorrow and the next day, to help him with the kids? Where would all this lead? Was it even remotely possible that Ben's bizarre scenario could end up being his life?

For now, at least, it was simple enough. The three of them were going to watch *Star Wars*. And it was obviously the right decision because Danny finally smiled when Matthew said to him, "Luke, how about using the Force and putting in the DVD?"

Having Amelia there was surprisingly nice. At least he knew her, and that fact in itself was comforting. He even knew her middle name: Elizabeth. He knew her favorite color: aqua. He knew her birthday and her favorite foods and that she had a bizarre attraction to the number four. Whenever they did the I'm-thinking-of-a-number game, he could freak her out with his psychic abilities simply by guessing four. She had a terrible memory for numbers; maybe that's why she stuck with four, the number of people in her own family growing up; she'd probably had to say it all the time at school, answering the teacher's question. He remembered this, too. "How many people are in your family, Matthew?" He hated that question because his dad would be out of the house on a bender for weeks at a time and he wanted to be honest with the teacher, but what was the honest answer, two or three? He used to stand there and blush like it mattered. Two or three? Who the hell cared? The truth was always a matter of perspective, or, to put it more bluntly, what most people called "truth" was usually bullshit.

Still, it was true, for the moment at least, that he was happy. Danny was sitting on the floor, a few feet from the TV, as always. Matthew was on the couch with Amelia's feet in his lap, watching a movie the two of them had seen many times, years ago, in a galaxy far, far away. When midnight came, they heard the city come alive with fireworks and yells and the blasts of a thousand car horns. Naturally, Isabelle heard all this noise, too, and she came stumbling out in full pout mode, clearly mad that she hadn't been invited to this little party. When Matthew collected her in his arms, she was still warm and floppy and half asleep, but she said "No!" repeatedly when he tried to take her to bed. So he gave up and settled her on the couch with them. He had no idea if she knew what was going on, but she was giggling as if she couldn't wait to see what would happen next, as if this was so special she wouldn't miss it for the world.

Acknowledgments

This is my fourth book with Simon & Schuster, and I feel very lucky to have found such a wonderful home for my work. My deepest thanks to everyone at S&S, especially my lovely editor and friend, Greer Hendricks; Judith Curr, a force of nature who also happens to have excellent taste in covers; Carolyn Reidy, who, in addition to running a publishing company, remembered to tell me that her sister had loved one of my novels, which made my BEA; and Lisa Keim, cosmopolitan jet-setter, hand holder, and dear friend. I'm also grateful to everyone on the Atria team, especially Kathleen Schmidt, Kim Curtin, Nancy Tonik, and Sarah Walsh; the hard-working S&S sales force; the awesome people at the warehouse at Riverside, including Barb Roach, Liz Monaghan, Gail Hitchcock, and Karyn Basso, and all those who have graciously hosted me at the trade shows, especially Tim Hepp and Terry Warnick.

Again, my heartfelt thanks to Megan Underwood Beatie and Lynn Goldberg of Goldberg McDuffie Communications for their enthusiastic support of my career. To all the booksellers who have championed my novels and all the readers who have written me. To my friends Sara Gordon, Joe Drabyak, Mary Gay Shipley, Michelle Zive, and Sarah Bagby. To Ed Ward, for sharing amusing anecdotes about his years at Hopkins, and Chris McNabb, for teaching me everything I know about golf. To Alix Rabin, endlessly patient listener, seeker of typos, and advocate of Metropolitan bakery. To Philly, my adopted city, for inspiring this novel and welcoming me home.

To my family, with love and gratitude for sticking by me through this very difficult year: Ann Cahall; Jim, Jeff and Jamie Crotinger; my girl and sweet visitor, Emily Ward, and her mother, Laurie, who wrote the daily emails that reminded me that no matter what I've lost, I will always have words and stories—and an amazing sister.

To Marly and Michael Rusoff, Kevin Howell, Pat Redmond, and Melisse Shapiro, who have been like family to me. Your support and love have meant more than I can say.

Miles, buddy, this is our book, isn't it? No matter what else happens, we were there. We whispered, we cried, we laughed with Matthew, and we survived Christmas. We might have been changed in ways we'll never understand, but we have lived through this. Thank you for being with me in this journey into the unknown. "He had a lion's heart, just like my son."